HIEROGLYPHS AND HOMICIDE

THE CLARISSA BELL MYSTERIES

BOOK ONE

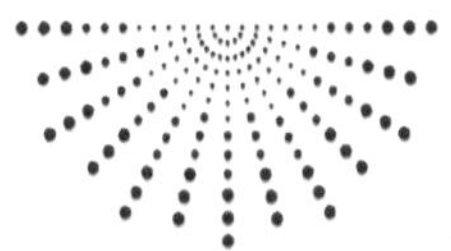

TRACY HIGLEY

CHAPTER ONE

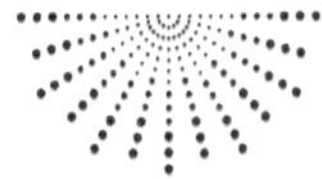

Cairo, Egypt
February, 1923

The second time I arrived at Cairo's Rameses Train Station, I vowed to avoid a repeat of my earlier experience, including getting involved in a murder plot. My archaeological expertise applied much better to people who'd been dead for several millennia.

Instead, I carried twelve books on Egyptian pottery, three trowels of varying lengths, and zero plan for convincing Dr. Bradford that a woman could identify artifacts by more than just their "pretty colors."

My father's goodbye echoed in my head: "get Egypt out of your system, my dear girl, then return to New York to do the sensible thing!" By which he meant, marry Richard, his business partner's son—a fate I'd recently decided would be equivalent to being entombed with the pharaohs, minus the dignity of mummification.

I'd already managed several years ago to defeat Daddy's objectives for me by training at Cambridge in England, a "silly notion for an American girl." But he was still smarting over my recent defection from my engagement to Richard.

Steam cascaded across the tracks of Ramses Station—built thirty years ago as part of Khedive Ismail's grand modernization plan for Cairo and designed specifically to impress European visitors with Egypt's progress toward Western standards.

The vapor rolled over marble floors as I gripped my battered leather satchel, watching the throng surge around me like the annual flooding of the Nile. Except with significantly more bowler hats and fewer crocodiles. The morning light fractured through the train station's arched windows, casting honey-gold geometric patterns across the polished stone.

I had grossly miscalculated the weight of my research materials. The human body was not designed to transport so many books, no matter how essential they might be. As I attempted to wrangle my ungainly collection of luggage, a porter materialized at my elbow, rattling off a rapid string of Arabic.

I straightened my shoulders and deployed one of the few Arabic phrases I'd managed to memorize on the journey from London.

"Astatie 'an akil haqayibi."

And then questioned whether I'd just declared I could carry my own bags or accidentally proposed marriage. Based on his startled expression, it could have been either. Or something else entirely.

A socialite in an elaborate hat swept past, her perfume causing my eyes to water. Notes of henna (common in Egyptian perfumes since the Old Kingdom), vanilla (Madagascar origin, suggesting French colonial trade routes), and something that reminded me distinctly of a Cambridge colleague's failed attempt at brewing coffee using soil samples. My overdeveloped sense of smell was rarely a blessing, and often a curse.

The atmosphere vibrated with a symphony of sounds— vendors shouting prices in three languages and the mournful call to prayer echoing from distant minarets. The Cairo heat bore against my skin, and what felt like half of Cairo's population jostled my carefully pressed linen ensemble—selected to project professional competence and now transformed into a study in wrinkles during the train ride from Alexandria. At this rate, I'd arrive at the dig site looking less like a serious archaeologist and more like something recently excavated.

I made a brief stop at my prearranged lodgings, a narrow room above the Nile View Café, which notably had no discernible view of the Nile. My tiny upstairs room also smelled of aniseed and what I prayed was not decomposing camel.

I changed into my excavation attire. The outfit consisted of practical trousers (scandalous), a loose cotton shirt (sensible), and boots that had seen better days, possibly during the Old Kingdom period.

The mirror above the washbasin reflected a face I barely recognized. My reddish-blonde hair had escaped its pins during the journey, creating a halo of unruly waves to my shoulders, while the Egyptian sun seemed to have already intensified the freckles across my nose. Nondescript gray-green eyes looked back at me, bloodshot from the dusty train ride. I tucked away the lapis lazuli pendant I always wore, smoothed down my cotton shirt, and sighed. Not exactly the image of a respected academic, but then, appearances had never been my primary concern.

My landlady, Madame Farah, met me at the bottom of the steps, the café behind her.

"Look at you," she clicked her tongue disapprovingly, eyeing my practical trousers. Her English was surprisingly good. "You run around dressed like man. Your mother would weep to see what has become of her daughter."

Her look suggested I was single-handedly destroying two thousand years of social progress. But traditional skirts were spectacularly impractical when climbing in and out of tomb shafts.

I smiled, nodded, and headed outside to the street.

Dr. Bradford, the dig director, had already arranged my immediate transportation to the Giza site. The drive in the back of a rattling Ford lorry was an exercise in staying alive while being tossed about like pottery sherds in a sieve. My fellow passengers—three crates of archaeological equipment and a chicken of uncertain provenance—seemed equally unenthusiastic about the journey. The chicken, at least, had the good sense to look terrified.

We arrived at the Great Pyramid looming before us, a geometric miracle that had survived four and a half thousand years. The recent discovery of Tutankhamun's tomb in November of last year had created an unprecedented "Egyptomania" across the Western world. Newspapers ran daily updates on Howard Carter's discoveries while wealthy tourists flocked to Egypt in record numbers, making the ancient monuments suddenly fashionable backdrops for society photographs. No doubt their guides were reciting tales of mummy curses and hidden treasures.

But it was impossible not to marvel. The morning radiance turned the limestone blocks to molten gold, while heat shimmer made the ancient monument dance on the horizon.

We bounced across to the dig site, sprawled well to the east, a grid of ropes and markers that made my heart beat faster. The site lay hidden from eager eyes, behind canvas screens and warning signs. Fascinating finds were no doubt being processed through the established stations: careful cleaning, precise measuring, meticulous sketching, and finally, labeling, using the dig director's specific system.

The Ford lorry lurched to a stop. I climbed out of the back and dusted my trousers.

This was it. I had made it. My chance to prove—

"I say, has someone mistaken this for a secretarial pool? This is a dig site, not a typing room."

I pivoted to find a cluster of men in various states of archaeological dishevelment. The speaker, a portly gentleman with an astonishing mustache, peered at me through a monocle that hadn't been cleaned since Rameses II was in nappies. My fingers instinctively twitched toward my field notebook, ready to document this remarkable specimen of *Academicus pompousis*.

Instead, I extended my hand. "Dr. Clarissa Bell. Cambridge

University. My credentials arrived last week with Dr. Sutherland's recommendation." I'd counted on Sutherland's presence to ease the introductions, but he wasn't among them. His absence sent an uneasy prickle down my spine.

The mustache twitched. The monocle dropped. Several of his companions developed sudden, fascinating interests in their boot tops.

"Ah yes, Sutherland's... protégé." He managed to make the word sound like a particularly distasteful skin condition. "You don't look like an archaeologist." His gaze flicked dismissively over my red-blonde hair and freckled skin. "I expected someone more... scholarly."

"I am sorry to disappoint."

"Hmm. Well. I am Dr. Nathaniel Bradford. I suppose you can help catalogue the pottery fragments coming out of G 3152. Sutherland's not here yet, which is most irregular." Bradford's voice carried a note of genuine concern that contradicted his dismissive demeanor. "But Phillips, my field photographer, can show you where to set up your... workspace." He flicked his hand toward a canvas tent that appeared to be losing an argument with the wind. "I shall introduce you around to the scholars later. We're all quite unavailable here at the moment."

Behind him, local workers navigated with practiced efficiency, their trowels creating a rhythmic *tink-tink* against limestone that sounded suspiciously like Morse code for "another foolish American." I noticed how they exchanged glances when I appeared—curious rather than dismissive—some even offering small nods of acknowledgment.

The dig site bristled with the tools of our trade: delicate brushes for cleaning, pointed trowels worn smooth by use, metal sieves that chimed like byzantine bells when the wind hit them right. My own toolkit, which I had ordered new from London, still gleamed with embarrassing brightness.

I smiled for Bradford, the way I imagined a sphinx might smile just before posing a riddle that ended in someone's gruesome death. "So kind of you." I nodded to each of the others. "And the team needs little introduction, as I've read all your work in preparation for joining you. I've published myself, on New Kingdom pottery classification systems. Perhaps some of you have read my work in the Journal of Egyptian Archaeology?"

Bradford's mustache performed a complicated maneuver that suggested extreme distress, possibly attempting to detach itself and scurry away to find a more enlightened host. "Yes, well. The pottery fragments are already broken, so they should suit your capabilities perfectly."

The words landed with all the subtlety of a tomb collapse. My jaw clenched involuntarily, teeth grinding together.

I retreated to my assigned table, keeping my spine rigid and my expression neutral, though internally I was cataloging every variety of academic condescension I'd encountered since my first day at Cambridge. This particular specimen ranked seventh on my scale of infuriating dismissals, somewhere between "Did you take notes for your husband?" and "Remarkable insight—did one of the professors help you with that?"

I devoted the next hour to sorting through pottery relics that looked about as exciting as my great-aunt Gertrude's china collection. If Gertrude had taken a hammer to it and buried it in the desert for several millennia. The work itself wasn't beneath me; the problem was that I could see the real excavation happening fifty yards away, where the men were carefully uncovering what appeared to be a previously undocumented structure.

Their trowels moved in practiced synchronization, scraping away years of sand while brushes swept clean any promising surfaces. String grids divided the ground into neat squares, while spirit levels balanced on surfaces ensured that even gravity was properly documented.

The pottery fragments that were spread before me formed a constellation of broken history, each one catching the light differently.

My fingertips traced the uneven surface of a sherd, feeling the ridges where an ancient craftsman's fingers once pressed into soft clay, creating a tactile connection across thousands of years. Each ceramic fragment had its own story to tell.

"What secrets have you been keeping, you poor broken thing?" I whispered to a particularly interesting sherd. "Did they toss you aside, once you weren't perfect anymore?"

A gust of wind sent my carefully arranged sherds skittering across the table. I lunged to catch them, nearly upending my rickety wooden chair in the process. "Oh, for the love of Tutankhamun's underpants—" My hand quivered as I scrambled to prevent the loss of an hour's meticulous sorting.

"Three-point-two meters per second, with a northeasterly vector of precisely forty-seven-point-five degrees, accounting for local thermal variations."

I glanced up to find that one of the team, Dr. Étienne Deveraux, had slipped beside my table with the efficiency of a well-dressed ghost. He was lanky and precise, with rimless spectacles perched on a narrow nose and fingers as delicate as the instruments he wielded. He held an anemometer in one hand and a leather-bound notebook in the other. The newest addition to Bradford's team had already gained a reputation for turning every excavation into an exercise in geometric perfection that would have made Pythagoras weep with joy. His jodhpurs remained mysteriously immaculate, as if he'd somehow convinced the desert to avoid sullying his Parisian tailoring.

"The wind speed." He extracted a set of silver calipers from his leather case with the reverence of a priest handling sacred relics. "Fascinating how it affects artifact displacement. That ceramic fragment—" he indicated with his polished pencil, "— must have traveled 50 centimeters before you caught it." He made another neat notation in his journal, the numbers marching across the page in perfect formation.

"How terribly useful." I pulled out my own notebook. "I've been meaning to calculate the exact aerodynamic properties of pottery sherds. Perhaps we could co-author a paper: 'Wind-blown Antiquities: A Mathematical Analysis of Archaeological Inconvenience.'"

I reached for the errant ceramic fragment, but Deveraux was already placing it back in line.

Dr. Bradford appeared, his other companions clustered behind him like a Greek chorus of disapproving mustaches and sand-dusted tweeds.

"Deveraux's not bothering you, I hope, Miss Bell?" He tugged at his too-tight collar.

I straightened. "Not at all. I was just noting the unusual fabric composition of this sherd. The inclusion of calcium carbonate suggests—"

"Yes, yes." Bradford waved his hand as if shooing away an annoying insect. "Just sort them by size and color. That should be simple enough, even for a..." He paused, his face contorting. "...lady archaeologist."

I felt something crack in my professional facade.

I had worked twice as hard as any man to earn my position, only to discover that in the end, it was my father's checkbook rather than my dissertation that had opened the door. His funding of the dig had secured my place on this expedition—a fact that burned like desert sun.

"If that is all that's required," I replied, my voice steady, "perhaps we should employ trained monkeys. I hear they're excellent at sorting by color, and less expensive to maintain than Cambridge-educated archaeologists."

CHAPTER TWO

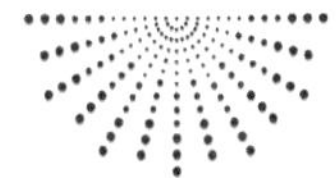

*B*radford's eyebrows shot toward his receding hairline at my impertinence.

Before he could respond, I turned my attention back to the pottery, effectively dismissing him.

His indignant huff as he retreated was followed by the muted chuckles of his companions.

Alone at my table, I lifted a pottery fragment to the light, examining its surface with exaggerated thoroughness while blinking back the hot moisture that threatened to blur my vision.

"Your loss, Bradford," I whispered. "This piece alone contains more history than your entire last publication."

I mentally archived Bradford's comment with other archaeological artifacts: *Male Ego (Common), Late Colonial Period, remarkably well-preserved specimen of academic fossilization.*

And I briefly considered explaining that sorting by dimension and pigmentation was about as scientifically useful as categorizing the Sphinx by how aesthetically pleasing its weathered features were.

"Deveraux! Stop measuring the girl's pottery and come examine this structural alignment. We need your exact measurements for the journal article."

"Of course." Behind me, Deveraux tucked away his calipers with loving care. "Though I should note that Miss Bell's table is precisely 82.6 centimeters in width, and could be more efficient—"

"Now, Deveraux!"

I watched him hurry away, then glanced down at my fragment. "Well," I shrugged, "at least you appreciate my expertise." The pottery, unsurprisingly, did not respond. Though I had to admit it was showing more intellectual curiosity than my colleagues.

The dig site sprawled before me like a vast, sun-baked chessboard where I'd been designated the most dispensable pawn. Canvas tents flapped in the hot breeze while the Great Pyramid loomed in the background—forty-five centuries of architectural triumph silently witnessing my professional humiliation. Even the ancient stones seemed to be exchanging judgmental glances at my expense.

Determined to prove my worth, I began documenting each pottery specimen with fanatical thoroughness, my pencil flying across the paper as I noted every minute variation in composition, every telling mark of ancient craftsmanship. If they wanted me to catalogue pottery, then by Ra, I would catalogue it so thoroughly future archaeologists would stand amazed. Father hadn't funded this expedition just to see me fail at pottery sorting.

The midday heat transformed the dig site into a shimmering mirage where sand met sky. I hunched over my work, sweat dripping onto my meticulous notes. The air hung still and expectant around us, as if the archaeological gods themselves were holding their breath to see how thoroughly I might redeem—or further damn—myself through pottery classification.

My assigned workspace resembled the archaeological equivalent of a dunce corner—a rickety table inside a worn-out tent with its sides tied back, positioned far enough from the main excavation that my feminine presence wouldn't contaminate the serious scholarship happening there.

I was so engrossed in my work, I didn't notice the approaching footsteps until a shadow fell across my meticulous notes.

I lifted my gaze to find Deveraux had rematerialized, this time clutching a water jug, which he held out to me. "We require water for the team."

Somewhere in the distance, a jackal laughed.

I couldn't blame it.

"It's not far." He nodded to the east side of the site, his tone apologetic. "The vessel is exactly twelve-point-four meters northwest of your current position, assuming a straight-line trajectory accounting for the natural topographical variance of the substratum, with a nine-degree incline that requires adjustment to your stride length—"

"I believe I can locate a water barrel without triangulating its position, Dr. Deveraux."

His perfect posture stiffened. "Ah, but precision in all things, *n'est-ce pas*? I find that approaching each task with mathematical rigor—"

"Creates a significant probability of dying of thirst while calculating the exact angle of dehydration?"

Deveraux consulted his pocket watch. "No, the team's current work rate suggests they will require hydration only within the next seven-point-three minutes."

I seized the water jug, and trudged across the site to fill it from the barrel. My pristine new excavation blade clicked against my belt with every step, its factory-fresh edge a contrast to the smooth, well-worn tools I could see hanging from the other archaeologists' belts.

I navigated around the ghost markers of Flinders Petrie's 1880s grid system, still visible to the trained eye despite nearly forty years of subsequent digs. The great man's methodical approach had revolutionized Egyptian archaeology while I, his unworthy successor, was relegated to water-bearing duties typically assigned to the youngest local boys. My New York debutante acquaintances would surely faint at the sight of Armand Bell's daughter performing manual labor in the desert heat.

As I trekked back to the site with the jug, I indulged in a brief fantasy of discovering something spectacular—perhaps a previously unknown pyramid, preferably one with my name carved conveniently above the entrance in hieroglyphs. "The Tomb of the Great Queen Clarissa." I stumbled as my boot caught on a rock, nearly dumping the jug. "Feared by lesser archaeologists, measurer of her own artifacts, destroyer of academic—"

"Careful there, Miss Bell. Water is precious here."

I nearly dropped the jug. Deveraux's measuring tape snaked across the excavation grid, its brass fittings catching the sun like ancient gold. He was examining the partially excavated wall of the next flat-topped mastaba tomb to be opened, with the sort of passionate intensity most men reserved for their first-born children or particularly fine whiskey.

"Just measuring my angles, Dr. Deveraux. Approximately three degrees of embarrassment with a trajectory toward complete mortification." The water sloshed dangerously close to the jug's rim.

He frowned.

I nodded toward his wall. "That limestone block displays particularly fascinating tool marks."

"Ah." He nodded with professorial gravitas. "Though that's actually sandstone."

Wonderful. I'd just misidentified one of the most basic building materials in Egyptian archaeology. Perhaps I could petition the gods to open up the ground and swallow me whole.

I straightened my spine. If my career was to be buried here, at least my dignity would be preserved for future excavation.

The water jug slipped.

Time slowed.

In that eternal moment, I had time to observe several things with perfect precision:

First, that Deveraux's expression suggested he was mentally calculating the exact orbit of disaster.

Second, that Bradford had chosen this moment to emerge from behind a tent, his mustache mid-twitch.

And third, that the water jug was about to introduce itself to a perfectly preserved piece of Old Kingdom pottery with all the grace of a scarab beetle browsing a ceramics shop during a sandstorm.

"I say," Deveraux's voice cut through my horror as the piece shattered. "Was that the vessel we uncovered this morning? The one Bradford was planning to photograph for his upcoming publication?"

Yes, apparently it was. Because if one is going to destroy a priceless artifact, one might as well destroy one that's central to the dig director's research.

I briefly considered mummification as a preferable alternative to facing Bradford's reaction.

The worst part wasn't Bradford's rage or my colleagues' silent judgment—it was the naked vulnerability of public failure.

I stood amid the pottery pieces, mentally composing my own funerary text. "Here lies Clarissa Bell, who survived twenty-six years of life only to be murdered by an angry archaeologist with a surprisingly violent mustache. May Anubis judge her heart lightly, as her brain was clearly missing to begin with."

Heat crawled up my neck, determined to reach my cheeks.

Bradford's face progressed through several fascinating colors, finally settling on a shade of purple that would have delighted any ancient Egyptian dye-maker.

"Do you realize what you've done?" Each word enunciated as if speaking to a particularly dim child.

Behind Bradford, several Egyptian workers exchanging knowing glances.

I looked at the pottery sherds, then back at him. "Created a practical exercise in archaeological reconstruction?"

The gathered crowd of archaeologists collectively inhaled.

Bradford straightened his jacket and touched his credentials hanging around his neck.

"Miss Bell," he managed through clenched teeth, "I believe

your... talents... might be better suited to literally anywhere else in Egypt. Preferably somewhere far from any breakable artifacts. Perhaps you could study the migration patterns of sand?"

A hot desert breeze swept across the dig, carrying dust devils that swirled around my feet. I opened my mouth to point out that sand migration was actually a fascinating geological process essential to site preservation, but a flash of movement caught my eye. Beyond Bradford's shoulder, half-hidden in the shadows of the entrance to tomb G 3152, a figure stood watching our little drama unfold.

Unlike the other men on site, he wore no academic tweeds or archaeological kit, but rather an elegantly cut Savile Row sort of suit that seemed to defy the desert sun. His perfectly knotted tie suggested both taste and wealth. And he was holding something—something that glinted like gold in the harsh light.

The man noticed my attention. His subsequent smile contained the precise combination of charm and danger that archaeological instinct warned should be cataloged under *Exhibits: Absolutely Do Not Touch*. Something about his posture—the casual confidence of someone who navigated the world without permission.

I frowned. Unauthorized access to tomb sites was strictly forbidden, and that man had definitely not been part of our excavation team. Unless, of course, Bradford was in the habit of hiring aristocratic-looking strangers in bespoke suits to lurk in doorways.

Then he slipped into the tomb's darkness, taking whatever he'd been holding with him.

"Miss Bell!" Bradford's voice cut through my thoughts. "Are you even listening?"

No, I was not, in fact, listening. I was too busy wondering why a well-dressed stranger would be sneaking around our dig site—and why he'd looked so damnably pleased about my spectacular failure.

CHAPTER THREE

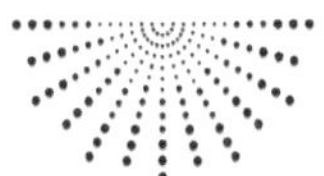

*N*o one else seemed to have noticed the stranger, so I followed him down into the tomb, boot heels echoing against limestone. The sensible thing would be to alert Bradford—though he'd likely diagnose me with a case of feminine archaeological hysteria, a condition apparently brought on by allowing women too close to ancient artifacts.

I cataloged my options:

Option A: Alert Bradford *(Common Resolution, Colonial Period, known to cause severe academic apoplexy)*

Option B: Follow suspicious stranger alone into dark tomb *(Rare Example of Archaeological Idiocy, Modern Period)*

Option C: Pretend I hadn't seen anything *(Cowardice, Well-Preserved Example of Career Preservation)*

After my spectacular contribution to pottery destruction this morning, I couldn't risk being wrong. Consorting with an unauthorized visitor could jeopardize the dig's permissions—career suicide served with a side of professional humiliation.

The tomb's blackness pressed around me, heavy with four thousand years of dust and rather more recent bat deposits.

If he claims to be lost, I'll cite regulation 7B regarding unauthorized site access. If he's a thief, I'll... My mind stuttered. What exactly did one do with a tomb robber? None of my courses at Cambridge had covered "Confronting Well-Dressed Criminals 101." Perhaps they should have taught it, given archaeology's tendency to attract the aristocratically larcenous.

A flicker of movement ahead gave me pause. The stranger's silhouette was bent over something, and in his hand, that same golden glint I'd spotted earlier.

My heart performed an acrobatic flutter. First day on the job, and I might catch my own tomb robber!

I should get reinforcements.

No. I squared my shoulders. I hadn't spent six years studying Egyptian archaeology to falter now. If I returned with Bradford, only to find nothing amiss, I'd be relegated to sorting pottery by color and size for the remainder of my natural life—possibly even in the afterlife, where I'd no doubt be assigned 365 ushabti figurines, one for each day of eternity.

Wait, did that make sense?

I stepped forward, forcing steel into my voice. "You there! Stop immediately!"

The stranger straightened, turning with the sort of unhurried grace that suggested he'd never had to rush for a train. Or chase down a tomb robber. He was taller than I'd realized, his expensive suit managing to look crisp despite the heat. And he was smiling, of all things—the kind of smile that belonged in a museum display case labeled *"Male Confidence (Excessive), Modern Period."*

"That's dig site property you're holding." I gestured to the golden object in his hand, trying to sound like someone who regularly confronted criminals. "Return it immediately, or I'll—"

"You'll what?" His baritone was rich with amusement, like honey poured over condescension. He stepped closer.

Subject demonstrates alpha-male behavioral patterns common to:

A) Wealthy aristocrats

B) Senior archaeologists

C) Particularly smug cats

I forced myself to stand my ground, though instinct suggested maintaining a safe distance from all three categories.

"Call the authorities?" He continued. "I'd be quite pleased to explain how a young lady archaeologist—" his eyes flicked to my trousers with barely concealed mirth "—caught me in the nefarious act of checking my watch."

He held up his hand. The golden glint was indeed just a pocket watch, though an expensive one.

Heat flamed up my neck but I pressed on.

"That doesn't explain why you're lurking about in this tomb." I lifted my chin, channeling my best impression of a museum curator. "This is a restricted archaeological site, and—"

"Lurking?" He clicked the watch closed with elegant precision. "My dear, I never lurk. I was merely examining—" He gestured to something in the alcove behind me.

I followed his eyeline, then caught myself. Standard diversionary tactic. "Don't change the subject. You've no proper authorization to be here, and—"

"Actually," he pulled a folded paper from his jacket with a flourish, "I've every proper authorization to be here. But you're adorably fierce in your defense of antiquities. Tell me, do you always charge into dark tombs alone to confront suspected criminals?"

His patronizing tone set my teeth on edge. Was it possible to mummify someone using only academic disdain? The research potential seemed compelling.

I grabbed the paper and scanned it. Apparently, he was doing some work for the Egyptian museum, though he was clearly British.

Before I could respond, he stepped past me toward the small alcove, his shoulder brushing mine in the narrow space. The contact sent an unwelcome shiver down my spine that I immediately filed under *Physiological Responses (Irrelevant, Modern Period, requiring immediate suppression).*

The tomb around us was a typical example of its type. G 3152 had been thoroughly looted in antiquity of all the items considered valuable, as all tombs were. Except, of course, for the recent and spectacular discovery of Tutankhamun's intact tomb in the Valley of the Kings.

This particular tomb had been uncovered a few months ago, and the systematic cataloguing of its remaining items, deemed worthless to tomb robbers, had been going on since then.

I stepped past the limestone niches—carved with hieroglyphs invoking abundance for the deceased in the afterlife. The artifacts left behind as worthless by ancient looters were spread across makeshift tables, awaiting proper documentation.

The small alcove where we now stood had once been a sacred space for offering rituals, its walls still bearing the faded ochre and blue pigments of pastoral scenes—grain harvests and bird hunting in the marshes, the eternal Egyptian fantasy of abundance.

He smiled over his shoulder, a gesture that probably opened doors at the finest clubs in London but merely made me question my academic objectivity. "Since you're here, perhaps you'd like to see what I was actually examining? Unless you're planning to arrest me with your nonexistent authority?"

He held out a notebook, and I stared at his sketches of a clay seal I knew the team had found weeks ago. His renderings were precise, capturing every detail, down to the subtle wear patterns that told the seal's story as clearly as any ancient text. To my annoyance, he was also mapping the precise location within the tomb layout, his spatial awareness as irritatingly competent as everything else about him.

"You have a good eye," I admitted. "Though you're missing the cartouche impression on the reverse."

"You mean this one?" He flipped the page with an elegant efficiency. "Fourth Dynasty, I believe. Though the string's composition suggests it may have been reused during the Fifth."

I blinked, momentarily thrown. "That's... actually a reasonable hypothesis."

"Try not to sound so shocked. Some of us can appreciate Egyptian artifacts without an alphabet of letters after our surname." His eyes crinkled at the corners when he smiled—a detail I again filed away under *Observations (Distracting, to be deleted)*.

"Appreciation is one thing." I launched into what my Cambridge colleagues called my 'lecture voice'—typically reserved for particularly dense undergraduate students. "But the systematic documentation of archaeological finds requires a thorough understanding of stratigraphic principles, context analysis, and—"

"—and the correlation between artifact placement and cultural significance," he finished with the smooth confidence of someone who'd never had to explain to a board of bitter old men why women should be allowed to dig up things besides their father's disappointment. "Just as the seal's position suggests ritual placement rather than casual discard, likely indicating—"

"I was about to say that." The words came out sharper than intended. I forced my voice back to proper neutrality. "The jar's positioning clearly demonstrates ceremonial significance, as evidenced by—"

"—the deliberate alignment with the tomb's eastern wall?" That insufferable smile again. "Do carry on, Doctor. Your expertise is rather fascinating."

Was he mocking me? I couldn't tell, which was even more infuriating. Was I defending historical integrity, or just repeating Cambridge doctrine like a well-trained parrot? In my years as an American woman at Cambridge, I'd learned well how to use my intellect, both as a weapon and a shield. I dove deeper into archaeological theory, wielding terms like "seriation analysis" and "typological classification," waiting for him to falter.

He didn't. Instead, he matched every point with casual ease, as if we were discussing the weather rather than complex archaeological principles. Worse, he kept noticing details I'd missed. Each observation squeezed my chest with the need to prove I knew more.

"Of course," I heard myself saying, "one must consider the implications of material degradation on chronological attribution..." I was babbling now, drowning him in terminology.

"Fascinating point." He leaned closer to examine the seal. "Though perhaps we should also consider the possibility that you're trying to impress me."

"I most certainly am not!" The traitorous stiffening of my spine suggested otherwise. "I'm simply ensuring proper academic rigor, which is clearly lacking in your... assessment."

"My assessment?" His laugh was warm, genuine. "I believe you mean my 'surprisingly well-informed observations,' as you noted earlier."

"I take it back," I muttered, though a traitorous part of me thrilled at a conversation that Dr. Bradford and his cronies would never have engaged in, at least not with me. "You're completely insufferable."

"And you're utterly captivating when you're being scholarly." He grinned. "Might we discuss pottery chronology next, then? I noticed some fascinating sherds in your tent earlier."

"You were spying on me?"

"Observing. It's an important skill in archaeology, wouldn't you agree? That's why I know you've been cataloging pottery all day, despite being far more qualified." He glanced at the dust on my sleeves. "The same way I know this dig is dramatically underfunded, making proper conservation of finds like this..." he gestured to the sketch, "...problematic at best."

"At least in a museum, it would be properly documented and available for scholarly study." I drew my shoulders back. "Not locked away in some private collection, gathering dust alongside hunting trophies and stolen artwork."

"Is that what you think private collectors do? How charmingly naive." He leaned closer, his voice dropping. "Would it surprise you to learn that several major museum discoveries of the past decade were only possible because of private funding?"

"Would it surprise you to learn that I don't believe a word you say?"

"On the contrary, I'd be disappointed if you did." He straightened. "You're far too clever for blind trust, I should think."

I spun to leave, but my elbow nudged a small pot perched on the table. *Not again.* If I broke another artifact today, Bradford's mustache might actually achieve liftoff and propel itself into orbit.

The stranger reached for the pot rolling across the table. "Allow me to—"

"Don't—" I lunged, but the awkward angle made it impossible to reach without disturbing the other artifacts. "I can manage."

"Clearly." He stepped in, his chest pressing against my back as he reached around me to steady the pot. "Though perhaps we could debate your stubbornness after saving the Fifth Dynasty vessel?"

The narrow confines of the tomb seemed to contract further as he pressed closer. "It's Fourth Dynasty, and I told you—" The words died in my throat as I became acutely aware of his presence, including warm breath on my neck. He smelled of sandalwood and leather-bound books—a combination I again filed under *Distractions (Dangerous)*. His hands were strong and surprisingly graceful for their size—the hands of someone used to handling delicate objects. Not that I was conducting a detailed analysis of his physical attributes. That would be most unscientific and embarrassingly unprofessional on at least seventeen different levels.

I extracted myself, irritated by my body's betrayal. Accepting help was bad enough without this inconvenient awareness of him.

"Thank you, but I had it under control."

"Of course you did." His smile suggested otherwise. "Just as the pot has Fourth Dynasty glazing techniques?"

I glared at him, annoyed to find his eyes dancing with amusement. "Fifth Dynasty. I was... testing you."

His distinctive tie, upon closer inspection, had a subtle pattern of tiny hieroglyphic symbols—a pretentious accessory that somehow managed to be both scholarly and fashionable.

"Who are you, anyway?"

"Forgive my bad manners." He tucked his notebook away. "Benedict Quinn, antiquities dealer, at your service. And I fancy I might help this dig achieve rather more than pottery catalogues."

"Antiquities dealer?" The words tasted bitter. My first impression had been accurate after all. I'd dealt with this sort nearly ten years ago, when I first visited Egypt. "You mean a glorified tomb robber."

"My clients have resources your museums can only dream of. Proper conservation, detailed documentation..." His eyes met mine, startlingly intense. "Freedom from the politics and budget constraints that keep brilliant minds cataloging pottery sherds."

"By selling our finds to private collectors?" I stepped between him and the table of fragments. The worst part was, I could see why some might be tempted. His argument was reasonable, practiced—and utterly wrong.

"As I said, these artifacts belong in museums. The preservation of history isn't for sale, Mr. Quinn."

"Everything's for sale, Dr. Bell. The only question is—"

Shouts erupted from outside the tomb, cutting him off.

We both turned toward the entrance.

"We are ready to open!" someone yelled.

The next mastaba tomb, awaiting our careful excavation, was ready to be entered.

For a moment, Quinn and I shared a look of pure, unguarded excitement—just two souls who lived for the thrill of discovery.

Then I remembered he was an antiquities dealer, and I was a proper archaeologist, and that some things, like mummies and moisture, were never meant to mix.

He slipped a business card into my hand, his fingers lingering just a moment too long. "If you want to see what real preservation looks like..." he murmured, leaving the invitation dangling like a partially translated hieroglyph.

I should have handed it back. I should have torn it to pieces. Instead, I tucked it into my pocket with the kind of swift efficiency that would have made Dr. Deveraux measure the exact velocity of my academic principles crumbling.

CHAPTER FOUR

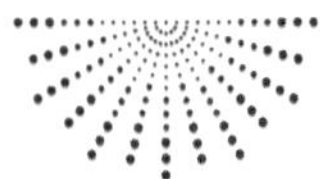

A week had passed since the opening of the new mastaba tomb, which proved considerably more interesting than my introduction to the dig site, though with fewer shattered pots. The new tomb was now designated as G 4215. (Archaeologists are very creative with naming conventions.)

These rectangular, flat-roofed structures served as both tombs and commemorative monuments, with G 4215 located in the Eastern Cemetery where nobles and high officials connected to the royal family were buried. Those who served Khufu during his reign nearly five thousand years ago competed fiercely for burial plots near their pharaoh during this golden age of pyramid building when the Great Pyramid and Sphinx were constructed, when Egypt maintained extensive trade networks stretching to Lebanon for cedar wood and Nubia for gold.

Early evidence suggested the tomb belonged to a scribe named Amenemhat. It was assumed he served Khufu from the Fourth Dynasty. Like most tombs in the vast cemetery sprawling at the Great Pyramid's feet, it had been ransacked in antiquity. Still, ancient thieves had left behind the less conventionally valuable items, presumably being too busy carrying off gold to appreciate the historical significance of more mundane artifacts. Their loss was our cataloging gain.

The opening might have been cause for universal celebration, if not for the Benedict Quinn incident. Bradford caught him making detailed sketches of the new tomb's layout without permission, leading to Dr. Bradford chasing him off site. Bradford accused him of industrial espionage, though Quinn claimed he was working for the Egyptian Museum. The truly irritating part? He was actually telling the truth—he had a legitimate contract as their consultant.

Deveraux, of course, had measured every millimeter of the new mastabas before being called away to Alexandria. Something about an urgent need for his precise calculations at a museum exhibition. His departure had left a blessed absence of wind-speed readings and trajectory calculations, though oddly, I yearned for his meticulous documentation of my various mishaps. At least someone had been paying attention to my work.

One week at this dig site had proven that archaeological success and personal humiliation were not, in fact, mutually exclusive.

By early Thursday morning, I was well-settled into my new "workspace."

A throat cleared behind me, the sound tentative and apologetic, barely audible above the background sounds of the dig.

"Miss Bell?"

I turned to find a slight young woman in dove-gray day dress with a fashionable dropped waist and subtle embroidery at the collar, clutching a carpetbag as if it might shield her from the desert heat.

"I'm Annie Evanwood." Your father sent me to... assist you."

She had the wide-eyed look of someone who'd never expected to find herself in Egypt, much less at an archaeological dig site.

"My father sent—" I stopped, shoulders tightening as comprehension dawned. "He didn't."

"Mr. Bell was most insistent that you have proper... support." Annie's cheeks turned rose pink. "Dr. Bradford arranged everything. He said it wasn't suitable for a lady of your background to be without... services."

Of course he had. Bradford probably thought having a lady's maid would remind everyone of my proper station—somewhere far from actual archaeology.

And Father? By sending Annie along a week behind me, he avoided my New York refusal of a lady's maid, and gave the poor girl no way to return home without his assistance.

Though looking at Annie's sweet, anxious face, I couldn't quite muster the appropriate indignation. She stood behind an upturned crate like a nervous sparrow, smoothing her immaculate skirts against the ever-present sand that infiltrated everything—not the romanticized silky desert sand of novels, but a coarser, more insistent variety that grated between pages of notebooks, scratched beneath fingernails, and somehow managed to infiltrate even sealed containers.

"Have you ever been to Egypt, Annie?"

She shook her head, then blurted, "But I brought all the necessary supplies for maintaining your wardrobe in the desert climate." Her determination to prove herself useful was touching. Her fingers twisted a handkerchief, before she squared her shoulders.

I glanced at my sand-encrusted work clothes and suppressed a smile. The idea of trying to maintain any sort of proper wardrobe here was laughably absurd. And yet. there was something rather pleasant about the thought of having someone to talk to who wasn't constantly measuring my scholarly worth.

"Does ancient Egypt interest you?"

"Oh, yes. All the novels—and the newspapers—make it sound so exotic." Her eyes brightened. "Though I do worry about all those curses they keep discovering. The papers in New York are full of stories about the terrible fates befalling those who disturb the tombs."

"Well then," I found myself warming to her, despite my

slight annoyance at the curse nonsense, "I suppose we'll make the best of it."

The morning heat pressed against us. While I had accepted the desert's brutal honesty—the way it stripped away pretension along with comfort—Annie's pinked cheeks and carefully concealed discomfort revealed how foreign it was.

Several of the younger archaeologists soon were finding reasons to pass by my tent more frequently, gawking at Annie as she efficiently organized my chaotic workspace into something resembling civilized quarters. Bradford clearly approved of her presence. Having a lady's maid no doubt made my archaeological pursuits more acceptably feminine.

I adjusted my classification cards for the fourteenth time that morning, clinging to the increasingly desperate hope that someone might actually notice my meticulous work. Although at this point, I'd settle for a passing "nice handwriting."

The rhythmic sounds of labor drifted from the main excavation—the clink of trowels against stone, the soft swish of brushes clearing sand, and the occasional triumphant exclamation. They were cataloging new finds from the G 4215 mastaba, while I was relegated to sorting the unremarkable finds from the last one.

A sparkle of sunlight on my brass magnifying glass brought a flash of irritation as I remembered Benedict Quinn's gold pocket watch glinting in the tomb's shadows, along with a recollection of the warmth of his hand near mine. The way he'd held the pocketwatch, fingers curled around the case with casual elegance, as if everything he touched naturally became more valuable—

I attacked the next pottery sherd with perhaps more vigor than necessary. No reason to waste mental energy on the man. Even if his suits fit him with mathematical precision.

"Is it true you went to Cambridge, Miss Bell?" Annie asked, carefully dusting sand from my field jacket—a hopeless task if I'd ever seen one.

"Doctor of Letters in Egyptology." I squinted at a particularly obstinate hieroglyph. "Though at the moment, my primary qualification appears to be 'person least likely to be missed if relegated to outer Mongolia.'"

Specimen: Female Archaeologist (Struggling), Modern Period, displaying symptoms of desperate need for validation while maintaining façade of indifference.

"And your father—" Annie hesitated, then continued with the air of someone who couldn't quite help herself, "I heard the other archaeologists talking. Does Armand Bell, the New York millionaire industrialist, truly approve of his daughter... digging?"

I grimaced, a tight knot forming in my stomach. Of course that would be the detail making rounds at camp. Not my published papers or my thesis on New Kingdom pottery classification. No, apparently my most noteworthy achievements were managing to disappoint both Daddy's social aspirations and my ex-fiancé's delicate sensibilities by choosing a career—*digging*—that involved more sand than soirées. Father had given me precisely one digging season to get Egypt out of my system before returning to New York and my "proper place in society."

"Father believes every problem can be solved by throwing either money or servants at the matter," I said, then immediately regretted my tone when Annie's face fell. "Though I must admit, he did show excellent judgment in sending you."

Annie brightened, smoothing her already immaculate dress. "He said you'd need someone with patience. And discretion. And..." she lowered her voice, "...a keen eye for suitable gentlemen from the proper families, who might entice you back to civilization."

I nearly dropped my classification cards, a sudden flash memory of Richard's disappointed face when I'd returned his ring making my fingers tremble. "He didn't."

"Oh yes." Annie's eyes sparkled with unexpected mischief. "Though I haven't seen many suitable candidates yet. Unless you count Dr. Sutherland with that dramatic alabaster streak in his hair. Rather distinguished, isn't he? Like a gentleman from a Gothic novel."

"Dr. Sutherland," I said with a dry smile, "is distinguished because he's one of the few men here who actually reads research papers like mine, instead of using them to wrap his lunch. The white streak came from a lifetime of actual archaeology, not romantic brooding in towers. Unlike Bradford, he values both academic precision and treating his colleagues as actual human beings, regardless of gender."

"It sounds as though you like him very much."

"Sutherland was a mentor to me, at Cambridge. Treated me like a scholar, not simply an American heiress on holiday. So yes, I do like him. In fact, I wouldn't be here, if it weren't for him."

Well, him, and Daddy's money.

Through the tent flap, I could hear our field photographer Roberts and Dr. Sutherland in conversation. Hopefully Sutherland hadn't heard Annie's romantic suggestion.

"Rosamund Fairchild's arriving next week," Sutherland called out. "Did you hear about her discoveries at Deir el-Bahari?"

"Remarkable work," Roberts replied. "Bradford's practically giddy about having her join us. Says she's exactly the sort of serious scholar we need."

I gripped my pencil harder, knuckles whitening and a familiar heat creeping up my neck. Someone might as well have carved the words in stone: *not* the sort of serious scholar they need.

It was more than that, though. Fairchild had been a professor of mine at Cambridge as well. Where the glowing reviews of her latest publication had conveniently failed to mention my contributions to her analysis of that pottery fragment just six months ago.

No matter. I'd do my job well enough that someone, somewhere would notice.

I scanned the minor finds pulled from the tomb, spread across my table. Which to work on next?

Perhaps the wooden scribe's palette. The foot-long piece of slim wood was beautiful—acacia wood, still smooth after millennia in the sand, with the desert having miraculously preserved its original reed brushes. Twin rows of shallow depressions ran its length, each still stained with traces of red ochre and kohl ink. The hieroglyphs painted along its edge were worn but legible, and the cord holes at one end suggested it had once been carried at its owner's waist, bouncing against his kilt as he walked the palace corridors.

Over four thousand years had passed since a living hand had last traced these hieroglyphs. Yet holding this palette, I felt a spark of connection transcending millennia. The wood grain beneath my fingertips told stories beyond what was written— of hands like mine that had once held it daily, of ink-stained fingers moving methodically across papyrus scrolls, of someone whose name now echoed only through these artifacts. In this moment, separated from the academic posturing at the main dig, I felt closer to the scribe Amenemhat than to my contemporary colleagues bustling importantly around their grids of string and stakes.

I ran a finger over its surface, imagining the scribe dipping his reed pen, recording the day's business in precise columns of text. When warmed by my touch, a surprising fragrance emanated from the palette—a subtle, resinous perfume of acacia preserved in desert dryness, carrying faint undertones of ancient oils and minerals from pigments long since dried but never completely vanished.

Most telling were the ink stains—not just the usual red ochre and kohl I'd first noted, but traces of blue pigment—not sky blue but deeper, more mystical. "Egyptian blue" was not typically used for documents. It was one of the world's first synthetic pigments, and must be a mark of the scribe's elite status.

"What were you used for, my blue-stained friend?" I murmured to the piece.

Egyptian scribes were among the few literate people in ancient Egypt—less than one percent of the population could read and write—and they held prestigious positions in society as the keepers of knowledge and royal records.

I examined the glyphs more closely. Would they yield a clue as to his court position?

Wait a moment...

"Annie, look at this." I traced the hieroglyphs with a careful finger. "These cartouches—they're not what we'd expect."

Annie leaned closer, her eyes sharp with interest. "How so?"

But I missed her question. My heart had begun to race as I translated the faded symbols, checking and double-checking my reading, my breath quickening until I nearly gasped. This couldn't be right.

"Miss?" Annie's voice seemed to come from very far away. "Are you all right? You've gone quite pale."

I swallowed hard, my throat dry. There was no mistaking what I was seeing.

CHAPTER FIVE

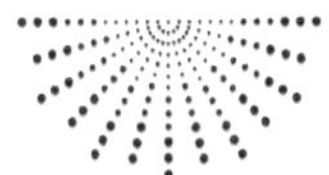

The afternoon heat pressed down like a physical weight as I stared at the scribe's palette, decoding the hieroglyphs for the tenth time. Perhaps I'd gone sand-mad. That would certainly be a more rational explanation than what I was uncovering.

The dating was all wrong—the symbols suggested New Kingdom rather than Old Kingdom origin, which would completely disrupt the established chronology of this tomb. If true, it would be a spectacular find here on the Giza Plateau, where New Kingdom burials were nearly non-existent.

My hand quivered as I pointed to the faded marks along the back, keeping my voice steady. "These marks here. They're not just standard scribe's notation. See how this cartouche links to—" A flash momentarily blinded me as Roberts, our photographer, seized the moment to immortalize my discovery. Wonderful. I'd appear in the official documentation looking like an owl caught in lamplight.

But none of that mattered. Because if I was right about what I was seeing, everything was about to change.

Dr. Sutherland materialized beside my cataloging table with his characteristic silent grace—a skill I suspected he'd perfected during decades of tiptoeing around fragile artifacts.

"What have you found, Dr. Bell?" His voice held none of Bradford's patronizing tone—only genuine scholarly interest.

The Egyptian Antiquities Service representative, Mr. Hassan, paused his conversation with two workers who'd been carefully screening soil nearby and ducked into my open tent. His pristine white linen suit gleamed in the sunlight with almost supernatural brightness against the dusty canvas backdrop. As the official guardian of Egypt's heritage, appointed by the Service to monitor foreign excavations, he had the power to halt our entire dig with a single word. The Antiquities Service, established more than sixty years ago, had begun pushing for more Egyptian control over excavations amid rising nationalist sentiment, creating an undercurrent of tension between Hassan and the European archaeologists.

I held the palette to Sutherland's bent form, running a gloved finger under the faded markings I'd noted.

"Most irregular," Sutherland murmured, producing a magnifying glass from somewhere within his rumpled field jacket. "This could suggest a direct royal connection..."

Bradford appeared so suddenly I wondered if he had some sort of supernatural ability to detect potentially significant finds.

"I believe I've made a significant discovery here, Dr. Bradford."

He leaned over the palette and squinted. The monocle dropped from his eye, but he caught it. "Good heavens, you can't possibly believe—"

"That our humble scribe Amenemhat worked for a much later king than Khufu?" I failed to suppress the triumph from my voice. My chin lifted. "That's exactly what I'm suggesting."

The next few hours dissolved into a flurry of documentation, photography, and heated debates about historical implications—during which I noticed my name being mentioned less and less frequently as the senior archaeologists began referring to "our discovery" and "the team's findings."

"This discovery could change everything." Bradford's chest was puffing visibly, his pitch rising. "The British Museum will surely increase our funding when they hear we've found evidence of New Kingdom burials at Giza. We might even attract other American patrons with deeper pockets than the Museum."

Mr. Hassan made careful notes in his own journal, while I observed several Egyptian workers huddled together, exchanging whispers while glancing toward the European archaeologists with undisguised suspicion.

But when I returned from the mess tent, after eating a sadly rushed affair involving something that might have been goat in a previous incarnation, I found my carefully ordered workspace in chaos. Cards scattered like confetti, reference books splayed open, and most importantly...

The scribe's palette.

It was gone.

My stomach plummeted. I stared at the violation of my workspace, back stiff and breaths turning shallow. With deliberate effort, I forced myself to analyze the scene.

Fine sand infiltrated everything, creating a persistent grittiness in my notebooks and coating the back of my throat with each breath—the desert's way of claiming even the most carefully maintained order.

It was truly gone.

At the news, the camp erupted into a frenzy. Workers retraced their steps, archaeologists ransacked their own workspaces, and at least three colleagues attempted to search the same empty crate simultaneously. The frantic shuffling of papers produced a sound like desert beetles scurrying through dry leaves, desperation growing louder as our search proved futile.

"It can't have just vanished." Bradford executed his elaborate throat-clearing routine, a performance that involved three distinct pitches and always preceded his most pompous pronouncements. "Unless you're suggesting we have a tomb ghost with a particular interest in scribal implements?"

"Certainly it was only misplaced." Sutherland's voice remained measured, though his darting glances at Mr. Hassan suggested he was thinking about exactly how many ways the Egyptian Antiquities Service could make our lives difficult if we'd managed to lose such a significant artifact less than twenty-four hours after its discovery.

I began composing my letter home: *Dear Father, Remember how you wanted me to pursue a career in something more respectable than archaeology? You'll be delighted to know I've branched out into losing priceless historical artifacts. Much more exciting than the debutante ball, really.*

Mr. Hassan's placid diplomatic demeanor was evaporating. "This is precisely why these artifacts belong in Egyptian institutions!" He gestured toward the dig site with an open palm. "Foreign expeditions treat our heritage like their personal property!"

"Now see here—" Bradford began, but Hassan wasn't finished.

"While you catalogue and classify our history, I remind you that these treasures were created by my ancestors, not yours." Hassan's voice lowered. "And in these times of change, the question of who truly owns Egypt's past becomes increasingly relevant to who will control its future."

Ignoring Hassan, Bradford pulled out his handkerchief, dabbed his forehead, and glared at me. "Well, it seems obvious we should start by questioning your little helper, Miss Bell. After all, your maid is the only stranger to arrive on site today." His pipe tobacco left a pungent cloud around him, mingling unpleasantly with the scent of wool too heavy for the Egyptian climate.

"Annie?" I couldn't help laughing. "I can assure you she spent the entire afternoon engaged in a tragically futile battle with my laundry, until I sent her back to her lodging with a headache brought on by, and I quote, 'Miss Bell's shocking disregard for proper garment storage.'"

Bradford's eyes constricted. "And you can be certain of this?"

"Absolutely. Annie may be determined to salvage my social graces, but she thinks these artifacts are, as she put it this morning, 'dreadfully dusty and in need of a good wash.' The very notion of her attempting to steal one is absurd."

Outside, the desert evening had transformed from merely cool to biting cold, the temperature plummeting as dramatically as my professional prospects. Beyond our discussion, the desert night provided its own symphony—distant jackals calling, the soft crunch of sand beneath pacing feet, and the almost imperceptible whisper of dunes shifting in the night wind.

Dr. Sutherland's glasses caught the lamplight as he studied my scattered cards, his obsidian-black hair with its dramatic white streak making him look like a living stratification line. "More to the point, this was clearly a deliberate search. Someone with enough archaeological knowledge to recognize the significance of what they were taking."

"Indeed." I gestured to how the cards had been scattered. "Look at how they searched—they ignored all the other artifacts and expensive tools, going straight for the palette. This wasn't some random theft. Someone knew exactly what those hieroglyphs meant."

Or someone who deliberately intended to undermine my success, and even my career.

Bradford paced. "This is a disaster. If word gets out—especially with the British Museum delegation arriving next week—"

The excavation tent, spacious during daylight hours, had contracted in the evening gloom, forcing us all uncomfortably close. Each gesture sent shadows leaping across canvas walls, and every raised voice seemed to press the air from the enclosed space.

"Actually," Dr. Deveraux cleared his throat in the way dons had been perfecting since the Middle Ages, "I may have a solution."

Attention shifted to him.

"Benedict Quinn."

Bradford's face flushed. He yanked out his monogrammed handkerchief and began polishing his monocle with vigor. "That charlatan? That... that tomb robber in a tailored suit?"

"That Egyptian Museum consultant," Deveraux countered, "with extensive connections throughout Cairo's antiquities community—both legal and, shall we say, less traditional?"

Bradford harrumphed.

"Quinn's expertise in tracking stolen artifacts is quite remarkable. The piece is likely to show up on the black market soon. Who better to locate it?" Deveraux adjusted his collar. "And given that the Antiquities Service is closely aligned with the Museum, giving them certain... rights—"

"Absolutely not!" Bradford's mustache achieved full defensive formation.

"Then perhaps," Deveraux said, "you'd prefer to simply apologize to the Antiquities Service, for losing a potentially royal artifact? I'm sure they'd be fascinated by your theories about tomb ghosts with a penchant for office supplies."

Dr. Sutherland removed his glasses and pinched the bridge of his nose. "I don't trust that man. Quinn. He's as likely to pocket the piece himself."

Bradford rocked forward on his toes, his hands clasped behind his back like a general planning a campaign. "Yes, well. We would need someone who can document everything Quinn discovers. Someone with impeccable attention to detail and a thorough knowledge of proper archaeological protocol. Someone who can ensure any recovered artifacts are handled correctly and documented properly."

Deveraux nodded. "Someone whose presence will ensure this remains an official archaeological investigation rather than a mere... treasure hunt. The British Museum would certainly feel more comfortable with one of our own scholars involved."

Bradford's expression shifted from outrage to calculation as he turned toward me.

"Miss Bell has certainly demonstrated her... thoroughness in documentation. And she's not currently essential to the excavation work." His eyes lit with a gleam as though the sudden inspiration had been his own. "Yes, perhaps this is the perfect assignment for someone of her... particular talents."

I stared at him, unconsciously fiddling with my collar before catching myself. "Surely you're not suggesting—"

"Miss Bell." Bradford whipped out his stained monogrammed handkerchief and dabbed at his forehead, a nervous habit that emerged whenever his authority was challenged. "Consider this your opportunity for redemption. After that unfortunate incident with the pottery—"

"You want me to work with Benedict Quinn? The man you just called a 'tomb robber in a tailored suit?'"

The man whose eyebrows arch in that infuriating way whenever he thinks he's being clever?

"Unless you'd prefer to return to sorting pottery fragments?" His smile sweetened. "By color and size, of course."

Dr. Sutherland's glasses caught the lamplight as he watched this exchange, his mouth pressed into a thin line. "An excellent suggestion. We can trust Dr. Bell's analytical abilities implicitly in this... investigation."

A flutter rose in my stomach—purely professional dread, of course. Although, perhaps this could be my chance—to do something significant enough to finally earn respect despite my gender. I'd need to remain vigilant, analytical.

Specimen: Career Opportunity (Dubious), featuring collaboration with irritatingly handsome antiquities dealer.

Notable elements include complete destruction of professional dignity, forced proximity to excessively tailored suits, and high probability of disaster. Typical.

CHAPTER SIX

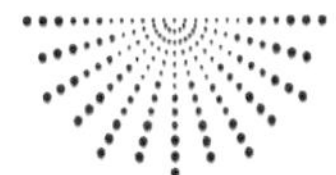

From the street, the café in Islamic Cairo looked exactly like the sort of place where respectable archaeologists went to destroy their careers. Brass lamps cast shadows that danced across intricately carved wooden screens. On the street in front, smoke from hookah pipes curled through the air like ancient apple-scented tomb gases.

I trailed Quinn toward the entrance, cataloging our descent into archaeological impropriety.

The café reeked of intrigue, over-steeped tea and question-able life choices.

I had already filed the experience under *Catastrophically Bad Ideas, Early 20th Century, Egyptian Subdivision.*

Quinn had agreed to help track down the missing artifact. "The Egyptian Museum prefers their consultants to prevent theft rather than facilitate it," he'd explained earlier, managing to sound both principled and shifty at the same time. "Besides, Dr. Bell, if someone's going to profit from your missing palette, it really should be me."

The worst part was, I couldn't tell if he was joking.

And now he'd orchestrated this entire meeting with the flair of someone accustomed to bending rules and people to his will.

The café's interior was a palimpsest of Cairo's history—Ottoman-era ceiling beams supporting British electrical fixtures, ancient stone floors worn smooth by centuries of footsteps beneath modern European furniture. Like my current moral dilemma, nothing was purely one thing or another, each layer obscuring and revealing the complexities beneath.

I scanned the room. A waiter with a jacket that hung oddly on one side—concealing something, perhaps. Two men at a corner table, who abruptly ceased their whispered conversation as we passed. My skin prickled with the distinct sensation of being watched.

"Your contact 'specializes in lost artifacts,'" I whispered as we settled at a corner table. "Which I assume is a polite pretense for 'trafficking in stolen goods'?"

Quinn smoothed his suit sleeves. His tall frame towered over most of the café patrons, dark hair just slightly too long for proper society, but combed back in waves. Those penetrating brown eyes missed nothing as they surveyed the room, his body positioned with clear sightlines to all entrances and exits. "Think of him as an informal curator of wandering antiquities."

"How charmingly euphemistic. Next you'll tell me grave robbers are 'freelance extraction specialists.'" I glanced around the room, where several patrons were doing their best to look like they weren't doing anything suspicious, which of course made them look supremely suspicious. "I don't suppose the Egyptian Museum knows about your alternative artifact acquisition strategies?"

"The Egyptian Museum?" Quinn's voice was infuriatingly calm. "I find most museums prefer not to keep abreast of such matters regarding how certain previously-missing artifacts find their way into their collection."

Honeycomb patterns of amber light danced across the walls, tossed there by perforated brass lamps hung from chains blackened by decades of smoke. Conversations in Arabic, French, and English ebbed and flowed, creating a linguistic tide pool where secrets and gossip seemed to swirl together, occasionally washing close enough for me to catch fragments before receding into the general murmur.

Outside, the evening was still hot, pressing down on Cairo like a physical weight, trapping the day's tensions. Inside the café, ceiling fans fought a losing battle against the temperature, their lazy revolutions mirroring my circling thoughts. The bitter scent of Turkish coffee mingled with the sweeter notes of apple tobacco from the water pipes, creating an aromatic tapestry as layered and complex as the city itself.

Quinn signaled for coffee with the casual authority of someone who considered the entire city his private club, effortlessly winning over a suspicious server with a smile and a few words of Arabic.

I watched with a mixture of irritation and reluctant admiration.

He turned to me. "So. The daughter of Armand Bell, steel magnate and patron of the arts. I imagine that arranging to have you work on this dig considerably simplified the funding arrangements for them."

I stiffened. "I earned my place through my doctoral work on pottery classification systems, not my father's bank account."

"Of course." His smile could have coaxed water from desert stone. "I'm sure Dr. Bradford found your father's generous contribution to the expedition purely coincidental."

"I specifically told Father not to—" I stopped as Quinn's knowing smirk spread across his face. My jaw clenched involuntarily. "How exactly do you know about that?"

"I make it my business to keep abreast of such matters." He leaned forward, his knee brushing mine. Close enough that I caught a whiff of expensive cologne. "Just as I know your thesis on faience glazing techniques in Middle Kingdom ceremonial vessels was brilliant, if tragically under-appreciated by the archaeological establishment."

My stomach clenched. Was I allowing myself to trust him simply because he flattered my academic vanity? I retreated into cool skepticism. "You've read my thesis?" I narrowed my eyes.

"Let me guess—professional interest in which sites might yield valuable artifacts for your less-than-legitimate acquisitions?"

"You wound me, Dr. Bell." He pressed a hand to his heart with theatrical flair, his other hand absentmindedly fidgeting with a small ancient coin he'd pulled from his pocket. "Though I must say, your conclusions about the Abydos specimens left me rather unconvinced."

"The Abydos—" I nearly upended my coffee. "Those conclusions were perfectly sound, based on extensive—"

"Analysis of surface wear patterns?" His eyes danced. "I found your methodology fascinating. Almost as fascinating as your decision to fund your own research rather than use your father's connections. Though I believe you missed the secondary chisel marks on the southern face of the ceremonial basin."

I heard my voice rise half an octave as I launched into defense of my methodology—a tell I thought I'd trained myself out of years ago. "No, I documented those clearly in appendix B, figure 14! They were consistent with—"

I stopped, blinking. "You really did do your homework."

"Professional interest." He adjusted his cuffs, a gesture I was beginning to recognize as his tell for actual sincerity. "Though I admit, I'm curious why someone with your resources would choose to dig in the dirt with academics who don't appreciate your genius."

"Because history doesn't care about social connections or family names." I met his gaze. "It only cares about who has the patience to uncover its secrets properly."

"Ah." He settled back, something like respect flickering across his features. "And here I thought you were just staging a rebellion against Daddy's plans for you to marry some wealthy industrialist."

"That was just a bonus." I shrugged. "Though I did accidentally break his favorite Ming vase when he suggested I consider a more 'ladylike' profession."

"Practicing your excavation techniques early, were you?"

"Well, one does need to start somewhere."

His laugh was unexpectedly genuine.

I smirked. "Though I suppose you started by selling your classmates' marbles as 'ancient gaming pieces.'"

"Not quite. 'Roman gaming spheres,' if you please. Made twice my pocket money that term."

I tried not to smile and failed miserably. Fortunately, I was saved from further unwanted camaraderie by the arrival of a man wearing an expertly fitted European suit that probably cost more than my entire academic salary, and a smile that suggested he found everything quietly amusing.

The café's layout created a natural intimacy—outer tables exposed to the street's view, inner sanctums shielded by carved screens and strategically placed hookahs. Quinn had positioned us at the perfect midpoint between secrecy and escape.

"Ah, Mr. Quinn." The English carried just a hint of French schooling. "And this must be the distinguished Dr. Bell. Your reputation precedes you, though I must say your academic papers failed to mention how lovely you are. I am Rashid Hafiz. I was most interested to hear about your... missing palette."

I nodded, trying for polite disdain. "How fascinating you've heard about it already. Considering the theft occurred less than twenty-four hours ago." I frowned. "One might suspect an established network of artifact redistribution specialists."

"Information, like the blessed Nile, nourishes those who know where to drink, Miss Bell." Hafiz produced a small folio with the flourish of a magician and turned to Quinn. His fingers drummed a precise rhythm on the leather—too measured to be unaware, too deliberate to be nervous. "Speaking of which, I've recently become informed of several pieces that might interest you. A remarkable set of canopic jars that simply appeared one morning, like a gift from Osiris himself. A royal seal that went on an unexpected journey. Some amulets that decided to relocate..."

Each casual mention felt like a physical blow to me. My stomach tightened with each item he listed. These weren't just stolen treasures—they were pieces whose disappearances had devastated legitimate excavations. Pieces that belonged in museums, being studied and shared with the world, not sold to private collectors like exotic pets.

"You speak as though these items *chose* to leave their excavation sites," I said coldly. "When in fact they were stolen from their rightful context."

Hafiz raised an eyebrow. "Perspective is everything, Dr. Bell. One might argue I'm merely returning balance to a system that has plundered my country for centuries."

I sat straighter. "How can you possibly justify—"

"The palette," Quinn interrupted, leaning forward with an intensity that made Hafiz draw back. "You mentioned you might have information?"

"Ah, yes." Hafiz nodded. "Though such information usually requires certain... considerations. Perhaps some flexibility regarding access to your current excavation site?"

I opened my mouth to tell him exactly what I thought about that suggestion, but movement near the door caught my attention. A familiar figure in wire-rimmed glasses and streak of white in his dark hair was making his way toward us. My nose caught the distinctive scent of his preferred tobacco—Virginia blend with hints of cherry—before he even reached our table.

"Dr. Sutherland?" I couldn't keep the surprise from my voice. "What are you doing here?"

"My dear, I was rather alarmed when word reached me of your excursion with Mr. Quinn," Sutherland smiled that carefully cultivated smile that had charmed countless university benefactors, but something about it seemed too practiced, his eyes never quite meeting mine. "This quarter of Cairo can be most perilous for a lady of scientific pursuits."

Quinn and Hafiz exchanged a look I couldn't quite interpret, Quinn's body language subtly shifting to place himself between me and Sutherland.

"How fortunate you found us." Quinn's voice carried an edge I hadn't heard.

"Indeed." Sutherland pulled up a chair. "I hope I'm not interrupting any progress on locating our missing artifact?"

Hafiz's smile didn't waver. "As I was explaining to your colleagues, I might be able to assist. My network is quite extensive. Though of course, such assistance would require certain considerations. Perhaps an opportunity to examine your dig site? I have such an... academic interest in your work."

"The world of archaeology is full of compromises," Sutherland sighed, a flicker of genuine weariness crossing his features. "We all make concessions to politics, funding, institutional demands. Sometimes one must bend to preserve what matters most."

I felt my integrity crumbling faster than a half-baked mud brick. The palette was important—potentially career-defining if my suspicions about its inscriptions were correct. It was the kind of discovery that could force the stuffed shirts of archaeology to actually read my papers instead of using them to level wobbly desk legs.

And if we could bribe Hafiz to help us recover it quickly, quietly...

No. I wouldn't compromise everything I believed about preservation and proper archaeological practice. I wouldn't become part of the very system I despised.

Apparently coffee was insufficient, because mint tea arrived at the table. I sipped, but it was scalding hot and barely sweet, its bracing flavor at odds with the murky moral waters into which I was wading.

I set the cup down and shook my head. "I'm afraid we couldn't possibly—"

But then I saw them. Partially hidden under Hafiz's leather folio. Detailed drawings of our dig site. The tomb layouts. The grid markers. The equipment placement. All sketched with precise detail that could only have come from someone with intimate knowledge of our excavation.

Knowledge that had to have predated the theft.

My heart hammered against my ribs as I grasped the ramifications. I suddenly felt cold despite the café's oppressive heat.

But before I could process this discovery, the café's atmosphere shifted like air pressure before a tomb collapse.

Several men had entered. Armed. Searching.

Conversations around us stuttered to silence.

Quinn's hand gripped my arm. "We need to leave. Now."

"But—"

He scowled. "Unless you fancy cataloguing their rather impressive collection of persuasion techniques?"

Quinn pulled me toward the back of the café.

The heavy wooden door to the back room creaked on iron hinges that had probably witnessed centuries of secrets being whispered, bargains being struck, alliances forming and dissolving.

I glanced back to see Sutherland still seated, calmly speaking with the newcomers as if discussing the weather, his eyes darting to the drawings when he thought no one was looking.

We burst into a narrow alley. The evening air pressed around us, thick with more than just heat and dust.

Quinn still held my arm, dragging me toward the open street.

The alley behind the café assaulted us with the pungent aroma of cumin, coriander, and fenugreek from a nearby spice merchant.

I yanked my arm free, but stayed close.

"Those drawings." I was breathless. "They had to have existed before the theft. No one's been allowed near the site since. What does it mean that Hafiz had them?"

"Perhaps your distinguished Dr. Sutherland is playing a far more complicated game than simple academic excavation."

I stopped short, my academic world tilting on its axis. "That can't be true. Dr. Sutherland mentored me, helped me get a place on this dig..."

Quinn's smile held no humor. "Welcome to my world, Dr. Bell. It's considerably grayer than your ivory tower."

Footsteps echoed across the alley behind us, and Quinn

pulled me into a shadowy doorway, his back to the street and shielding me with his body.

I pressed against ancient stones that had probably witnessed centuries of similar desperate attempts.

"Why are we hiding?" I kept my voice low.

He shook his head. His shoulder pressed against mine.

I became acutely aware of his breathing, the rhythm oddly synchronizing with my own.

The footsteps receded.

"Has anyone ever told you," Quinn said, his voice low, "that your eyes are rather extraordinary? Like ancient jade with flecks of gold when you're angry." His gaze roamed my face, down to my neck. "Which seems to be most of the time in my company."

I inched away from him as much as the space allowed. "Has anyone ever told you that commenting on a colleague's physical attributes while hiding from potential murderers is deeply inappropriate?"

"Frequently," he admitted with an unrepentant smile. "Though usually with less eloquence."

He hesitated, then stepped into the darkening street, and continued walking as though the incident had been an everyday occurrence.

"Hold on a second! Are you going to explain—"

He shrugged. "Some past difficulties, trying to catch up with me. Nothing that concerns you." He continued on.

I followed. Where were we going?

The soft clattering of copper pots from a nearby kitchen echoed through the narrow passage, temporarily drowning out the clip-clop of donkey hooves and the persistent calls of street vendors. The evening sun, nearly gone, slanted through the alley at a sharp angle, turning dust motes into floating gold and casting our elongated shadows against walls the color of aged papyrus.

"So..." I watched Quinn's broad silhouette outlined by sunset. My voice sharpened. "You are saying I have two choices. Either trusting the devil I know—that's you, in case that wasn't clear—or the devil who might have a Cambridge fellowship plus a side job in artifact theft."

"Devil? I prefer to think of myself as more of an ethically flexible guardian angel."

"Yes, because nothing says 'divine intervention' quite like back-alley meetings with suspicious art dealers." I sighed. "You know what's truly tragic? I'm starting to think your morally ambiguous approach to archaeology might actually be necessary."

Quinn's laugh was barely a breath. "You've now met preservation in Egypt, Dr. Bell. Where sometimes the best way to protect history is to bend the rules."

"That's absolutely horrifying." I straightened my jacket and stopped walking. "Where are we going?"

"I've got something rather important I'd like you to examine. I need your expertise."

"Another shady café?"

He turned, smiling. "No. In my hotel room."

I waggled my eyebrows. "Why, Mr. Quinn, how forward of you. But I require at least three scholarly debates and a formal disagreement over pottery dating techniques before visiting a gentleman's quarters."

He tilted his head and exhaled with some amount of frustration. "Some documents about a few other recent finds, which I think have bearing on your current situation."

"You're trying to bribe me with academic resources." I grinned. "That's remarkably astute of you."

"I do pay attention."

Our eyes met in a moment of shared humor.

"Right then." I squared my shoulders. "Lead on, my Morally Ambiguous Guardian Angel."

CHAPTER SEVEN

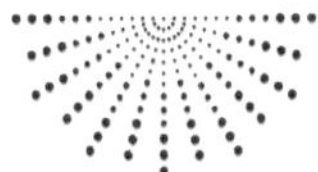

The front of Shepheard's Hotel boasted a grand colonial facade and towering palm trees lining the entrance. Inside, the alabaster columns caught the honeyed light of brass chandeliers, transforming ordinary limestone into luminous pillars that absorbed and reflected Cairo's golden sunsets.

I tugged at my tweed jacket, while around me, Cairo's elite glittered and preened in the crystal-dripped lighting, their gowns and dinner jackets spangled with precious gems. Throughout the lobby seating, glasses clinked like delicate wind chimes, punctuating the hushed murmurs of colonial administrators exchanging secrets over gin cocktails and exaggerated expedition tales.

The scene reminded me of my father's New York society gatherings—brilliant, beautiful, and equally focused on who belonged and who didn't. I'd escaped those gilded cages for dusty dig sites, much to his ongoing disappointment.

Shepheard's had been the epicenter of British colonial society in Cairo for more than sixty years. The hotel was where archaeological discoveries were often first announced—and expedition funding secured—over brandy and cigars.

I trailed after Quinn into his natural habitat, to the base of the grand marble staircase, where several society ladies were giving me glares.

"I'm beginning to wish you'd suggested meeting some-where less—"

"Magnificent? Sophisticated? Civilized?"

"I was going to say 'riddled with people who look like they've never seen a woman in practical clothing.'"

"Perhaps they're stunned by your innovative approach to evening wear. Not everyone appreciates the bold statement of excavation-ready fashion at eight in the evening."

I could practically hear their clucking: *shocking disregard for propriety by visiting gentleman's quarters unescorted.*

Quinn's suite proved to be less of a hotel room and more of a museum curator's fever dream. Maps and documents blanketed every tabletop and credenza, while artifacts that belonged in glass cases perched casually on side tables as if they were common ornaments. The suite's opulence felt like a physical manifestation of Quinn himself—gorgeous, impressive, and utterly divorced from the dusty reality of proper archaeological work, where artifacts earned their context through meticulous documentation rather than purchasing power.

"Please, make yourself comfortable." Quinn motioned to a Louis XV armchair upholstered in pomegranate-red silk damask, its gilt frame gleaming and carved legs ending in lion's paws. "I believe you'll find this rather interesting."

The damask upholstery felt slick and cool beneath my fingertips, its silk threads arranged in patterns that mirrored motifs I'd seen on New Kingdom wall paintings—beauty echoing across millennia. I realized with a jolt that the chair was likely brought to Egypt during Napoleon's 1798 campaign and subsequently claimed as a "souvenir" by British forces after the French defeat—making it an artifact with its own history. It reminded me of the Louis XVI piece in Father's study where I'd first announced my intention to pursue Egyptology rather than marry his business partner's son. The memory of his thunderous expression still brought a small smile to my face. Breaking my engagement with Richard last month had been painful but necessary—both men had expected marriage would "cure" my archaeological ambitions.

But my first visit to Egypt at the age of seventeen had instilled a reverence for these pieces that even six years at Cambridge couldn't formalize away. These weren't merely objects to be possessed—unlike what my father's millionaire friends seemed to believe when they displayed their 'exotic souvenirs.'

"I'm seeing quite enough already." I picked up a small ushabti statuette with obvious Dynasty 18 characteristics. "How did you end up in this ridiculous collection, you poor thing?" I looked up at Quinn. "Do you always travel with a portable museum of questionably acquired antiquities?"

"Only the ones that help me track down their missing friends." He unfurled a series of documents across his desk. "Speaking of which..."

Quinn's maps spread across the table like a visual confession of his reach. The comprehensive network simultaneously impressed and infuriated me—how many proper excavations had I been denied while this man traversed the ancient world at will?

Quinn trailed his finger along one of his maps. "These are the theft locations of the pieces I've been tracking. Some of them stolen from private collections, not just digs or museums. Whoever is doing this is rather more clever than that."

I leaned over the table, devouring the documents with my eyes.

He tapped the map. "These people aren't just common thieves—they're organized, methodical."

"Unlike your filing system." I began straightening a stack of documents near me, imposing order on the chaos.

Quinn stopped my fidgeting with a light touch on my hand.

I jerked back as though I'd received a shock.

"My system serves its purpose splendidly." He shifted a stack of parchments, revealing what appeared to be a Dynasty 19 scarab amulet used as a paperweight. I noticed how he subtly positioned himself between me and certain artifacts on his desk—particularly an ornate gold ring and a small limestone carving.

"Yes, I can see that." The papyrus fragments rustled with a distinctive dry whisper as Quinn shifted them, a sound so familiar from my excavation work that it momentarily transported me from his luxurious suite back to the dig site's artifact tent.

"Dr. Bell." He tilted toward me, his expression serious. "There's something bigger happening here. Look at these artifacts—all items vanishing shortly after discovery. Someone has access to information, now apparently including excavation details, before finds are even documented."

I studied the papers, academic curiosity battling with my moral outrage.

"Are these... do they all..." I glanced at Quinn.

He shrugged and shook his head, as though confused.

After a moment's consideration, I made a conscious decision to throw distrust to the wind. "Look. This lapis-inlaid scarab from the Metropolitan Museum. And this inlaid ritual knife from the museum here. They both have the Egyptian blue frit. So do some of these others..."

Quinn frowned. "Frit...?"

"It's basically the world's oldest synthetic pigment, made from copper, lime, silicone, and an alkali, fired very hot to create a glassy blue material that can be ground down into a pigment." My voice automatically shifted into my academic tone, clipped and formal.

He nodded. "This is the Egyptian blue that was so popular?"

"Yes, tomb walls, pottery, furnishings. Even portraits at one point. It mimics the lapis lazuli stone in color." I leaned forward, my words quickening. "Its formula was lost with the fall of the Roman Empire, then rediscovered by modern chemistry in the 1800s."

"And each of these items—"

"Yes, see, here? Not every item on your list, but most of

them, they have at least some of the Egyptian blue pigment. Or at least, they have blue pigment. It's possible, but unlikely, that it's actually the more expensive lapis lazuli stone, ground down to use as pigment."

"Like your pendant?"

I touched the chain around my neck. How had he seen the piece I always kept tucked away? I'd worn it since my first trip to Egypt, a memento with more importance than I cared to explain at the moment.

"Yes."

Quinn leaned over the list, his brow furrowed in concentration. The lamplight caught the angles of his face—the sharp cheekbones, the strong jaw, the slight crook in his nose that suggested it had met something solid at least once in his adventurous career.

He smoothed a hand over his hair, then adjusted his tie. "This situation appears to be getting a touch complicated. We must handle our little enquiry... unofficially."

"Unofficially?" I arched an eyebrow. "Like how you 'unofficially' acquired that rather obvious Sixth Dynasty calcite vessel you're using to hold your fountain pens?"

"Would you prefer it ended up destroyed by amateurs who don't know what they're handling?"

That hit uncomfortably close to my own recent pottery-breaking incident.

But before I could form a suitably cutting reply, a document caught my eye. The inventory list was familiar—too familiar. My hand shook as I picked it up.

"This is from our dig site. Other items that haven't even been officially cataloged yet." The implications settled in my stomach. "Where did you get this?"

"It was passed to me by one of my contacts yesterday. Now you understand why we can't go to the authorities. We can't know who is involved." Quinn's voice was grim. "The question is, Dr. Bell, are you prepared to work outside your carefully ordered academic world?"

I stared at the document. This situation was rapidly deteriorating from *Professional Crisis (Minor)* to *Career-Ending Catastrophe (Imminent)*. The worst part was, he was right.

Because I recognized the penmanship.

"This is Sutherland's handwriting. He wrote this list."

"Your Dr. Sutherland has been busy." Quinn's voice was unnervingly gentle.

"I'm telling you, he wouldn't."

A flash of memory surfaced—Rosamund Fairchild taking credit for my analysis of the pottery fragment, claiming it was "how the game is played." The sense of betrayal burned fresh again.

A sharp knock at the door made me jump, nearly upsetting a teetering stack of papyrus fragments.

Quinn retrieved a telegram from a hotel boy, his expression darkening as he read. "The Graeco-Roman Museum in Alexandria was robbed yesterday. Three pieces taken. All recently excavated."

He passed me the telegram.

I scanned the message.

ALERT STOP THREE ARTIFACTS TAKEN FROM ALEXANDRIA MUSEUM STOP TWO CONTAIN BLUE PIGMENT MATCHING YOUR SPECIFICATIONS STOP PROCEED WITH CAUTION

I raised my eyes, outrage rising with them. "*Two contain blue pigment*? You've been tracking this pattern all along!" I slapped the telegram onto his desk, scattering several papyrus fragments. "You already knew."

Quinn shrugged, leaning against his desk with infuriating nonchalance. "I had to be certain. For all I knew, you might have been working with your father to acquire antiquities for his private collection. I needed to see if you'd recognize the pattern on your own. And," his mouth curved into that maddening half-smile, "I wanted to see just how clever Cambridge's rising star really is."

I glared at him, fingers itching to throw something suitably heavy and historically significant at his perfectly groomed head. "Next time you decide to test my integrity or intelligence, Mr. Quinn, I suggest you do so from behind reinforced glass."

Indignation spent, I sank into the obscenely expensive chair, my mind racing through implications. "The palette translation—everyone on the site saw it. They know what we found."

Quinn's controlled breathing and precise movements became more pronounced. "What exactly *did* you find?"

I met his gaze. Did I trust him with the truth?

"Evidence the mastaba was a New Kingdom burial in Giza. Which would at least challenge everything we thought we knew about royal burial practices of the New Kingdom. But potentially overturn accepted chronology of the Giza plateau." My voice cracked. "If I'm right about those hieroglyphs... We're not just dealing with stolen artifacts. We're dealing with stolen history."

"That piece is even more valuable, then."

"The value, Mr. Quinn, is in what it can teach us about Egyptian history."

Again, that smile. Condescending, or appreciative of my conviction, hard to say.

"The history doesn't pay nearly as well as the mystery, Dr. Bell." Quinn's voice held an edge of challenge. "Though I suspect you're about to tell me exactly how wrong I am about that."

"Someone has to maintain academic standards." I gestured at his impromptu museum of misappropriated antiquities. "Since your ethical compass appears to be pointing due profit."

I glimpsed a fleeting look of genuine hurt cross his face, but it quickly dissolved into his usual charm.

"It's not just about finding pretty things, Quinn. Every artifact tells a story, and if we don't document it properly, it's like ripping pages out of history's only copy of its own biography."

I tried to shake off my judgmental attitude and squared my shoulders.

"The Egyptian blue—" he waved a hand over the documents, the maps, the telegram— "there must be more to this.

Why would anyone be stealing such a commonly used pigment? And why would the pieces end up back in circulation, going into private collections?"

"I want to go to the auction with you." The words tumbled out before I could properly catalogue them.

Quinn's eyebrows rose. "I don't recall mentioning an auction."

"Please." I waved a hand at his collected evidence. "A sophisticated operation dealing in high-value artifacts needs a laundering mechanism. Given the social circles you inhabit—" I glanced pointedly at the hotel's gilt-edged opulence, "—there's clearly an upcoming event where these pieces will emerge, freshly packaged with conveniently vague provenance. If the palette's going to show up, it'll be there."

A slow smile spread across his face, infuriatingly smug.

"Very good, Dr. Bell. Tomorrow night, as it happens. Though I should warn you, evening dress required. Something considerably more elegant than your current..." His gaze swept over my practical attire. "...archaeological chic."

"I do own evening wear." I straightened my jacket. "Shocking as that may seem to someone who apparently thinks ancient artifacts make appropriate desk accessories."

"Then I'll collect you at eight." He stepped closer, supposedly to gather some papers, but his proximity sent my cataloging abilities into alarming disarray. "Assuming you won't have changed your mind by then."

"Unlike some people's ethical standards, my decisions tend to remain firm."

At a noise from the balcony, we both froze.

Quinn moved fast, reaching the French doors in two strides, immediately positioning himself between me and potential danger.

I followed.

I glimpsed a shadow, but it was already gone, leaving only the flutter of gauze curtains and the distant sounds of Cairo's nightlife—the distant tinkling of *oud* music from nearby cafés melding with automobile engines and the distant, haunting call to *Isha*, the night prayer.

I scanned the empty balcony and leaned over the edge.

Quinn placed a protective hand at the small of my back.

My skin flashed with a conflict between annoyance and awareness of his touch.

If there had been someone on this balcony, he—or she, I wouldn't discriminate—must have taken advantage of the conveniently placed drainpipe that ran down the side of the hotel.

"Perhaps," Quinn's voice was dangerously close, "we're not the only ones interested in tomorrow night's activities."

A sudden desert wind snatched at our clothes and hair—the same khamsin wind that had uncovered countless buried secrets throughout Egypt's history.

I studied the street below, and then the sky. Beyond the balcony, the Cairo night hung low and intimate, stars dimmed by the city's haze but the moon appearing impossibly close, as if one could reach out and brush fingertips against its pock-marked face.

Should I be upgrading my situation from *manageable crisis* to *life-threatening adventure*? I gestured over my shoulder, back into his room. "Got any wadjet eye amulets in that collection of yours? I suddenly feel the need for protection."

"I thought you disapproved of private ownership of artifacts."

"Yes. Well. I'm willing to make an exception if it keeps us alive long enough for me to properly lecture you about it later."

CHAPTER EIGHT

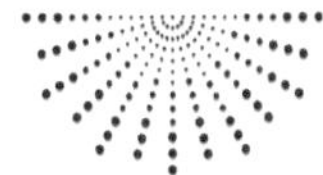

*B*enedict Quinn was grumpy.

Despite agreeing last night to escort me to this evening's auction, he seemed to resent my presence in the gleaming Bentley he'd hired to drive us to the estate of one Elias "Eli" Hawke, Cultural Liaison to the Foreign Office, one of the British Museum's largest private donors, and a respected collector of Egyptian antiquities.

"Officially," Quinn's voice took on a dry edge, "he's above reproach."

The mansion, sprawled across the Nile's Gezira Island, rose from manicured gardens like a monument to imperial hubris—part English country estate, part Eastern fantasy. Palm trees stood in formations more rigid than the British guards. The entire arrangement seemed designed to announce that even Egypt's ancient mysteries had been conquered, cataloged, and commodified for display.

I fidgeted with the beaded edge of the small purse in my lap, which contained a tiny notebook and fountain pen rather than cosmetics. "I still don't understand how a shipping magnate ends up in one of the largest estates in colonial Cairo."

"The same way he acquired his artifact collection." Quinn's jaw tightened. "By knowing which palms to grease and which threats to make. Half the British administration relies on his shipping contracts for military supplies, and the other half wishes they had his direct line to the Colonial Office. Meanwhile, he positions himself to do a different sort of business here. And his appointment as Cultural Liaison to the Foreign Office was particularly convenient. It gives him diplomatic credentials to transport 'cultural materials' between countries without the usual customs inspections. The perfect cover for his real business."

I filed this information away. A government position with diplomatic immunity would certainly explain how so many artifacts moved through Hawke's hands without official scrutiny.

The wrought-iron gates of the Hawke Estate loomed before us, their elaborate Islamic geometric patterns an ironic testament to the wealth extracted from Egypt by its colonial occupiers. Two uniformed guards stood at attention, their stances suggesting military training rather than household staff.

We glided through the gates, along a private drive to the estate. The mansion could have rivaled Ramesses the Great's palace complex.

I extricated myself from the automobile to find Quinn offering his arm with a slight bow. The touch sent an irritating tingle up my arm.

My shoulders tensed beneath the beaded silk, as if the weight of my assumed identity pressed down alongside the fabric. The sheath dress, while perfectly appropriate for New York society, felt out of place here. The midnight blue silk fractured the lamplight, its beaded fringe catching the light, like stars in the desert sky. The backless design left me feeling more exposed than if I'd arrived wearing nothing but field notes. I longed for my dig clothes with their useful pockets and complete lack of glitter.

"I feel rather like an artifact displayed in the wrong exhibit case."

"Well, you look rather like a well-dressed starlet." His voice held that infuriating hint of amusement. "Though I've never seen one quite so..."

"If you say 'charmingly disheveled,' I shall be forced to find something precious to break."

"I was rather thinking 'elegant.'" He tightened his arm around mine. His perfectly selected tie somehow matched the blue of my dress. "Shall we brave the lion's den?"

"More like the jackal's den," I muttered, but stepped forward anyway. After all, even Isis occasionally had to deal with unsavory characters.

Inside, the ballroom's vaulted ceiling arched overhead, European orchestral music clashing with the architecture. The grand salon stretched before us and the amount of cultural artifacts on display made me want to murder someone with my trowel.

Quinn's hand at my back guided me deeper into the crowd, his touch as usual both steadying and destabilizing. His hand registered through silk as five distinct pressure points, warm and steady. Despite the evening's coolness, heat crept up my neck.

"That chap by the Roman vase is the French Ambassador," Quinn's whisper was warm against my ear. "The woman in purple is a notorious collector from Vienna. And that distinguished-looking fellow running his fingers carelessly across an ancient papyrus—"

"Is a complete fraud," I finished. "That's not how a real archaeologist examines artifacts. He's performing for his audience."

"Very good. Now, what do you make of our host's latest acquisition?"

I followed his gaze to a limestone relief that made my pulse stutter. "That's from the Valley of the Kings. It can't be here legally." My fingers twitched toward my notebook, ready to document the evidence.

Quinn's fingers caught my hand. "Best tread carefully. The man watching us is one of Hawke's personal guards. They're dressed as servants, but note the way they stand."

I did note it, along with the warmth of Quinn shifting his stance to subtly position himself between me and the guard.

Two guards seemed to follow our movements with subtle turns of their heads, their casual poses belied by the alertness in their stance.

Elias Hawke navigated his crowded ballroom with the confidence of a man who owned not just the space but everyone in it. He created territories with his movements— approaching too close when speaking to some, backing others away with subtle shifts in posture. The room expanded for him and contracted for others.

We mingled, until finally a voice behind us, with the precise cultured tones of an expensive education, raised the hair on my neck.

"Ah, Dr. Bell."

I turned to find myself face to face with our host. His silver hair and aristocratic features suggested old money, but his eyes flashed with calculating gleam of someone who'd fought his way to power. Every elegant inch of him radiated cultured menace.

He extended a hand toward me. "Your monograph on New Kingdom pottery classification was fascinating." Hawke's smile didn't reach his eyes. "Particularly your observations on the correlation between firing temperature and structural durability in Predynastic vessels. Quite... illuminating."

I felt Quinn tense beside me.

"How kind of you to take an interest in pottery classification." I took the proffered hand. "Most find it rather... dusty."

"On the contrary." Hawke's gaze was uncomfortably penetrating. "I find your research uniquely valuable."

"The true value lies in what these artifacts reveal about ancient Egyptian technological advancement," I replied, unable to resist correcting him. "Their monetary worth is merely a modern construct."

Quinn chuckled. "But rather a construct we can profit from, eh, old chap?"

It was, perhaps, an interjection to soften my bluntness.

Quinn also subtly shifted position to break Hawke's territorial advantage.

"Speaking of value," Quinn smiled, "I understand you've acquired a rather exceptional lapis scarab amulet from the Middle Kingdom. I've come tonight with particular interest in bidding on it."

Hawke's eyebrows lifted fractionally. "Ah, Mr. Quinn. Always with an eye for the exceptional pieces. Yes, that item will be available during our... private auction later this evening. I should think you'll find its provenance quite satisfactory." The way he said "provenance" made it clear the documentation was as fabricated as his concern for archaeological integrity.

Hawke nodded at Quinn. "Please feel free to join a select group in my private gallery in about thirty minutes. We're having a rather specialized viewing."

His careful wording left me wondering whether the invitation included me.

I felt my indignation rising through my chest, threatening to reach my lips.

Quinn cleared his throat softly in warning.

"We would be delighted." He answered for us both, his tone pleasant but his posture suggesting he was ready to tackle me bodily from the room if necessary. I filed that image under *Thoughts to Examine Never.*

We took a few turns around the grand salon, drank a bit of champagne, which tasted of cold stones and distant vineyards, its effervescence masking an undertone of bitterness that matched my mood. European perfumes battled with each other in invisible clouds—French jasmine, English rose, and German amber—all failing to disguise the unmistakable mineral scent of ancient limestone that clung to the stolen artifacts.

A pompous collector approached, gesturing to a small statuette. "Magnificent Third Dynasty piece, wouldn't you agree?"

"Fifth Dynasty, actually," I replied. "The carving technique and proportional system weren't developed until at least two hundred years after the date you're suggesting. The material is also inconsistent with Third Dynasty royal workshops."

Quinn expertly diverted the man's embarrassment with a question about his collection while giving me a look that mixed exasperation and reluctant admiration.

We moved toward Hawke's "private gallery," which proved to be behind a set of carved doors that would have looked more appropriate on an New Kingdom tomb.

The gallery held the hushed reverence of a temple and the tasteful lighting of a museum, but the possessive energy of a dragon's hoard. Glass cases gleamed with subtle spotlights that highlighted the artifacts' best angles while conveniently obscuring any evidence of their questionable provenance.

As we entered, I began methodically cataloging everything I saw, my heart rate increasing with each item.

Predynastic ceremonial palette. Stolen from Abydos, 1921. Unmistakable.

Middle Kingdom jewelry collection. Matching description of pieces missing from recent dig sites.

New Kingdom ceremonial collar with lapis lazuli inlay. Reported missing from Luxor last month.

The artifacts rested on black velvet like actors on a stage, spotlights creating halos around each piece while shadows pooled in their crevices, hiding centuries of stories in darkness.

It was clear that those invited were merely taking in the items on display, then moving back into the ballroom.

"Remarkable collection," Quinn commented smoothly. He brushed his sleeve against mine, the pressure firm enough to communicate caution, as though he knew I was already reaching for my notebook, ready to sketch the identifying marks that would prove each item's origin.

My attention was briefly captured by a woman examining a display of canopic jars. When she turned, I glimpsed striking features—high cheekbones, penetrating dark eyes, and a composed expression that suggested she assessed the artifacts with genuine knowledge rather than mere acquisitive interest.

Hawke appeared at my shoulder.

"Do you dance, Dr. Bell?"

"Only when cornered by social obligation."

He laughed, the sound genuine enough to be truly unsettling. "Then perhaps I can tempt you to join me, with promises of academic talk?" He extended a hand toward the ballroom. "The next waltz is beginning."

"Actually," Quinn cut in, "I believe Dr. Bell promised the next dance to me."

I had done no such thing, but given the choice between Hawke's oily charm and Quinn's questionable morals, Quinn seemed the lesser evil.

"Another time, then." Hawke's smile suggested he had all the time in the world. "Do enjoy examining the collection. Though I should mention—" his voice dropped to a confidential murmur, "—my security staff are quite serious about preventing any... detailed documentation of the pieces. We wouldn't want any accidents."

He drifted away, leaving me to contemplate how many of the attending staff were actually armed guards. Based on their vigilant gazes, I estimated at least six. Possibly eight.

"Well," I whispered to Quinn, "that wasn't remotely threatening."

"You're managing admirably, all things considered." His eyes crinkled at the corners. "Now, shall we actually dance, or would you prefer to continue cataloging threats to our immediate survival?"

"I'm quite capable of doing both simultaneously."

We moved to the dance floor, and Quinn guided me into the waltz with practiced ease. We moved in perfect synchronization despite our distraction, my body somehow attuned to his leading steps in a way my mind refused to acknowledge.

After the dance, we mingled with various guests, some of whom Quinn seemed to know well. His smile for the Viennese collector was perfect—too perfect, compared to the uneven quirk of lips he occasionally directed at me.

A man in a server's uniform approached him and whispered something that made Quinn's expression harden momentarily before he smoothly resumed his charming smile. What was that about?

I'd come with a plan, though I wasn't sure Quinn would approve.

So I waited until he was thoroughly engaged, then slipped away with the practiced stealth of someone who'd spent years avoiding social interactions at academic functions.

Specimen: Academic Espionage (Novice Attempt), Modern Period. Notable for conflicting intellectual integrity and necessary deception.

No one would miss one socially awkward "lady archaeologist" while she behaved badly, right?

And what was one more catastrophically bad decision in an evening already featuring a dress without a single practical pocket?

CHAPTER NINE

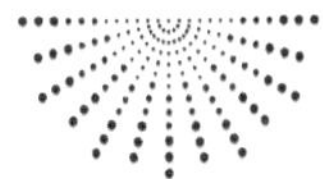

*H*awke's study wasn't difficult to locate. A locked door flanked by "decorative" urns (New Kingdom, likely stolen) practically advertised its importance. The urns—looted from the tomb of a Fifth Dynasty queen at Saqqara, if I wasn't mistaken—featured delicate lotus motifs that once held offerings of sacred oils meant to sustain the deceased in the afterlife.

The door's lock proved surprisingly simple for someone who regularly had to break into her own office due to misplaced keys. I'd brought a handy little pick from the digsite, anticipating just such a necessity.

The study was a temple to colonial excess, where genuine Egyptian artifacts rubbed shoulders with garish reproductions. A massive desk dominated the space, flanked by bookcases. Oil lamps cast shifting shadows across walls decorated with fake tomb paintings, their colors vibrant. The overall effect was rather like someone had attempted to recreate the Egyptian Museum using only auction catalogs and questionable taste.

I moved quickly to the desk, its surface cluttered with papers, illuminated by the amber glow of a brass lamp shaped like the god Thoth. Shipping ledgers were immediately visible

—apparently criminal masterminds were no better at filing than archaeologists.

Port of Alexandria... Expected shipment... Royal Museum artifacts...

My pen raced across my notebook pages as I copied dates and details.

I scanned a handwritten letter, still needing to be typed and not addressed to anyone. Copied phrases into my notebook like *finder's fee, recovered artifacts,* and something about *maintaining the established historical narrative,* which struck me as strange, given Hawke's apparent disdain for maintaining anything.

A floorboard creaked behind me.

I spun, heart thundering, but it was only Quinn. "What are you doing here?" I hissed.

"Preventing you from getting killed." He closed the door silently. "Hawke's heading this way. We need to—"

The handle turned.

Quinn moved with shocking speed, pulling me into a narrow map room adjoining Hawke's office, barely more than a closet, lined with rolled charts and surveys. His decisive action left no room for discussion or alternatives. Typical. He pressed me between the wall and himself, his body effectively trapping me in place.

Why did we always seem to end up smashed together in hiding places? I could feel his heart racing, though whether from danger or proximity was unclear. For scientific purposes, I noted my own pulse was equally elevated.

The small map room closed around us. The musty scent of aged paper and Quinn's cologne mingled in the stale air, creating an atmosphere that felt both suffocating and oddly intimate.

My fingers brushed against the cool wall behind me, a contrast to the warm pressure of Quinn's body. And noticed for the first time the exact shade of his eyes—a deep brownish-gold that caught what little light filtered into our hiding place. A small scar near his temple raised questions I wanted to ask.

"—in my study," Hawke's voice drifted through the doorway. "Just need to retrieve something."

"Dr. Bell." Quinn's whisper was a breath against my ear. "Stop thinking and focus on not breathing."

"I am focusing," I whispered back. "I'm focusing on not noticing that your left hand is on my—"

"I'm helping you balance."

"That is *not* my balance point."

The door clicked shut. Footsteps retreated.

We emerged from the alcove, both crimson-cheeked. I smoothed my dress while Quinn straightened his tie with meticulous care, then adjusted his cuffs with a precision that seemed absurd given our recent brush with discovery. Neither of us quite met the other's eyes.

"We should return to the party," he said finally.

"Yes, well." I waved my notebook. "I have what I need."

"Be careful." Quinn's expression turned serious. "Hawke's watching you too closely. He'll suspect you've found something."

"Well, then I will simply throw him off the scent."

"How?"

"I'll dance with him."

His eyebrows lifted. "That's your brilliant plan? Waltz with a potential criminal mastermind?"

"It's the last thing he'd expect me to do after finding evidence against him. He'll assume I would want to avoid him."

"You should avoid him."

"Precisely why I won't."

The muscles in Quinn's jaw rippled beneath his skin. "Right then. But should he threaten to feed you to the crocodiles, I shall place the blame squarely on your shoulders."

"Crocodiles are sacred animals." I smiled sweetly. "He's more likely to have me thrown into a pit of snakes."

"Your knowledge is impressive."

"Keep this safe." I pressed my notebook into Quinn's hand. "And if I'm not free in ten minutes, assume I've been fed to historically accurate sacred animals."

His fingers closed over mine. "Five minutes. Then I'm coming to get you."

"That would be tremendously unhelpful."

"I specialize in unhelpful." His thumb brushed my wrist. "Especially where you're concerned."

When I reached the grand ballroom, Hawke materialized from the shadows by a marble colonnade as if summoned, extending his hand with practiced grace. "Dr. Bell. I believe you owe me a dance."

The grand ballroom's architecture mimicked the hypostyle hall at Karnak Temple, with columns carved to resemble papyrus bundles—an Egyptian sacred space transformed into a venue for the wealthy elite's entertainment.

The waltz swept us into its rhythm. Hawke's perfectly timed steps were a contrast to my usual method of navigation. His hold was exactly what the dance manuals prescribed— proper, precise, and somehow more threatening for its correctness.

I felt a moment of discomfort as Hawke angled his body toward mine, his face closer than propriety dictated, creating an illusion of intimacy. And then a flash briefly illuminated us.

A photographer wielding a bulky Graflex camera had captured our dance.

"For the society pages." Hawke smiled. "The Cultural Liaison to the Foreign Office must maintain certain appearances, after all."

"I must compliment you on your collection." I aimed for academic enthusiasm while my stomach coiled, and kept my expression detached. "Particularly that remarkable predynastic necklace with the falcon motif."

"I'm much more interested in items *you* have found. Rare pigments, surprising locations..." Hawke's smile remained fixed and glacial, his teeth gleaming against the artificial warmth of his tanned skin.

"I don't know what you're talking about."

His smile didn't waver. "No?" We turned, his steps forcing

me to follow or stumble. "Then let's discuss what you found in my study instead."

My heart stopped. "I'm afraid I—"

"Was admiring my closet? Yes, it is rather compelling up close, isn't it? Though the space is rather tight for two people."

I found myself speechless.

"I should mention," Hawke continued pleasantly, "that my upcoming shipment from Alexandria is rather important to certain interested parties who are putting together special collections. Parties who would be—disturbed—by academic interference."

"Are you threatening me, Mr. Hawke?"

"Not at all." His smile remained. "I'm merely suggesting that some discoveries are better left unexcavated. For everyone's safety."

He took us through another turn.

"I've heard your father's cotton investments in Egypt are particularly vulnerable. The processing facility in El-Mahalla El-Kubra would make a spectacular fire."

My blood turned to ice water.

The music ended. He released me with aristocratic disdain. "Do give my regards to your father. I'm sure Armand would be devastated if anything happened to his only daughter."

I felt Quinn's presence beside us before his fingertips grazed my arm. "Everything alright?"

"Perfectly," Hawke answered for me. "Dr. Bell and I were just discussing the unfortunate accidents that sometimes befall archaeologists in the field. Tomb collapse, snake bites, unexpected falls... Egypt can be so dangerous for academics who stray into unsafe areas."

I kept my voice steady. "How fortunate that I have expertise in identifying things that should remain buried."

"Indeed." His gaze shifted to Quinn. "Though some things have a way of surfacing despite our best efforts. Good evening."

He melted into the crowd, leaving me shaking with both fury and fear.

"What did he say?" Quinn's voice was tight.

"That we're dealing with something far bigger than a stolen palette." I turned to him. "And that he knows exactly who I am, what I've found, and how to make me disappear."

Based on the events of the evening, Quinn thought it best we exit before the clandestine auction began.

The drive back to my lodgings felt longer than an entire dig season. I stared out the ink-black window, trying to remember the items on the list I'd copied in Hawke's office.

Cairo's night streets slipped past the windows like a dark river, punctuated by the occasional golden glow of oil lamps illuminating doorways where figures huddled in conversation. The city held its secrets close, ancient and modern conspiracies layered like strata in an excavation. I was perhaps merely the latest archaeologist attempting to decipher which layers contained truth and which were mere distractions.

"You're being unusually quiet." Quinn's voice was tight.

"I'm trying to decide if being murdered would damage my academic reputation more, or less, than being caught with an antiquities dealer inside a closet."

"At least his stolen cartographic collection was properly archived."

Despite everything, I laughed. It came out slightly hysterical. "Yes, that will look wonderful on my tombstone. 'Here lies Clarissa Bell, found in compromising position in properly archived map closet with known artifact smuggler while being threatened by criminals.'"

The automobile slowed to a stop in front of the Nile View Café. Neither of us moved.

"I won't let him hurt you," Quinn said finally, his concern masked behind a casual tone.

"That's reassuring." I turned to face him. "But I don't need protection. I need to stop whatever's happening in Alexandria."

"Alexandria?"

I explained about the shipping manifest and Hawke's contracts.

"I need to get there before more artifacts disappear into

private collections. Especially the scribe's palette, but I think it's much bigger than that."

"Even if it gets you killed?"

"Better than letting history be stolen and sold piece by piece."

His hand found mine in the darkness. "There are other ways, I daresay. Less dangerous paths we might bloody well explore."

"Yes, well." I withdrew my hand, though part of me wanted to lean into the unexpected comfort of his touch. "Those ways seem to involve sneaking around with questionably ethical dealers, so I'm not sure they're actually better."

"Questionably ethical?"

"Did you prefer 'morally flexible'?"

He smiled, though it didn't reach his eyes. "I'd prefer you alive."

I filed that under *Statements Too Meaningful to Examine* and fumbled for the automobile's door. My instinct to refuse his help warred with the increasingly obvious fact that some excavations required a partner. "Then help me figure out what's happening in Alexandria. Before Hawke decides to make me a permanent part of the archaeological record."

"Clarissa." His voice stopped me. "Next time you decide to break into a criminal mastermind's study, perhaps warn me first?"

"Why? Would you have tried to stop me?"

He held my gaze for a long moment before he shrugged. "No. But I might have wanted to watch."

I stepped out into the Giza night, oddly warmed by this thoroughly unhelpful declaration of support.

Quinn's Bentley purred away into the streets, nearly silent.

My pulse quickened as I watched him go, for reasons I refused to acknowledge had nothing to do with our narrow escape.

The café below my lodgings still buzzed with late-night activity, the scent of tobacco and coffee mixing with what was probably the same decomposing camel from the day of my arrival.

My landlady, Madame Farah, materialized from within.

"Telegram, Miz Bell." She thrust the paper at me. "Man in fancy clothes bring it. Very important, he say. Though not so fancy as your friend in motor car." Her lips pursed with the kind of disapproval that could have withered pharaohs in their day, though genuine concern lingered in the depths of her eyes.

I unfolded the telegram. The message was brief:

MUST MEET URGENTLY STOP POMPEY PILLAR TOMORROW NOON STOP TELL NO ONE STOP MATTERS OF GRAVE IMPORTANCE STOP BRING ALL NOTES STOP SUTHERLAND

"Grave importance?" I muttered. "Really, Dr. Sutherland, must we resort to mortuary puns?"

I tucked the telegram into my beaded evening bag.

What was Sutherland up to? Why ask to meet me at Pompey's Pillar in Alexandria, more than a hundred miles north of Cairo? And was it purely coincidence that I was already planning a trip there?

Madame Farah still stood, arms folded, watching me, shaking her head.

"Better to meet no one alone." Her announcement came with the confidence of someone who had witnessed four thousand years of poor decisions in her café. "Men who send secret messages, they are like bad dates at market—look sweet, taste bitter."

I gave her a noncommittal smile and retreated upstairs to my cramped lodging.

My room seemed to shrink further as I contemplated Sutherland's message. Outside, the moon slipped behind gathering clouds, casting my small window into darkness.

I agreed with Madame Farah. Those inventory documents at the café were uppermost in my mind. There was no way I would fail to meet Sutherland. But I should be smart about it.

"Well," I announced to my reflection as I undid my hairpins, "if one must choose between possible criminals, better the charming one who can probably afford a first-class train ticket. Nothing adds insult to potential homicide like having to face it in third-class at an ungodly hour of the morning."

And at least if everything went horribly wrong, I could comfort myself with the knowledge I'd soon be providing future archaeologists with a fascinating murder mystery to excavate. Assuming, of course, they could find my remains among the Roman ruins. Knowing my luck, they'd misfile me as "scattered architectural debris."

Late as it was, I would need to wait for Quinn to reach his hotel in Cairo, before I could head down to the café to use the telephone.

Would he agree to come? I hadn't given him much reason to accommodate me.

But nothing says "I'm beginning to trust you" quite like "Want to come prevent my possible murder in Alexandria?"

CHAPTER TEN

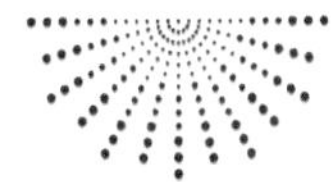

The dining car of the Cairo-Alexandria Express offered an exemplary gallery of suspicious characters, which I observed while pretending to be fascinated by my thoroughly mediocre coffee. The liquid was doing a remarkable impression of mud that had briefly considered a career change into beverage form before giving up halfway.

Specimen A: Male, Mid-50s. Demonstrates unusual interest in gazette, given he's been staring at that article about the latest finds catalogued in Tutankhamun's tomb for 27 minutes. Either illiterate or terrible at espionage.

Specimen B: Male, Late 30s, Gloves Too Expensive for Third-Class Ticket. Hat pulled suspiciously low. Attempting nonchalance with all the success of a hippopotamus trying ballet.

Specimens C and D: Two Males, Various Ages, All Displaying Classic Signs of Hired Muscle (Origin: Streets of Cairo, Dating: Contemporary, Notable Characteristics: Suspiciously Bulging Jacket Pockets and collective IQ equal to their shoe size).

Quinn dropped his voice, leaning across our table. "I count at least four rather unsavory characters who could be following us."

I took another sip of my coffee, immediately regretting the

decision as my taste buds filed a formal protest. "Five, actually. You missed the porter who's been polishing the same doorknob for the past quarter-hour. Though in fairness, Egyptian Railways' cleanliness standards have improved dramatically since the war."

His eyebrows arched. "I'm impressed."

"Don't be. In archaeology, observation is everything. For instance, I've also observed that your left coat pocket contains a revolver, and your right appears to be harboring what I suspect is a stolen scarab amulet. Really, Quinn, a museum piece as a good luck charm? That's like using the Rosetta Stone as a paperweight."

He shifted, almost imperceptibly. "It's a replica."

"The micro-cracks in the glazing suggest New Kingdom, possibly 18th Dynasty. The only replicas that convincing are in the British Museum's conservation lab, which you visited last month." I paused. "I do hope you at least left them a receipt. Perhaps written on the back of your moral compass, which appears equally missing."

"How in blazes could you possibly know—"

"Your coat shifted when you laid it down in our compartment, revealing a distinctive outline against the wool. So I investigated when you were in the restroom. Really, for a man in your profession, your concealment techniques are disappointingly amateur. You might as well have pinned a note saying 'illicit antiquity here' with a helpful arrow."

The corners of his mouth twitched. "We should return to our compartment. This car is becoming rather crowded."

"Indeed. Though I can't imagine anyone trying anything in such a public place. Even hired thugs have standards, presumably."

The remaining two hours of our trip passed uneventfully, as we watched the changing landscape of the Nile Delta region pass before us. I was looking forward to whatever light Dr. Sutherland could shed on this whole mess. And hopefully we'd learn more of whatever Hawke was planning, no doubt at the

Graeco-Roman Museum, where the recent thefts had occurred.

We arrived at Alexandria's Misr Station, which also bore architectural scars of its colonial conception—graceful Islamic arches awkwardly married to European industrial design, like a camel forced to wear a top hat.

We stepped from the station's grandeur into Alexandria's breathless afternoon heat, where the Mediterranean sun seemed determined to reclaim the city for Egypt by force. The sky stretched impossibly blue overhead, devoid of clouds or mercy.

"I don't like this." Quinn gestured around us. "Too many places for someone to hide."

"How delightful." I dodged a porter wielding a steamer chest like a battering ram. "And here I was worried this expedition might become dull."

Quinn's voice was low. "Stay close. We need to find somewhere defensible—"

"Actually, I have a better idea." I shifted my leather satchel. "We split up. Make it harder for them to follow. I'll head toward the Pillar, you take the—"

"Out of the question, Clarissa." His normally smooth brow furrowed into what I mentally cataloged as *Expression #7: Academic Woman Has Suggested Something Perfectly Rational But Inconvenient To Male Ego.*

I squared my shoulders for battle. "Your protective instincts would be charming if they weren't suffused with male condescension, but—"

He shook his head. "This isn't about being protective, it's about basic survival. The black market is filled with people who aren't just common thugs. They're organized and determined."

"Fine. Then follow at a distance. If I'm walking into a trap, you can swoop in for a heroic rescue. I'm sure your ego would appreciate the opportunity."

We took a winding route through the market stalls, moving quickly in an attempt to lose any potential tail through the labyrinth of ancient streets, where the smell of spices mingled with less appealing aromas.

Far ahead, the towering column of Pompey's Pillar thrust skyward, a twenty-five-meter pink Aswan granite monument that was actually erected by the Roman Emperor Diocletian around 300 AD—not Pompey at all. It originally stood alongside a magnificent temple to Serapis that rivaled the Great Library of Alexandria before zealots destroyed it in 391 AD. Now the pillar stood alone, surrounded by a maze of partially excavated walls, scattered limestone blocks, and tourists posing for photographs with expressions suggesting they believed looking deeply contemplative would somehow improve their snapshots.

I slowed to a stop and turned to Quinn. "I want to go on alone. Dr. Sutherland specifically said to tell no one I was meeting him here." I pointed to a crumbling half-wall. "You stay here. I'll holler if I need you. Perhaps I'll develop a special distress call. Three short screams, two long ones, followed by the opening bars of 'God Save the King.'"

"Clarissa—" Quinn called after me, frustration evident in the tight set of his shoulders.

I lifted my satchel. "Don't worry. I have several volumes of George Andrew Reisner's archaeological surveys. Any assailant will be unconscious before they reach chapter three. His writing style is more effective than chloroform."

"I would strongly advise against that course of action." His expression suggested he was assessing all the ways this could go horribly wrong.

"Most of archaeology is terrible ideas executed with exceptional precision." I turned toward the pillar, adjusting my grip on my satchel, in which I'd brought my drawings and notes about the stolen palette, as Sutherland's telegram insisted.

"Clarissa!"

But I was already weaving toward the landmark, feeling rather pleased with my tactical brilliance. I still didn't trust Quinn. Not completely. I was determined to get answers, and I wanted to do it alone.

I circled the archaeological precinct methodically, noting the two sphinxes flanking the pillar and the various shadowy alcoves between the ancient walls—perfect for both scholarly observation and, unfortunately, less academic pursuits like ambushes, kidnappings, and other activities not covered by my Cambridge education.

I pressed my palm against the pillar. The granite was polished to glassy smoothness in some spots, while elsewhere the surface had roughened like crocodile skin under centuries of wind-driven sand.

It was nearly noon. Perhaps my mentor had given up on me.

"Dr. Sutherland?" I called through the site, but my voice echoed off ancient limestone. "Your message said to meet you here..."

The only response came from a stray cat, who gave me a look suggesting I was the most disappointing thing it had seen since the collapse of the Ptolemaic dynasty. The feline yawned with deliberate insolence before slinking away.

Movement caught my eye—a flash of violet behind one of the massive sphinxes.

I squinted, recognition dawning with a jolt that nearly had me dropping my satchel. That distinctive violet hat—I'd seen it before, at Hawke's mansion during the auction. And before that, hadn't I seen it at the café where Quinn and I had met with Rashid Hafiz? The same woman had been hovering in the background, watching us.

Oh, Ramesses' razors. Had I just walked myself straight into a trap? Somewhere, Quinn was composing a lecture on the dangers of excessive independence, likely with detailed footnotes and several cutting remarks about my judgment.

I retreated toward the half-excavated passageway beneath the pillar's eastern platform, where ancient priests had once conducted their mysteries. Today's mystery appeared to be "How Many Ways Can Clarissa Bell Endanger Herself Before Lunch?"

More movements in the alcoves. I counted at least three

figures converging on my position, none of them displaying the distinctive gait of Oxford-educated archaeologists.

The woman in the violet hat emerged from behind the pillar's massive limestone base.

I cocked my head. Now that I could see her fully, her features were crystal clear. Those dark eyes, the carved cheekbones. Yes, the same woman from Hawke's mansion, and the café before that. She'd been following me for days.

"You're not Dr. Sutherland," I observed, demonstrating my keen archaeological deduction skills.

"No, Dr. Bell." She smiled without warmth. "But I have you alone, finally."

"Finally? Have I been that elusive? I should add it to my academic credentials. Dr. Clarissa Bell: Expert in Pottery Classification and Difficult to Corner."

In response, she extracted a diminutive Colt pistol from her purse with casual elegance. "You've been remarkably well-protected since the palette was stolen. Until now." She gestured to my satchel. "Your notes, if you please. Your drawings of the palette are particularly interesting to us."

I had once cataloged forty-seven different types of ancient Egyptian traps, from elaborate pulley systems to simple pit designs. How ironic that I was about to be done in by the most basic trap of all: human stupidity, specifically my own. I should have listened to Quinn, a thought I would take to my grave before admitting aloud.

The woman—whom I would now classify as *Specimen B: Female (Antagonistic), Early 30s, Carrying Firearm (Small Caliber), Violet Hat Still Remarkably Well-Positioned Despite Villainous Activities*—gestured with her handbag.

"Your satchel, Dr. Bell. Slowly."

I clutched my bag to my chest. "I'm afraid I simply couldn't. These are first editions of Reisner's surveys. Do you have any idea how difficult it is to find—"

The distinct click of a safety being released suggested she did not share my appreciation for literature.

"The satchel. You're the only one who's documented the palette properly before it was taken."

Two more figures emerged, carrying guns.

My usual rapid-fire cataloging system stuttered to a halt as I realized the full implications of her words. Perhaps they didn't have the palette. Someone else had stolen it—and they thought my drawings and notes were the key to finding it.

"Dr. Bell." A familiar voice echoed through the ancient sacred precinct. "I believe the lady made a request."

Benedict Quinn emerged from behind the western sphinx.

My heart sank like a stone dropped into the Nile. Of course. The one person I'd started to trust, however reluctantly.

He smiled—not his usual charming grin, but something darker. "I do apologize for the theatrics, Dr. Bell, but perhaps next time you'll heed my counsel about venturing off alone."

Another specimen update. *Benedict Quinn (Traitor), Recently Demoted from "Intriguingly Roguish" to "Absolute Rotter."*

The woman's perfectly plucked eyebrows drew together. "Mr. Quinn. I wasn't aware you had an interest in this particular acquisition."

I opened my mouth for a scathing accusation of Benedict Quinn, possibly involving several choice hieroglyphs not suitable for academic publication.

And then Quinn half turned toward me and winked.

The next few moments could only be filed under *Chaos (Orchestrated)*.

Quinn's hand moved with speed, producing something that glinted in the sunlight.

Violet Hat spun, her gun tracking the wrong target.

A familiar scarab amulet sailed through the air, catching the light—and providing the perfect distraction for Quinn to tackle both me and my apparently precious satchel behind a fallen column, then pull me toward a half-hidden entrance between massive foundation blocks—one of Alexandria's ancient cistern access points.

The scarab distracted them just long enough for us to slip into the narrow gap. As they fumbled to retrieve the amulet—a moment's hesitation over whether to pursue us or secure the artifact—Quinn pulled me into the cistern entrance that gaped like a mouth to the underworld.

"The El Qabari tunnels connect through here," he whispered, helping me down into the darkness. "Part of Alexandria's water system—some chambers date to Ptolemaic times. Might I suggest we hurry? They're rather damp."

Stone crumbled beneath Quinn's foot as we descended. He stumbled, suppressing a grunt of pain as his shoulder slammed against the ancient wall.

"Are you—"

"Perfectly fine." He straightened his collar one-handed, the other arm rotating at an awkward angle. "Just don't tell the Antiquities Service we're using their precious water system as an escape route."

"Fascinating construction." We waded through ankle-deep water, surprisingly silken against my ankles, neither warm nor cool. "Late Ptolemaic waterworks, judging by the ashlar masonry. The vaulting technique here suggests Roman influence, though the channel dimensions follow Egyptian proportional systems—a perfect architectural reflection of Alexandria's cultural hybridization."

"As always, Clarissa, your observations stagger me. But do move quickly. They can't be far behind."

"That was the British Museum's scarab, wasn't it?"

"A replica, as I said. Consider it a donation to the cause." He yanked me around a corner as footsteps reverberated behind us. "Though I do hope you're noting the value of having connections in dangerous situations. I wouldn't have known of these tunnels without my network of local contacts."

The cistern air carried the mineral perfume of standing water against limestone—cool, metallic, with undertones of ancient mortar and the distant, indefinable scent of time itself.

Quinn's hand gripped mine, his fingers tightening painfully.

"I'm noting you're insufferably pleased with yourself." But I surrendered to his lead. "Though I suppose I might have been somewhat... overconfident."

"Somewhat?"

"Don't push it, Quinn."

We were losing the light, dwindling behind us, and the passageway narrowed, forcing us to press against each other to squeeze through. My mind noted the measurements of the channel—designed for water, not people—while my traitorous body cataloged the pressure of Quinn's hand around mine.

Dust from our hasty descent coated my tongue —chalky, acrid, with an iron undertone that might have been from the water or my own bitten lip.

We emerged a moment later into sunlight, then dashed toward a side alley.

Had we lost them?

The alley squeezed itself between buildings of at least four distinct eras—Ottoman balconies sagging above Greek stonework, built upon Roman foundations, themselves resting on something far older. Alexandria was a city of perpetual resurrection, each generation building atop the bones of its predecessors until history became less a timeline and more a layer cake of civilizations.

We stood there, catching our breath, hands linked. Our eyes met, sun-blind from the tunnels. For a moment, something electric passed between us before we both looked away.

Another beat, and our hands separated

Perhaps some undertakings benefitted from collaboration.

But a pressing question remained:

Why, exactly, were my palette drawings worth killing for?

CHAPTER ELEVEN

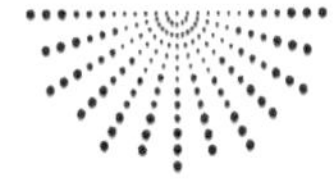

"For the last time," I dabbed ineffectively at the tunnel muck on my jacket, "my satchel contains nothing but three volumes on ceramic typology and my field notes."

Quinn and I had taken refuge in a shadowy café near the harbor after our escape through Alexandria's ancient waterways.

The proprietor took one look at our bedraggled state and wordlessly brought us strong Turkish coffee and a plate of dates. The rich, cardamom-laced aroma of Turkish coffee curled around us, a welcome contrast to the stagnant tunnel air that still clung to my clothing.

The café's cracked plaster walls, stained with decades of coffee steam and tobacco smoke, was weathered, disreputable, yet somehow still functional. Rather like us.

"It makes no sense." Quinn frowned into his coffee cup. "Why would they follow us all the way from Cairo, only to attack you here? And why didn't Sutherland appear at the pillar as his telegram promised?"

The coffee settled in small brass cups with ornate handles, the black liquid leaving a silty residue of finely ground beans on my tongue that tasted of charcoal. I pushed away the plate of dates, glistening crystallized honey and attracting flies.

I pulled out the crumpled message, studying it again. "It sounds like him. But really, I should have known. Anyone could have sent it."

"Again, if it was our friend from last evening's auction, why send you a telegram to lure you to Alexandria? Or if the telegram is genuine, did something—or someone—prevent Sutherland from meeting us?" Quinn's expression darkened. "The museum theft occurred just days ago. If he was investigating..."

"Yes, the Graeco-Roman Museum." I sat up straighter. "That's where the artifacts were stolen. That's where we'll find Sutherland, if he's truly here. And you have contacts there?"

"Somewhat less than legal contacts," he reminded me, his mouth quirking.

"At this point," I sighed, brushing tunnel debris from my hair, "I believe we're well past concerns about proper archaeological protocol."

"Did that hurt to admit?"

"Tremendously." I gathered my begrimed satchel. "Though possibly less than the lecture I'll endure when Cambridge discovers I've abandoned proper channels entirely."

"Consulting," Quinn corrected, throwing some coins on the table. "We're consulting. It sounds much more respectable."

"Yes, I know, you're the tomb robber in a top hat."

His wounded look was entirely unconvincing. "I thought we agreed on 'antiquities redistribution specialist.' And I do not wear top hats!"

Outside the café, Quinn flagged down a passing hantour. The driver, his red vest gleaming with gold embroidery, eyed our mud-streaked clothing with visible concern for his upholstery.

We clip-clopped through Alexandria's sprawling chaotic vibrancy—merchants hawking wares in three languages, the persistent Mediterranean breeze carrying scents of spice and salt water, administrators striding purposefully past locals who watched with carefully neutral expressions.

The Graeco-Roman Museum rose before us, its neo-classical columns a jarring sight after weeks among Egypt's ancient monuments. It housed one of the most important collections of Hellenistic artifacts from Alexandria's golden age as a center of learning.

"Fascinating architectural choice," I murmured as we stepped out of the horse-drawn carriage. "Nothing says 'we respect local heritage' quite like building a Greek temple to house Egyptian artifacts."

As we stepped from the hantour, Alexandria's khamsin wind had begun to stir, carrying fine particles of sand that scratched against exposed skin and infiltrated clothing—an abrasive reminder of Egypt's power to wear down even the most imposing structures, given enough time.

Quinn shrugged. "At least they're preserving the artifacts."

"Yes, rather than selling them to private collectors."

"About that." Quinn straightened his tie, which had acquired a distinctly rakish tilt during our escape. "I should mention I have an... arrangement with one of the guards."

"Let me guess. This 'arrangement' involves either bribery or blackmail."

"Informal cultural exchange." He flashed that infuriating smile that somehow managed to be both charming and thoroughly untrustworthy. "Unless you'd rather spend the afternoon filling out official paperwork?"

A distinguished-looking guard approached, his brass buttons gleaming in Alexandria's harsh sunlight. Quinn stepped forward, speaking Arabic far more fluent than my own awkward attempts. Money almost certainly changed possession, though Quinn's sleight-of-hand rivaled that of a street magician.

"Your disapproval is noted, Miss Bell." He gestured toward the now-open side entrance. "Shall we proceed with our completely unauthorized investigation?"

I glanced at the museum's main entrance, where proper

visitors queued with their proper paperwork, doing things properly. Then I thought of Sutherland's cryptic telegram and the violet-hatted woman who'd tried to kill us. *Proper* seemed rather beside the point now.

"I suppose needs must." I sighed, following Quinn through the door. "Though if we're caught, I'm telling Bradford this was entirely your idea."

"Naturally. I doubt he'd believe his 'lady archaeologist' capable of such impropriety, anyway."

"True. He'd likely expire from sheer shock."

The side entrance door hinges protested with a rusty groan that echoed through the narrow corridor, announcing our illicit presence to anyone with ears to hear. The guard led us down a narrow corridor that smelled of dust and furniture polish. My fingers itched to examine the artifacts we passed—a Ptolemaic funerary mask, late period, likely from the Fayum region, with distinctive gilding techniques typical of Alexandrian workshops—but Quinn's hand at my elbow kept me moving.

My mud-encrusted boots left faint betraying prints on the polished museum floor, each step marking our unauthorized path like dirty breadcrumbs.

I stopped short as we entered the main gallery. "Oh... oh my."

Alexandria's ancient history as a cosmopolitan port city founded by Alexander the Great was evident everywhere, where Greek, Egyptian, and Roman cultures intermingled to create a unique Alexandrian identity still visible in the artifacts surrounding them. The marble bust of Marcus Aurelius caught the afternoon light streaming through the high windows, his stone eyes seeming to follow our movements with imperial disapproval.

"Quite impressive, isn't it?"

The cultured voice behind us made me spin around so quickly I nearly knocked over Marcus.

Quinn's hand shot out to steady both me and the emperor.

Dr. Rosamund Fairchild stood in the gallery doorway, looking exactly as formidable as I remembered. Her platinum blonde hair was elegantly coiffed, her expensive suit unwrinkled despite Alexandria's punishing humidity. She held a long-handled lorgnette like a queen might hold a scepter, ready to pass judgment on lesser mortals who dared exist in her presence.

I glanced down at my own appearance: dust-covered jacket, wild hair, clear signs of recent flight from murderous pursuers. I looked like I'd been dragged backward through a dig site.

"Dr. Fairchild." I managed not to squeak. Mostly. "We weren't expecting to see you in Alexandria. I thought you weren't due at Giza until next week."

Where every man on my team eagerly awaits your remarkable and serious scholarliness.

Her gaze swept over me. At least she didn't raise the lorgnette glasses to her eyes. "And I had not expected to see you at all, Dr. Bell, especially not here."

I tottered forward, off balance for some reason. "I've just joined the Giza dig."

"I see. Though I find myself more intrigued by why you're here in Alexandria. In this museum. Through the service entrance, no less."

She didn't wait for an answer, turning a shoulder to me in dismissal.

"And Mr. Quinn," she turned to him with a smile that could only be called seductive. "How absolutely lovely to see you again."

Quinn's jaw tightened. "Rosamund, we're investigating the recent—"

Fairchild cut him off with a refined hauteur. "I must confess, I'm surprised to find you working with Dr. Bell." She turned to me. "I was informed of the letter you wrote to the Cambridge Archaeological Journal. Making certain... accusations."

My stomach dropped like a stone down a well. Six months

ago, after she'd published findings on a pottery fragment that were unquestionably mine, without so much as a footnote acknowledgment, I'd written a rather strongly worded letter to the journal suggesting their editorial board examine attribution practices.

"No, I wasn't—I only wanted them to be aware—"

Quinn cleared his throat. "Perhaps we could discuss scholarly publications after we investigate the rather pressing matter?"

"The theft?" Rosamund's lorgnette glinted as she tilted it toward the light. "Yes, I suppose we should. But why is Cambridge's rising star in pottery classification suddenly interested in black market antics?"

I exchanged a quick glance with Quinn. How much did she know? How much should we tell her?

"Unless," she added with a razor-sharp smile, "this has something to do with your missing palette from Giza? I've been sent here by the British Museum specifically to investigate this recent string of thefts. Your missing palette has only heightened the urgency of my inquiry."

Quinn tensed beside me.

"You're here officially as a British Museum representative?" I couldn't keep the surprise from my voice. The last I'd heard, she was still at Cambridge, though there had been rumors.

"Indeed. My position at Cambridge is... transitioning." Her smile suggested she was moving upward, not laterally. "Something rather more significant on the horizon. The Museum felt my expertise would be valuable here, given recent events."

I tried to reconcile this with the woman I'd once idolized. As a first-year student, I'd worshipped Professor Fairchild, hanging on her every word about Egyptian artifacts and research methodologies. For years, I'd sought her approval, followed her academic path. Until the betrayal of the pottery fragment publication that still stung like a fresh wound.

"And have you learned anything about these thefts?" I tried to keep my voice neutral, professional.

She extended a hand to the back of the gallery. "Please, join me in the records room. I've been given special access." Her gaze lingered on me with an uncomfortable intensity. "Though I must admit, Dr. Bell, finding you here raises rather interesting questions about coincidence and opportunity."

The implication hung in the air: that I was somehow involved in the theft. The audacity nearly left me speechless.

Quinn's shoulder brushed mine, a subtle show of support. "Clarissa was with me when the theft occurred. I can personally vouch for her whereabouts."

Fairchild's eyebrow arched delicately. "How fortunate for her."

The chemistry between Quinn and Fairchild was palpable, like static electricity before a desert storm. Then Egyptian archaeological world was a small one, but still, there was clearly history there—the kind that involved broken hearts or professional betrayal. Possibly both. I filed this observation away for later examination.

The records room smelled of leather bindings and aging paper—again, a scent that usually calmed my nerves. But watching Rosamund unlock a cabinet with practiced efficiency, my stomach jumped in anticipation.

"These are the recent acquisitions logs I've been able to examine." She spread the first ledger open on the mahogany desk, pushing aside other documents. "The three artifacts stolen a few days ago from this museum were all recent additions. Primarily from private donations. But here," she slid another sheet across the desk, "are other recent thefts. Perhaps there is some connection."

The ledger's pages whispered against each other with the dry papery sound of autumn leaves, a sound that always made my pulse quicken with anticipation.

Her gaze lingered on me, her expression somewhere between suspicion and disappointment, like a mentor who'd expected better. I'd once craved that approval; now I just wanted to be free of her judgment.

I leaned closer, scanning the neat columns of entries.

We already knew the connection. The Egyptian blue pigment was present on all of them.

But I'd be mistaking a cartouche for a crocodile before I gave up a bit of information to Rosamund Fairchild.

CHAPTER TWELVE

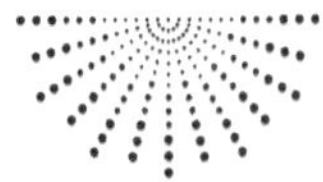

*A*ll of these pieces are mysteriously vanishing shortly after cataloging." Rosamund tapped the ledger. "Someone's collecting them systematically. But why these specific pieces?" She was watching me with sharp interest. "You believe these thefts are connected to something larger?"

A gentle throat-clearing saved me from answering.

A distinguished older gentleman stood in the doorway, his suit perfectly pressed, his silver hair and beard neatly trimmed.

"I thought I recognized your voice, Dr. Fairchild." His smile created a web of kindly wrinkles around his eyes. "And this must be Dr. Bell—I've been following your work with great interest." He stepped into the room with the careful movements of a seasoned archaeologist accustomed to navigating fragile artifacts. "And Mr. Quinn! How wonderful to have such distinguished visitors in our humble museum."

"Dr. Montague." Quinn's posture shifted subtly. "Your reputation precedes you."

"Oh, hardly worth mentioning compared to your recent discoveries." Montague's eyes twinkled as he pulled up a chair, settling in as if for a pleasant scholarly discussion. "But what brings you to the records room? Perhaps..." His eyes flickered to our notebooks. "Something to do with our recent difficulties?"

Quinn started to speak, but Montague waved him off. "No need for explanations. These are troubled times for our profession, aren't they? So many artifacts going missing..." He sighed heavily.

Rosamund folded her arms across her chest. "I've been perusing the visitor logs, Dr. Montague. Did you know, Gregory Sutherland was here just last week, examining the artifacts that were stolen only days later?"

I straightened. "Dr. Sutherland was here?" A pang of betrayal stabbed through me—my mentor working this angle without including me, another reminder of how easily I could be sidelined in my profession despite my expertise.

Montague shrugged. "I did see him briefly—didn't know what he was here to see. He seemed quite agitated about something. I do hope he's all right. He left rather suddenly."

She pursed her lips. "Does it not seem coincidental? Sutherland's pulling pieces for study, and then those very same pieces, stolen?"

Montague stood with surprising agility. "Why don't we continue this discussion in my office? A cup of tea seems warranted."

Through the window behind him, I spotted two burly men crossing the courtyard. They moved nothing like the usual museum guards, and looked familiar.

Quinn's hand found my arm. "Another time, perhaps. We have a prior engagement."

"What a shame."

Montague's hand shot out as I tried to pass, catching my wrist. "Your palette," he said softly. "The one from Giza. I assume you were able to translate some of the inscription before it... disappeared?"

I met his eyes and saw a familiar academic hunger. I'd experienced enough of it myself.

My satchel rested against my hip, the detailed translation and my notes burning a hole in it.

"I'm afraid not," I lied, feeling only a bit guilty. "Just a few initial observations."

"Pity." He stepped back, adjusting his gold pocket watch chain. "Do be careful in Alexandria, Dr. Bell. The streets can be so... unpredictable."

We left the records room at a pace that straddled the line between dignity and flight. Behind us, I heard Montague speaking quietly to someone—probably Rosamund, though when I glanced back, she was gone.

We made it exactly three steps out of the museum before everything went wrong.

The "guards" from the courtyard materialized on either side of us.

The harsh Alexandria sunlight beat down on the limestone steps, bleaching all color and creating sharp-edged shadows that offered no hiding places.

"Run," Quinn said pleasantly, as if suggesting we take a stroll by the harbor. Then he drove his elbow into the nearest guard's throat.

I didn't need to be told twice. My heart hammered against my ribs and my mouth went dry, fear transforming composure into pure survival instinct. I sprinted down the museum steps, my satchel of books and notes thumping against me. Behind me came the distinctive sounds of Quinn introducing faces to various pieces of architecture.

A flash of violet caught my eye—the woman from the train station was here too, emerging from a doorway.

I swung my satchel at her face with what I considered rather impressive accuracy for an academic.

"Left!" Quinn was at my shoulder. "The market—"

Something whistled past my ear.

Quinn yanked me sideways into a narrow alley just as another shot cracked against the stones.

The rough stone walls brushed against my shoulder as we navigated the narrow passage.

"Now they're shooting at us?" I gasped, ducking under a

line of drying laundry. Somehow I'd believed Violet Hat's pistol was mostly for show.

"Welcome to peer review in the antiquities trade." Quinn rushed me into a narrow alley, his hand firm against my back, moving in instinctive coordination.

He jerked suddenly, spinning me behind him as another shot rang out. The acrid scent of gunpowder cut through the market's blend of turmeric and brass polish.

He grunted, a hand to his shoulder, and shock flashing in his eyes for an instant before a mask dropped over his expression.

"Quinn!"

"Keep moving." His voice was tight. "Nearly there."

We plunged into a square where copper merchants hammered their wares. The rhythmic clanging masked our footsteps. The crowd swallowed us—a sea of *galabeyas* and *abayas*, silver bangles flashing in filtered sunlight.

Bodies pressed against us from all sides—the brush of linen, the occasional cold touch of jewelry, inevitable bumps and jostles.

Quinn steered us from the tourist sections toward the authentic local areas, his familiarity with the "real" Alexandria evident in his confident navigation through areas most Westerners never saw.

We weaved through fruit stalls, past a woman haggling over turquoise-studded jewelry, around a cart laden with carpets.

Quinn directed us toward a doorway half-hidden behind a cart of mounded dates. Blood darkened his jacket's shoulder, spreading like spilled wine across the linen, dark and insistent.

"In here." He pushed open the door. "Quickly."

Once inside, he locked the door and sagged against it. The immediate temperature change was striking—from the sweltering heat of pursuit to the cool shadows inside, with dust motes dancing in the thin beams of light filtering through shuttered windows. The distant sound of ship horns from Alexandria's harbor mixed with the merchant's haggling.

I decided not to question how and why he knew of a bolt-hole in the middle of Alexandria.

"Let me see." I helped him out of his jacket, trying to ignore how his breath hitched. "It's just a graze, but I'll need something to bind it."

"Handkerchief," he managed. "Inside pocket."

"You know Rosamund Fairchild."

I wrapped the bandage, watching his face. After weeks of studying ancient artifacts, I'd gotten rather good at spotting forgeries. The pain in his expression seemed genuine. Then again, he'd already proved himself an excellent faker.

"Yes. And so do you."

"But it seems like you two go way back. Personally."

He winced as I tied off the bandage. Tightly. "We aren't friends."

"I seem to keep discovering things I should have already known about you. For all I know, you're behind the thefts yourself."

"If I were, would I have just taken a bullet protecting you?"

"Perhaps that's part of your act too. And you hardly 'took a bullet.' It'll heal in no time."

He laughed, then grunted in pain. "You really do have a suspicious mind."

"Scholarly skepticism."

"It has to be Sutherland. Behind all of it. The thefts, probably even—"

"The attack at the pillar." I didn't want to believe it, but we seemed to be one step behind.

"Which means we're both in considerable danger." He caught my wrist, his grip surprisingly strong. "Clarissa. Whatever connects these artifacts—the reason they are being targeted—it's bigger than a few stolen treasures."

I met his eyes, seeing my own realization mirrored there. "You think this is about more than stealing Egypt's past."

"Yes." He grimaced. "Somehow, I rather think they're trying to control its future."

Through the window, we heard shouting as men searched

the square. I looked down at Quinn's shoulder, then at my blood-stained hands, shaking despite my attempts at nonchalance over his injury.

We slipped out the back door into the far edges of the market, where the smell of fresh-baked flatbreads and grilled meat mixed with the salt breeze off the harbor. A woman in black haggled over a mountain of pomegranates while her children played among baskets of dates.

Quinn guided us through the crowd with practiced ease. "The pieces I've been investigating are part of my investigation for the Egyptian Museum. Officially, I'm tracking stolen artifacts. Unofficially..." He paused to let a cart laden with melons pass. "I believe someone's building a private collection of interconnected pieces. But for what larger purpose, I can't discern."

"And you didn't think I might help with that investigation?"

"Honestly?" He steered me past a stall selling kebabs, the smoke making my empty stomach growl. "I was trying to protect you."

"I don't need—"

"From yourself," he finished. "You're brilliant, dedicated, and utterly incapable of backing down from a puzzle. The moment you understood the full scope of what we're dealing with, you'd dive straight into danger."

"As opposed to your careful, measured approach of getting shot?"

"Exactly. I'm a professional at getting shot. You're still an amateur."

I opened my mouth to retort, but something caught my eye. Through a gap in the crowd, past a display of brass lamps that belonged in a fairy tale, I spotted a familiar figure.

"Quinn." I gripped his arm. "By the spice merchant's stall. Isn't that—"

"Hawke." Quinn's voice hardened. "What's he doing in Alexandria?"

Eli Hawke stood examining a tray of saffron, looking absurdly out of place in his London suit. A local man in a finely embroidered *galabeya* stood beside him, speaking urgently.

"That's one of the men who was chasing us," Quinn murmured. "The one who wasn't shooting at us."

I watched them exchange something—too quick to see what passed between their hands.

"Follow them?"

Quinn's smile held no humor. "Now you trust me?"

"Not remotely. But right now you're the only untrustworthy person I've got."

Our positioning shifted as we followed Hawke—initially with Quinn leading, then gradually moving to side-by-side. The patterns of light and shadow cast by market awnings created a dappled effect that made tracking them like following figures through a kaleidoscope. We moved deeper into the market's maze of stalls and secrets, following Hawke's aristocratic shoulders through the crowd.

Whatever game my new partner Quinn was playing, whatever unspoken lies still lay between us, one thing was becoming clear: all of this was larger than we understood.

It was beginning to feel uncomfortably like a conspiracy.

CHAPTER THIRTEEN

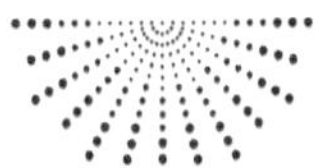

$\mathcal{A}$lexandria's streets carried the ever-present undertone of donkey dung, human sweat, and poverty, an authentic perfume of its back alleys tourists that rarely encountered. I was feeling the curse of my overly keen sense of smell today.

We slipped through narrow corridors, tracking Hawke's distinctive silhouette through the marketplace crush and under washing lines that drooped between crumbling facades like ancient suspension bridges.

Quinn glided with surprising elegance for a man in hand-made Italian leather shoes and a shoulder wound. His normally immaculate linen suit now carried the dust of tunnels and a gash of blood, giving him a disheveled appearance that suited him irritatingly well.

Hawke's silhouette disappeared down a side street, past children playing with wooden tops on the dusty ground.

"He's turning left," I whispered.

We quickened our stride, careful to stay hidden. Rivulets of sweat traced my spine, and my lightweight cotton clothing clung to my skin in a manner that would scandalize my father's New York associates.

"There," Quinn murmured, his breath warm against my ear

as he gestured toward a small teahouse nestled between a coffee merchant and what appeared to be a fortune teller's shop.

Hawke hesitated at the beaded curtain entrance, surveyed his surroundings, then vanished inside.

As everything else, the teahouse looked like it had survived multiple regime changes—Ottoman arches, French shutters, British ceiling fans. We crept toward it, Quinn steering me toward a partially shuttered window where sun-bleached curtains stirred in the meager breeze.

"Perfect," Quinn breathed, positioning us against the wall where we could hear but remain unseen. The window's wooden shutters tilted at a fortuitous angle, providing just enough of a gap for eavesdropping without exposure. The sun-baked plaster of the building felt rough and crumbly under my fingertips, tiny pieces breaking off between my nails, leaving chalky white residue on my skin.

Inside, teacups clinked against saucers and bitter-sweet scents mingled with tobacco smoke. The rhythmic bubbling of water pipes came from the corner where elderly Egyptian men sat playing with game pieces. A ceiling turbine rotated lazily overhead, its creaking punctuating the low murmur of conversation.

"You're late. Again." The voice from within was unmistakably familiar.

I froze, my fingers digging into the crumbling plaster, my breath catching audibly. "That's Sutherland," I hissed, then took a step away from the wall.

Quinn's hand clamped firmly over mine before I could move. "Wait," he whispered, his expression darkening.

Hawke's smug voice replied. "Couldn't be helped. The streets are crawling with British officers."

"And your Cambridge... inconvenience?" Sutherland's tone was clinically detached.

"The Bell woman has proven irritatingly resilient."

"Tell me you at least secured her notes?" Sutherland asked.

My mind raced. The notes about the palette?

Hawke grunted. "I'm afraid they slipped through our fingers, much like their owner."

Quinn's grip on my wrist tightened in warning.

Sutherland didn't reply, but Hawke sighed heavily. "We have no choice but to accelerate our timeline. The Egyptian Museum Gala is in only three days."

"The main exhibition hall will be heavily guarded, with the new Tutankhamun items on display," Sutherland was saying. "I still think the curator's auxiliary display in the east wing, where they've had to relocate collections due to the new pieces, remains the best opportunity for approach."

"The samples must be acquired immediately." Hawke's voice held a nasty undertone. "All of them. He was quite specific."

Quinn's brow furrowed at me. "He?" he mouthed silently.

"I'm well aware of the timeline," Sutherland snapped.

Hawke grunted. "Just ensure your contacts at the museum have disabled the necessary security by eight o'clock. My men will handle the rest."

Chairs scraped against floor tiles, announcing the meeting's end. The soft padding of footsteps approaching the window sent my heart racing.

Quinn and I locked eyes, panic flashing between us. A shadow fell across the dusty street as someone inside moved toward the doorway.

As I shifted my weight to retreat, my boot caught on an uneven cobblestone. A stray tabby cat—mangy and battle-scarred—yowled indignantly as I disturbed its afternoon nap. The sound seemed to echo through the narrow alley.

Quinn pulled me sideways into a small alleyway and pressed me against the wall.

"Don't move," he whispered, his body shielding mine as we pressed into the alley's bricks.

Seriously, again? If I could figure out how he was doing it, I would swear he was engineering these pull-you-into-a-tight-place-and-invade-your-space moments.

Quinn's heartbeat thundered against my chest, our bodies

aligned from shoulder to knee. His normally composed face was inches from mine, jaw tight with tension.

My quickened pulse was likely visible at my throat, a warmth spreading across my chest that once again, wasn't entirely due to fear.

Heavy footfalls approached.

Quinn pressed closer, one arm braced against the wall above my head, his body completely shielding me from the street. His eyes held mine, steady and unflinching, as we shared the same shallow breaths.

The pressure of his chest against mine and the slight stubble forming along his jaw at this late hour built a heat in my limbs.

A man's shadow fell across our hiding place, accompanied by the acrid smell of strong Turkish cigarettes.

Time stretched like warm amber. The man muttered something in colloquial Arabic, no doubt about the romantic spectacle we presented. The cat that had betrayed us reappeared. After what felt like several geological ages, the man chuckled, tossed something to the feline traitor, and retreated.

Neither of us moved for several heartbeats. Though the immediate danger had passed, Quinn remained frozen in place, his expression oddly vulnerable. Something shifted in his eyes —a fleeting glimpse beneath the carefully maintained façade of the hardened antiquities dealer. For a moment, he wasn't the infuriating rogue who'd been complicating my investigation, but simply a man placing himself between danger and someone he... valued.

"He's gone," I whispered, my voice barely audible, a whisper against his jawline.

Quinn blinked, awareness returning to his features. He stepped back with uncharacteristic awkwardness, clearing his throat while straightening his dust-streaked jacket.

I brushed some of the plaster from his lapel, then dropped my hand, embarrassed by the unconsciously intimate gesture.

We retreated swiftly down the alley.

"We have to warn the museum," I said once we were headed past the docks, toward the train station.

Quinn shook his head. "A telegram would be worse than useless in this situation. Every museum guard, curator, and night watchman in Cairo has a price, and Hawke knows all their rates."

"We can't simply do nothing!" I raised my voice as we navigated around porters unloading crates of fish, their pungent cargo drawing seagulls that screamed overhead.

"Any warning would reach Hawke's ears before the ink had dried on the telegram." Quinn ran his hand through his disheveled hair, somehow making it look more stylish than before.

I stopped short, forcing a donkey cart to swerve around us. "Then we telegraph Bradford or Deveraux—"

But no, Deveraux had left for Alexandria a few days ago. Supposedly. Could he be part of all this as well?

I shook my head. "You're right. At this point, we can trust precisely no one. But one thing I will say—" I jabbed a finger at my satchel. "Someone wants my notes and drawings of the scribe's palette to disappear. So the best thing I can do is just the opposite. Make them public."

Quinn smiled. "You are extraordinarily fearless, Dr. Bell."

We reached Misr Station after a ten-minute walk, but the winter sun was already dropping below the horizon. The evening locomotive to Cairo towered like an iron beast, belching steam into the twilight air.

We boarded with a wary caution, checking each car for Hawke's men before settling into a private compartment—the last available space on the crowded train.

"Then we will need to devise our own strategy." I grabbed the seat cushion as the train lurched forward, then collapsed against the back. The scratchy upholstery abraded my neck, my muscles ached from tension, and the persistent grit of Alexandria dust seemed to have infiltrated every fold of clothing. I rested my satchel on my legs. I'd pull out my notes, as soon as I'd rested a minute.

Quinn dropped to the seat next to me, nodding. "By alerting authorities, we'd only cause Hawke to change his timing, not abandon the theft entirely. We can best stop him by catching him in the act."

The clacking of wheels against tracks filled our silence as Egypt's coastal landscape gave way to moonlit fields of delta farmland. Villages passed like ghosts, small flickers of lamplight marking human existence against the vast darkness.

The notes could wait.

"How exactly did someone like you end up in antiquities?" I asked, partly from genuine curiosity, partly to distract from the growing awareness of our isolation together.

Quinn's mouth quirked in a half-smile and he said nothing.

I sighed. "Yes, yes, I assumed you followed the money."

"That came later." He shifted, stretching his long legs in the compartment's close quarters. "I had a mentor once—brilliant archaeologist, impeccable credentials. He took me under his wing when I was studying ancient Mediterranean trade networks at Oxford."

The revelation that Quinn had formal training surprised me.

"What happened?"

"I discovered he was falsifying provenance documents for wealthy collectors." Quinn's expression hardened. "Not just mistaken attributions—he was aging modern forgeries using a technique involving calcium carbonate solutions and controlled heat exposure. When I confronted him, he ensured I was implicated in the scandal. University administrators slammed their doors rather permanently after that."

I studied him with interest, seeing him with new eyes— recognizing the intelligence and integrity beneath his exterior. Our gazes held longer than necessary, until he looked away. "So you joined what you couldn't defeat?"

"I became a bloody pragmatist. The antiquities world operates by its own rules, whether we approve or not." His eyes met mine. "But I've never falsified a document or stolen an artifact from its rightful context."

"Just facilitated their movement into private collections."

"Things aren't nearly as tidy as your Cambridge dons would have you believe, Dr. Bell." There was no malice in his tone, only weariness.

The train swayed through a turn, momentarily pressing my knees into his. When it straightened, neither of us moved to restore the proper distance.

I closed my eyes. "I understand the disillusionment. I thought Dr. Fairchild was a mentor to me. At Cambridge. I believed she'd hung the moon—until she published some of my ideas without crediting me."

"That must have stung. Did you call her on it?"

"Yes. She advised me to 'play the game' rather than challenge the establishment."

"Meaning?"

"She told me to stop making waves, to accept that the field would never truly respect women scholars, so we each had to do whatever we had to do."

Quinn surprised me by gently covering my hand with his. "Explains why you're so determined to prove yourself."

"I sometimes wonder if I'm fighting a losing battle." I gazed out at the darkness. "Dr. Fairchild has somehow managed it—earned respect."

"Rosamund Fairchild has her own complicated history," Quinn said cryptically.

I turned to study him, and something shifted in the air between us—a current as tangible as the static before a desert storm.

His eyes dropped briefly to my lips, then back to my eyes.

I exhaled, tension, dropping away.

"I daresay we ought to find something to eat." Quinn abruptly stood. "The dining car should still be serving."

"Yes. Food. Excellent idea."

The narrow corridor swayed beneath our feet as we made our

way through three carriages to reach the dining car. Crystal glasses clinked softly against white tablecloths as the train rocked along the tracks. Egyptian waiters in crisp uniforms navigated the space with practiced ease. The tablecloths had a distinctive smell of starch and lemon oil that triggered memories of formal dinners in New York, making me momentarily homesick despite myself.

Over plates of somewhat dubious chicken and surprisingly excellent tahini with the nutty bitterness particular to Egyptian sesame paste, we discussed strategies. Quinn sketched the museum layout on a napkin, marking potential entry points and guard rotations based on his detailed knowledge.

I watched the precise movements of his hands—steady, methodical, revealing that artistic ability I previously glimpsed.

"The east wing where Hawke mentioned the auxiliary display," he circled an area with his pencil, "it's connected to the main hall by a staff passage here. The different wings house collections organized by historic period—Old Kingdom, Middle Kingdom, and so on."

I nodded, committing the layout to memory while stifling a yawn.

When we returned to our compartment, the awkwardness threatened to resurface. I busied myself organizing my notes while Quinn sat beside me on the narrow bench, looking over my shoulder at what I'd collected.

The train compartment, initially spacious when we boarded, seemed to contract with the darkness outside, creating an intimate bubble of lamplight that separated us from the world rushing past.

Despite my determination to remain alert, the gentle rocking of the train conspired with exhaustion. My eyelids grew heavy, my head gradually tilting toward Quinn's shoulder. The last thing I remembered was Quinn draping his jacket over my shoulders as I dozed off. He hesitated, his hand lingering near my face.

I dreamed of blue pigment and betrayal, of hands reaching through darkness.

When I woke, harsh electric lights from Ramses Station

flooded through the window, casting sharp-edged shadows. My head still rested on Quinn's shoulder, his cheek pressed against my hair. For a moment, neither of us moved, caught in the strange liminal space between sleep and full awareness.

Then the train whistle announced our arrival, and reality crashed back.

We sat up simultaneously, adjusted rumpled clothing and avoided each other's eyes.

"Ready to stop a museum heist?" Quinn asked, his familiar half-smile returning.

I nodded, pushing aside all thoughts except the mission ahead. "Let's catch some thieves."

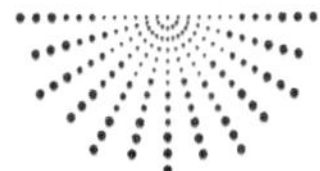

CHAPTER FOURTEEN

Three days had passed since our Alexandria adventure. I'd retreated to the dig site, cataloging the steady stream of artifacts emerging from the scribe's tomb. The simple, methodical work provided a welcome respite from murderous antiquities dealers and international conspiracies.

I'd even managed to steal away for a solitary visit to the Great Pyramid—my first since I'd been here at age seventeen. The ancient limestone blocks towered over me with the same indifferent majesty that had gone unchanged for millennia, while empires rose and fell around them. If only human affairs could maintain such dignified stability.

Quinn, of course, had a plan for the gala, delivered even before we'd exited Ramses Station.

"We'll attend as guests." He had sidestepped a porter smoothly. "Position ourselves strategically to intercept Sutherland and his accomplices."

I stopped short, nearly causing a collision with an elderly gentleman behind me. "Have you forgotten that minor detail where neither of us is actually invited? The Egyptian Museum doesn't typically welcome self-appointed artifact vigilantes."

Quinn's mouth curved into a smile. He pulled a small

leather notebook from his breast pocket and tapped it meaningfully.

"Fortunately, my dear Dr. Bell, I happen to know several people who owe me favors. By Friday evening, we'll be sipping champagne among Cairo's elite while we prevent a historic theft."

I narrowed my eyes. "Why does your solution always involve dubious connections and social schmoozing?"

"For the same reason yours always involves dusty books and righteous indignation." He shrugged. "It works."

I had no suitable retort, which was irritating.

It wasn't until two days later, standing in Annie's room at the Mena House Hotel, that I felt a flicker of excitement over Quinn's idea.

The opulent surroundings of Annie's accommodations served as yet another reminder of my father's long-reaching influence. He'd insisted on providing my "lady's companion" with quarters befitting the Bell family status—a lavish suite at Giza's most prestigious hotel, complete with a view of the pyramids and service that bordered on obsequious.

But I preferred my academic squalor to my father's gilded cage, even by proxy.

Annie fussed with my hair, pinning the red-blonde strands into a fashionable style that somehow tamed their usual rebellion. "You have such lovely coloring, Miss Bell. This emerald gown brings out the green in your eyes something magnificent."

I glanced down at the beaded silk draped over my athletic frame. I'd brought it from New York at my father's insistence —he'd commissioned it from a French designer for the party celebrating the opening of the new Bell Steel headquarters. I'd worn it precisely once, standing dutifully beside him while he paraded me before potential business partners like a prized *Specimen: American Heiress (Reluctant), Modern Period, Notable for Temporary Compliance with Social Expectations.*

"It will do, I suppose," I murmured. But I had to admit, the color complemented my fair, freckled skin rather well, and I'd kept my lapis pendant around my neck, with the dress pulling out the green highlights in the stone. "And anyway, it doesn't matter. Tonight is about gathering information, not gathering admirers."

"No? Because... that Quinn fellow..." Annie fanned her face with her hand. "I don't imagine one meets many antiquities dealers who look like they stepped out of a moving picture. Most of the archaeologists I've met have been..." she shrugged, as if thinking of Bradford, "I'd say, considerably less dashing."

"Yes, well, Quinn catalogs rather neatly under *Dangerously Attractive Nuisance*, right alongside *cobra*." I adjusted the emerald earrings at my lobes. "Though I suppose a cobra can at least be relied upon to be straightforward about its intentions."

Annie's tinkling laugh followed me as I gathered my evening bag. The tiny beaded affair could barely hold a handkerchief, let alone the measuring tools, specimen bags, and notebook I'd typically carry. Fashion, it seemed, was fundamentally opposed to archaeological practicality.

The journey from the hotel to the Egyptian Museum reminded me of all the reasons I preferred excavation sites to social gatherings. My corset, intended to flatten my bust and hips into the straight line that was currently fashionable, was instead impeding breathing and rational thought.

The Main Hall of the Egyptian Museum was ready to throw a party. The room buzzed with the distinct blend of British military officers in dress uniforms, colonial administrators with their wives in imported Paris fashions, and the aristocratic Britons and Americans who treated Cairo as their exotic playground from November through March, discussing the horse races at the Gezira Sporting Club and comparing notes on their Nile cruises while sipping champagne beside priceless artifacts. The officers' medals gleamed under the chandeliers, while the distinctive red tabs of staff officers formed bright spots among the black and white of formal wear.

But along with the elite, scholars in formal attire who usually squinted at potsherds through magnifying glasses now squinted at each other through monocles and lorgnettes, academic rivalries temporarily masked behind champagne and insincere smiles.

I stood at the entrance, cataloging possible escape routes, when a sudden hush fell over those nearest the door. For one horrifying moment, I thought some social faux pas had already marked me as an interloper. Then I realized they weren't looking at me—they were looking past me.

Benedict Quinn appeared at my elbow, resplendent in a perfect tuxedo that managed to look both conventional and dangerous. His dark hair was impeccably styled, and his usual roguish demeanor had been polished to a glossy social sheen. Only the barely perceptible quirk at the corner of his mouth betrayed the troublemaker beneath the gentleman. He entered a room like someone to be *seen*. The antiquities world's version of Rudolph Valentino, heartthrob of the silver screen.

Quinn's eyes widened fractionally as he took in my appearance, his gaze traveling from my elegantly styled hair to the emerald gown, with an attention to detail that would have impressed Deveraux. Something flickered in his expression— appreciation tinged with surprise, as if he'd discovered an unexpectedly valuable artifact in an otherwise ordinary dig.

"Dr. Bell," he murmured, with a small bow. "I believe you've managed to render me momentarily speechless."

I adjusted my gloves, ignoring the unwelcome warmth creeping up my neck. "Enjoy the novelty while it lasts, Quinn. I expect your regular verbal deluge will resume momentarily."

We moved further into the hall, threading through clusters of Cairo's elite who parted with subtle deference to Quinn's confident stride, passing a cluster of British officers, their reminiscences of their stations in India punctuated with barking laughter. The marble floor gleamed beneath our feet, reflecting the warm glow of crystal chandeliers and gilded sconces.

"Stop fidgeting." Quinn handed me one of the two champagne flutes he'd procured. "You look perfectly at home."

A blatant falsehood. I'd cataloged at least seven disapproving glances from women whose jewelry could pay for three of me. Their eyes lingered on my practical shoes, visible beneath the gown's hem when I walked.

"I attended an event just like this, six years ago. Actually, at your very hotel."

Quinn raised his brows. "You've been to Egypt before? How did I not know this?"

"Once. When I was seventeen." I touched the pendant at my throat. "That's when I purchased this piece. "Father was negotiating cotton exports and dragged Mother and me along to be decorative. I was supposed to flutter my eyelashes, but instead ended up helping solve a murder."

Quinn nearly choked on his champagne. "I beg your pardon?"

"Oh, it was fairly straightforward. You'd have been quite interested. It was all about illegal artifacts—bronze dagger, my stolen pendant, plus a morally bankrupt antiquities dealer. All the hubbub was mostly dealt with in the course of an evening." I waved at a passing waiter offering canapés.

"You helped solve a murder. At seventeen." Quinn studied me with what appeared to be a recalibration of his already complicated assessment. "Why am I simultaneously shocked and not surprised at all?"

"It cemented my love for Egypt." I smiled at the memory. "Not the murder, obviously, but the time I spent examining artifacts while the police bumbled about. I returned home determined to study Egyptology properly." I swept my gaze across the museum. "Though I didn't anticipate quite this much excitement on my return visit."

"With you, Dr. Bell, I'm beginning to expect nothing less." Quinn's expression warmed me with its admiration before he cleared his throat and turned to the scene before us.

The massive hall soared upward, its coffered ceiling designed by someone who clearly believed that if one skylight was good, thirty-seven must be divine. Columns marched along both sides, supporting a balcony that wrapped around the upper level where, no doubt, the most prestigious artifacts were displayed—far from the reach of sticky tourist fingers and archaeological assistants who, like myself, had reputations for breaking priceless pottery.

In preparation for today's exhibition, they'd rearranged the central space. Display cases formed a labyrinthine path through the hall, each containing artifacts behind glass buffed to within an inch of its life. Large stone statues of pharaohs and gods stood along the perimeter, their imperious faces frowning at me.

Gold placards announced in three languages that we were privileged to witness "Royal Treasures: Sacred Artifacts of Tutankhamun," sponsored by none other than Elias Hawke. His name appeared ninety-seven percent larger than any actual historical information.

"Subtle," I muttered.

A massive statue of Thoth—the ibis-headed god of wisdom and writing—dominated the center of the exhibition, newly positioned to oversee the proceedings like a disapproving headmaster. His expression seemed particularly judgmental as it gazed down at the cocktail-wielding archaeologists below, as if to say, "I invented writing, and this is what you do with it?"

"Our targets," Quinn whispered, "are in the northeast corner. Three artifacts with the highest concentration of Egyptian blue."

We wandered over, trying to appear subtle.

The artifacts in question were arranged in a special case—two fragments of painted limestone from a tomb wall, and a small faience figurine of a scribe, all containing the precious blue pigment created from heated copper, limestone, and silica.

"Security is heaviest near that display," Quinn nodded toward a guard who looked as if he'd been carved from the same granite as the nearby statues.

I stepped forward, only to feel Quinn's hand close gently around my wrist.

"Perhaps we should circulate. Appearing too interested in these specific items might draw attention."

The massive arched doorways leading to adjacent galleries stood like portals to other archaeological realms—Greek and

Roman antiquities to one side, mummies and sarcophagi to another. In normal circumstances, I would have happily spent days here, meticulously examining each artifact while making insufferably detailed notes.

Today, however, I had more pressing matters. Somewhere in this museum, amid the gleaming marble and priceless antiquities, Hawke and his conspirators were planning to steal artifacts that might hold the key to understanding why Egyptian blue pigment had suddenly become worth killing for.

"I've identified three potential conspirators," I whispered, accepting another champagne but not drinking. "The man with the imperial mustache by the Ramesses bust hasn't looked at a single artifact, only the exits. And those two by the sarcophagus look pained to be here."

Quinn's eyes scanned the room with practiced casualness. "Observant. Now watch a master at work."

He slipped seamlessly into conversation with a portly museum patron, his laugh carrying across the room with practiced ease. Within minutes, he was charming some sort of information from the man's wife.

The exhibition speeches droned on, each museum official more self-congratulatory than the last. I positioned myself near an archway that led to the museum's west wing, where less popular exhibits languished in relative obscurity. My archaeological instincts tingled with warning.

A museum guard consulted his pocket watch, then conveniently wandered away from his post. Moments later, two well-dressed men slipped into the hallway, their movements precise and practiced.

I caught Quinn's eye across the room and touched my pearl necklace—our agreed signal. He nodded, then turned back to the corpulent patron who had cornered him, laughing with apparent delight at whatever tedious anecdote the man was sharing.

The seconds stretched. Quinn remained trapped in conversation, his eyes darting to me with increasing frequency. The thieves would be halfway through the west wing by now. Not at all where we expected them to strike.

I made my decision.

Abandoning my position, I followed the men down the dimly lit corridor, my practical shoes—the very ones that had earned society ladies' disdain—now silent on the marble floor. The exhibition's distant chatter faded, replaced by the pounding rhythm of my heart.

Around a corner, I found them: four men efficiently dismantling a display case containing a royal scribe's ledger from the Eighteenth Dynasty—the blue pigment clearly visible on its ancient surface.

"Stop!" The word escaped before I could consider its wisdom.

They turned, startled—then one launched himself toward me, gun clearly tucked into his jacket.

I swung my beaded bag like a makeshift weapon, connecting with his jaw before a second man's arm caught me hard across the shoulders.

I stumbled against an iron bench, then hit the floor as they fled with their prize, deeper into the museum through a narrow doorway.

~

"Of all the reckless, impulsive—" Quinn's words tumbled over each other as our horse-drawn carriage clattered through Cairo's drowsy evening streets, each cobblestone sending a fresh jolt through my already battered dignity. He knelt awkwardly on the carriage floor, dabbing at the cut on my leg with his monogrammed handkerchief. "Why didn't you listen to me? You could have been killed!"

"Fascinating how you've managed to make my injury about your feelings." I winced as he pressed too hard on the gash. "Perhaps you could channel some of that outrage into your first aid technique. Medical practice usually works better without emotional commentary."

Our carriage driver, a wizened man with a face as textured as ancient papyrus, kept glancing back at us with undisguised interest, clearly adding our conversation to his collection of foreigner anecdotes to share at the coffeehouse later.

"While you were busy impersonating a social butterfly with the aristocracy, actual crimes were occurring." I snatched the handkerchief to apply proper pressure. "What was I supposed to do? Leave a polite note for the thieves? 'Dear Sirs, Kindly postpone your larceny until Mr. Quinn has finished his third glass of champagne and exhausted his supply of charming anecdotes. Sincerely, The Management.'"

Quinn's face contorted through several fascinating expressions before settling on exasperation. "I was gathering information!" His voice rose enough to startle our horse, which offered its own commentary with a disgruntled snort.

The carriage swayed as we rounded a corner, forcing Quinn to grab the seat to avoid tumbling into my lap—a catastrophe I wasn't prepared to navigate.

"We need to go to the authorities." My decision crystallized. "Sutherland, Hawke, the thefts—all of it. This has gone beyond academic rivalry to armed robbery."

Quinn huffed. "The authorities? Half the Cairo police force is in Hawke's pocket. You'd be handing them a convenient list of witnesses to eliminate. Including yourself."

"So your solution is vigilante justice? Chasing thieves through museums while they systematically loot Egypt's heritage?" I straightened, ignoring the sharp protest from my leg. "Some of us still believe in doing things properly."

"Some of us actually want to succeed," he shot back, eyes flashing in the intermittent lamplight filtering through the carriage windows. "Law and order make a lovely theory, Dr. Bell, but I deal in the real world."

I leaned forward, rapping sharply on the driver's seat. "Change of plans," I called. "Return me to the museum immediately."

Quinn's eyebrows ascended toward his hairline. "The museum? Now?"

"I'll get a driver from there to my lodgings." What did it mean that I was beginning to lie so smoothy? Quinn was having a detrimental effect on my morals, no doubt. "Some of us need a good night's sleep before continuing this investigation."

In reality, I intended to track down Dr. Sutherland and the truth—assuming both could be found in the same location.

The carriage rattled to a stop outside the museum's imposing entrance.

Quinn dismounted first, turning to offer me his hand with the frustrated gallantry of someone who'd prefer to lecture me about recklessness.

"We'll meet tomorrow morning." His voice was tight. "At my hotel. You've done enough solo investigating for one day, unless you're attempting to set a record for injuries sustained while wearing an evening gown."

I accepted his hand with as much dignity as possible for someone sporting a torn dress and what would surely become an impressive bruise collection.

"Hmm. Perhaps your mother should have changed your given name from "Benedict" to "Bene-dictator.""

"Funny."

"Fine. Tomorrow morning, at your hotel. And I'll expect a full report on what your 'socializing' uncovered, preferably with footnotes and proper citations."

I sent him off, waiting until the carriage had turned a corner before ascending the museum steps.

The guard recognized me from earlier and waved me through. The gala continued without upset. Apparently no one had yet noted the theft.

It took only three or four well-placed questions to learn that Sutherland had, not surprisingly, also shown up for the exhibit.

I spotted him in a side gallery, bent over a display case with the intensity of a man searching for salvation in ancient artifacts.

"Dr. Bell." His voice wavered, hands fidgeting with his spectacles. The white streak in his hair seemed more pronounced under the museum lights. "I was just—"

"Meeting with your conspirators?" I kept my voice low but steady. "I overheard you at the teahouse in Alexandria, planning today's theft with Hawke."

His face drained of color. His eyes darted to the doorway.

"Not here." His voice thinned with panic. "They might be listening."

"Who?" I demanded. "And how could you be betraying—"

"Please," he clutched my arm, hand trembling. "My room at the Mena House in Giza tomorrow morning. I can explain everything—but it's bigger than you know." He released me, looking hunted. "Far more dangerous than you realize."

With that, he pushed past me and hurried from the gallery.

I let him go. Tomorrow would be soon enough.

I headed back to the Tahrir Square Street, to find yet another carriage. Unfortunately, there was still someone I needed to speak with.

Quinn opened his hotel room door before I could knock, as if he'd been pacing near it since he arrived. His expression shifted from surprise to relief to carefully constructed neutrality.

"He's terrified," I said without preamble, stepping past him into the suite. The lamps had been dimmed, casting the room in a golden light that softened the edges of our earlier argument. "Sutherland. Not guilty—frightened. He insisted on meeting tomorrow at the Mena House."

Quinn closed the door, leaning against it. "Where did you—"

I waved away the question. "Back at the museum, I confronted him."

His sigh spoke volumes—irritation and a bit of resignation. "And you believe him?"

"I believe fear." I sank onto the damask chair. "His hands were shaking. Whatever's happening involves something that scares even Sutherland."

Quinn moved to the bureau, pouring amber liquid into

two crystal glasses. "I've heard rumors." He handed me a glass. "British Museum board members with connections to nationalist movements pushing for Egyptian independence. Political machinations disguised as archaeological interest."

Egypt had been declared an independent kingdom last year, but Britain still retained control over defense and military affairs, including the Suez Canal and control of the Sudan. The Wafd Party was pushing for full independence, and the presence of British troops was a constant source of tension between Egyptian nationalists and the British government.

But Sutherland involved in all this?

The whiskey burned pleasantly as I considered this new angle. "You think the thefts are politically motivated?"

"I think waiting until we hear Sutherland's explanation before alerting the authorities might be prudent."

Not a direct answer. And it wasn't capitulation—I would still insist on proper channels eventually—but it was a truce of sorts.

"One day," I conceded, rising to leave. "Then we do things properly, go the authorities."

Quinn's smile flickered in the low light. "Of course, Dr. Bell."

At the door, I paused. "For the record, Quinn, this partnership—" I gestured between us, "—remains a highly questionable archaeological experiment."

He smiled—the smile that was all sincere charm. "Yet with remarkably compelling data," he murmured.

I slipped into the hall, the door closing behind me.

Encounters with Benedict Quinn: Equal Parts Infuriating and Intriguing. Excavation Status: Dangerously Incomplete, Proceed with Caution and Possibly a Protective Helmet.

CHAPTER FIFTEEN

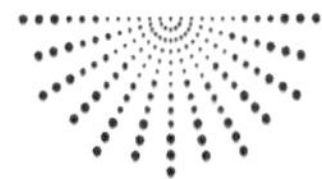

The sun had barely begun its ascent over Giza when I knocked on Dr. Sutherland's door at the Mena House Hotel.

The grand colonial-era building loomed like a well-dressed British gentleman trying too hard to look comfortable in the desert—imposing, expensive, and utterly incongruous with its surroundings.

No answer came from within Room 237. I knocked again, harder this time, my knuckles protesting against the heavy mahogany. The corridor remained tomb-silent, but the rich aroma of Turkish coffee drifted from the hotel's dining room, mingling with lingering traces of perfumes and pomades from the previous night's socializing.

"Dr. Sutherland?" My voice echoed in the empty hallway. "It's Clarissa Bell."

A nearby service door cracked open, and a sleepy-faced hotel employee peered out.

"The gentleman in 237 left very early, miss. Before dawn." He rubbed his eyes. "Said something about urgent business at his dig site office."

I thanked him with a nod and the last of my pitifully small supply of Arabic pleasantries.

I left the Mena House behind, my boots crunching on the path that wound toward the dig site, and my leather bag stuffed full of notes and journals slung over my shoulder. The morning air still held the night's coolness, a brief reprieve before the sun remembered its job description as Egypt's premier torture device.

Dawn painted the Great Pyramid in hues of gold and rose, and the path was deserted. Soon, workers would be streaming toward the site like ants to a picnic. Only silence accompanied me, broken occasionally by distant bird calls. My skin prickled with unease despite the pleasant temperature.

Dr. Sutherland's "dig site office" was a generous description for what amounted to a canvas tent with a military surplus desk. Located at the eastern edge of the excavation, it offered a modicum of privacy for the senior archaeologist's records and personal effects—hardly the secure storage one might hope for when dealing with Old Kingdom artifacts dating to the Fourth Dynasty, but apparently adequate.

The early morning light cast long shadows across the site as I approached the tent. Something felt wrong. The canvas flap hung partially open, which violated Sutherland's notorious obsession with keeping sand out of his workspace.

I paused at the entrance, suddenly reluctant to push aside the canvas.

"Dr. Sutherland?"

The silence that answered held a weight to it.

I pushed the flap aside, and the familiar scent hit me before my eyes adjusted to the dim interior. The musty scent of canvas baking under the Egyptian sun mixed with the metallic tang of blood.

Dr. Gregory Sutherland lay sprawled across his paper-strewn desk, his wire-rimmed glasses askew on his face, the distinctive white streak in his hair matted with crimson. The collar of his normally immaculate oxford shirt bloomed with a dark stain that spread outward like a spilled inkwell.

"Dr. Suth—!" I stepped back, colliding with a camp stool that clattered to its side. My heart hammered against my ribs.

I should run, I knew that. Find Bradford, alert the authorities, do any of the sensible things a normal person would do upon discovering a colleague thoroughly and definitively murdered.

Instead, I catalogued details with a detached precision.

A surveying theodolite's wooden tripod lay discarded beside the desk, its brass mounting plate dark with what could only be blood. The expensive instrument itself was still in its protective case on his desk. Sutherland had been mapping tomb locations yesterday; the tripod should have been cleaned and properly stored with its instrument.

The angle of the body suggested he'd been seated when attacked. No signs of a prolonged struggle. The papers on his desk were disturbed but not scattered—he'd been working when it happened. And there, partially concealed beneath his outstretched hand, lay our stolen palette—now broken into two distinct pieces.

I leaned closer, careful not to disturb anything. The blue pigment on the palette's surface caught the light oddly, appearing iridescent.

I squinted, examining the break pattern. The palette hadn't been smashed in a struggle—it had been deliberately snapped, the fracture lines too precise for accident.

Beneath the broken palette lay a sheet of paper, partially concealed by Sutherland's outstretched hand. The top corner contained calculations for carbon dating estimates of Third Dynasty pottery—ordinary archaeological notes. But in the center of the page, scrawled in rusty brown, were the letters 'FOR C' with the 'C' smudged at the bottom as though he'd trailed off.

I glanced at the desk surface—no pen within reach. A chill crawled up my spine despite the growing heat of the morning.

The grim realization hit me—Sutherland had used his own blood to write this message.

From outside, heavy, purposeful strides were moving quickly toward the tent.

I straightened, scanned for a weapon, ignored the bloody

tripod and reached for Sutherland's prized brass magnifying glass. It would have to do. I gripped it tightly, its weight surprisingly satisfying against my palm. I slipped to just inside the tent entrance and raised it above my head, muscles coiled with tension.

The canvas flap was thrown aside, flooding the tent with morning light and the imposing silhouette of Benedict Quinn.

"Put that down before you hurt someone, Clarissa." He stepped inside, eyes darting between me and Sutherland's body. The clean scent of his aftershave momentarily overpowered the smell of death in the confined space, giving me a split second of relief before reality reasserted itself.

"Good heavens! What have you done?"

"Nothing! This wasn't me."

He stepped around me and bent to the body, navigating the small space with careful precision, maintaining a professional distance while examining the evidence. "No, of course not, my apologies. But please tell me you haven't touched anything."

"How did you know I was here—"

"My contact at the hotel overheard you asking about Sutherland." He moved beside me, his expression grim. "I was coming to warn you he might be dangerous. Apparently, I'm too late."

"For him, certainly." I reluctantly set down my makeshift weapon. "Not for me. Although your concern is... noted."

Quinn's explanation for his presence here didn't make sense. The drive from Shepheard's, where he and I were supposed to meet, would have taken longer than my twenty minute walk from the Mena House, even if he'd gotten an immediate phone call from his "contact." But I'd deal with that later.

Quinn crouched beside the desk, studying the scene. "The palette." His voice dropped to a whisper. "He had it all along."

"Not quite." I pointed to the blood spatter on the desk, which formed a pattern underneath the broken palette. "It was placed here after the main event. So maybe it was left here after he was struck."

"Or he had it tucked away and pulled it out as he was dying." Quinn peered closer at the fracture points. "These breaks look deliberate."

"Because they are. Look at how clean the edges are. And look at the blood smear, here, on both ends of the piece, and here, on his fingers. You're right, I think Sutherland broke it himself." I leaned in, careful not to disturb anything.

"'FOR C'—maybe 'For Clarissa'? You think he was writing you a note, wanting you to have it?"

I shrugged and blew out a breath. "Maybe. Perhaps he stole it himself, and wanted to return it to me? Felt guilty about harming my career?"

I moved around the desk, studying the blood pattern that decorated the papers. The stifling quality of the air grew worse as the morning heat built.

"The palette was deliberately broken," Quinn murmured. "But why would he do that?"

"Perhaps he didn't want it sold off?" But the explanation fell flat.

Quinn's expression darkened. "The timing can't be coincidental—after all the trouble to steal it, it suddenly reappears beside his body?"

"He must have uncovered something significant about it—something worth killing for." I tapped my finger against my chin. "The blue pigment has always been unusual. Perhaps there's something hidden in the composition itself, or inscriptions visible only under certain conditions."

"Or perhaps he simply discovered who stole it," Quinn suggested, "and confronted the wrong person at the wrong time."

"Either way, Sutherland knew something dangerous," I replied, the academic detachment in my voice a thin veneer over growing unease. "And now that knowledge—whatever it was—died with him."

"Clarissa," Quinn put a hand on my shoulder and delivered

his concerned expression. "There's a dead body between us." He gestured toward Sutherland. "This isn't an academic exercise."

"I know that." I swallowed hard against the tightness in my throat. Sutherland had been the only person at this dig who'd treated me as a colleague rather than an inconvenience in skirts. I couldn't afford to process that loss now—not while standing in his blood. Compartmentalization: the archaeologist's most underrated skill.

I moved toward a leather case tucked beneath the desk, careful to avoid disturbing the blood pattern.

Quinn glanced toward the tent entrance where the sound of a truck engine rumbled across the desert, growing louder.

The archaeological team arriving for the day's work, blissfully unaware.

Quinn stepped to the tent entrance, one eye peering through the slit. "We have approximately three minutes before this tent becomes the most popular attraction in Giza. Whatever revelation you're pursuing had better be worth potential arrest for murder."

"We can't just leave! There's a dead man and crucial evidence—"

"Think, Clarissa. Do you want to be found standing over a dead body? I can assure you that my reputation will land me in an Egyptian cell immediately."

"So we just flee a murder scene? That's your solution?" I fought to keep my voice down.

"Not flee. Strategic retreat."

Quinn's head swiveled to take in the items in Sutherland's tent, then lunged toward Sutherland's field camera—a folding Kodak Autographic.

Before I could consider the consequences, he was shooting photographs of Sutherland from all angles, of the palette, of the scattered documents, then lifted the strap around his neck.

He grabbed my hand. "Satisfied?" He pointed. "Back exit."

I grabbed up my own bag. Then Sutherland's personal satchel. Ignored Quinn's raised eyebrows.

We slipped through a seam opening at the back of the tent and hurried away, keeping low behind a ridge of excavated sand. The open desert around us felt simultaneously threatening and protective—offering no hiding places but also vast space for escape. We'd barely made it twenty yards, to a stack of pottery crates, when the first yell announced the discovery of Sutherland's body.

"Now what?" I whispered as we crouched behind the stack of empty crates. "Did you drive here? They'll see your motor car!"

"I left the driver down by the tourist entrance near the Sphinx."

Even at this hour, it would likely blend in with the other autos ferrying camera-wielding visitors to the 'exotic Orient.'

I pointed along the back side of the site. "They're all occupied up there. We just need to get down to the—"

Quinn took the satchel, grabbed my hand, and we ran.

CHAPTER SIXTEEN

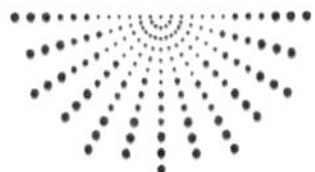

The Model T lurched away from the pyramid site. In the rear seat, I clutched Sutherland's notes to my chest as the scent of exhaust mingled with desert dust.

I tapped the leather satchel, with a glance at the driver in front of us. "We need somewhere private to examine these."

"My hotel suite?"

I sighed.

"Don't worry, Dr. Bell. I would never presume that discovering dead bodies together constitutes proper courtship."

"Well, when you put it like that, how can a girl refuse?"

Quinn leaned forward to study the crowded morning street through the windscreen, his shoulder touching mine in the narrow space. Outside, vendors calling their wares in Arabic and the chatter of European tourists exclaiming over trinkets created the chaotic symphony of Cairo streets.

"You do have a talent for finding trouble."

"I believe trouble found me quite effectively on its own this time." I leaned against the cool side panel. Even in morning, the Egyptian sun beat down on the Model T, making the metal exterior hot to the touch and intensifying the closeness between us in the stuffy interior. "Sutherland wasn't a traitor."

"You sound certain."

"I'm not. But I knew him, and I believe he was a good man. I think perhaps he was trying to stop something. Maybe from the inside. Maybe that's why he was meeting with Hawke—not betraying us, but trying to track the thefts."

"Well, it got him killed."

The reality of Sutherland's death suddenly hit me with full force. "I accused him of being a traitor, and now he's dead. I was so certain, so arrogant..."

My voice broke, and I turned away, embarrassed.

Quinn's hand covered mine on the seat of the auto.

The leather seat crackled beneath my palm as the car lurched.

"You couldn't have known."

"I should have." I blinked rapidly, fighting tears. The taste of dust in my mouth made me swallow hard when Quinn looked at me. "I'm supposed to question assumptions, examine evidence objectively—that's what archaeology demands. Instead, I let my personal paranoia cloud my judgment."

"I don't think you are paranoid, Clarissa."

I swiped at my face. "But I am. I'm always thinking that others are out to discredit me."

"Perhaps with good reason?"

I shrugged. His fingers were warm against mine, his presence unexpectedly comforting.

"Only since I was twelve years old."

"Twelve?"

He was distracting me, obviously. But I unfolded the memory anyway. "Yes, my first brush with academic treachery came when I was twelve." I traced a figure-eight in the dust on the Model T's window as we bumped along, each pothole threatening to rearrange my internal organs. "I'd spent weeks researching an obscure pharaonic dating method—terribly exciting stuff for a socially awkward adolescent who'd rather catalogue pottery sherds than discuss which classmates had been invited to Millicent Porter's birthday soirée."

The car lurched, sending my shoulder colliding with Quinn's. I straightened quickly, still gripping the leather seat.

"The night before presentation day, Walter Hammond—whose intellectual prowess began and ended with his ability to belch the school anthem—somehow presented my exact findings. When I confronted him, our teacher looked at me like I'd suggested the pyramids were built by trained flamingos wearing tiny construction hats."

Quinn's mouth twitched. "I'd pay good money to see that."

"My father's response was even better." I cleared my throat, adopting the regal posture of Armand Bell addressing the help. "'Clarissa, dear, why must you be so emotional? Surely you're overreacting.'"

I shrugged, bouncing as we hit another miniature canyon in the road. "That was the day I learned two fundamental truths: men would always be credited for women's ideas, and righteous indignation was merely 'hysteria' when expressed while female."

A grin found its way to my lips. "I also learned to document everything. Poor Walter never quite recovered from the twenty-seven-page annotated bibliography I nailed to his desk. With actual nails."

"And here you are, still fighting to uncover the truth." His smile was gentle. "That's rather brave."

"Or foolish." I sighed. "The jury's still out."

"I've always found the line between bravery and foolishness to be remarkably thin." His gaze dropped to my mouth, then back to my eyes. "Like the line between antagonism and attraction."

An unexpected turn slid me toward him again. The laws of physics, apparently delighted by awkward situations, conspired to keep me pressed against his side despite my best efforts.

The air in the Model T suddenly felt thick. Quinn's arm, casually draped along the back of the seat, might as well have been a high-voltage wire crackling with tension.

"Clarissa..." His hand moved to brush a strand of hair from my face, his fingers lingering against my cheek, as if cataloging each freckle for future reference.

My traitorous skin shivered. Every nerve ending suddenly

remembered it was alive—and apparently had very specific, very inappropriate opinions about Benedict Quinn. My pulse thundered in my throat, and my mouth went suddenly dry.

I leaned closer. My body hummed with a complex symphony of desire, curiosity, and absolute mortification. Heat pooled in my cheeks.

"Quinn..." The name escaped on a breath that was equal parts warning and invitation.

Our lips were mere inches apart when the driver hit what must have been the Grand Canyon's Egyptian cousin. The car bounced violently, sending us knocking foreheads like a pair of mountain goats establishing dominance.

"So much for the romance of archaeology," Quinn muttered, rubbing his forehead while I straightened my blouse and attempted to resurrect my dignity.

The remainder of our journey passed in awkward silence—punctuated by the occasional strategic cough or glance out the window.

Shepheard's Hotel soon loomed before us. The driver left us at the entrance, and we passed through the polished marble lobby where ceiling fans lazily cut through the heavy air. Egyptian staff moved deferentially around European guests.

In his suite, Quinn tossed his hat onto the bed.

I watched the hat bounce, then settle.

"Shall we?" Quinn gestured toward Sutherland's satchel under my arm.

He cleared an area from the cluttered desk. We spread the satchel's contents across the space and leaned over them.

Morning light slanted through half-drawn curtains, creating patterns of shadow and light across the scattered documents. From somewhere down the hall, a gramophone played a popular tune.

"He was tracking the pieces. He knew there was a pattern, too. There must be a systematic reason. If I can just find it."

Quinn watched my actions with the fascination of a naturalist observing a volatile scientific specimen. He leaned against the desk, arms crossed, while I paced the room, sorted and rearranged papers, and mumbled through my racing thoughts.

"Clarissa." His tone suggested practical concerns were about to be introduced. He tugged at his tie, loosening it slightly at the knot. "We should discuss—"

"Shhh."

He tried again. "We're potentially being hunted by—"

"Mmhmm." I didn't look up, fingers dancing between photographs like a concert pianist mid-symphony.

Exasperation rolled off Quinn in waves. "You do realize we might be in actual danger?"

He grabbed at my hand, knocking a stack of documents. They tumbled in a cascade, sheets scattering like startled birds.

I scrambled to pick them up. Then froze.

"Quinn," I whispered, "you magnificent accidental genius."

He looked terrified.

Spread before me, the papers had realigned themselves into coherence.

I snatched up the pages and started assembling them on the desk, setting some aside.

"I think..." My voice hit that pitch reserved for academics on the verge of a breakthrough. "I think all of these pieces— well, most of them—involve math and science."

Quinn circled to look at the pages.

"We've been so focused on the blue pigment. But if we only look at these," I jabbed a finger at several pages in succession, "but ignore those," I pointed to the few that I'd pushed to the side, "and also include this one. And this one." My voice trailed off as I assembled more than ten pages, then a few more.

"Yes?"

"Sorry. Yes, it's quite a few of them, all the with the blue pigment, but also with symbols that reference things like geometry, astronomy, medicine. Much like the New Kingdom stelae from Deir el-Medina showing medical and astronomical records. Howard Carter might dismiss these as 'mundane' compared to his golden treasures, but surely they're far more significant to understanding Egyptian scientific knowledge."

I grabbed his forearm in excitement. "This must mean something! We need to get these to an expert."

He placed a warm hand over mine.

I looked up into his face. Fought the flare of distraction that looking into his eyes invariably brought, and the desire to tangle my fingers in his. We were too close to let something as trivial as attraction slow us down now.

He exhaled, studying me. "Clarissa, about earlier. Driving here..."

I shook my head. "A mistake."

One eyebrow—his trademark weapon of mild provocation —arched. "Mistake?"

I summoned up the commentary that had been running behind everything since our near-miss in the Model T.

"Listen, Quinn. I have an archaeological mystery to solve, no time for romantic entanglements, and—most crucially—I would rather spend a week trapped in one of Bradford's lectures on Mesopotamian irrigation systems than become romantically involved with an illegal antiquities dealer."

Quinn looked simultaneously wounded and impressed—a combination I was discovering was his particular specialty. "Ouch."

"Sorry. That could have been delivered more gently." And more truthfully.

I turned back to my research, aware that he stood too close, too silent, reading my traitorous thoughts.

The moment shattered with a knock on the door.

Sharp. Deliberate. Definitely not housekeeping.

We both froze, our eyes meeting in shared apprehension. Someone had found us.

CHAPTER SEVENTEEN

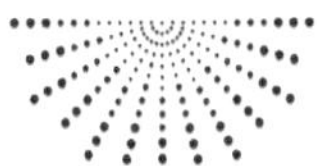

The knock at the door resonated through Quinn's suite —three sharp raps followed by an ominous pause.

Quinn and I exchanged glances, his hand moving subtly toward the inside pocket of his jacket.

"Mr. Benedict Quinn?" A heavily accented voice called.

Quinn motioned for me to stay back as he approached the door.

I slid Sutherland's papers into his satchel, feeling the texture of the worn leather against my sweating palms.

"Yes?" Quinn's expression betrayed nothing as he opened the door, his posture transforming instantly into casual aristocratic boredom.

Two men stood in the corridor. The first wore the crisp white uniform of Cairo's police force, adorned with the epaulets and insignia of a senior officer. His companion, dressed in a less impressive uniform, stood a half-step behind, his hand resting deliberately on his holstered sidearm.

"I am Captain Mahmoud of the Cairo Police." The officer's eyes, dark and calculating, moved from Quinn to where I stood by the writing desk, pausing briefly on Sutherland's satchel. "And this is Sergeant Aziz. We would like to ask you some questions about the unfortunate death of Dr. Gregory Sutherland."

Quinn's voice remained perfectly steady. "Dr. Sutherland is dead? How terrible. When did this happen?"

His performance was remarkable. If I hadn't personally witnessed him photographing Sutherland's blood-spattered body mere hours ago, I might have believed his shock.

"This morning, at the Giza excavation site." Captain Mahmoud stepped forward, uninvited, into the suite. The sound of their polished boots clicked against the marble floor tiles, echoing in the tense silence. "A Ford Model T was seen leaving the area shortly after the body was discovered. The vehicle matches the description of one you hired from Cairo yesterday evening."

Specimen: Evidence (Circumstantial), Colonial Policing Era, Notable for its Inconvenient Accuracy.

"I have indeed rented such a vehicle." Quinn's voice was smooth as honey-soaked konafa. "But I assure you, Captain, I was nowhere near Giza this morning."

"And yet here you are, with dirt on your shoes." Captain Mahmoud glanced pointedly at Quinn's shoes, then at mine—both still bearing the distinctive pale limestone dust of the Giza plateau.

The dry Egyptian heat seeped through the windows, making the collar of my shirt stick to my neck.

Captain Mahmoud moved through the room with deliberate authority. The scent of bay rum and tobacco clung to him.

Sergeant Aziz's gaze settled on me with intensity. "And you are...?"

"Dr. Clarissa Bell." I squared my shoulders. "I'm an archaeologist from Cambridge University, working at the Giza excavation."

Captain Mahmoud's eyebrows rose fractionally. "Indeed? And what brings a Cambridge archaeologist to Mr. Quinn's hotel room so early in the day?"

Quinn opened his mouth, but I spoke first, tasting fear.

"Professional consultation. Mr. Quinn is assisting Cambridge in recovering artifacts stolen from our dig site."

"Is that so?" The captain made a show of examining the room, his eyes lingering on the rumpled bedspread where our papers had been spread, Quinn's jacket draped over a chair, and my satchel bulging with Sutherland's documents. "Most archaeological consultations I've observed take place in museums or universities. Not hotel bedrooms."

His implication hung in the air.

I felt heat rise to my cheeks, my pulse hammering in my throat as my fingers tightened around the leather strap of Sutherland's satchel.

"The consultation required privacy." Quinn gave Mahmoud his charm-smile. "Museum staff have been implicated in the thefts."

"I see." Captain Mahmoud's tone suggested he saw entirely too much. He deliberately positioned himself so Quinn had to look up at him. "And why were you observed at the exact location where Dr. Sutherland was murdered, at the time of his death?"

Nice try.

"That's preposterous." The indignation in my voice was genuine, if somewhat misaimed—given that we had, in fact, been precisely where they claimed. "Mr. Quinn was assisting me in tracking down documentation related to our stolen artifacts. We've been comparing notes all morning."

"All morning?" Sergeant Aziz spoke for the first time, his voice softer than his superior's but no less pointed.

"Since breakfast." I met his gaze with the practiced confidence of someone who has defended questionable interpretations before hostile academic committees.

Captain Mahmoud pulled a small notebook from his breast pocket and consulted it with a theatrical flourish. "Interesting. Because the concierge reports that Mr. Quinn left the hotel at 6:15 this morning. Alone."

If Quinn was troubled by this accurate timeline, he didn't show it. "I always take an early morning drive. It clears the head. I picked up Dr. Bell afterward, and we've been reviewing documents since."

"And Dr. Bell, where were you early this morning?" The captain turned his attention to me, emphasizing "Dr." with slight skepticism about my credentials.

I looked him directly in the eye, feeling the strain of maintaining a composed posture while being inspected. "At my lodgings in Giza, above the Nile View Café, preparing for today's work."

"Can anyone confirm this?"

"My landlady, Madame Farah." I hoped fervently she hadn't noticed my pre-dawn departure. I couldn't help but imagine how my father would react to seeing his daughter questioned by Egyptian police in a man's hotel room.

"You seem unusually interested in Dr. Sutherland's death, given that he was not a local." Quinn cleared his throat. He adjusted his tie, a subtle tell that his carefully managed exterior had been disturbed. "Was there something distinctive about the crime scene?"

It was a dangerous gambit. If we hadn't been there ourselves, we wouldn't know to ask such a question.

Captain Mahmoud's eyes narrowed. "Why do you ask, Mr. Quinn?"

Quinn shrugged with elegant nonchalance. "Professional curiosity. In my experience, police don't typically question hotel guests based solely on a similar vehicle being spotted nearby. There must be something more specific connecting me to the scene."

In the silence that followed, distant sounds of Cairo filtered through the window—the clatter of wooden shutters being opened for the day, the occasional automobile horn, the shouts of children playing in the street below.

Diversionary Tactic (Bold), Attempting to Extract Information While Under Suspicion.

"Indeed." The captain studied Quinn for a moment. "The murderer left something unusual at the scene. A broken artifact."

"How tragic!" I channeled my genuine distress into a performance. "What sort of artifact?"

"I believe your colleagues called it a scribe's palette. Egyptian. Quite old." The captain watched me closely.

I allowed myself a controlled reaction of professional interest. "A palette? How strange—we had such a piece stolen a few days ago. I wonder if it could have been connected to the murder?"

Mahmoud's eyes narrowed. "I don't believe I mentioned it was murder, Dr. Bell."

Quinn moved casually to stand beside me, our shoulders nearly touching. The brief contact sent electricity through me, triggering a dual reaction, as always. "If there *has* been a murder at the dig site, surely you should be questioning Dr. Bradford and the other archaeologists who were actually there when it happened?"

"We are." He tipped his head back, watching us through half-slit eyes. "But not everyone fled the scene in a Ford Model T."

"We didn't—"

Quinn's slight pressure against my arm silenced me.

"Captain, we're as shocked by this news as anyone. Dr. Sutherland was a respected colleague. If there's any way we can assist your investigation—"

"Indeed there is." Captain Mahmoud gestured to Sergeant Aziz, who withdrew a folded document from his pocket. "We would like to examine your belongings, Mr. Quinn. And those of Dr. Bell."

Quinn accepted the paper, studying it briefly. "A warrant. You work quickly."

"Signed by the British Commissioner himself," the captain confirmed with the annoyance of a man representing the newly established Egyptian independence. "Your reputation precedes you, Mr. Quinn."

For the next excruciating forty-five minutes, the officers methodically searched Quinn's suite. The Cairo heat built throughout the process, initially tolerable but gradually becoming oppressive as the questioning intensified, mirroring my growing discomfort and the tightening net around us. Small beads of perspiration formed at Quinn's temples.

They examined clothing, correspondence, even the contents of his toiletry case. Sergeant Aziz meticulously cataloged each item in a notebook, while Captain Mahmoud conducted the search with the delicacy of a rhinoceros in a pottery display.

I clutched the satchel with Sutherland's documents protectively, but when Mahmoud extended his hand expectantly, I had no choice but to surrender it.

"These are my personal research materials."

He emptied the contents onto Quinn's writing desk. "And what research would that be, precisely?" The captain sifted through the papers, his expression growing more interested as he examined them. The weight of the Egyptian air hung unusually still and heavy, as if the hotel itself were holding its breath during the investigation.

"Analysis of pigments used in Old Kingdom artifacts," I replied promptly. "I'm examining the correlation between pigment composition and scribal notation systems."

Captain Mahmoud looked at me with new assessment. "You read hieratic script, Dr. Bell?

"Of course." I stepped forward, pointing to one of Sutherland's notes that was, thankfully, actually about pigment analysis. "This section discusses the molecular composition of Egyptian blue. It's quite technical."

The captain studied me rather than the paper. "And this research relates to the stolen artifacts?"

"We believe the thefts are targeting items containing specific pigments," Quinn interjected. "Dr. Bell is the foremost expert on ancient Egyptian coloring agents."

This extravagant exaggeration nearly made me choke, but I maintained my composure.

"Indeed?" Mahmoud replaced the papers in my satchel with surprising care. "And have you shared these theories with your colleagues at the dig site?"

"Not yet," I admitted, my mouth dry and chest tight. "We wanted more evidence before presenting our findings."

Sergeant Aziz, who had been examining the bathroom, emerged holding Sutherland's camera. "Sir."

Captain Mahmoud took the device, examining it with interest. "You're a photographer, Mr. Quinn?"

Quinn tensed beside me. "A hobby. Landscapes, mostly."

The captain opened the back of the camera, removing the film canister. "I'm afraid we'll need to develop this."

"That's private property," Quinn protested, with the first genuine emotion he'd shown during the entire interview.

"And this is a murder investigation." Captain Mahmoud pocketed the film. "If there's nothing incriminating, you'll get your photographs back."

My stomach twisted. How were we going to explain those pictures?

After another fifteen minutes of increasingly uncomfortable questioning, Captain Mahmoud finally signaled to his sergeant. "We'll be watching you both closely." He paused at the door. "Please don't attempt to leave Cairo without informing us first."

"Of course not," Quinn bowed. "We are at your disposal."

The door closed behind them with the finality of a sealed tomb.

Quinn immediately moved to the window, watching until the police officers emerged onto the street below. A tense silence fell as we waited to ensure the officers were truly gone. Only then did he exhale slowly. "Well, that was unfortunate."

"Unfortunate?" I sank into the nearest chair. "They have your photographs of the murder scene! They know we were there! They'll have that film developed by the end of the day."

"Unlikely." Quinn's mouth curved into a small smile. "The film in the camera wasn't even the right type for that camera. I'd already removed the exposed roll."

I stared at him. "Where is it?"

He reached into his waistcoat pocket and produced a small metal canister. "I always carry the important things close."

"You're infuriating," I told him, though relief undermined the accusation.

"So I've been told." He moved to the writing desk, extracting his amber bottle of liquid from a drawer. "Drink? I believe we've earned it."

"It's not yet noon."

"We've been accused of murder. I think normal hours no longer apply." He poured two glasses anyway, setting one near my hand. The liquid caught the late morning sunlight, creating honey-colored patterns on the desk's polished surface.

I ignored the drink, running my fingers through my already disheveled hair. "We need a plan. They'll be back once they realize that film is blank."

Quinn took a sip from his glass. "We need to determine whom we can trust."

"About that..."

He quirked an eyebrow.

"Do you want to explain how your man at the Mena House managed to get word to you so quickly that you magically appeared in Sutherland's tent not thirty minutes later?"

He dropped his gaze. "There was no man. I had no intention of letting you meet Sutherland alone. I was minutes behind you at the hotel, and followed you to the dig site."

"I see."

"Clarissa, you can trust me."

"Hmm. But no one else, apparently." I began pacing, my mind racing through options. "Bradford will likely believe we killed Sutherland. The police clearly suspect us. Hawke is involved in the scheme, possibly with Sutherland. Fairchild appeared in Alexandria too conveniently. Deveraux is conspicuously absent..."

"What about your Egyptian contacts?" Quinn picked up the glass and placed it into my hand. "Someone outside the European archaeological community?"

I paused mid-stride. "Actually... there is someone. Dr. Waseem Abbas at Al-Azhar University. He's a mathematician who's been systematically denied recognition by European academics, despite his brilliant work on ancient calculation methods." In the growing tension between foreign archaeological missions and Egyptian authorities regarding antiquities ownership, Dr. Abbas would understand all too well.

"And you think he'd help us?"

"He has no reason to protect the colonial archaeological establishment." I retrieved the satchel, checking that the contents remained intact. "And if these artifacts contain some kind of pattern, he'll be the one who understands them."

Quinn drained his glass and set it down with decision. "Then let's visit this mathematician."

CHAPTER EIGHTEEN

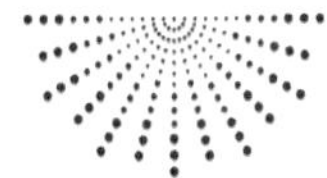

After our excited decision to visit Dr. Abbas, we reconsidered and detoured to yet another contact of Quinn's who could spend a few hours developing our photographs from Sutherland's murder scene.

We'd left the hotel through a service entrance, like thieves escaping with particularly disappointing loot—nothing but a roll of film and a satchel full of papers that might get us killed.

Quinn assured me that his "associate" Gerhardt Mueller, a stooped German expatriate with nicotine-stained fingers and the permanent squint of someone who spends too much time in darkrooms, would be nothing but discreet.

By the afternoon, armed with the photos and all our notes, Quinn himself drove his hired Bentley through Cairo's chaotic streets, the engine's rumble matching my internal turmoil, deciding against his occasional driver with the Model T, spotted earlier.

I stared at my reflection in the window glass, ghosted over the passing cityscape. The scent of exhaust mingled with aromas of nutmeg and cinnamon from street cooking, while occasional wafts of hibiscus drifted from hidden courtyards.

Specimen: Archaeologist (Female), Modern Era, Currently

Experiencing Existential Crisis While Fleeing Murder Accusations.

"You look positively funereal." Quinn navigated around a donkey cart with more optimism than skill. "Having second thoughts about our life of crime?"

"I'm a Cambridge-trained archaeologist with a specialty in ceramic classification systems." My mouth had gone dry, and I found my fingers unconsciously tracing patterns on my satchel. "I catalogue pottery. I publish in respectable journals. I do not flee police interrogations or investigate murders."

"And yet here we are."

"Here we are indeed." I straightened, studying my window-self more carefully. The woman reflected back had a wild-eyed look.

What exactly was I doing? I'd spent years fighting for academic respectability, only to throw it all away on a mad adventure with a questionable antiquities dealer. Bradford would fire me. Cambridge would disavow me. My father would say "I told you so" in that insufferable way of his, before arranging a socially advantageous marriage. And my pottery classification skills would be limited to selecting dinnerware.

And yet.

Sutherland died for these artifacts. Perhaps for knowledge someone desperately wanted hidden. Knowledge that could perhaps rewrite Egyptian history.

"If you're having regrets," Quinn murmured, "I can take you back to your lodgings. You could claim ignorance, distance yourself from me. Bradford would welcome you back eventually."

I met my reflection's eyes directly. The woman looking back wasn't just the dutiful academic, cataloging by color. She was someone else too—someone willing to risk everything for truth, for justice, for the messy, gloriously complex reality of the past.

"And miss the chance to completely destroy my career, reputation, and possibly get murdered by artifact-forging criminals?" I adjusted my dust-laden field scarf, still bearing traces of

Giza limestone, and turned to face him. "What kind of archae-ologist would I be?"

Quinn grinned. "A sensible one?"

"Precisely why it's out of the question." I fixed him with my most determined expression. "Drive faster, Mr. Quinn. We have history to uncover and highly questionable choices to make."

It had taken only a few phone calls to learn Dr. Abbas's whereabouts and his address. The afternoon sun bore down on the narrow streets of the neighborhood surrounding his modest home near Al-Azhar University, creating pockets of scorching heat and slivers of blessed shade. This area bore little resemblance to the splendor of downtown Cairo or the tourist comforts of the Giza plateau. Narrow, winding streets teemed with the vibrant chaos of everyday Egyptian life. Vendors called their wares, children darted between buildings, and women carried baskets on their heads with perfect balance.

Our arrival in Quinn's automobile drew immediate atten-tion—unwelcome attention, judging by the suspicious glances and whispered comments that followed us as we made our way to Abbas's address.

"I feel like we might as well be carrying a banner announcing 'Interfering Europeans.'" I nodded to several older men in the small courtyard, engaged in what appeared to be an intense game of dominoes.

"We *are* interfering Europeans." Quinn offered his own respectful nod to the men, who deliberately ignored him.

"Speak for yourself. I'm an American."

"Which makes you even more suspicious in certain quar-ters." Quinn guided me toward a modest doorway with a small brass plaque bearing Arabic script. "I believe this is our destination."

Before we could knock, a young boy of perhaps ten years emerged from the alleyway beside the house. He addressed us in Arabic, his expression openly hostile.

Quinn replied in the same language, his tone courteous but firm.

The boy's eyes widened before his face settled back into suspicion.

"What did he say?"

"He wanted to know why British police are bothering his uncle again." Quinn straightened his tie. "I explained we aren't police, just academics seeking Dr. Abbas's expertise."

"And that worked?"

"Not particularly. But he's gone to inform his uncle we're here."

We waited in uncomfortable silence, the weight of neighborhood scrutiny pressing against us like the desert heat. Several minutes passed before the door finally opened to reveal a man in his fifties, dressed in a simple *galabeya* with a *taqiyah*, a white embroidered skullcap that marked him as a religious man. Wire-rimmed spectacles perched on his nose, and his beard was neatly trimmed with threads of silver throughout.

"I am Dr. Abbas," he said in perfect English, his expression guarded. "My nephew says you claim to be academics."

"Dr. Clarissa Bell, Cambridge University." I extended my hand, which he regarded with hesitation before briefly shaking it.

"Benedict Quinn, consultant to the Egyptian Museum," Quinn added.

Abbas's eyebrows rose. "The Egyptian Museum. Yet you are British. How interesting. Have you come to borrow more of our heritage? Or simply to explain why it's better preserved in London than Cairo?"

"Neither," I assured him. "We've discovered something that requires your expertise—expertise that has been deliberately overlooked by European institutions."

"And suddenly my expertise is valuable?" Abbas's smile didn't reach his eyes. "How convenient."

I gave him a contrite smile. "Dr. Abbas, I understand your skepticism. European academics have consistently stolen credit for discoveries made by Egyptian scholars. I've read your papers on ancient calculation methods—the ones Oxford and Cambridge refused to publish."

This caught his attention. "You've read my work?"

"Your analysis of the Moscow Mathematical Papyrus was brilliant. Particularly your observations on the volumetric calculations for truncated pyramids." A flash of pride in my academic thoroughness quickly evaporated into empathy for this brilliant, marginalized mind.

Abbas studied me with new interest. "Those papers were not widely circulated."

"My mentor shared them with me." Slight pang there, as I had a flash of Sutherland's body, bent over the desk in his tent. "He found your conclusions revolutionary."

Some of the hostility faded from his expression. "And what is it you believe requires my expertise, Dr. Bell?"

I glanced around the street, aware of watching eyes and listening ears. "An artifact—a matter of some delicacy—and potentially significant historical importance. May we speak inside?"

Abbas hesitated, torn between suspicion and intellectual curiosity.

Quinn remained silent, wisely allowing me to lead this negotiation. The restraint, so unlike him, had his fingers tensed at his sides.

"Why should I trust you?" Abbas asked bluntly. "Your British colleague here claims ownership of artifacts my ancestors created. Your Cambridge professors dismiss Egyptian scholarship as derivative."

I answered him with equal directness. "Because I believe the truth of Egypt's achievement matters more than American or European pride."

Abbas's eyes sharpened. Behind his spectacles, I could see a fierce intelligence.

"What artifact?"

I lifted my satchel. "May we come in?"

For a long moment, he said nothing, weighing my words against a lifetime.

Finally, he stepped back from his doorway, a mathematician's curiosity overcoming political prudence.

The interior of Abbas's home was a refreshing contrast to the oppressive heat of the streets. The blessed coolness of shade enveloped us, and I felt the smooth, worn mosaic tiles beneath my feet, heat leaching away. The central courtyard was laid with intricate blue and white patterns, worn smooth by generations. Bookshelves lined every available wall, stacked with volumes in Arabic, English, French, and German.

From an interior doorway emerged a woman in her sixties, frowning. She wore a simple blue gown, her hair covered with a patterned headscarf that wrapped lightly around her neck. She positioned herself between Abbas and us, her stance protective.

"My wife, Fatima," Abbas extended a hand. To her, he said only, "Academics with questions."

"Welcome to our home." She spoke in accented English, and her tone carried the warmth of an English January. "I will bring tea."

She disappeared into another room, leaving behind the distinct impression that poison in the teacups remained a viable option.

Abbas led us to his study where a massive brass astrolabe dominated a corner of his desk—not merely a paperweight but an ancient technology from Islamic scholarly tradition. A chalkboard covered in equations dominated one wall.

The lingering scent of hookah tobacco and aged paper filled the space, while the muted sounds of family conversations from adjoining homes floated through the windows.

"Now," Abbas settled behind a desk. "Show me this artifact."

CHAPTER NINETEEN

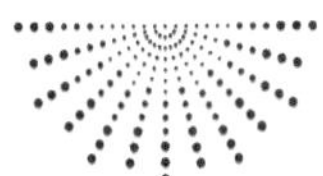

I extracted the documents from my satchel and spread them carefully across the one clear corner of his desk. "These are from Dr. Gregory Sutherland's private papers. They are copies of various artifacts recently stolen from museums, private collections, and even dig sites. You may be familiar with some of them. We noticed they all contain at least some Egyptian blue. But there is more than theft going on, and we believe something must link these pieces besides the blue pigment."

Abbas adjusted his spectacles and hunched over the papers with the intensity of a man deciphering the coordinates to buried treasure—which, intellectually speaking, was precisely what we were offering. The soft rustling of documents filled the otherwise quiet room, his breathing quietly intense as he studied each piece.

Quinn leaned against a bookshelf, attempting to look casually uninterested but watching Abbas's reactions with focused attention.

Abbas sat back, shaking his head. "These are not new. I have seen many of these, or photographs of them, from museums. A few in private collections."

"Yes, but all of these have been stolen. Recently. And we believe there must be a pattern, a reason. Perhaps the math?"

He leaned forward again, his gnarled fingers spreading the photographs, sorting them with methodical precision.

"You have his field journal?" Abbas held out a palm, as though confident I would place Sutherland's journal in it.

"No. I'm afraid not. It wasn't with his papers."

I'd noticed the missing journal the moment we'd dumped his satchel onto Quinn's bed at Shepheard's. What additional light could it shed, if we'd found it? I chastised myself for not searching his tent before fleeing.

"You assume these are all Egyptian blue," Abbas said, tapping several photos. "Some could be lapis lazuli pigment."

He was surprisingly knowledgeable. I wouldn't have expected the lapis observation.

Quinn leaned in. "Why would they use lapis lazuli instead of Egyptian blue?"

Abbas's eyes lit with scholarly passion. "Lapis was far more valuable—imported from Afghanistan at great expense. It was reserved for only the most significant royal or religious documents. Egyptian blue was common; lapis lazuli signified something of extraordinary importance, meant only for the eyes of scribal elites or royalty."

"Would that be a reason to steal them?"

Abbas shrugged and returned to studying the documents.

Fatima returned with a tray bearing small glass cups of mint tea. Fragrant steam rose from the delicate glass cups, and the aroma mingled with the musty smell of ancient texts. She placed it on a side table, her gaze lingering on the documents with unmistakable interest before she slipped away again, casting a warning glance at her husband.

"Interesting," Abbas murmured after several minutes of silence. His finger traced symbols I could barely make sense of, following patterns invisible to my untrained eye. "You could be right."

"What do you see?"

"These are not just mathematical notations, Dr. Bell. Many

of them refer to comprehensive mathematical principles that were not 'discovered' in Europe until thousands of years later." His finger stabbed at different sections. "Here—calculus concepts. Here—astronomical calculations of remarkable precision. Here—engineering formulas utilizing seked measurements for pyramid construction. And here—" he tapped another section, "medical calculations for drug preparations, anatomically precise surgical procedures."

I felt my pulse quicken, my fingers gripping the cool metal of my chair as a sudden silence fell over the room while we all processed the implications. I caught Quinn's eye, our glance acknowledging we'd stumbled onto something significant.

"The stolen artifacts," Quinn pushed himself away from the bookshelf. "They're not just random pieces with blue pigment."

"No," Abbas confirmed. "If I must guess, I would say perhaps some—likely not all of them—could have been created in the same scribal workshop, perhaps using the rare lapis lazuli pigment, and form a sort of loose collection of knowledge."

I leaned forward, nearly knocking over my untouched tea. The bitter-sweet aroma wafted toward me, but my focus remained entirely on Abbas. "The same scribal workshop—perhaps the New Kingdom scribe whose tomb we just found at Giza?"

"You mean Old—"

I shook my head. "No." I pulled out the photograph of the broken palette, careful to leave the images of Sutherland himself in my satchel, though there was little to disguise his hand and the "FOR C" written in blood. Thankfully, the gray-black shades made it impossible to tell exactly what had been used to ink his final message.

"This scribe's palette was stolen from our Giza dig site last week, and recently recovered, although sadly it had been damaged. You can see here," I pointed to the relevant markings, "it's likely New Kingdom."

Abbas picked up the photo and brought it close to his eyes,

leaning it left and right as if he could see the piece from a different angle.

He frowned. "I do not understand. Why would there have been a forged artifact in a mastaba in Giza?"

My stomach dropped. "Forged?" I pulled the photo back from his hand.

"You see, here? The glyph spacing is too precise." Abbas pointed to several hieratic symbols. "No ancient scribe worked with such uniformity. And here—" his finger traced an ink well, "—the wear patterns on these indentations are artificially created. Real palette wells would show asymmetrical wear from years of a scribe dipping his reed on one preferred side." He smiled in sympathy. "I am sorry to disappoint. But whomever is in this photograph clearly knew it was forged, yes?" He tapped Sutherland's message. "He began writing FORGERY, just here."

My shoulders dropped and I exhaled heavily. Suddenly the trailing off of the message after the "FOR C" made the final letter look much more like a "G."

I tilted the photograph toward Quinn. "That's why he broke it. It wasn't a message for me at all."

Quinn's smile was sympathetic. "Perhaps it still was. He was trying to tell you about the piece."

"But how would a forgery have gotten into a newly opened—"

Wait just a minute.

I scrambled through my satchel for my field notes, made that morning of the original find, and yanked the drawings out to spread on the table.

All three of us bent our heads over the drawings, then sat back, trading glances.

I tapped my notes. "I wasn't crazy. The piece I examined wasn't a forgery." My original drawing clearly showed slight changes in the hieratic script. I laid a hand on the photograph of the broken palette. "But this is."

Quinn folded his arms over his chest. "None of this makes

sense. Why create a forgery, but make it deliberately different, so that it was obviously a fake?"

"But the only proof that the piece I first analyzed was different is in my notes."

Quinn nodded. "The notes someone seemed intent on taking from you in Alexandria."

"So..." I fought to form a coherent story out of this mess. "Someone steals the piece, creates a forgery, which Sutherland ends up with. They try to destroy any proof that the forgery was created. But Sutherland wanted us to know it was a fake."

Quinn drummed his fingers against the wooden desk. "And at least some of these pieces are connected, both the advanced scientific concepts and possibly the lapis lazuli pigment."

Abbas tapped the papers listing the various stolen artifacts. "Modern laboratory analysis could potentially identify chemical markers unique to specific pigments and even manufacturing locations. But such technology is rare, especially in Egypt where British authorities control access to advanced scientific equipment."

We sat in silence for a few moments, still processing this information. I didn't bother to explain my own familiarity with pigments.

Finally, I sighed and looked to Abbas. "So, you're saying a sophisticated scientific tradition existed in ancient Egypt that predates European 'discoveries' by millennia," I summarized. "And it is knowledge that someone seems to be systematically removing from museums and private collections."

"Yes. Of course, these discoveries are already known." He shrugged. "But perhaps someone wishes to suppress the organizing, the publicizing of it." Abbas's voice lowered. "Consider the implications, Dr. Bell. If ancient Egyptians possessed mathematical understanding that Europe supposedly only discovered in the seventeenth century, what does that say about the narrative of Western intellectual superiority that justifies British colonial rule?"

Quinn whistled softly. "That's quite the diplomatic powder keg."

I nodded. "It could explain why someone might kill to suppress it."

Abbas looked sharply between us. "Kill? You didn't mention murder."

"Dr. Sutherland was murdered for these artifacts." My voice was steadier than I felt. "For knowledge that someone wants buried deeper than any tomb."

Abbas frowned. "As I am certain you know, powerful interests—the British Museum, Oxford, Cambridge—all have built their Egyptology departments on certain fundamental assumptions about the progression of human knowledge."

Fatima appeared in the doorway again, speaking Arabic to her husband.

Abbas's expression darkened as he turned to us. "My nephew reports men asking questions about us in the neighborhood." He began gathering the papers with urgent efficiency. "Europeans. Not police, but carrying weapons."

Quinn moved to the window, peering carefully around the edge of a woven curtain.

My posture stiffened, breath quick. "I think our stay has reached its natural conclusion."

"If what you suspect is true, Dr. Bell, these specific artifacts, when taken together as a body of knowledge from one scribal workshop, could challenge the very foundation of colonial authority in Egypt." Abbas jotted something on a slip of paper, then pressed it and the other documents back into my hands before we followed him to the back door of his home.

Outside the door, the lengthening shadows of late afternoon created a maze-like quality to the streets. We stepped from the dimly lit interior, exposed.

Abbas half-bowed before releasing us. "Be careful whom you trust."

I nodded and touched his hand in gratitude. "We're rapidly running out of options in that department."

CHAPTER TWENTY

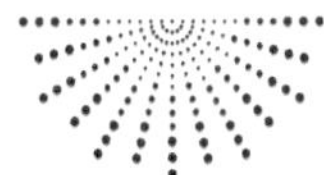

I don't understand why we're still debating this." I adjusted my hat against the morning sun as Giza bustled around our outdoor table at the Nile View Café. "The forged palette is obviously significant. Someone is replacing genuine artifacts with forgeries, and poor Dr. Sutherland died for discovering it."

We sat outside the small café beneath my apartment, surrounded by the morning cacophony of vendors, donkeys, and the occasional automobile backfiring.

I'd phoned Dr. Bradford early, receiving the news that the team was back at work today, despite yesterday's tragedy. He magnanimously informed me that now that the scribe's palette —albeit a forgery—had been found, there was no need for me to continue my distasteful partnership with Benedict Quinn. I was expected back at the site today.

Quinn stirred his coffee with a practiced air. "The forgery itself isn't what matters." He leaned back and crossed one leg over the other. "It's what the thieves are collecting—and why. Now that Dr. Abbas has confirmed these artifacts contain mathematical and astronomical knowledge that predates European discoveries, we need to put pressure on that contact he wrote down for you."

I sighed. *Academic Disagreement (Circular), Early Morning Variety, Notable for its complete inability to reach a conclusion despite two allegedly intelligent participants.*

"I still say we should focus on Eli Hawke." I absently smoothed a crease in my linen skirt. "Unlike Abbas's contact, he is clearly involved, and significantly less dead than Dr. Sutherland, which makes him more useful for questioning."

"An excellent point, though your standards for useful conversation partners are distressingly low."

I was formulating a suitable response when a young boy approached our table. Without a word, he handed me a folded piece of crisp, expensive stationery and darted away, disappearing into the street crowd.

"Well, this is not ominous at all." I unfolded the note, scanning the elegant handwriting.

Dr. Bell, I have information regarding the recent museum thefts that may be of interest. Meet me at the Hammam Al-Sultan at noon today. Come alone—this matter requires discretion. Yours, Dr. Rosamund Fairchild

Quinn leaned across the table, his coffee forgotten. "What is it?"

I passed him the note. "An invitation from Dr. Fairchild to discuss the thefts. At a hammam, of all places."

"Ah, the ancient tradition of combining personal hygiene with academic espionage." Quinn frowned, a slight tightening around his eyes and an uncharacteristic fidget of his fingers. "You're not seriously considering going alone?"

"Of course not. I'm bringing my collection of pointed archaeological implements as conversational aids." I rolled my eyes. "Though a bathhouse is an interesting choice. They're typically gender-segregated, so she likely believes I won't bring you."

Quinn's eyebrows lifted. "Excellent point. Although some of the more touristic establishments have modernized sections. Rosamund is no doubt counting on Western prudishness to ensure privacy."

I noted again his use of her first name, and the implied history. "I'm not letting you come with me to a hammam."

"You most certainly are. May I remind you that the last person who arranged a private meeting with you ended up dead at his desk?"

I stared at him. Was his concern genuine or part of some game he might be playing? The fact that I still couldn't entirely trust him was as irritating as sand in my undergarments.

"You were quite familiar with Dr. Fairchild at the museum, which you still haven't explained." I traced the rim of my coffee cup with one finger, aiming for casual. "Former colleagues? Rivals? Something more personally calamitous?"

Quinn's expression shifted to his cultivated mask of charming inscrutability. "I've dealt with Rosamund professionally on several occasions. She's formidable—probably trustworthy, but I still don't like your meeting her alone."

"How fortunate my father insisted on sending me a lady's companion, then." I stood, gathering my satchel. "Annie can accompany me. Problem solved."

Quinn laughed. "Your maid? Against Rosamund Fairchild? That's like bringing a teaspoon to excavate the King's Valley."

"Annie is considerably more capable than you give her credit for." Though I had to admit, the thought of sweet-natured Annie facing the razor-sharp Rosamund Fairchild was concerning. "Fine. You may accompany me, but you'll maintain a respectable distance and intervene only if I'm in imminent danger of being murdered, kidnapped, or subjected to tedious academic small talk."

"I make no promises regarding the latter." Quinn stood, placing coins on the table. "Besides, I'd love to see the interior of the Hammam Al-Sultan. It was built during the Mamluk period, though it incorporates elements from multiple dynasties, including several architectural features looted from Pharaonic temples."

I blinked at him, cataloging this new information. *Benedict Quinn (Unexpected Academic), Notable for Scholarly Knowledge When Least Expected.*

"That was... surprisingly informed."

"Don't look so shocked. I do occasionally read something other than forged provenance documents."

~

Our journey through Cairo's streets built tension with each step, the cityscape transforming from European-influenced thoroughfares to the more ancient, winding alleys that had resisted redesign for centuries.

The Hammam Al-Sultan rose before us, its elegant dome punctuated by star-shaped skylights that cast dappled light across the entrance. The façade sported a column capital featuring papyrus motifs from the 18th Dynasty incongruously supported by an Islamic arch, the juxtaposition jarring to my archaeological sensibilities. In archaeological terms, it was the equivalent of discovering a mummy wearing a wristwatch.

Inside, the building created its own microclimate—a transition from the harsh, dusty street to the cool, shadowed entry.

"Through here," Quinn murmured as we entered, "the hammam has three sections—the cold room, warm room, and hot room. Rosamund will likely be in the warm room, which serves as a social area."

"I'm familiar with the basic architectural principles of a hammam, thank you." Though in truth, I'd never actually visited one, having limited my Egyptian bathing experiences to the questionably sanitary basin in my rented room.

The attendant at the entrance gave us a curious look as we approached. I explained we were meeting Dr. Fairchild, which earned us an understanding nod and directions to a private bathing chamber that had been reserved for "the English lady doctor."

"A private chamber?" Quinn frowned. "That's not standard practice."

"Perhaps she truly values discretion. Or she's planning to murder me without witnesses." I straightened my shoulders. "Either way, we're about to find out."

The interior of the hammam unfolded like an archaeological layer cake of history. We passed through the maslakh—the changing room—where marble benches lined the walls beneath intricately carved wooden screens. The air grew progressively warmer and more humid as we were led deeper into the building, carrying the mingled scents of eucalyptus oil, rosewater, and mineral-rich steam that coated my lungs with each breath, making me feel I was inhaling liquid history.

My palm steadied against the slick, cool feel of ancient marble, the polished stone worn into subtle depressions by centuries of wet hands seeking balance.

We reached what was apparently the private room, but the attendant—a stern-faced man—blocked our path with the sudden authority of a pharaoh.

"No, no, no." He tutted, scandalized. "You cannot enter hammam dressed as English museum display." He gestured frantically at our clothing. "You must change. Is tradition."

I opened my mouth to protest, but Quinn cut in with diplomatic smoothness.

"Of course. We'll observe proper customs."

The attendant handed us each a bundle of fabric and pointed down separate corridors. "Lady goes there. Gentleman goes there." He fixed Quinn with a withering look. "After changing, gentleman goes to men's section. Only lady joins Dr. Fairchild."

"Certainly," Quinn agreed with a smile that wouldn't have fooled a nearsighted donkey.

We separated, and I slipped into a small changing room lined with ornate wooden screens. The "proper attire" consisted of a near see-through cotton wrap.

Bathhouse Attire (Inadequate), Modern Period, Notable for maximizing embarrassment while minimizing coverage.

After several minutes of fabric wrestling, I emerged wrapped in what felt like an ambitious tea towel. My dignity had retreated, leaving behind only burning cheeks and the desperate hope that Rosamund Fairchild would appreciate my commitment to cultural authenticity.

I stepped cautiously into the corridor, clutching my satchel (which I'd refused to relinquish) against my cotton-wrapped chest.

Quinn was waiting, leaning against the wall with infuriating composure. He wore the traditional men's wrap around his waist, leaving his chest bare—an architectural feature I had not previously had occasion to study in such detail. Objectivity momentarily abandoned me.

"You look..." His eyes performed a thorough survey that likely violated several British Museum protocols. "...suitably cultural."

"And you look indecently pleased with yourself." I adjusted my wrap with as much dignity as possible, which amounted to none. "Where's our official guardian of tradition?"

"Explaining proper hammam etiquette to another unfortunate tourist." Quinn glanced down the corridor. "We have perhaps thirty seconds before he returns to ensure my proper banishment to the men's section."

"Then we'd better move quickly."

We slipped toward Rosamund's private chamber, my wrap threatening rebellion with every step. Quinn's hand hovered at the small of my back, not quite touching but close enough that the air between us seemed charged with electricity. Which seemed a bad idea in such a damp environment.

"You realize," I whispered as we approached the door, "that if Rosamund is trying to frame me for theft and murder, wandering around dressed like an aspiring harem girl probably won't improve my scholarly credibility."

"On the contrary." Quinn's whisper tickled my ear with unnecessary proximity, his words carrying the faint scent of honey, and warm against the condensation on my neck. "No one would believe a Cambridge-educated archaeologist would voluntarily wear that outfit if she weren't being coerced."

"Your logic is as flimsy as this fabric."

His gaze did another reconnaissance mission across my cotton-draped form. "I wouldn't say flimsy. Revealing, perhaps. Interesting, certainly."

"If you value the continued functionality of your limbs, you'll redirect your interests immediately."

A smile quirked at the corner of his mouth. "Just maintaining my cover as your protective companion."

"Is that what we're calling it now?"

For one alarming moment, standing outside Rosamund's door with nothing but thin cotton between us and a complete abandonment of professional boundaries, Quinn looked at me with an expression that had nothing to do with artifacts or investigations. My internal cataloging system experienced a brief but catastrophic failure.

The moment dissolved as voices approached from the hall.

Quinn straightened, all business. "Ready?"

I nodded, gathering both my wrap and my composure.

"For the record," he murmured as I reached for the door handle, "traditional hammam attire suits you far better than it has any right to."

"For the record," I replied with more breathlessness than scholarly dignity should permit, "if you mention this particular cultural experience to anyone, ever, I will personally ensure your next archaeological discovery is your own skeleton."

His laugh followed me through the door, warming me more effectively than the hammam's steam ever could.

CHAPTER TWENTY-ONE

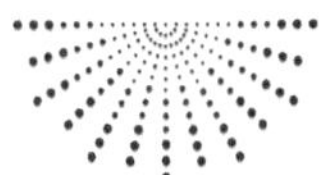

The interior of the chamber was larger than I expected. We paused inside the door, where the scent of bitter orange and rose water mixed with the hammam's steam, creating a distinctly Middle Eastern perfume that would likely cling to our clothing and skin long after leaving.

"I still don't like this," Quinn whispered. "Private chambers aren't typical unless someone has paid handsomely for exclusivity."

"How fortunate I brought my trusty companion, then." I adjusted my dishcloth with delusions of grandeur for the fourteenth time.

Quinn's expression suggested he found my choice of weaponry amusing. "Stay alert. Rosamund Fairchild is not known for her straightforward approach to... well, anything."

The octagonal chamber was stunning. Dominated by a central marble fountain, with steam rising from the shallow pool, creating ghostly shapes that danced in colored light filtering through stained glass inserts in a domed ceiling. Wall niches were filled with copper water vessels and small oil lamps that cast a golden glow across the mosaic floor. The whole effect was rather like being inside a sultan's jewel box – beautiful, expensive, and entirely too confining.

Seated on a marble bench, wrapped in a silk robe and looking absurdly composed despite the humid environment, was Rosamund Fairchild. Her pale blonde hair was twisted into an elegant knot, not a single strand daring to frizz in the steam-filled air. Next to her sat a tray with a steaming teapot and small glasses. Dappled patterns of colored light from the stained glass danced across her skin, painting her in subtle tones that shifted with the movement of steam.

"Dr. Bell." Her gaze shifted to Quinn, one perfectly sculpted eyebrow arching with the precision of a mathematical equation. "And Mr. Quinn. How unsurprising you've ignored my request for privacy."

"Antiquities dealers are notoriously bad at following instructions." Quinn plucked at his towel. "We tend to show up where we're told not to."

"Indeed." Her smile contained that same flirtatiousness I'd noted earlier. "Please, join me."

I remained standing, cataloguing the room's exits (one door, no windows large enough for escape) and potential defensive implements (copper water vessels, slippery marble floor, my overwhelming sense of inadequacy).

"You summoned me here," I said, attempting to sound dignified. "Something about urgent information?"

"Direct as ever." Rosamund gestured to the bench opposite her. "Please, sit. The steam is quite beneficial for opening both pores and conversation."

I reluctantly sat, feeling the cool, slick marble bench against my thighs while the hot, humid air pressed against my face and neck, making my towel stick uncomfortably.

Quinn positioned himself deliberately between Rosamund and me, leaning against a marble column with the casual air of a man prepared to spring into action at any moment.

"You seem to be everywhere, Rosamund. In Alexandria, here in Cairo."

"Yes, I only just arrived in Cairo late last night." She poured tea into small glasses with grace. "I needed to wash Alexandria off of me, hence the hammam. The poverty there has a way of infiltrating everything."

The hammam's steam thickened around us, making the air feel like soup – thick, hot, and uncomfortable to breathe.

"But I wanted to speak to you immediately, Dr. Bell, so forgive the unconventional meeting place. Although hammams have been places of business and negotiation for centuries." Her smile was a masterpiece of condescension. "But I do understand Western sensibilities can be... delicate."

I bit back a retort. The calculation was clear: Rosamund wanted me off-balance, uncomfortable, exposed. But why?

I shifted on the slippery marble, trying to maintain the arrangement of cotton barely covering my essentials.

"I've been investigating a series of thefts across several museums." Rosamund began pouring tea into small glasses. "Artifacts disappearing, records altered, catalogues mysteriously updated to exclude certain items."

"We have noticed a pattern," I admitted cautiously.

"Is that right?"

I glanced at Quinn.

He shrugged.

"Yes, the items all contain Egyptian blue."

Her eyebrow arched. "Impressive observation. However, I'm afraid there is another pattern that's rather... troubling." Her voice hardened. "I'm aware of your father's activities, Dr. Bell."

My stomach dropped. "My father's activities?"

"Armand Bell's 'private collection' contains numerous pieces illegally exported from Egypt." Rosamund sipped her tea with infuriating calm. "Pieces that mysteriously disappeared from archaeological sites over the past decade."

"That's absurd." My voice echoed off the marble, bouncing back at me like an accusation. "My father's collection was acquired through legitimate dealers and auctions."

Quinn shifted uncomfortably against his column, a microscopic movement that nonetheless sent warning signals flaring through my brain.

"Was it?" Rosamund reached beside her and withdrew a leather folder, somehow perfectly dry despite the steam-bath environment. She flipped it open to reveal photographs of artifacts I recognized with sickening familiarity—pieces proudly displayed in my father's New York mansion.

"These items were documented at excavation sites in Luxor and Saqqara before mysteriously vanishing." She tapped one photograph with a manicured fingernail. "This particular statue was cataloged at a British Museum excavation in 1919, then disappeared during transport. It next surfaced in your father's Manhattan dining room."

I struggled to keep my expression neutral while my mind raced through a panicked inventory of my father's collection. The bronze Bastet statue. The alabaster perfume jars. The faience amulets. All displayed without a hint of shame or secrecy, their provenance never questioned—at least not in my presence.

"And you think I'm involved?" The accusation hit like a slap. "That I've been helping my father smuggle artifacts?"

"You're a trained archaeologist with connections to multiple excavation sites." Rosamund's voice remained cool and factual. "Someone with your expertise would be invaluable for identifying significant pieces worth... acquiring."

"I've devoted my career to preserving archaeological context, not destroying it!" The steam suddenly felt suffocating, pressing against my lungs like a physical weight. "I would never participate in artifact theft."

"And yet you've lived alongside your father's collection, presumably without raising any concerns about its suspicious origins." She closed the folder with a decisive snap. "One might wonder why."

"I am not my father's representative. I've spent what feels like half my life distinguishing myself from him!" The words were sharp, even bitter. I clenched my teeth, regretting the honesty.

Quinn finally spoke, his voice carrying a note of caution. "Rosamund, I think you're making unfounded accusations."

"Am I?" Her gaze locked with his, some unspoken communication passing between them. "I find it rather convenient that artifacts continue to disappear from sites where Dr. Bell has connections, only to resurface in private collections like her father's. Perhaps Dr. Sutherland discovered what she was up to and intended to make accusations..."

Quinn harrumphed. "No one would have believed him. Clarissa has no motive for theft or murder."

"Doesn't she?" Rosamund tilted her head. "A brilliant female archaeologist consistently overlooked by her male colleagues? Relegated to sorting pottery while men claim the significant discoveries? Perhaps she decided to create her own collection—or her own scholarly breakthrough by 'discovering' connections between stolen artifacts."

The accusation hung in the steam-filled air, heavy and oppressive as the humidity.

"If I wished to murder my way to archaeological prominence," I dabbed at the perspiration forming on my upper lip, "I would have started with Dr. Bradford and his insufferable mustache, not Dr. Sutherland, who was one of the few people who actually respected my work."

Quinn coughed, though it sounded suspiciously like a laugh hastily disguised.

"And that doesn't explain why you were at Dr. Sutherland's tent the morning of his murder."

"We were meeting him to discuss the thefts." Quinn shifted his weight against the damp column, leaving a perfect silhouette of his shoulder on the condensation-slicked marble. "He contacted us the previous evening, claiming he had vital information. Unfortunately, we arrived too late."

I shot him a warning glance. The less we revealed about what we'd found at Sutherland's tent, the better. And how did she have such abundant knowledge? Was she working with the Cairo police?

"I see." Rosamund gathered her papers, sliding them back into her bag with deliberate care. "And have you reported this to the authorities?"

"The Cairo police have already questioned us," I flicked a droplet of water from my arm, watching it disappear into the steamy air. "Though they seemed more interested in Quinn's movements than the actual murder."

"Unsurprising. Mr. Quinn's reputation precedes him in most archaeological circles."

Quinn smiled thinly. "As does yours, Dr. Fairchild."

Something unspoken passed between them, a current of shared history that made me suddenly feel like I was excavating a site without a proper map.

Rosamund turned her attention back to me. "I would tread carefully, Dr. Bell. These accusations against you would be taken very seriously should they come to light. The British Museum is particularly concerned about potential scandal."

"As you know, the British Museum often employs me as a consultant," Quinn pointed out. "They trust my judgment, and I vouch for Dr. Bell's innocence."

Rosamund's laugh echoed off the marble walls. "Your judgment, Benedict? The man who once authenticated a 'Ptolemaic' sculpture that turned out to be manufactured in Birmingham circa 1905?"

"That was before I learned to detect resin casting techniques," he replied stiffly. "And entirely irrelevant to the current situation."

I glanced between them, adding this exchange to my catalogue of their mysterious connection.

"In any case," Rosamund rose gracefully, "I've delivered my warning. If you're truly innocent, Dr. Bell, I suggest you find evidence to prove it—quickly. Otherwise, your promising archaeological career may be entombed alongside your reputation."

My mind spun like a defective compass, unable to find true north. Was this why Quinn had been watching me? Sticking close? Because he suspected me of being some sort of archaeological double agent?

The thought stung worse than the humid heat.

"I need to investigate this matter thoroughly, Dr. Bell."

Rosamund's tone suggested she'd already reached her conclusion. "And I suggest you consider your position carefully. Family loyalty is admirable, but there are lines that shouldn't be crossed."

She moved toward the door, then paused. "Oh, and Dr. Bell? Be careful with Elias Hawke." She offered a smile like a scorpion offering its stinger. "He's not as charming as he seems."

With that parting shot, she glided from the room, leaving behind only the lingering scent of lotus perfume and unmistakable menace.

The door closed behind her with a soft thud that somehow sounded like a death knell for my career.

I turned to Quinn, whose expression had shifted to something I couldn't quite read—concern? Guilt? Suspicion?

"Did you know about my father's pieces?" The question escaped before I could contain it.

His hesitation was answer enough.

"Let's discuss this elsewhere." He glanced toward the door. "This isn't the place."

We dressed quickly, rejoined near the entrance, then stepped from the hammam into the harsh sunlight. I felt scoured raw—not by the bath's steam but by the realization that Quinn's interest in me might have been nothing more than surveillance.

The shock of moving from dim interior to bright street disoriented me. I blinked against the midday sun, using the moment to gather my fragmented composure.

"You suspected me all along." My voice was low, tight with controlled fury as we walked away from the hammam. "That's why you've been following me, inserting yourself into my investigation."

Quinn's silence confirmed my accusation.

"I need to know, Quinn." I stopped walking, forcing him to turn and face me. "Have you been watching me because you thought I was helping my father steal artifacts?"

His eyes met mine, his expression uncharacteristically serious. "When we first met, yes. Your father's collection has... raised eyebrows in certain circles."

The betrayal hit like a physical blow. All our shared dangers, the moments of connection, the growing trust—all of it potentially built on his suspicion that I was nothing more than a tomb robber using my academic credentials as cover.

"And now?" I demanded, hating the slight tremor in my voice.

"Now I know you better." He stepped closer, lowering his voice. "I know you would never compromise your archaeological principles, not even for family."

"How magnanimous of you to finally recognize my basic professional integrity." My words dripped with sarcasm that could have corroded bronze.

"Clarissa—"

"Dr. Bell." My voice was icy. "I think we've established our relationship is strictly professional, and apparently based on mutual suspicion."

"That's not fair."

"No? Then explain why you didn't tell me about my father's collection being under investigation. Why spend all this time at my side without once mentioning it?"

"Would you have believed me?" His voice sharpened. "If I'd approached you with accusations about your father, would you have listened, or dismissed me as just another untrustworthy antiquities dealer?"

I had no answer for that. The truth was, I probably wouldn't have believed him. My father was many things—controlling, overbearing, disappointed in my career choices—but a criminal? The idea seemed absurd. Yet now, uncomfortable doubts began to surface.

Quinn ran a hand through his hair, disarranging it in that way annoyingly appealing manner. "The important thing is that Rosamund believes it. And she could cause trouble for you. But I don't understand her objective. Sutherland's dead, so warning you about his possible accusations seems pointless. And the warning about Hawke—"

"Completely unnecessary, as he is already our number one bad guy."

"Right. But I know her well enough to know, history is her life. She would do anything to protect these artifacts."

He started again down the street.

I didn't follow him. "There's something you're not telling me about Rosamund Fairchild." I waited until he turned. "Your history is more complicated than mere professional acquaintance."

Quinn sighed, the sound nearly lost amid the street noise. "The British Museum has been quietly recovering stolen artifacts for years—without public scandal. I've occasionally assisted in these discreet recoveries. Rosamund has been involved in that program."

"You're suggesting the British Museum sanctions theft?"

"Not sanctions—remedies. When items go missing, sometimes it's easier to recover them quietly, than to cause an international incident."

"And your relationship is nothing more than that?" I hated myself for asking.

"Nothing more."

"And can this all really be about Egyptian independence, as Dr. Abbas suggested?" I asked, temporarily setting aside my personal feelings to focus on the larger puzzle.

Quinn shrugged. "It seems as though someone is willing to kill to control that narrative. They may have decided you're in their way."

I squared my shoulders, my scientific curiosity temporarily overriding both my sense of self-preservation and my hurt feelings. "Well then, we'll simply have to get in their way more effectively, won't we?"

Even as I said it, I wasn't sure if "we" still existed. The ground beneath our partnership had just shifted dramatically, and I wasn't certain it would hold.

CHAPTER TWENTY-TWO

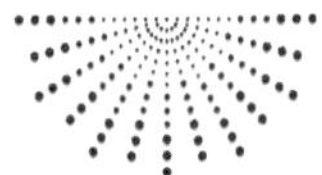

One week of amateur detective work had taught me precisely three things: how to flee from armed pursuers through ancient tunnels *(bring better shoes)*, the exact dimensions of a Turkish bathhouse towel *(insufficient)*, and that my career trajectory had abandoned academia for what could only be classified as *Catastrophic Professional Suicide (Spectacular Variety), Early 20th Century.*

The morning sun transformed the Giza plateau into a shimmering golden expanse as the rickety hired Fiat jolted toward the dig site. The Great Pyramid loomed ahead, casting an elongated shadow across the sand. I felt exposed and insignificant—the vastness of the desert and the monumental scale of the pyramids reduced human concerns to momentary specks against the backdrop of millennia, though I felt watched from all angles, vulnerable to whomever had targeted Sutherland.

I'd left Quinn at the café, poring over photographs of the forged and stolen artifacts. Our parting had been a study in awkward non-communication, perhaps a result of the bathhouse debacle:

"So you're really going back to Bradford?" He'd leaned

against the chair back with practiced nonchalance, tension visible in the set of his shoulders.

"Yes, well, someone needs to investigate from the inside, and I don't recall you having a degree in Egyptology."

"I have many talents you haven't discovered yet, Dr. Bell."

"I'm sure they're all equally useful for ending up in prison."

His grunt had followed me into the Fiat, settling somewhere between my shoulder blades like an irritating, oddly comforting weight.

The truth was I had no choice but to return. Sutherland deserved justice. The artifacts—the real ones, not the forgeries—needed protection. And frankly, after spending the past several days in close proximity to Benedict Quinn and his collection of roguish smiles, I needed the stabilizing influence of dusty pottery sherds and academic tedium.

The auto ground to a halt at the edge of the dig site, kicking up a swirl of sand. I disembarked and approached the excavation area, where the grid of string markers following Petrie's methodology for recording artifact provenance rippled in the morning breeze like an elaborate spiderweb.

No one seemed to have marked my arrival, so I headed to the sorting tent.

Inside, a hand-wringing Annie jumped from an overturned crate.

"You don't have to do this." Her normally cheerful face was pinched with worry. "We could still catch the afternoon train to Alexandria, then a ship to—"

"To where, exactly? The Antarctic? I hear penguins are marvelously nonjudgmental about failed archaeologists." I adjusted my field hat against the glare, feeling the uncomfortable dampness where my hair stuck to the back of my neck. "Besides, Bradford expects me back today."

The mention of the dig director inspired a magnificent eye-roll from Annie. "Dr. Bradford couldn't find his own reflection without a team of assistants and a mirror-polishing service."

I smiled. It would appear I was rubbing off on Annie already. "Ah, but his pomposity has its own gravitational field.

Small artifacts probably orbit him when no one's looking." I peered through the dust toward the familiar canvas tents visible in the distance. "Like tiny academic moons trapped in his self-importance."

Annie squeezed my arm in solidarity, her hand lingering and communicating more than words.

The man himself appeared a few moments later.

"Miss Bell! How good of you to return." His handkerchief made its habitual appearance, dabbing at his forehead in a complex choreography. "Most of the team scattered after—well, after the unfortunate business with Sutherland."

I noted the careful avoidance of words like "murder" or "bludgeoned with his own tripod."

"I thought I might be more useful here than hiding in Cairo." I adjusted my satchel.

"Yes, yes, quite right. Excellent attitude." Bradford nodded. "I've moved your workspace into the main documentation tent. With Sutherland gone and Deveraux jumping at shadows, we need all hands cataloging the new finds."

This unexpected promotion nearly caused me to check the sky for flying pigs. "The main tent? Not sorting pottery by color?"

"Don't be ridiculous, Miss Bell. You're Cambridge-trained, after all. Your expertise might be particularly valuable now."

Ah. Of course. With Sutherland gone, I'd been elevated from "lady archaeologist" to "available expert on the thing we need." Still, I'd take pragmatic sexism over the dismissive variety any day. The irony wasn't lost on me that it took a murder for my male colleagues to finally acknowledge my expertise.

"What about my work with Mr. Quinn?" I asked, testing the waters.

Bradford's twitchy concern faded. "That business is concluded, thank God. As I've said, the man's a menace in tailored linen. I've informed the Museum we no longer require his... services."

I nodded neutrally.

But added *Continue Secret Partnership with Menace in Tailored Linen* to my day's agenda.

Annie coughed delicately. "I'll take our things to Miss Bell's new tent, then."

As Annie departed, Bradford leaned closer, his voice dropping to what he presumably thought was a conspiratorial whisper. "The police have been asking questions, Miss Bell. About Sutherland."

"I'm not surprised."

"They seem to think his death is connected to these thefts we've been experiencing."

"How fascinating."

"Yes, well." He tugged at his collar nervously, the fabric scritching against his neck. "They mentioned you and Quinn were seen at various... questionable establishments in Cairo."

"Archaeological research often requires unorthodox methods, Dr. Bradford."

He tugged at his collar so vigorously, I half expected him to remove his entire shirt like a magician's tablecloth trick. "Indeed. Well, I've assured them you're a perfectly respectable scholar, despite your... modern tendencies."

I bit back a laugh. If Bradford knew that my "modern tendencies" now included fleeing murder scenes, impersonating society women at auctions, and nearly being kissed by antiquities dealers in Model Ts, not to mention nearly disrobing in front of said antiquities dealer, he would probably petition Cambridge to revoke my degree on moral grounds.

"Your confidence is appreciated." I gestured toward the main tent. "Shall I get started?"

"Yes, yes. Deveraux has just returned. He is inside, measuring... well, everything, as usual. Though he is rather jumpy."

I made my way across the camp, noting how the workers averted their eyes. News of Sutherland's murder had transformed the academic excavation into something darker and more dangerous. In the distance, I could hear the calls of workers carried on the hot breeze.

As I approached the main documentation tent, I could

hear Deveraux muttering measurements to himself inside, the familiar rhythm of his obsession like a metronomic lullaby.

"Seventeen-point-three centimeters, northern orientation, slight discoloration on the upper quadrant, approximately two-point-two millimeters in diameter, possibly post-firing oxidation..."

The tent's interior was a climate unto itself—hot, dusty, and smelling of scholarly exhaustion. Wooden tables groaned under the weight of artifacts, field notes, and measuring equipment, arranged with organizational logic.

Deveraux stood in the center, his silver calipers in one hand and a notebook in the other. He resembled a heron that had somehow acquired academic credentials—all angles and intense focus.

He looked up and nearly dropped his calipers at the sight of me. "Miss Bell! You've returned!"

"Dr. Deveraux." I set my satchel down on a nearby chair. "I see your measuring continues unabated. The caliper industry must send you thank-you notes at Christmas."

He swallowed, Adam's apple bobbing like a desperate swimmer caught in a whirlpool. "Precision is... essential in our work." His accent seemed to have thickened since my departure, as if he'd spent the intervening days marinating in additional Frenchness.

I moved to examine the pottery fragment he'd been measuring—an Eighteenth Dynasty faience fragment displaying characteristic red and ochre pigmentation common to Amenhotep III's reign.

"This is similar to the palette that was stolen, isn't it? At least in terms of pigment composition."

The caliper in Deveraux's hand trembled like a tuning fork struck against his evident terror. "I wouldn't know. I never had the opportunity to measure the palette properly before it was... taken."

"Strange." I picked up the fragment, turning it in the morning light filtering through the tent canvas. "I could have sworn you were also documenting it before it disappeared."

I knew this to be untrue, but Deveraux's nervousness—the slight tick at the corner of his eye, the perspiration beading along his hairline—prompted me to push a bit.

A bead of sweat trickled down Deveraux's temple. "Perhaps... perhaps you are mistaken."

"I'm rarely mistaken about documentation practices, Dr. Deveraux." I set the pottery fragment down and reached for his notebook, which he clutched to his chest like a shield against barbarian invaders. "May I? I'm particularly interested in any measurements of items that have subsequently gone missing. I'm developing a theory that artifacts flee in direct proportion to how precisely they've been measured. Sort of an escaping-scrutiny hypothesis."

"That would be... highly inappropriate." His knuckles whitened around the notebook edges. "My notes are private until formally submitted to the expedition record."

I smiled in what I hoped was a disarming manner but, based on his expression, might have more closely resembled a predator selecting its lunch. "Dr. Deveraux, we both know something unusual is happening with these artifacts. I believe your measurements might help solve the mystery."

"There is no mystery." He took a step back, bumping into the table behind him. "Only carelessness and common thieves. The everyday hazards of archaeological work."

I moved closer, lowering my voice to a conspiratorial whisper. "You knew the palette was a forgery, right?"

The effect was immediate and dramatic. All color drained from his face. For a moment, I feared he might actually faint, which would have been both inconvenient and difficult to explain to Bradford.

"I—I don't know what you mean." The words emerged as a strangled whisper.

"I think you do." I glanced toward the tent entrance, ensuring we were alone. "Sutherland discovered it. That's why he was killed."

Deveraux's clipboard clattered to the ground. "I had

nothing to do with any murder!" His voice rose to a fevered pitch. "Nothing!"

"But the forgeries?" I stepped closer, invading his carefully measured personal space. "Your measurements would be invaluable for creating perfect replicas, wouldn't they? Every dimension, every shade of pigment, every crack and chip cataloged with your famous precision."

It wasn't much of a leap—Quinn and I had discussed this possibility during one of our strategy sessions. If someone was replacing authentic artifacts with forgeries, who better to provide the specifications than the most obsessively precise measurer in archaeology?

"I—" Deveraux paused, then glanced furtively around the tent as if expecting eavesdroppers to materialize from behind pottery shelves. He moved closer, and I caught the distinctive scent of absinthe on his breath. Apparently French courage came in liquid form. "Not here. Too many ears."

Well. That was unexpected. I'd anticipated denial, perhaps tears, possibly even righteous academic indignation. Instead, I'd gotten cloak-and-dagger intrigue from a man whose most dramatic life decision until now had probably been whether to use ink or pencil for preliminary measurements.

"Very well." I nodded toward the back of the tent. "Shall we step outside?"

Deveraux shook his head vigorously, then reached into his waistcoat pocket. He withdrew not a confession or a weapon, but what appeared to be a small envelope sealed with distinctive dark blue wax. "This came yesterday. I was instructed to deliver it to the usual location."

"The usual location?"

"The postmark is from Cairo. They all are." He pressed the envelope into my hand, his fingers trembling against mine. "I don't deliver them personally. I leave them at the Continental-Savoy, with a porter named Nasir. He handles the final delivery."

I examined the envelope. High-quality stationery, the expensive kind with rag content rather than wood pulp. The wax seal bore a distinctive impression—not a family crest or official emblem, but what appeared to be an ancient Egyptian ankh symbol intertwined with a lotus flower. The envelope itself was addressed simply to "The Curator" in an elegant, slanting hand.

"You fill these requests?" I turned the envelope over. "For whom?"

"I don't know." Deveraux's voice dropped to a whisper. "But they have their ways of ensuring compliance."

"Threats?"

"My family in Marseilles. My mother and sisters. They received... visits." His eyes darted toward the tent entrance again. "A woman with a British accent. She made it very clear what would happen if I didn't cooperate."

"This woman—did she identify herself?"

"Never by name. But she was elegant, educated. Like you, but with the warmth of a tomb at midnight."

A chill ran down my spine despite the tent's oppressive heat. Violet Hat, perhaps?

"And your measurements?" I pressed. "They're used for creating forgeries?"

Deveraux shrugged helplessly. "I assume so. I document everything Bradford asks me to catalogue—dimensions, composition, pigment analysis. Then I receive these envelopes." He gestured to the one in my hand. "Always with the same seal. Always containing new instructions and... compensation."

"How long has this been going on?"

"Eight months, two weeks, four days. It began with small items, things that seemed unimportant. But lately..."

"They're getting more ambitious."

He nodded miserably. "The palette was different, though. I never measured it, never documented it. It disappeared before I could examine it properly." His eyes met mine, fear mingling with something that might have been guilt. "If Sutherland discovered forgeries—if he was killed because of what I've done—"

"Not what you've done." I carefully placed the envelope in

my satchel. "What you've been forced to do. There's a difference."

Relief flashed across his features, quickly replaced by renewed panic. "What are you going to do with that? If they discover I've given it to you—"

"They won't." I straightened my jacket. "As far as anyone knows, I cornered you about missing artifacts, you denied everything, and I left in a scholarly huff. You'll deliver the envelope to your usual contact at Continental-Savoy."

"But how—"

"Leave the rest to me." I picked up his clipboard from the floor and handed it back to him. "In the meantime, I suggest you develop a sudden family emergency requiring your immediate return to France."

He blinked. "But Bradford—"

"Will manage without your measurements for a few weeks. Your family's safety is more important than precise documentation of pottery fragments." I moved toward the tent entrance, then paused. "Dr. Deveraux?"

"Yes?"

"Sutherland suspected something, didn't he? That's why he was examining your records."

Deveraux's shoulders slumped. "He asked to see my notes last week. Said something about inconsistencies in the artifact registry. I was terrified he would discover..." He trailed off, staring at his calipers as if they had betrayed him.

"Thank you." I ducked through the tent flap, emerging into the blinding Egyptian sunlight that seemed to sear away shadows—both physical and metaphorical.

My thoughts raced. The information about Nasir at the Continental-Savoy was a solid lead to whomever was orchestrating this elaborate forgery scheme. The watermark, the unusual seal, the hotel connection—pieces of a puzzle slowly assembling themselves.

Annie appeared at my elbow, materializing with the silent efficiency that made her invaluable and slightly terrifying. "Your original tent has been searched," she murmured.

"Nothing obvious taken, but someone rummaged through your notes. They tried to make it look undisturbed, but I noticed your system was disrupted. Your 'Questionable Methodologies' folder was between 'Pottery Classification' and 'Pigment Analysis' rather than after 'Suspicious Colleagues.'"

"Thank you, Annie. Your attention to my filing system may prove more valuable than you know. Did you notice anything else unusual?"

"I don't believe so." Annie didn't smile, her normally cheerful face now arranged in what appeared to be her attempt at spy-movie seriousness. "You're not safe here, Miss Bell."

"I'm not safe anywhere, Annie. Not until we figure out what's happening." I ran my fingers through my hair. "But I believe I've found our next lead."

I looked up at the Great Pyramid, silent and imposing against the cloudless sky. For thousands of years, it had kept its secrets hidden beneath sand and stone. Now I needed to unearth a modern mystery with potentially ancient implications.

"Tell Bradford I've gone to document some findings." I straightened my shoulders with newfound determination. "I need to find Benedict Quinn and pay a visit to the Continental-Savoy."

CHAPTER TWENTY-THREE

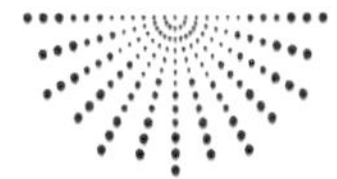

The Continental-Savoy Hotel stood amid the bustling heart of Cairo, complete with the familiar ornate balconies, palm-fringed gardens, and an air of entitled superiority. But unlike Shepheard's, where Quinn took his nightly brandy and charmed the staff, this competing establishment offered the one luxury he couldn't purchase elsewhere: anonymity.

I'd filled my partner in on the details of Deveraux's confession, and we'd made our way here, to investigate further.

We approached the front desk, and Quinn leaned in, to murmur in my ear.

"Married, wealthy, desperately seeking delivery of valuable family heirlooms." He circled my waist with his arm. "Follow my lead and try to look like someone who enjoys having money rather than digging up junk."

"I beg your pardon?" I hissed, but had no time to protest further.

The concierge desk loomed before us—a mahogany monument to bureaucratic gatekeeping, behind which stood a thin Egyptian man with a pencil mustache and a dead-eyed stare.

"Mr. and Mrs. Huntington-Bell." Quinn unleashed the full

wattage of his charm, slamming it down on the counter like a winning hand of cards. "We're looking for Nasir. We understand he's taken up a position here."

I nearly choked on the masquerade.

"My wife is absolutely distraught," Quinn continued, pulling me closer with an arm that felt uncomfortably natural. "Family heirlooms—a jewelry case with her grandmother's emeralds. The delivery was arranged through Nasir. It's absolutely vital we recover it immediately."

"I don't know any Nasir," the concierge replied with practiced boredom, examining his fingernails.

Quinn pressed what appeared to be an obscene amount of Egyptian pounds into the man's palm. "Perhaps this will refresh your memory? We're terribly desperate. My wife hasn't slept in days." He lowered his voice to a stage whisper. "She's becoming quite unstable. Yesterday she tried to catalogue our dinner courses by pharaonic dynasty."

The money disappeared with a sleight-of-hand efficiency.

"Ah, yes. Nasir." Pencil Mustache nodded toward a side entrance, suddenly afflicted with total recall. "One of our staff. But he's not here today."

Quinn's jaw tightened. "When will he return?"

"He won't. Left two days ago. Very sudden." The man leaned forward, lowering his voice to a conspiratorial whisper. "But his cousin Farouq took over his... special arrangements. Works in the mail room. Ask for the monk's delivery service."

"Monk's delivery?" I echoed, forgetting momentarily that I was supposed to be playing the role of distressed society wife rather than curious archaeologist.

"The old abandoned monastery. Outside the city." He straightened as a pair of British tourists approached, his helpful demeanor evaporating. "Now if you'll excuse me, Mr. and Mrs. Huntington-Bell."

Quinn steered me toward the exit, his hand still proprietarily placed at my waist like he'd won me in a card game.

"Do you ever get information without a bribe?" I hissed as we descended the steps.

"Cultural exchange program."

"And I'm not your wife."

"Would you have preferred to be my sister? Cousin? Illicit lover?"

"I would have preferred to be Dr. Clarissa Bell, archaeologist, who needs information for legitimate scholarly purposes."

"Well, Mrs. Huntington-Bell, it seems we have a new destination."

"Call me that again, and I'll excavate your eye socket with my fountain pen."

"Such violence from Cambridge's finest."

"So, shall we find this Farouq?"

He shrugged. "Why not simply go directly to the source, this suspicious abandoned monastery?"

Quinn flagged down a taxi with aristocratic efficiency. "There's only one abandoned monastery near enough Cairo to serve as a delivery hub." He opened the door with a flourish. "Deir al-Matruh. About an hour's drive northeast of the city."

It turned out the address would lead us far beyond Cairo's bustling center, past the fringe of the city where buildings thinned out. The road deteriorated until it became little more than a suggestion of where one *might* drive, if one had a particularly optimistic view of what constituted a "road."

The hot leather seat stuck to my skin through my clothing as we bumped along, sweat trickling down my neck. The taxi rattled over stones and ruts with what seemed like deliberate malice.

Our driver deposited us at the dusty end of civilization, pointing vaguely toward a structure barely visible in the distance. After much negotiation (and the promise of triple fare), he promised to wait for us.

The building squatted on the landscape like a forgotten artifact, its limestone walls bleached nearly white by countless Egyptian summers. Once grand arches had partially collapsed, and what might have been a bell tower now resembled an architectural shrug.

"Deir al-Matruh." Quinn extended a hand like a tour guide.

"Abandoned in the 17th century after a particularly ambitious Ottoman tax collector decided that devotion to God should include substantial devotion to the treasury."

"You're a walking encyclopedia of cheerful historical anecdotes, aren't you?"

"I save the truly depressing ones for special occasions."

The complex loomed larger as we approached—a jumble of buildings surrounding a central structure. The silence was absolute, broken only by the occasional skittering of small creatures and our labored breathing.

"I don't see any recent tracks." Quinn pointed to the ground. "At least not on this approach."

"Perhaps there's another entrance." I studied the structure. "Monasteries typically had multiple access points—supply routes, escape tunnels in case of attack."

"Or in case the tax collector showed up," Quinn added.

We circled the perimeter until we found a smaller door partially obscured by drifting sand. Unlike the rest of the weathered structure, the hinges on this door looked suspiciously well-oiled.

Quinn positioned himself ahead of me before catching himself. "Ladies first?" He gestured with exaggerated gallantry.

"How progressive of you." I stepped forward.

"Since you are 'perfectly capable.'" He mimicked my earlier tone with devastating accuracy.

"I am. And your respect is noted for the record." I pushed past him and eased the door open, wincing at the faint creak.

The monastery's interior was a study in contrasts—ancient stone walls and floors juxtaposed with the occasional jarring evidence of modernity. Electric wires ran along ceiling beams. A metal door had been installed at the end of the corridor, looking out of place.

"Someone's been renovating." Quinn's voice echoed.

We followed the corridor to the metal door. It was unlocked—a detail that immediately raised my suspicions. Either someone was careless, or they were confident no one would find it. Or perhaps they wanted it to be found.

Beyond the door lay what had once been the monastery's refectory, now transformed into a makeshift laboratory. Long tables bore equipment I recognized from chemical analysis facilities. Microscopes, scales, distillation apparatus, and dozens of containers of minerals and compounds lined the walls on metal shelving.

"This is... not what I expected." Quinn moved to a table covered with small ceramic pots of pigment in various hues.

"It's a pigment analysis and reproduction facility." I examined a notebook filled with chemical formulas. "And quite a sophisticated one."

In the corner stood an array of delicate glass beakers, test tubes, and Bunsen burners connected to gas lines.

I scanned a nearby cabinet and its collection of hydrochloric acid, sodium hydroxide, and various reagents necessary for decomposition tests. Several watch glasses contained powder samples in various stages of chemical analysis, and a mortar and pestle showed traces of the distinctive blue pigments being ground for testing.

I picked up a testing plate with residue of a deep, vibrant blue and examined it under the light. The realization hit me with sudden clarity.

"They're specifically testing for ultramarine—the signature component of lapis lazuli. It contains sulfur-rich sodium aluminum silicate, while Egyptian blue is calcium copper silicate. To the naked eye they might appear similar, especially in ancient artifacts, but chemically..." I tapped the testing apparatus, "they're entirely distinct signatures."

Quinn looked over my shoulder. "Why?"

"I don't know. But someone is going to extraordinary lengths to determine which artifacts use genuine imported lapis and which use domestically produced Egyptian blue."

The centerpiece of the room was a large worktable covered with artifacts in various stages of analysis—or reproduction. Some appeared to be ancient pottery and papyrus fragments, while others were clearly modern recreations, being painted with meticulous care to mimic the patina of age.

"Here's where they're replicating artifacts. Creating perfect forgeries."

A momentary flash of insecurity swept through me—would my own archaeological knowledge be sufficient to detect such expert fabrications? Had I already examined forgeries without realizing it? The thought was deeply unsettling.

"The question is why." Quinn moved to a cabinet, carefully opening drawers. "And what is being done with the originals?"

I traced my finger over a ledger book, flipping through pages of meticulous notes on pigment compositions. "This is extraordinary work. The level of detail in matching the chemical signatures of ancient pigments..."

"Someone with extensive archaeological and chemical knowledge," Quinn agreed. "And resources."

I flipped to the most recent entries in the ledger. "These measurement specifications... I recognize this handwriting."

Quinn joined me at the desk. "Whose is it?"

"Deveraux's." I traced my finger along the precise measurements, each recorded with his characteristic obsessive attention. "These are exactly what he described—the specifications the British woman blackmailed him into providing."

I found a series of notations that made my blood run cold: 'D's measurements of G 4215 artifacts accurate to 0.02mm. Reproducing physical dimensions exactly as specified. Chemical analysis confirms blue consistent with New Kingdom standards.'

While Quinn examined a series of locked cabinets along the far wall, I moved to a desk cluttered with correspondence. Letters from museums across Europe and America—the British Museum, the Louvre, the Metropolitan Museum of Art—all thanking the recipient for their generous donations or expert consultation.

"Quinn," I called, holding up one of the letters. "These are addressed to Hawke."

"Well, that's confirmation, then."

I continued sorting through papers. "He appears to be

supplying museums with authentication services for Egyptian artifacts. Specifically ones with..." I paused, finding a pattern in the correspondence. "With notable pigments."

The growing Egyptian nationalist movement had recently increased pressure on museums to prove the legitimate provenance of their acquisitions, creating a climate where authentication services like Hawke's would be particularly valuable. With the international spotlight on Egyptology following Carter's discovery of Tutankhamun's tomb, there was both a market for forgeries and intensified scrutiny of artifacts.

Quinn had managed to open one of the locked cabinets and was carefully removing a wooden box. "I think I've found something that might interest you."

The box contained dozens of glass vials, each labeled with a number corresponding to entries in yet another ledger. Inside each vial was a sample of blue pigment in varying shades.

"Egyptian blue," I breathed, picking up one of the vials, reading the label. "Calcium copper silicate. But not just any Egyptian blue. These are samples from different time periods, different regions. The formula changed subtly between the Old Kingdom and Middle Kingdom periods." I examined another vial, labeled 'lapis.' "And it was manufactured differently in Upper versus Lower Egypt. Someone has been systematically collecting and analyzing the composition of blue pigment across dynasties."

Quinn moved to another table where several microscope slides were laid out. "These appear to be from the palette stolen from your dig site."

I examined the slides, noticing tiny fragments of pottery and wood with traces of blue pigment. "These aren't just from our palette. There are samples here from at least a dozen different artifacts."

I noticed distinctive tool marks on several fragments—techniques specific to different Egyptian dynasties. The firing patterns and pigment application methods varied in ways that would typically be used for authentication. With Deveraux's detailed measurements, these differences could be exploited to create nearly undetectable forgeries.

I privately admitted that Quinn's methods, while ethically questionable, had an efficiency I grudgingly appreciated. Without his "cultural exchange program" at the hotel, we wouldn't have found this laboratory.

While Quinn continued searching the cabinets, I noticed a small leather-bound journal partially hidden beneath a stack of technical papers. Opening it revealed not scientific notes but personal observations.

"Listen to this: 'The British Museum acquisition will be the most challenging yet, but with H's position of trust, we should be able to access the necessary items without raising alarms.'" I frowned. "H must be Hawke. He's a donor to the British Museum."

Quinn had moved to a large wardrobe in the corner. Inside were dozens of garment bags, each labeled with a name and institution.

"Museum conservator uniforms." He pulled one out. "British Museum, the Egyptian Museum, Metropolitan Museum of Art... they could walk into any major institution looking like staff."

As I continued searching the desk, my hand brushed against a folder. Inside I found a stack of photographs.

"Quinn, look at these." I spread the photographs on the desk. "These are surveillance shots of archaeological digs. Including ours."

A distant sound—perhaps the ancient building settling, or something else—briefly distracted me, then faded. A momentary draft swept through the room, out of place in the enclosed space.

And then an acrid, chemical odor reached my nostrils— kerosene. The smell cut through the laboratory's blend of ancient dust and chemical preservatives, first tickling the back of my throat before registering as danger.

We both froze, heads snapping up at the same moment. A

rush of something sent my heart hammering against my ribs before my mind fully processed the threat.

"Do you smell—"

A whooshing sound interrupted Quinn.

Followed immediately by a burst of flame that erupted along the far wall.

CHAPTER TWENTY-FOUR

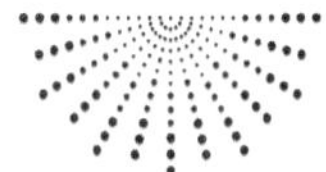

Flames raced along what appeared to be a deliberately laid trail of accelerant.

"Someone's burning the evidence!" I grabbed as many of the photographs and documents as I could stuff into my satchel.

Quinn seized the ledger and several of the blue pigment samples, shoving them into his pockets.

The fire spread with unnatural speed. Smoke filled the room, thick and acrid, forcing us into a crouch.

"The door we came in through." I pointed, but flames had already blocked that route.

"There has to be another way out." Quinn grabbed my arm, pulling me toward the back of the twelfth-century monastery as flames engulfed the workbenches.

The heat was intense, the smoke disorienting.

We stumbled through a doorway into what had once been the monastery's kitchen.

The fire pursued us, hungry and determined.

Through watering eyes, I spotted a narrow window high on the wall. "There!" I doubled over, coughing.

Quinn immediately interlaced his fingers to create a step for me. "I'll boost you up."

"What about you?" I shouted over the roar of the flames and the groaning of ancient timbers collapsing.

"I'll find another way! Go!"

With his boost, I scrambled through the window, scraping my sides on the rough stone. I tumbled onto the hard ground outside, rolling to absorb the impact.

Seconds later, Quinn burst through a different window opening, landing with considerably less grace than I had managed.

We scrambled away from the building as flames consumed the ancient wooden roof beams.

From a safer distance, we watched as centuries of history and a wealth of evidence burned before our eyes, the scent of charred wood and stone hanging heavy in the air.

Movement caught my attention—a figure standing on a small rise about a hundred yards away. The dark form seemed to watch the inferno with the satisfaction of a job well done, then turn and disappear over the ridge.

"Were they waiting for us?" I struggled to catch my breath. "Was this a trap?"

Quinn shook his head, his face smudged with soot. "Not a very effective one, if their goal was to kill us. And I don't see how they could have known we'd be here."

"Perhaps that wasn't the goal." I patted my satchel, confirming our salvaged evidence was intact. "Perhaps they just wanted to destroy whatever we found in there."

The realization struck me that I had not hesitated before taking evidence from what was technically a crime scene. A month ago, I would have written a strongly worded letter to the Archaeological Society about proper documentation procedures. Now I was fleeing burning buildings with evidence stuffed in my satchel, my Cambridge reputation smoldering as thoroughly as the monastery behind us. My father's warnings about archaeology being "no place for a Bell" echoed in my mind, followed by the defiant realization that I'd never felt more alive than when I was in danger, pursuing truth.

It was probably time for reclassification...

Specimen: Respectable Academic (Pristine); Now classified under Archaeological Renegade (Soot-Covered Variety).

The most disturbing part was how little I minded the transition.

"Do you know," I said as we caught our breath, "I believe I'm getting rather good at this detective business."

Quinn raised an eyebrow. "What gave you that impression? The fact that we're watching crucial evidence burn, or that we nearly became specimens ourselves?"

"Neither. It's that I considered stealing that brass magnifying glass on the desk before the flames reached it. For evidence, of course."

His smile was equal parts approval and concern. "Dr. Bell, I believe I'm a terrible influence on you."

Quinn pulled a vial of blue pigment from his pocket, holding it up to catch the light. "The question is, what's so important about this that someone would burn down an entire building to keep it secret?"

I stared at the flames consuming what had once been a sacred place of worship, then a laboratory of deception. "More importantly, did they know we'd be here?"

The monastery continued to burn, sending a column of black smoke into the cloudless Egyptian sky—a signal to anyone watching that another piece of history had been sacrificed in the name of something far more dangerous than archaeology.

There was nothing to be done, so we started the walk back to where we'd left our taxi driver.

But despite the fistful of piasters Quinn gave him to wait for us, the taxi was gone.

Quinn scanned the horizon. "Six miles to the nearest village." He squinted at the setting sun. "Less than two hours if we're quick."

I glanced down at my boots. "At least we have comfortable walking shoes and a delightful aroma of smoke to accompany us." I set off with a stride that suggested more energy than I possessed, rolling my shoulder where I'd landed during my escape.

Quinn fell into step beside me, occasionally clearing his throat from smoke irritation. "Always the optimist, Bell."

"Hmm. If so, my optimism is merely a failure to properly analyze available data." I wiped soot from my cheek, likely creating a more elaborate mess. "The evidence indicates we may have been followed, our proof is currently being converted to ash, and we smell like we've been baptized by a campfire."

The sun began its slow descent, casting long shadows across the dusty landscape. We walked in silence for several minutes, our footsteps crunching a steady rhythm on the packed earth road. Around us, the Egyptian countryside sprawled in golden hues, beautiful and utterly unhelpful.

I adjusted my satchel, wincing as it pressed against a bruise from our hasty exit. "The question is whether they were watching us, or the monastery."

"Both, I'd guess. They're eliminating evidence and witnesses. Someone is desperate to keep whatever's in those artifacts from becoming public knowledge."

The growing darkness wrapped around us like a blanket. Stars emerged overhead, the same stars ancient Egyptians had once mapped with extraordinary precision—possibly using the very mathematical knowledge someone was now willing to kill for.

In the distance, the haunting call of desert wildlife made me instinctively move closer to Quinn. We continued walking as night fully claimed the landscape.

Quinn broke our silence. "You're unusually quiet. For you."

"I'm conserving energy for the inevitable moment when we're attacked by bandits or wild dogs."

He chuckled, the sound warm in the cool night air. "You realize normal people don't anticipate calamity with quite your level of enthusiasm."

"Hmm. Never been normal, I guess."

The moon emerged fully now, casting enough light to navigate by. In the distance, faint lights twinkled—the village, seemingly retreating as we walked, like truth staying just beyond our reach.

Quinn cleared his throat. "Can I ask you something, Bell?"

"Proceed."

"Why do you care so much about these artifacts? Beyond the academic interest."

I considered this. "Because it could be that someone is using them to rewrite history. To erase evidence of accomplishments that don't fit their preferred narrative. Or perhaps there is more truth to be learned, more to add to what we know. I can't let that knowledge stay buried."

Quinn was quiet for a moment. "And why do you assume I don't care about that?"

"You're an antiquities dealer," I said, the words emerging more harshly than intended. "Your profession literally involves moving artifacts from their historical context to private collections where they... disappear."

"Is that what you think I do?"

"Evidence suggests it's precisely what you do."

Quinn stopped walking. "You've analyzed the evidence incorrectly, Dr. Bell."

Something in his tone made me pause. I turned to face him, his features half-illuminated by moonlight, half in shadow —rather like the man himself.

"Enlighten me, then." I crossed my arms, ignoring the twinge of pain from a bruised elbow.

"You assume I sell to the highest bidder without concern for what happens to the pieces." Quinn's voice was low, controlled. "That I'm motivated purely by profit."

"Aren't you?"

He ran a hand through his soot-streaked hair. "No."

For once, I remained silent, waiting.

Quinn resumed his pace and I joined him.

"I was eleven when my family lost everything." Quinn's eyes fixed on the distant horizon. "My father made bad investments, trusted the wrong people. We lost our home, our position, everything—including a small collection of antiquities that had been in our family for generations."

The night seemed to grow still around his words.

"My mother fell ill a few years later, after my father... moved on. We had nothing to sell except a small Roman coin—my grandfather's. It was the last thing of value we owned." His jaw tightened. "I took the coin to an antiquities dealer, hoping to get enough money for medicine."

I could already guess what happened. "He cheated you."

Quinn nodded. "Paid me almost nothing, mocked my ignorance, my desperation. Six months later, I saw that same coin in a collector's home, with him boasting its value at ten times what the dealer paid me."

The pieces were rearranging themselves in my mind, my categorization of Benedict Quinn shifting uncomfortably.

To catalogue and classify based on incomplete evidence was a professional habit that might serve archaeology but perhaps failed in understanding complex human motivations.

"I became an antiquities dealer to ensure that didn't happen to others." He adjusted his cuffs, his habitual gesture rendered absurd by his disheveled state. "I pay fair prices. I document provenance meticulously. And most importantly, I make sure artifacts go to people who will preserve them, appreciate them, and occasionally—yes—even make them accessible to scholars."

"But still not to the public," I pointed out, though with less certainty than before.

"The 'public' you speak of—who are they, exactly?" Quinn's voice took on an edge. "The British Museum visitor who glances at a display for thirty seconds before moving on to the next? The wealthy colonial tourists who gawk at Egypt's treasures while knowing nothing of their significance? Or do you mean the Egyptian public, from whom these treasures are systematically stolen to fill European museums?"

I felt as though I'd been caught in a logical trap of my own making.

"Museums aren't always the sanctuaries of knowledge you

imagine, Bell. They can be monuments to conquest—filled with artifacts acquired through dubious means, displayed according to narratives that reinforce superiority."

"And private collectors are better?" My tone challenged, though my conviction was wavering.

"Some are worse," he admitted. "But the ones I work with? They fund research. They allow scholars access. They preserve pieces that would otherwise be lost to bureaucracy or destroyed in political upheavals."

We had resumed walking, our pace slower now as the conversation deepened.

"What happened to your mother?" I asked, my voice soft.

Quinn's shoulders tensed. "She died. The medicine came too late."

The admission hung between us, weighty with sadness. My hand lifted instinctively to touch his arm in sympathy, then stopped. "I'm sorry," I said, the words inadequate but sincere.

He nodded once, acknowledgment without elaboration. We walked in silence for several minutes, the rhythm of our footsteps the only sound beyond distant night creatures.

"The point is," he finally continued, "not everything is as black and white as 'museums good, private collections bad.' The world of antiquities is far more complex than that."

"Like most worthwhile subjects of study," I conceded.

A smile flickered across his face, visible even in the moonlight. "Did you just admit I might know something about antiquities, Dr. Bell?"

"I admitted the possibility of nuance in a complex field. Don't overinterpret the data."

Despite my words, something had shifted between us—a wall crumbling.

The sound of wheels and hoofbeats interrupted our conversation. We turned to see a carriage approaching, lanterns swinging on its sides.

I sighed. "Well, either salvation approaches or we're about to be efficiently murdered."

"Optimistic as ever."

The carriage slowed as it reached us. The driver, an elderly Egyptian man with a face carved by decades of desert sun, peered down at us suspiciously. The scent of tobacco, spiced tea, and leather wafted from him, momentarily transporting me away from our dire situation.

Quinn approached, speaking rapid Arabic with the fluid competence of someone who'd spent years navigating Cairo's markets. Money changed hands. The driver nodded reluctantly.

"He'll take us into the city." Quinn offered his hand to help me climb aboard.

"How fortuitous." I accepted his assistance with as much dignity as my smoke-damaged clothing and exhausted limbs allowed. "Did you happen to mention we're fleeing from a burning building and may have assassins in pursuit?"

"I told him we were archaeology enthusiasts who got lost." Quinn settled beside me, closer than strictly necessary in the small carriage. "Thought that might sound better than your version."

"Practical as ever." I grabbed for his arm as the carriage lurched forward.

The steady clip-clop of hooves provided a soothing rhythm, and we settled into silence, until the carriage deposited us near Shepheard's Hotel.

As we stood on the sidewalk, the awkwardness between us had transformed into something more complicated—a shared vulnerability I didn't know how to navigate.

"We should separate for now," Quinn said finally. "I'll investigate Hawke's connections, see what I can learn about his operation."

I nodded, suddenly reluctant. "I'll pursue the contact Dr. Abbas gave us, see if she can help identify where the original artifacts might be hidden."

"Be careful." Quinn's eyes met mine, concern evident. "Whoever's behind this won't hesitate to eliminate problems."

"I beg your pardon. I am far more than a 'problem.'" I

grinned. "I am, at minimum, a catastrophe of considerable magnitude."

His laugh was genuine, if brief. "Meet me tomorrow evening? How about that church I wanted to show you—Al-Mu'allaqah—say six o'clock?"

"I'll be there." I adjusted my satchel, acutely aware that we were standing too close, yet neither of us moving away. "Try not to get murdered before then."

"I'll do my best." He hesitated, then stepped back, breaking whatever spell had momentarily bound us. "Goodnight, Dr. Bell."

"Goodnight, Mr. Quinn."

I watched him walk away, his silhouette melting into the hotel lobby. Only then did I allow myself to acknowledge that my categorization system was once again experiencing a critical meltdown.

Benedict Quinn had somehow migrated from *Irritating Antiquities Dealer (Morally Questionable)*, to something entirely defying my careful taxonomies.

Something dangerously close to *Essential*.

CHAPTER TWENTY-FIVE

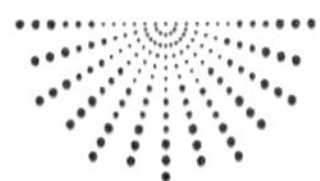

The Egyptian University's gardens blazed with late afternoon light, transforming its neo-Moorish architecture into a study in gold and shadow. The gentle splash of water from ornamental fountains created a deceptive sense of serenity.

Dr. Abbas's contact was ten minutes late, which I'd come to understand was the standard conversion rate between British Imperial Time and Cairo Local Time. I'd used the waiting period to observe the small groups of students clustered beneath palm trees, their animated discussions punctuated by the occasional burst of laughter or emphatic gesture. Several male students had glanced my way with expressions ranging from curiosity to outright disapproval of my decidedly unfashionable attire. Unlike at Cambridge where immediate dismissal was the norm, here I received lingering curious glances—a subtle shift that made me both more comfortable and more conspicuous.

I'd returned their stares with what I hoped was my most intimidating "I've-catalogued-scarier-things-than-you" expression.

"Dr. Bell?"

I turned to find a woman about my age approaching with

purposeful strides. She wore Western clothing—a practical skirt and blouse—but with Egyptian jewelry that caught the sunlight, silver pieces cool against her copper skin, representing her navigation between two worlds. Her dark eyes held a gleam of intensity.

"Miss el-Masri?" I extended my hand.

She shook it with surprising firmness.

"Please, call me Nadia." Her English carried the melodic cadence of Arabic underneath. "I would have suggested meeting somewhere less... conspicuous, but as a woman, I find university grounds safer for meetings. Men assume I am merely a student's sister or a secretary."

"I'm rather familiar with that assumption." I nodded toward a secluded bench partially shielded by a bougainvillea. "Shall we?"

The bench offered an excellent vantage point of the main path while keeping our conversation reasonably private. As we sat, I noticed Nadia's hands—the unmistakable calluses from delicate brushwork along her index fingers.

"You have experience with archaeological work." I gestured to her hands.

"And you have the observational skills Dr. Abbas mentioned." Her smile was brief but genuine. "I studied archaeology at the Sorbonne before returning home to discover neither the British nor my own countrymen particularly valued a female Egyptian archaeologist."

"So you became a tour guide instead."

"Officially." She withdrew a small package from her bag, carefully wrapped in linen. "Unofficially, I document what is being taken from Egypt, by whom, and where it goes. This sometimes grants me access to... restricted information."

The package contained several folded papers and what appeared to be official memoranda on British government letterhead, complete with the distinctive red border and embossed crown of the Foreign Office, marked with "Confidential" stamps in faded red ink.

"Dr. Abbas says you are to be trusted. These are classified

communications regarding artifact assessment procedures." Nadia's voice dropped lower. "The British Museum and Foreign Office have a systematic policy for determining which artifacts receive public display and academic publication."

I scanned the documents, my training allowing me to identify key phrases buried in the verbose prose:

"...artifacts demonstrating advanced scientific knowledge must be subject to additional verification procedures before public exhibition..."

"...care must be taken to contextualize Egyptian achievements within the appropriate historical framework to avoid misrepresentation of primitive technological capabilities..."

"...items potentially contradicting established chronologies of scientific development require Foreign Office approval before academic publication..."

"Good heavens." I looked up at Nadia, the bitter taste of morning tea lingering on my tongue.

Her expression remained carefully neutral.

"This is essentially a policy to suppress evidence contradicting European narratives of scientific progress."

"Precisely." She pointed to a signature at the bottom of one document. "Note the authorization."

The name "E. Hawke" appeared beneath his official title: "Cultural Liaison to the Foreign Office."

"How does the British government even trust this man?" I struggled to reconcile the ostentatious collector with a governmental role.

"His position allows him to identify potentially 'problematic' artifacts and ensure they receive proper... contextualization." Nadia's tone made the euphemism transparently clear. "Dr. Abbas believes the stolen items collectively document mathematical and astronomical knowledge that predates similar European discoveries by centuries."

"Yes, the theory is that they're not stealing these artifacts to sell them—they're removing them from circulation to control the historical narrative."

"A narrative that conveniently justifies continued British

presence in Egypt." Nadia reclaimed the papers, returning them to her bag. "If Egyptians built the pyramids using advanced mathematics while Europeans were still figuring out how to stack rocks in circles, it rather undermines the claim that we need 'civilizing,' doesn't it? The British Residency and High Commissioner's office have structured an entire administrative system around maintaining this narrative."

I smiled. It was rather more complicated than that, but her point was well taken.

"And Rosamund Fairchild? Do you know anything of her involvement in all this?"

Nadia lifted one shoulder. "I heard she arrived on Wednesday to consult at the Giza site. My hope is that she will have more success than others have, in proving who is responsible."

Sunlight dappled the path before us as students began dispersing for the evening, their shadows stretching across the manicured lawn. I wondered how many of them realized they were studying in an institution designed to carefully control which parts of their heritage they were permitted to claim.

"There's more." Nadia hesitated. "It's possible Dr. Sutherland discovered this policy and began documenting inconsistencies between initial archaeological reports and published findings. He was building a case showing systematic removal of evidence of advanced Egyptian knowledge."

"And that's why he was killed." My stomach clenched at the thought of Sutherland's lonely death.

"I assume so. But he wasn't working alone." She withdrew a final paper—a list of names. "These are scholars who have been quietly documenting discrepancies. Some are missing. Others have had unfortunate 'accidents.'"

I scanned the list, my blood running cold as I recognized several names from archaeological journals. Their mysterious disappearances or sudden deaths had been discussed in academic circles as unfortunate hazards of field work.

"This isn't just about artifacts," I murmured. "It's political."

"Everything about archaeology in Egypt is political, Dr.

Bell." Nadia stood, smoothing her skirt. "Figures like Saad Zaghloul have been making this argument for years. The question is whether you're willing to acknowledge it."

As she walked away, her words echoed uncomfortably in my mind, like footsteps in an unexplored tomb.

~

The Hanging Church appeared to defy both gravity and architectural good sense, perched atop the ancient gatehouse of a Roman fortress with a reckless disregard for structural anxiety. Like everything else in Cairo, it was a visual record of civilizations stacked atop one another—Roman foundations, Coptic design, Islamic influences, and the unmistakable fingerprints of European restoration.

I climbed the stairs to the elevated choir gallery where Quinn and I had arranged to meet, my footsteps echoing against stone worn smooth by centuries of faithful feet. I hadn't yet visited Al-Mu'allaqah, and Quinn insisted I see it. I'd arrived more than thirty minutes early, to explore on my own, my mind still processing the revelation that archaeology in Egypt was inextricably linked to political control.

The gallery offered an excellent vantage point of both the nave below and the intricate iconography adorning the walls. The evening light filtered through windows, creating pools of illumination that seemed to deliberately highlight different sacred images as the sun moved across the sky—a divine slideshow presentation that predated electricity by several centuries.

The interior air carried the complex olfactory history of centuries of worship: aged wood, old incense, candle wax, and that particular dust that seems to exist solely in sacred spaces—as if holiness itself produced a distinctive sediment when left undisturbed. Marble columns supported a wooden ceiling designed to evoke Noah's ark, while intricate geometric patterns demonstrated that religious mathematics transcended cultural boundaries.

I was cataloguing the stylistic periods in the iconography when movement below caught my attention.

Benedict Quinn entered through the main doors, his linen suit standing out against the ancient stones. He wasn't alone.

Eli Hawke followed close behind, his expensive walking stick tapping against the stone floor with metronomic precision. The sound reminded me uncomfortably of a beetle trapped in a specimen jar—persistent, rhythmic, and faintly menacing.

I instinctively stepped back into the shadows of the gallery.

I needed a way to get close enough to hear their conversation.

A narrow passageway to my right led around the gallery toward a smaller overlook. I moved quietly, my practical boots making less noise than fashionable heels. The ancient wooden floor occasionally protested my weight with alarming creaks that I was certain echoed throughout all of Christendom, but neither man glanced upward. I pressed my fingers against the ancient wood grain as I steadied myself.

"—becoming increasingly concerned about your progress, Quinn." Hawke's voice drifted upward, the acoustics of the church carrying his words with unexpected clarity.

"I've kept you informed." Quinn's tone was casual, but I detected the underlying tension of someone navigating a minefield.

"Informed, yes. Given me results, no." Hawke tapped his walking stick for emphasis. "The Bell woman was supposed to be a convenient distraction, not an actual investigator. You assured me you would handle her."

My stomach dropped. A cold sensation spread through my chest, down my arms, into my clenched fingers.

"I am handling her." Quinn's voice hardened. "Nothing for you to worry about. And I'm well aware of the timeline."

Quinn's voice sounded so coldly professional, I barely recognized it.

"And the Bell woman trusts me completely. She's sharing everything she discovers, which gives us the advantage of knowing exactly what she knows. Which, trust me, is next to nothing."

I bit my lip so hard I tasted blood.

That calculating, manipulative, archaeological desecrator of human decency! I'd trusted him—confided in him—almost kissed him, for the love of Hathor! And all along, he'd been reporting to Hawke, monitoring me like some laboratory specimen, feeding me information to—to what? Distract me? Use me?

"See that you maintain the advantage." Hawke moved toward a side chapel, where the light struck his profile. "The recovery operation at the university tomorrow will proceed as planned, with or without your assistance. But we could make could use of her."

"Trust me, it's not worth your trouble. She would never agree."

Quinn's smooth confidence made me want to drop a heavy textbook on his perfect head.

Hawke grunted. "I still think eliminating her entirely would be simpler."

My blood froze. Surely he couldn't mean—

"Too messy, too public." Quinn waved a dismissive hand. "I'll keep her distracted until after the operation. Then she becomes... irrelevant."

The two men moved deeper into the side chapel, their voices becoming indistinct murmurs.

I retreated back to the main gallery, my mind spinning. Every interaction with Quinn replayed in my memory, now tainted with suspicion and betrayal. My heartbeat changed rhythm—first stopping, then racing, then steadying into a determined cadence.

I had minutes to decide my approach: confront him immediately, or play along to gather more information? The archaeologist in me preferred careful excavation of evidence, but the woman who'd been thoroughly duped wanted immediate and spectacular confrontation.

When Quinn finally appeared at the top of the gallery

stairs, his expression brightened at the sight of me. The utter believability of his performance only fueled my anger.

"You're early." He moved toward me with the easy confidence of someone expecting a welcoming reception rather than imminent evisceration. "Have you figured out—"

"That I've become an inconvenient liability to be handled?" I stepped back, crossing my arms.

Quinn froze, his expression shifting from surprise to something more complex. "Clarissa—"

"Dr. Bell." My tone had iced over. "I believe we've established I'm merely an academic resource to be managed, rather than a colleague to be respected."

"That's not—" He glanced around the gallery, lowering his voice. "What you heard wasn't what it seemed."

"Really? Because it seemed remarkably straightforward. You've been reporting on me to Hawke, using me to track information about the artifacts, and apparently keeping me 'distracted' while some operation proceeds tomorrow."

"I was feeding him misinformation." Quinn stepped closer, his voice urgent. A muscle tensed in his jaw. "He and I have both worked in Egypt for years, and have a certain amount of mutual understanding. If I refused to work with him, he'd have simply assigned someone to follow you—someone who wouldn't hesitate to eliminate the 'liability' you present."

"How noble of you to volunteer. And I suppose calling me 'irrelevant' is also for my protection?"

"Yes, actually." Quinn ran a hand through his hair. "Hawke is planning something. I've been trying to figure out what. But in the meantime, the less important he finds *you*, the better."

"So you are pretending to betray me. How convenient that your version of protection and utter deception look identical." For a moment, I almost believed him, his explanation momentarily fitting into place like puzzle pieces—but I caught myself, reinforcing my intellectual resolve against emotional vulnerability.

"Clarissa—" He reached for my arm.

I stepped back.

"You called me 'the Bell woman.'" The words tasted bitter. "Like I was some specimen to be classified and controlled."

"I was playing a role!" His voice echoed in the vaulted space. "Do you think Hawke would believe me if I referred to you as my brilliant partner whose archaeological insights I've come to respect and—"

"Don't." I held up a hand. "Whatever you're about to say, don't. I trusted you, against every logical instinct. I defended you to everyone. I even—" I cut myself off, unwilling to admit how close I'd come to genuine feelings for him.

"I don't think you understand the gravity of the situation." Quinn stepped closer, his voice lowered.

I became acutely aware of how he seemed to command space—not just with his considerable height and broad shoulders, but with a kind of contained energy that made the air between us feel charged. His brown-gold eyes, normally bright with mischief, had darkened like the sky before a desert storm.

"Listen to me," Quinn's voice took on a new urgency. "Tomorrow morning, Hawke's people are raiding the university's archaeological storage facility. They're after the remaining blue pigment artifacts."

"And again, how convenient, that you have this information now that I've caught you."

"I've been trying to pinpoint their target for days! That's why I arranged this meeting with Hawke—to confirm my suspicions. Why would I have taken the chance on meeting him here, knowing you were coming?" Quinn stepped closer, his eyes intense. "You're walking into a trap if you go there tomorrow. They know you've been talking with Nadia el-Masri."

"And how exactly would they know that?" I raised an eyebrow. "Unless someone has been reporting my movements."

The flash of guilt across his face told me everything.

"I thought so." I turned to leave, my posture shifting from defensive crossed arms to straight-backed academic authority. "I'll solve this case myself, Mr. Quinn. I don't need a duplicitous antiquities dealer to explain Egyptian history to me."

"Clarissa, wait!" His hand caught my elbow. "The artifacts are just one part of a larger plan—we don't really understand what is going on here."

"Remove your hand before I remove it for you." My voice could have preserved a mummy for another three thousand years.

He released me. "I'm telling you, you're walking straight into their hands if you try to intervene tomorrow."

"Perhaps." I faced him one last time, channeling every ounce of academic disdain I'd accumulated from years of being underestimated. "But unlike some people, I don't abandon my principles when they become inconvenient. Those artifacts represent Egyptian scientific achievements that deserve recognition, not suppression."

"I agree! But how will you protect those achievements if you're dead?" His voice rose in frustration. "Think like an archaeologist! What matters more—the evidence or your pride?"

"Both, as it happens." I turned away, heading for the stairs. "Goodbye, Mr. Quinn. I do hope your next archaeological partnership proves more profitable."

"Clarissa!" His voice echoed through the ancient church as I descended.

I kept walking, his words following me. Whatever truth might exist in his claims, I'd excavate it myself—without the dubious assistance of Benedict Quinn.

The evening air hit my face as I exited the church, carrying the scent of baking bread and automobile exhaust. Cairo continued its chaotic symphony around me, unaware of betrayals and conspiracies hidden within its ancient streets.

Tomorrow, I would find a way to stop whatever Hawke planned at the university. Alone.

Right now, I only wanted to go home.

CHAPTER TWENTY-SIX

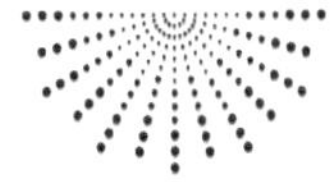

The taxi lurched over a pothole, launching me a good three inches off my seat. The worn leather cracked beneath my weight as I shifted, the scent of the driver's hair pomade mingling with tobacco smoke.

I barely noticed, mind straying backward to the Hanging Church, even as the taxi bore me back to the Nile View Café.

I'd splurged on Cairo's most expensive taxi service, but frugality seemed a distant concern when one's professional reputation, personal safety, and embarrassingly naive emotional attachments were simultaneously crumbling.

How ridiculous that I'd begun to consider a partnership—perhaps even more—with Benedict Quinn.

"A bit slower, please." We careened around a corner, nearly flattening a man on a bicycle.

The driver responded by accelerating with renewed purpose, as if "slower" in Arabic translated directly to "please endanger more locals."

The evening air smelled of roasting meat mixed with diesel fumes. Limestone buildings had absorbed the day's heat and now released it in waves that made the night air shimmer. The city hummed with evening activity—merchants closing shops, families gathering for meals, and antiquities dealers betraying the trust of archaeologists who should have known better.

The Bell woman trusts me completely, Quinn had said.

The sheer calculated precision of his betrayal...

The taxi screeched to a halt before my lodgings.

I overpaid the driver with money I couldn't afford to waste, but the alternative—counting out precise change while fighting back tears—seemed worse.

The bitter aroma of Turkish coffee bubbling in brass vessels wafted from the café, still bustling with nighttime patrons. Small porcelain cups clinked and Arabic conversations rose like steam.

My landlady, Madame Farah, intercepted me before I could reach the stairs to my room, her substantial form materializing from behind the counter.

"Miz Bell!" She waved a telegram at me with enthusiasm, her jewelry-laden fingers brushing against my hand as she passed it over. "Your father, yes? Very bad business!"

Oh, what now?

Madame Farah tapped the telegram with a stained finger, her numerous gold bracelets jangling like wind chimes. "You pay rent still, yes? If father not give you money?"

I chose to ignore the outrage of her reading my mail, and answer her question. "My finances are entirely separate from my father's," I assured her.

This was both completely true and entirely false. While I maintained an independent bank account with my modest academic salary, my excavation funding came largely from my father's deep pockets—a fact I preferred not to advertise to either colleagues or landladies. I'd tried to distance myself from his wealth while simultaneously relying on it—a contradiction I'd never fully reconciled.

"Good, good." She didn't sound convinced. "Also, second telegram come." She produced a folded paper from her apron pocket, already unsealed and well-creased. "I am not your delivery person. Not your assistant."

Two in one day? I was getting popular.

I took the two missives without comment, refusing to give her the satisfaction of reading them in her presence. Her disappointed expression suggested she'd been hoping for a public performance of my personal catastrophes.

"Thank you for your discretion." I tucked both into my satchel.

My room, when I finally reached it, presented the same depressing tableau I'd left that morning—narrow bed with sheets as thin as tissue paper, wobbly desk covered in notes, window that offered an exceptional view of the neighboring building's brick wall. The room smelled of burnt coffee, and the wooden floorboards creaked in the distinct pattern I'd mapped during sleepless nights while thin curtains fluttered.

Through my window, Cairo's night sky was visible, stars obscured by the city's haze, with occasional breaks revealing constellations the ancient Egyptians would have used for navigation.

I sank onto the bed, extracting the second telegram handed to me. It was from Cambridge University.

CONCERNS RAISED REGARDING RECENT BEHAVIOR STOP RESEARCH POSITION UNDER REVIEW STOP COMMITTEE MEETING SCHEDULED UPON YOUR RETURN STOP

I stared at the words until they blurred. My mind flashed back to my first day at Cambridge, how I'd felt invincible with academic potential. Now that same institution was treating me as disposable. First Bradford and his dismissive pottery sorting, then Quinn with his elaborate deception, and now Cambridge itself questioning my professional standing. My entire academic identity—the only identity I truly valued—was being stripped away, one betrayal at a time.

The walls seemed to close in as my panic rose, the ceiling pressing down with the weight of my unraveling career. I paced the small confines of my room.

The palette theft had consumed my reputation. I'd gone from respected Cambridge scholar to suspected criminal and now, apparently, academic pariah.

And tomorrow, Hawke's people seemed to have some kind of plan to destroy evidence of ancient Egyptian scientific advancement, all to maintain the illusion of British intellectual superiority. The implications were staggering. And I was somehow caught in the middle of it, being manipulated by forces beyond my control.

The telegram from my father was also brief, the headline being that he'd already received word of Sutherland's murder, and "AS REPEATED MANY TIMES, EGYPT NO PLACE FOR YOUNG LADY." He's certainly splurged on the extra words, just to include his version of an "I told you so." And apparently, tickets for passage back to New York for both myself and Annie awaited us at the Marseilles train station.

So, I was to be shipped back to my country of origin against my will.

A knock at my door interrupted my spiraling thoughts.

Annie herself stood in the hall, her round face flushed from exertion. The scent of expensive French perfume wafted from her, jarringly out of place in my spartan room.

"Oh, Dr. Bell! Thank goodness you're here!" She clutched a package to her chest as if it might attempt escape. "I've been looking everywhere for you!"

"Annie? What are you doing here?" I stepped aside to let her enter, noticing her worried glance at my sparse accommodations.

She waved her handbag at me.

"Dr. Bradford had several boxes of Dr. Sutherland's personal effects delivered to the dig site this afternoon. Papers, journals, all manner of academic detritus." She shook her head. "He mentioned that sorting through them would be, and I quote, 'an excellent task for Miss Bell's particular talents.'"

I couldn't help but laugh. "Of course he did."

"I may have taken a peek through the boxes." Annie's cheeks flushed. "When I saw this..." She extracted Sutherland's leather-bound journal from her bag with reverence. "I thought you'd want to see it immediately."

I took the journal, my fingers automatically noting the

worn leather, the slight oiliness of the binding from frequent handling. Sutherland's field journal, and his constant companion during excavations.

"The police never saw it?"

Annie snorted with uncharacteristic inelegance. "Apparently they glanced through his professional papers but then dumped them all on Bradford as unimportant."

I flipped open to the first page. Would I finally get some answers about whatever Sutherland was doing that got him killed?

Annie sat on the bed, her skirts rustling. "What will you do now?"

I pointed at the telegram from my father. "Well, there is one option."

She scanned it, then looked up with wide eyes. "Are you thinking—"

"I'm going nowhere, don't worry."

"Perhaps you should consider your father's offer." Annie's voice was gentle. "New York is glamorous... and safe. And adventures are less appealing when they involve actual danger."

I was about to respond when a faint noise from outside the door caught my attention. Not the typical ancient-apartment-creaky-noises, but something more deliberate—the scrape of a boot on a step.

I raised a finger to my lips, motioning Annie to silence.

Instinct sent me to my small shelf, where I pulled out the heaviest item in my possession—Petrie's definitive volume on Old Kingdom burial practices.

Instinct also had me shoving Sutherland's journal deep into the waistband of my trousers and then making certain it was covered by my shirt.

"Dr. Bell, what—" Annie's whisper was cut short by the sound of splintering wood as my door gave way with a spectacular crack.

A man in dark clothing jumped through the doorway, followed immediately by a second.

My body automatically shifted into the balanced stance I use when navigating unstable excavation floors.

I gripped Petrie's volume and swung it with the precision of a cricket player who'd spent more time in libraries than on fields. The satisfying thunk as it connected with the first intruder's head suggested that Professor Petrie's verbose writing style had finally found its true purpose.

"Annie, run!" I shouted.

Annie scrambled toward the door, only to shriek as a third intruder entered.

I launched the text like a discus, but my aim wavered, and it merely grazed his shoulder.

The first man recovered from his academic concussion and lunged toward me.

I dodged, sending him crashing into my desk.

The second attacker circled behind me, cutting off my escape route.

I managed to get two steps closer to the door before rough hands seized my arms, pinning them. I kicked backward, connecting with a shin, but the grip only tightened.

Annie screamed as the man at the door grabbed her.

These were not common thieves. Coordinated movements and efficiency spoke of professional training.

"You'll regret this." I spat, thrashing against my captor. "I have influential—"

A cloth covered my mouth and nose, cutting off my breath and my threat. A smell like overripe fruit left too long in the sun assaulted my senses.

I held my breath, but the room was already spinning, furniture and attackers blurring into a jumble of shapes and shadows.

As darkness crept into the edges of my vision, another figure appeared in the doorway.

"Careful with that one." The accent was British, cultured. He nodded toward me. "She's rather more trouble than she appears."

It was the last thing I heard before a chemical darkness claimed me.

CHAPTER TWENTY-SEVEN

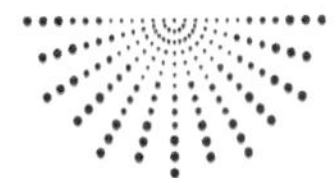

I regained consciousness with the distinct feeling my brain had been removed, examined, and reinserted by an amateur mummifier with a grudge. And my mouth cottoned like I'd been gargling liquid papyrus.

I attempted to catalogue my surroundings while keeping my eyes firmly shut, excavating each layer of sensory information.

The surface beneath me was hard and cold—concrete, judging by the gritty texture against my cheek. Uneven patches dug into my skin. The air smelled of motor oil, dust, and despair—a bouquet I labeled Eau de Impending Doom, with distinctive notes of metallic machinery tang, musty rat droppings, and the lingering chemical bite of chloroform.

A distant mechanical hum suggested industrial equipment. Occasional metallic clangs echoed through what must be a cavernous space. The unnaturally cold night air seeped through cracks, making my bound limbs ache with each small movement.

When I finally dared to open my eyes, the world swam into focus with alarming reluctance. My vision doubled momentarily before settling. I was sprawled on the floor of what appeared to be an abandoned warehouse. Shafts of moonlight speared through broken windows, creating geometric patterns that shifted slowly across the floor, illuminating dust motes that sparkled like tiny constellations in the darkness.

My wrists were bound with rough rope that scratched with every movement, leaving my skin raw. A fierce pounding drummed in my head.

I struggled to a sitting position, limbs unnaturally heavy and uncoordinated. My ankles were also bound, though with less expertise.

"Ah, Dr. Bell. Welcome back."

Eli Hawke stepped from the shadows. His expensive shoes struck the concrete with precise, measured steps that bounced sharp echoes through the empty space. His suit appeared freshly pressed, the fabric pristine in the decaying industrial setting.

"Lovely establishment." I surveyed the decrepit warehouse, once a productive center of commerce. "Though the decor is a bit sparse. Perhaps some ancient Egyptian throw pillows might liven things up?"

Hawke's smile never reached his eyes. The scents of pipe smoke and brandy concentrated around him like a shield, creating another layer of separation between him and the squalid surroundings.

"Your humor is noted, if not appreciated. I trust your accommodations are adequate for our short time together."

"Adequate? Absolutely. I've always dreamed of being drugged and bound in an abandoned building."

He circled me, head tilted. "I must admit, you've proven far more troublesome than anticipated. When Quinn suggested using you as a distraction, I had my doubts about involving an academic at all."

"Quinn." The name tasted bitter on my tongue. "I suppose he's waiting outside for his reward for delivering me to you?"

Hawke's eyebrow lifted with what appeared to be genuine surprise. "Quite the contrary. Mr. Quinn has been advocating rather forcefully for your safety. He seems to think you're worth protecting—a sentiment I find both puzzling and inconvenient, especially in light of recent developments."

This information failed to compute. An unwanted flush of warmth challenged my neat categorization of Quinn. Ally or enemy?

"Well, at least you had Sutherland to do your dirty work."

He laughed. "He was no better. Refused to use the perfectly good evidence against you I'd collected."

"So you killed him."

"Let's not get bogged down in accusations, my dear. Or explanations."

"Then what do you want?"

"You've been under surveillance since your arrival in Egypt, Dr. Bell." Hawke removed a silver cigarette case from his jacket pocket, lighting one with practiced style. The rich scent of expensive Turkish tobacco with hints of clove floated through the air, contrasting with the warehouse's industrial odors. "Your meeting with Nadia el-Masri was documented. You've walked a remarkably direct path to your own downfall, with no assistance required from Mr. Quinn."

I tried to process this revelation while simultaneously working at the ropes binding my wrists, a division of attention that yielded limited success on both fronts. I contorted my body, trying to reach the knots, each movement sending fresh pain through my raw skin.

Amazingly, the hard edge of Sutherland's journal still pressed against my hip where I'd hidden it in my waistband. If Hawke discovered it, I'd lose our only evidence. But trussed up like a holiday goose, I couldn't even check if it was still secure, let alone read its contents.

"Quinn has become a liability." Hawke exhaled smoke with aristocratic precision. "He's developed an unfortunate attachment to you—a softening I hadn't anticipated. I've relieved him of his responsibilities in this matter."

"How charitable of you." I finally succeeded in loosening the knot. "And what matter would that be, exactly? Suppressing evidence of advanced Egyptian scientific progress?

Destroying proof that undermines British narratives? Or just general villainous gloating?"

Hawke studied me with newfound interest. His cultured veneer had cracked somewhere between kidnapping and interrogation. The smooth, aristocratic collector now revealed flashes of something rawer—a desperation belying his manicured appearance. "You understand more than you should. That makes you particularly dangerous—and, ironically, particularly useful."

He snapped his fingers, and one of his goons materialized. Hawke murmured instructions, and the man disappeared, returning moments later with a leather portfolio.

"Your academic work on pigment composition across dynasties is quite impressive," Hawke remarked, extracting a paper I recognized as my own publication from the Journal of Egyptian Archaeology.

A treacherous spark of professional pride flared in my chest before I remembered the context. How pathetic that even in my current predicament, academic validation could still provoke such a response.

"Your ability to identify specific signatures in pigments and relate them to particular time periods is precisely the expertise we require."

"I'm not in the habit of giving impromptu lectures to kidnappers."

"Tomorrow morning at nine o'clock, my team will enter the Egyptian University's archaeological storage facility." Hawke flipped through my paper with disturbing familiarity. "We need to identify and remove specific artifacts containing the pigment variations you've so helpfully cataloged. With your expertise, we can complete the operation in minutes rather than hours."

"And why would I help you?" I strained against my bonds, achieving nothing but rope burn. "I'm an archaeologist. My entire profession is devoted to revealing history, not suppressing it."

Hawke sighed. "Because, Dr. Bell, your devoted assistant is

currently enjoying our hospitality in another part of this facility."

My blood froze. A metallic taste of fear flooded my mouth. "Annie?"

"Charming girl. Rather tearful, but otherwise unharmed." Hawke tapped ash from his cigarette. "Her continued well-being depends entirely on your cooperation."

"If you harm her—"

"Threats require leverage, Dr. Bell, which you notably lack." Hawke consulted his pocket watch with a frown. "I'm operating on an extremely tight schedule. I have a very specific, non-negotiable deadline, and I've wasted considerable time tracking down items that ultimately proved useless. Your expertise will expedite matters considerably."

"You're asking me to help erase history." My voice sounded steadier than I felt. "To destroy evidence that could rewrite our understanding of ancient scientific development."

"I'm asking you to be practical." Hawke extracted a document from his portfolio, unfolding it with deliberate care. "Help us identify the relevant artifacts, sign this confession stating you orchestrated the thefts for personal academic gain, and your assistant remains intact."

"What? Now you want me to take the fall as well? And if I refuse?"

"Then Annie suffers the consequences of your idealism, and we simply take everything of interest from the storage facility, destroying a significant portion of the university's legitimate archaeological collection in the process." Hawke's smile was mathematical in its precision and complete lack of humanity. "Either way, the evidence disappears. I can also make things significantly difficult for your father and his "special collection." So, it seems the only variable is how much additional damage occurs."

I stared at him, calculating escape scenarios, coming up with nothing.

My father had prepared me for many situations in life, believing my scholarly pursuits would keep me safely within libraries and museums. Kidnapping negotiations had been conspicuously absent from his parental curriculum.

And Richard, my ex-fiancé? He would have been apoplectic at the sight of me now. 'Really, Clarissa,' I could hear his condescending tenor, 'this is precisely why you should have stayed in New York.'

At this moment, tied up in an abandoned warehouse with a villainous art collector, I couldn't help thinking Richard and my father might have had a point.

"I'll leave you to consider your options." Hawke placed the confession document on a crate beside me, along with a fountain pen that gleamed with gold inlay and mother-of-pearl accents. "You have until dawn to make your decision. I suggest you think practically rather than academically."

He paused at the door, turning back with theatrical timing that suggested he practiced villainous exits in front of a mirror. "Oh, and Dr. Bell? Mr. Quinn believes you're capable of making the right choice. I, however, have significantly less faith in your judgment. Let's see which of us proves correct."

With that parting shot, he left, the heavy metal door clanging shut with all the finality of a tomb sealing. I heard the distinctive click of a lock, followed by receding footsteps.

For a moment, I sat frozen, the full weight of my situation settling over me. Then determination returned with a surge of adrenaline that temporarily cleared my chloroform-fogged mind. I renewed my efforts on the ropes, twisting my wrists until the skin burned. The knots remained stubbornly intact.

I surveyed my surroundings, searching for anything that might serve as a tool. Broken crates, dust, abandoned machinery parts—all tantalizingly useless for my current predicament. The moonlight had shifted, leaving me in deeper shadow, a fitting metaphor.

The confession document gleamed white against the wooden crate, its official letterhead mocking me.

Academic Career: Decimated. From Cambridge scholar to suspected artifact thief.

Professional Reputation: Extinct. Future employment prospects limited to perhaps sideshow fortune-telling.

Benedict Quinn: Complicated. Apparently not directly responsible for my kidnapping, but still consorting with Fairchild and operating in ethically ambiguous territory that required its own classification system.

Current Situation: Catastrophic. Bound up in an abandoned warehouse with a moral dilemma that would give Aristotle a migraine.

The impossible choice loomed. Help Hawke identify the artifacts, betray everything I believed about archaeological integrity, and sign my professional death warrant—or refuse and bear responsibility for Annie's suffering, my father's reputation, and perhaps even more archaeological destruction.

History and truth versus immediate human safety. Academic principles versus personal loyalty. The greater good versus individual harm.

It was the kind of ethical problem academics loved to debate in comfortable university offices, never expecting to face it while bound with rope in a disused warehouse with a pounding chloroform headache.

Annie—sweet, capable Annie who had done nothing to deserve this situation beyond the misfortune of being associated with me. Did she sit frightened in some dark corner of this building, perhaps bound as I was, wondering if anyone would come for her?

And my father—difficult, controlling, but ultimately concerned for my welfare. His investments represented more than money; they were the foundation of his identity. The destruction of his reputation would devastate him in ways that went beyond financial loss.

Not to mention the artifacts themselves—silent witnesses to ancient achievement, carriers of knowledge that had survived millennia only to face erasure due to modern imperial politics. If they were destroyed or hidden away, how many generations would pass before such evidence surfaced again?

The confession document stared up at me. Hawke had

crafted a perfect trap, using my own expertise against me, leveraging my connections, and exploiting my divided loyalties.

Dawn approached inexorably. The watery pre-morning light seeped through the broken windows, bringing with it a cold sharpness.

I had run out of time, options, and witty observations. The evidence was clear, the stratigraphy of my situation unmistakable: I was thoroughly, undeniably, and comprehensively trapped.

For the first time since arriving in Egypt, I found myself without a system adequate to catalogue the depth of my despair.

CHAPTER TWENTY-EIGHT

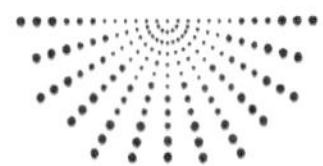

The first hint of dawn crept through the warehouse's broken windows, casting long fingers of golden-amber light across the concrete floor. I'd spent hours battling the ropes binding my wrists, achieving nothing but raw skin and a comprehensive catalogue of Egyptian profanities that would have made a hardened camel driver blush.

A rusted nail protruding from a nearby crate had caught my attention ten minutes earlier. Thinking I could maneuver myself against it and saw through the fibers, I had worked my way to it, awkwardly shuffling on my knees across the rough concrete that sent shooting pains through my legs.

The nail snagged the rope, and now I worked it against the coarse hemp fibers with desperate determination. The smell of rust mingled with the coppery tang of blood from my raw wrists. Tiny splinters embedded themselves in my already tender skin, each movement bringing fresh sparks of pain.

Sweat trickled down my spine. My once-crisp khaki work shirt stuck uncomfortably against my skin in the warming air.

As I labored, I sorted the evidence accumulated over the past days. The stolen palette. Sutherland's murder. The monastery laboratory. Forgery. The common Egyptian blue pigment and the rare lapis lazuli version. Fairchild's threats. Hawke's operation. Benedict Quinn.

These pieces remained frustratingly disconnected, like sherds from different vessels that I kept trying to force together into a coherent whole. My systematic analysis—one piece at a time, each in its proper context, properly positioned by period, location, and cultural significance—simply was not working.

Something wasn't right about my approach.

"You're so busy cataloging each pottery sherd separately," Quinn had told me once. "But you have to see how things fit together to understand what once was."

I'd missed connections.

Perhaps deliberately. Emotion was messy, subjective, unreliable—I'd built an academic career on its absence.

Was Quinn right? Did I catalogue the world to keep it at arm's length, creating taxonomies instead of relationships? Deliberately turn people into specimens to avoid the risk of genuine connection?

My heart lurched painfully in my chest, then settled into a stronger, more determined rhythm.

My mind flashed to twelve-year-old Clarissa Bell, proudly displaying her research on Egyptian dating methods, only to discover Walter Hammond had claimed it as his own. The humiliation burned as fresh now as it had then. I thought of how that same child had spent countless hours reorganizing her father's library by subject and period when she was only eight, much to the housekeepers' amusement. Even then, I had been imposing order on chaos, keeping the world neatly contained.

I'd learned my lesson early—collaboration leads to betrayal. Better to work alone, trust no one, keep everyone classified and contained in specimen jars where they couldn't hurt me.

The rope frayed against the nail. I redoubled my efforts, mind racing, even as my shoulders burned from hours in this position. My throat felt paper-dry, my head pounding with dehydration and exhaustion.

Hadn't I been doing the same thing with Quinn? The

evidence suggesting his loyalty had been there—his protection during our escape from Alexandria, his warning about the monastery fire, his consistent pattern of showing up when I needed help. Yet I'd refused to consider it, preferring to file him under "Untrustworthy" where he couldn't breach my defenses. Even now, I had to admire his relational intelligence—a quality my Cambridge professors had trained me to dismiss as irrelevant to serious scholarship.

What would those same professors think of my current predicament?

But I'd been so determined to prove I didn't need help, I'd landed myself in an abandoned warehouse, bound and facing an impossible choice. This wasn't independence; it was self-sabotage.

My father's voice echoed in my mind: "Clarissa, your brilliance is matched only by your stubbornness." For once, he might be right.

The rope gave, a few more fibers yielding to my persistence.

Yes, I'd been approaching this investigation like an excavation—meticulous, isolated, documented with academic precision, using the stratigraphic method I'd championed at my dig site rather than the hasty treasure-hunting of previous generations. But criminal conspiracies weren't artifacts to be cataloged; they were human endeavors driven by greed, ambition, and desperation.

While I'd been maintaining my scholarly detachment, people had been manipulating, threatening, and killing one another.

Despite my preference otherwise, the world was messy, interconnected, and fundamentally human in ways my classification systems couldn't adequately capture.

Perhaps I had held myself apart from that humanity—from Annie's warmth, from Quinn's complicated integrity, even from my father's concern—while convincing myself it was academic objectivity rather than emotional fear.

Specimen: Personal Epiphany (Uncomfortable), Modern

Period, featuring recognition of one's complete and utter misapplication of social skills.

I paused in my cataloging, surprised by the rush of emotion, both terrifying and strangely liberating.

The nail sliced through another strand of rope, bringing a flush of victory.

What would it be like to work alongside Quinn rather than against him—his intuitive leaps complementing my methodical analysis, his network of contacts expanding my research possibilities. The thought sent an unexpected flutter through my stomach.

The warehouse door creaked open. I shifted from the nail, assuming a defeated posture despite the small victories against my bonds.

The blue-gray shadows of the warehouse interior had yielded to the strengthening dawn light, revealing the true colors of my surroundings—ochre walls and rust-colored stains on the concrete floor. Massive wooden support beams crossed overhead, and the remnants of pulley systems hung like industrial skeletons, hinting at the building's former purpose as a storage facility. Around me, I could still see the ghostly impressions where crates had once been stacked, now empty except for forgotten debris.

Eli Hawke strode in, flanked by two armed men with expressions professionally blank.

"Good morning, Dr. Bell. I trust you've had adequate time to consider my proposition?"

I calculated my options. The rope remained too strong to break. The progress I'd made was in my attitude, not my escape skills.

"Where's Annie?" My voice remained steady despite my parched throat.

"Safe, for now." Hawke tapped his bottom lip with a manicured finger. "Her continued well-being depends entirely on your cooperation."

"I want to see her."

"You're not in a position to make demands, Dr. Bell." He

towered over me, smiling like a friend. "Have you reached a decision regarding our arrangement?"

I allowed my shoulders to slump in defeat, wincing at the sharp pain the movement caused. "What choice do I have? I'll help you identify the artifacts."

"And sign the confession?"

I hesitated, appearing to struggle with the decision. In truth, I was mapping my strategy with newfound clarity.

"Yes." I hissed the word through clenched teeth. "But I want assurances that Annie will be released immediately."

Hawke consulted his pocket watch again, frowning at what he saw. "She remains in our custody until the operation is complete."

"Then how do I know you'll keep your word?" I allowed genuine anger to surface. "For all I know, you've already harmed her."

Hawke sighed with exaggerated patience. "You misunderstand our relationship, Dr. Bell. I don't need your trust—only your compliance."

"Fine. But I need proof she's alive and unharmed before I help you with anything."

Something in my tone made Hawke study me more carefully.

"Very well." He nodded to one of his men, who disappeared through the door. "A reasonable request. You'll have your proof shortly."

Hawke checked his watch a third time, his movements growing more agitated. "Time is becoming a factor, Dr. Bell. My employer has set a non-negotiable deadline, and we've wasted precious days tracking artifacts that weren't relevant."

"Your employer?" I asked, trying to sound merely curious. But the revelation that Hawke was not the top man in this entire disaster surprised me. Again, the "he" Hawke had referred to earlier?

"Someone who values efficiency," Hawke replied curtly. "Someone who's becoming increasingly... insistent."

While we waited, I maintained my posture of defeat while

mentally refining my plan. The warehouse's shadows continued to shrink as dawn progressed.

The guard returned, roughly escorting Annie. Her face was tear-streaked but unmarked, her clothes disheveled but intact.

She gasped when she saw me.

"Dr. Bell! Are you—"

"Silence." Hawke interrupted.

Annie's eyes met mine, and in that brief moment of silent communication, I saw both her fear and her resilience.

"You've seen she's unharmed, Dr. Bell. Satisfied?" Hawke demanded.

I caught Annie's eye, hoping to communicate reassurance. "For now."

"Excellent." Hawke gestured to his men, who escorted Annie from the room. "Now, shall we discuss the operation details? With your expertise, we can work far more efficiently to identify the most valuable items at the university's storage facility."

Minutes later, I was hauled to my feet and shoved toward the door.

The "operation" had begun.

CHAPTER TWENTY-NINE

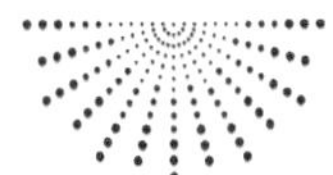

The Egyptian University's archaeological storage facility stretched beneath the earth like a forgotten tomb, with cool, damp air carrying the distinct scent of limestone dust and preservation chemicals. An underlying mustiness of ancient papyrus and wood made my nose twitch.

Hawke's grip on my arm looked gentlemanly to any observer but contained all the gentleness of a crocodile's bite. Two of his "assistants" flanked us.

I cataloged potential escape routes.

Exit Routes (Homo desperatus escapii), Early 20th Century Cairo, Notable Characteristics: main entrance (currently blocked by Thug #1), service door (likely locked), windows (nonexistent), miraculous divine intervention (statistically improbable).

"Remember our arrangement, Dr. Bell." Hawke's hot breath against my ear made my skin crawl, while his overpowering cologne—expensive but not enough to mask the underlying tang of nervous sweat—infiltrated my nostrils. "Your cooperation ensures Miss Evanwood's continued well-being. Any... rebellions will have immediate consequences."

"Your concern for my assistant is touching. Almost as touching as the revolver your friend is pressing into my back."

Sutherland's journal, hidden beneath my clothing, felt like

it was made of hot coal rather than leather, burning against my skin with the weight of dangerous knowledge.

The revolver's pressure increased, as if in appreciation of my observation.

"Merely insurance against your well-documented impulsivity."

The basement's enormous oak doors swung open at Hawke's approach, revealing the facility's guardian—a thin Egyptian man with a weary face and anxious eyes that darted between us. His eyes widened at the sight of our party.

"Mr. Hawke! We were not expecting your delegation until—"

"Change of plans, Mr. Kareem. The British Museum requires immediate access to examine certain items for the upcoming exhibition. Dr. Bell here will be assisting with authentication."

Kareem's suspicious gaze swept over me, lingering on what must have been spectacular bruising along my jawline from last night's chloroform party.

"Is the lady archaeologist well? She appears..."

"Overworked." My voice sounded unnaturally chipper. "The hazards of academic passion. You should see me during examinations."

Hawke's fingers dug warning impressions into my arm.

Kareem hesitated, then produced a ring of ancient-looking keys. "The British Museum authorization papers—"

"Were filed with your superiors last week." Hawke's impatience surfaced before disappearing beneath his aristocratic veneer. "Surely you don't expect us to carry such documentation for a pre-arranged visit?"

Kareem wilted at the quiet threat in his tone. "Of course not, sir. Please, follow me."

The storage facility's main chamber opened before us like a forgotten palace of knowledge. A stone corridor with multiple arches disappearing like a funhouse mirror stretched before us, and yellowish, inadequate bulbs cast long shadows between shelves. The artifacts seemed to shift and move in my peripheral vision, as if even inanimate objects were attempting to escape Hawke's clutches.

Row upon row of industrial shelving stretched into the shadows, laden with nailed wooden boxes, labeled with excavations and a few dates scrawled in thick black ink. Tens of thousands of items, languishing underground. Boxes arranged like courtiers waiting for an audience that never comes.

My heart ached at the sight. So much history, carefully extracted from its resting places but hidden away.

"Impressive, isn't it?" Hawke noted my expression. "The finest collection of Egyptian antiquities not currently in European museums."

"And yours for the taking, apparently." Sutherland's final research, his hidden evidence, pressed uncomfortably against my hip with every movement, containing what I suspected were damning revelations. If only I could find a moment alone to read it properly.

"I have to give you credit, Hawke. Your man Quinn certainly played his part well."

Hawke grunted. "Quinn is worthless. Let's just say I won't be working with him again. And neither will my employer."

I seized on the repeated reference. "Employer? I was under the impression you were the mastermind behind this little archaeological shopping spree."

Hawke's eyes narrowed. "Enough talk." He gestured toward a worktable.

A woman I recognized stood beside it. She wore immaculate clothing over her starched posture, with dark hair twisted into a severe bun and wire-rimmed glasses.

"Dr. Bell." Her voice carried the precise intonation of British academic corridors. "Your reputation precedes you."

"Dr. Louise Armstrong. I'm surprised to find Britain's preeminent expert on dynastic chronology participating in grand theft archaeology." I tilted my head. "Though I suppose your recent paper rejecting early mathematical developments makes more sense now."

Her lips tightened into a bloodless line as she shifted closer to me.

Hawke gestured toward the worktable. "Enough pleasantries. Dr. Bell, you will identify artifacts with specific blue pigment compositions. Dr. Armstrong will verify your assessments. We have a strict timeline to maintain."

A pair of cotton gloves landed on the table before me with a soft finality.

"The items we're interested in are noted in this ledger." Armstrong pushed a leather-bound book toward me. "Storage section E, shelves 17 through 24. Primarily Ramesside Period with several Middle and Old Kingdom outliers."

I pulled on the gloves with deliberate slowness, feeling a growing tension across my shoulders and a pressure building behind my eyes. "How convenient they're already cataloged. One might suspect prior planning."

"One might suspect you're stalling." Hawke nodded to one of his men, who immediately produced a small radio transmitter. "Perhaps a reminder of what's at stake? I can have my colleagues at the warehouse send their regards to Miss Evanwood."

My stomach clenched. "That won't be necessary."

The ledger contained categorized listings of artifacts, each with a registration number, brief description, and storage location. Certain entries were marked with a small blue dot—Hawke's hit list. I counted forty-three marked items.

"Shall we begin with the Amenhotep scrolls?" I suggested, selecting the furthest item on the list. "Their pigment composition is particularly complex and will establish an excellent baseline for—"

"Start with the nearest items." Louise's voice could have scoured limestone. "Section E, shelf 17."

I struggled to keep my expression neutral as she eliminated my stalling strategy.

"Of course. Practicality before archaeological method. How refreshing."

I approached the designated shelving unit, trailed by my

unwanted entourage. The shelf contained a collection of papyrus fragments, wooden writing boards, and small ceremonial palettes similar to the one stolen—and forged—from our dig site.

With exaggerated care, I selected and unwrapped the first marked item: a a delicate papyrus containing astronomical calculations, the blue pigment still vibrant along its edges where star charts were meticulously painted. Under normal circumstances, I would have been ecstatic to examine such a piece. Instead, I was facilitating its disappearance from scholarly access.

I carried it to the worktable as if it were made of spun sugar rather than plant fibers, my gloved fingertips registering the subtle irregularities and worn edges that told a story my eyes couldn't fully see in the dim lighting.

Why was I stalling? Hoping for rescue? From whom? The journal's weight seemed to increase with each passing minute, its contents burning to be read.

"Late 18th Dynasty under Amenhotep III." I began my analysis with perhaps excessive detail, handling the piece with the meticulous care Petrie himself had drummed into his students—even under duress, certain standards must be maintained.

"The distinctive edge patterns suggest royal workshop production rather than provincial craftsmanship, while the pigment traces show the characteristic malachite and azurite mixture favored during Amenhotep's reign. Note the hieroglyphic cartouche in the upper right corner—slightly damaged but still legible—"

"Is it on the list or not?" Hawke growled.

"Given adequate time to properly analyze the chemical composition—"

"Yes or no, Dr. Bell."

I straightened, meeting his gaze directly. "Yes. This is one of your prizes."

Hawke nodded to one of his men, who immediately wrapped the artifact in cotton and placed it in an acid-free box, his rough handling making me wince with professional indignation. The case went into a larger box held by one of the thugs.

And so it began. I moved through the shelves with glacial precision, providing elaborate academic analyses that would have put the most long-winded Oxford don to shame. My hands began to shake as I worked, requiring increasing concentration to maintain the steady touch these treasures deserved. Each artifact received a comprehensive examination including historical context, artistic significance, and chemical composition theories, which I largely invented on the spot.

"Fascinating how the scribal notation here includes what appears to be a proto-algebraic formula for calculating cylindrical volume using the standard royal cubit and palm measurements—centuries before similar mathematical concepts appeared in Mesopotamia." I held a wooden writing board to the light, turning it with exaggerated care, my touch reverent where Hawke's men were careless.

Hawke snatched it from my hands. "This is on the list. Next item."

"But the historical implications—"

"Are not your concern." Hawke checked his pocket watch. "We're behind schedule. Work faster."

He was giving up no more information, apparently.

I moved to the next shelf, my fingers trailing along artifact labels. My mind raced beneath my carefully maintained facade of academic absorption. The weight of the underground chamber pressed down like a physical manifestation of Hawke's threats, the air growing thicker with each passing minute. Why these specific items? The blue pigment connection was obvious, though we knew there was more. Abbas had discerned the mathematical and astronomical knowledge, but the artifacts contained diverse subject matter, from medical texts to agricultural records.

As I worked, I scanned the facility for anything useful. Near the stairwell, a newly installed phone sat on a table— tantalizingly near and utterly useless under such security.

The need to examine the journal grew overwhelming. I had to know what Sutherland had discovered, had to confirm my suspicions about why he was killed. The pressure of the leather against my skin felt like a maddening itch I couldn't scratch.

By shelf 21, Hawke's patience had visibly deteriorated. His pristine appearance remained intact, but a muscle in his jaw twitched with metronomic precision.

"For someone with your academic reputation, Dr. Bell, your pace is remarkably torpid."

"Proper analysis requires attention to detail. Unless you'd prefer I accidentally overlook something significant?"

"I would prefer you value Miss Evanwood's continued well-being over academic pedantry."

The threat hung in the air. I swallowed hard and increased my pace.

By shelf 23, desperation fueled inspiration. I deliberately misidentified a spectacular example of Middle Kingdom mathematical notation, describing it as "a common inventory record with minimal historical significance."

Louise pounced immediately, her voice icy. "You're mistaken. This clearly shows advanced geometrical calculations for pyramid construction using the seked system."

"Does it?" I peered at it with exaggerated confusion. "The notation style suggested standard list making to me. Perhaps in this lighting—"

"It's item seventeen on our list," she snapped, snatching it from me.

"My apologies. The symbols for 'grain calculation' and 'pyramid volume' are remarkably similar in Middle Kingdom notation."

Louise narrowed her eyes. "They are nothing alike."

"Perhaps my training at Cambridge emphasized different interpretational methodologies."

Hawke stepped forward, his patience evaporated. "Dr. Bell, this childish attempt at sabotage ends now."

He nodded to one of his men, who immediately spoke into the radio transmitter. "Initiate extraction protocol."

A cold wave of horror washed over me. "What are you doing?"

"Providing motivation. Your assistant will be moved to a more...permanent location."

"You promised she wouldn't be harmed if I cooperated!"

"And you have failed to uphold your end of that arrangement." His smile contained all the warmth of a cobra's gaze. "Perhaps you need a reminder of the consequences of defiance."

A garbled voice responded through the radio's static. I couldn't make out the words, but Hawke's satisfaction was clear.

"It seems Mr. Quinn's interference has been definitively addressed as well," he added casually. "Quite permanent, I'm afraid. He should have known better than to follow us here."

My blood froze. Quinn? Here? My throat constricted, cutting off air as a surprising surge of emotion overwhelmed my usual self-sufficiency. Not Quinn. The thought of him lying broken and still sent a pain through me entirely disproportionate to our professional relationship.

"You're lying," I whispered.

"The body in the alley behind the university administration building would suggest otherwise." Hawke consulted his pocket watch again. "Now, shall we continue with actual cooperation, or would you prefer to join them?"

My mind raced through possibilities, each more desperate than the last. Annie in immediate danger. Quinn possibly dead. Sutherland's journal—likely containing crucial evidence —just within reach but impossible to retrieve without being seen.

I had precisely zero good options.

"I need to use the facilities," I announced suddenly.

Louise scoffed. "This is hardly the time—"

"Unless you'd prefer I demonstrate the effects of stress-induced gastric distress on priceless artifacts?" I pressed a hand to my stomach. "I assure you, it would be both academically notable and spectacularly unpleasant. The British Museum might appreciate your thoroughness in acquiring these pieces, but I doubt they'd be thrilled to receive them with my personal contribution to their preservation history."

Hawke's distaste was evident. "Fine. Johnson, escort Dr. Bell. And do be thorough in your supervision."

The largest thug nodded, his expression suggesting this assignment ranked among his least favorite duties.

The restroom was a small, utilitarian affair with a single window too narrow for escape. The steady drip of a leaky faucet echoed against the tile, marking time like a countdown to whatever fate awaited Annie and me.

Johnson positioned himself directly outside the door. "Two minutes," he barked.

Inside, I quickly pulled Sutherland's journal from my clothing, frantically flipping through the pages. The leather was worn smooth at the edges from handling, with a subtle crack of the spine as I opened it. The distinctive musty-sweet scent of aging paper rose to meet me. His meticulous handwriting filled each page with observations, sketches, and measurements—exactly what I'd expect from the cautious archaeologist.

I scanned quickly, finding a section underlined twice: *Infiltrated H's operation as requested. Documenting systematic removal of artifacts showing advanced mathematical and astronomical knowledge. Not random theft—targeted suppression of evidence contradicting European scientific primacy. H answers to someone with significant government influence. Artifacts being dispersed to private collections worldwide to prevent scholarly access.*

Tucked into the back cover was a small paper envelope containing what appeared to be blue powder samples and a folded note. With shaking fingers, I extracted the note and read: *Blue pigment samples from genuine artifacts compared with forgeries. Chemical analysis confirms modern compounds in all recent "discoveries." Unknown party overseeing program. Document proves official sanction.*

I thumbed the pages again, and this time found a carefully pressed letter on Foreign Office stationery, authorizing "containment of problematic historical narratives that could inflame nationalist sentiments."

It was signed by Hawke, with a handwritten note in the margin: "Operation Indigo proceeds with full authorization. Items acquired by any means necessary."

The evidence was here—proof of a government-sanctioned operation to suppress historical evidence and replace genuine artifacts with forgeries. And more importantly, confirmation that Sutherland had been working undercover within Hawke's operation, not betraying us as Hawke had claimed.

"One minute!" Johnson called.

I quickly tucked the envelope and document back into the journal, then returned it to its hiding place against my skin, the leather warming quickly.

"Time's up!"

With one last adjustment to ensure the journal was securely hidden, I straightened my clothing and flushed the empty toilet for appearance's sake.

When I emerged, Johnson grabbed my arm and marched me back to the main room, where tension had visibly escalated. The storage facility had begun to feel like a tomb, shadows stretching longer as time ran out for all of us.

"We need to get out," Hawke was saying. "The university staff will be arriving in less than an hour."

One of his men looked up from packing artifacts. "We've acquired thirty-two of the targeted items."

"That will have to suffice." Hawke turned as I approached. "Ah, Dr. Bell. Feeling better? Good. We're concluding our business here."

"What about Annie?"

"Miss Evanwood will be joining us for the next phase of our journey." His smile didn't reach his eyes. "As will you. Your expertise has proven valuable, despite your childish attempts at obstruction."

Fear clutched at me. Whatever "next phase" meant, it clearly didn't involve releasing us.

"Our transportation is waiting." Hawke gestured toward the steps. "After you, Dr. Bell."

We ascended back to the main lobby of the facility. Hawke and his men carried leather cases and wooden crates filled with our stolen treasures.

The storage facility's guardian, Mr. Kareem, now lay unconscious behind his desk.

I moved toward the front doors, mind racing. The journal was secured, but it would do no good if I didn't survive to share its contents. Quinn was possibly dead. Annie and I were being taken to some unknown fate.

As we reached the doors, they suddenly swung open, flooding the space with morning light. The brightness momentarily blinded me after the underground gloom.

A familiar figure stood silhouetted in the doorway, bloodied but very much alive.

CHAPTER THIRTY

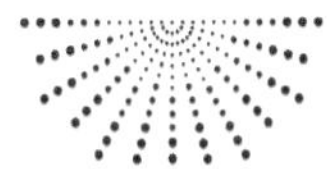

Quinn's face was a study in barely contained fury, his normally immaculate appearance now featuring several artistic splashes of blood and an impressive bruise around his eye socket.

My mind shifted from shock to tactical assessment in the space of a heartbeat. I noted his injuries even as relief flooded me: *laceration above left brow, contusion to right zygomatic arch, split lower lip.*

Hawke and his men stood frozen in momentary surprise.

My mouth went dry, pulse quickening with the hyper-awareness of every sound around us.

Quinn held open the door. "RUN!"

Hawke lunged toward me, manicured fingers grasping at air. "Stop her!"

Quinn intercepted and they collided with impressive force, creating a domino effect that sent Louise stumbling backward.

The university's emergency bell clanged out, as Quinn tackled one of Hawke's men. Someone—certainly not Mr. Kareem—had activated the alarm.

"Clarissa, get out of here!"

I bolted into the grassy quad. Behind me, the sounds of combat suggested Quinn was keeping Hawke's men occupied.

I sprinted across the grass. The journal pressed against my hip with each breath, its leather binding digging uncomfortably into my side. Sweat trickled down my spine.

I needed to get the journal—and myself—to safety, then mount a rescue for Annie.

Students milled about, glancing my way.

I slowed to a brisk walk.

Shouting increased behind me. So much for my head start.

I quickened my pace, navigated around a cluster of students.

"There!" The distinctive voice of one of Hawke's intellectually underwhelming associates carried across the quad.

I abandoned all pretense of calm and broke into an outright sprint. Students scattered before me and a professor carrying a stack of academic papers stared in horror as I dashed past.

The university wall became my immediate objective—a brick-laid barrier between imminent capture and potential freedom.

I darted past a fountain and headed toward the perimeter, risked a glance back to see Hawke's men leading the charge, followed by confused university security guards.

"Stop her!" Hawke himself had joined the pursuit. "She's stealing valuable research!"

The security guards accelerated.

My lungs burned as I pushed myself harder toward the low wall separating the university from a busy Cairo street. Excavation work could be demanding, but had not prepared me for sprinting. My thigh muscles screamed in protest.

The wall loomed, its decorative stonework offering potential handholds. I gathered the remaining fragments of my energy and accelerated toward it.

Thankful again for my practical khaki trousers and field jacket, I jabbed the toe of my sturdy leather boot into a crevice, grabbed the top of the wall, and vaulted myself over it. Rough stone scraped against my palms as I pushed upward, then experienced a momentary weightlessness before landing on the other side.

The morning sun cast sharp-edged shadows across the street, offering no place to hide. I ran along the street, refusing to glance backward.

Moments later, a rough hand grabbed my arm.

Instinctively, I drove my elbow backward, hard. It connected, with an audible crack.

The resulting grunt suggested effective contact.

"Heaven's sake, Bell," a familiar voice wheezed. "Must you aim for vital organs?"

I spun around to find Benedict Quinn doubled over, hand to his chest while attempting to maintain his dignity.

"Quinn! What—how—"

"I'd answer, if I could catch the breath you just knocked out of me."

"You snuck up on me after I've been kidnapped, threatened, and chased by half of Cairo's academic community. Did you expect a handshake?"

"Point taken." He glanced behind us toward the university. "I see your talent for creating catastrophic situations remains undiminished."

"My talent? I was kidnapped because of you!" The words emerged with more force than intended. "Hawke's men said they'd 'dealt with you permanently.'"

Something shifted in his expression. "They tried." He gestured toward his bloodied appearance. "Obviously with limited success."

He grabbed my elbow, steering me into the crowded street. "Time to disappear. Try not to look like you're fleeing for your life."

We dove into the crowd, weaving between morning commuters and market-goers. Cairo's street scene enveloped us —street sellers, pedestrians, donkey carts, and automobiles, all mingling with the occasional blare of automobile horns competing with the scraping of chairs from sidewalk cafés and porcelain cups clinking against saucers. The crowd provided excellent camouflage, though my Western clothing still marked me as conspicuous.

I caught my reflection in a shop window as we hurried through the Cairo streets and barely recognized myself. My strawberry blonde hair was windblown from our hasty escape, my freckles standing out against skin gone pale with adrenaline. The practical shirt and trousers I'd donned yesterday were now covered in dust and smudges.

Yet there was something else—a brightness in my gray-green eyes, a flush to my cheeks that had nothing to do with exertion. It was the look of someone alive in a way that cataloging pottery sherds had never managed. I turned away quickly. The last thing I needed was Quinn realizing how this dangerous partnership was affecting me.

I navigated through the narrow space between two street vendors' market carts, then ducked into a tiny alleyway barely wider than my shoulders.

Quinn followed close behind, his breathing as ragged as my own.

The high walls of the alleyway created a momentary sanctuary of shade and cool air.

"I think... we've... lost them," Quinn managed between gasps.

"Temporarily." I pressed myself against the stone wall, the temperature difference providing relief from both fear and the morning heat.

No one followed us into the alley. After sixty seconds of controlled hyperventilation, I cautiously peered around the corner. The distinctive smells of roasting nuts and coffee wafted from a nearby kitchen window.

"Still on our own?"

"Looks that way." I patted my hip where the journal was hidden. "I have Sutherland's field journal. It contains evidence of something called 'Operation Indigo'—just as Abbas suspected, a government program to suppress evidence of ancient Egyptian scientific advancements."

"Clarissa Bell, you are a walking disaster magnet." Quinn

muttered, though his tone lacked genuine irritation. "Carrying evidence of a government conspiracy while being hunted by both criminals and authorities."

"It's been an eventful morning." I peered around the corner again. "We need somewhere safe to examine this journal properly."

"My hotel is compromised. Your lodgings are definitely being watched."

"What about Dr. Abbas?"

Quinn nodded. "That could work. His home is in a neighborhood where Europeans stand out. Any surveillance would have been immediately noticed by the community."

"But that means you and I will be immediately noticed."

"Better than immediate arrest."

"We need to rescue Annie first."

I quickly explained how Hawke took Annie as leverage, holding her in the abandoned factory.

"How are we supposed to find—"

"It's near the Nile docks. It has a faded blue peacock painted on a water tower beside it."

"Fine." Quinn's expression hardened, his fingers curling into tight fists at his sides as his jaw muscles tensed. "If needed, I have contacts who can help us—people who owe me favors."

"Legitimate favors or the criminal variety?"

"Does it matter?"

I hesitated, intellectual disdain for operating outside legal channels warring with necessity. "No. It doesn't."

"I'll contact my associates and head to the factory immediately." He checked his pocket watch. "You should go to Abbas. I'll meet you there once Annie is safe."

"If Hawke's men have hurt her—"

"They won't live long enough to regret it." The cold certainty in his voice should have been alarming, but I found it oddly reassuring

He reached into his pocket and extracted a crumpled piece of fabric. "In the meantime, you might want to put this on."

It was a hijab, the traditional head covering worn by many Egyptian women. I took it with a questioning look.

"For disguise." Quinn pointed to my head. "Your distinctive hair color is somewhat conspicuous."

"Where did you get this?"

"I have a certain talent for acquiring necessities under pressure."

"You stole it."

"I'll leave some money on the vendor's cart on our way out." He straightened his own bloodied jacket with a grimace. "Unfortunately, I couldn't acquire a change of clothes for myself without attracting attention."

I wrapped the hijab around my head with what I hoped was reasonable accuracy, tucking my gold strands beneath the fabric. The light cotton felt strange against my skin, yet provided a bit of anonymity and protection.

Quinn studied the result with a critical eye, then stepped forward and gently adjusted the fabric where it had bunched awkwardly at my neck. His fingers brushed against my skin with unexpected gentleness, creating a moment of tension before he stepped back to practical matters.

"It won't do much. You still look American, but less obviously so. Keep your head down."

We slipped out of the alley and into the flowing river of Cairo's street life.

Quinn's hand rested lightly at the small of my back, the warmth of his palm through the fabric of my jacket creating an unexpected anchor amid the chaos. I kept my gaze fixed on the ground.

"Abbas's home is nearly two miles from here." I glanced across at him. "I'll never make it on foot without being spotted."

"You're not walking the entire way." Quinn steered me toward a small café with tables spilling onto the street. "In here."

He disappeared deeper into the establishment. When he returned a minute later, he was grinning.

"I've secured transportation. The owner's nephew has agreed to drive you in his delivery van."

"In exchange for what?"

"A small fortune in Egyptian pounds and my promise to come back and teach him all the English curse words." Quinn shrugged. "Cultural exchange at its finest."

The "delivery van" proved to be a dilapidated vehicle that had clearly experienced several past lives, none of them gentle. From the smell, its current incarnation seemed to involve over-ripe melons. My feet stuck to the floor where juice had dried into a tacky residue, and lazy, heat-stupefied flies buzzed.

I placed my hand on Quinn's arm, fingers closing around the blood-stained fabric of his jacket. "Promise me you'll get her out safely, Benedict."

His eyes widened at his first name, his expression softening almost imperceptibly before regaining its determined focus.

"You have my word," he said quietly. Our eyes locked in a moment of shared determination. Perhaps more. "Now go, before Hawke's men expand their search perimeter."

I climbed into the van, clutching Sutherland's journal as though it contained the Book of the Dead itself. As the engine sputtered to life, I caught a final glimpse of Quinn—bloodied, disheveled, and remarkably determined—before he disappeared into the crowd.

My fate now rested on the reliability of a delivery van and the driving skills of a teenage boy, while Annie's life depended on Benedict Quinn's mysterious network of Cairo contacts.

A man I'd once again, apparently, decided to trust.

CHAPTER THIRTY-ONE

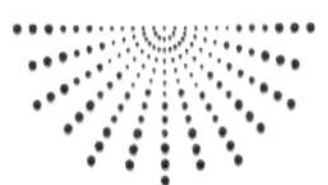

Two hours later, Dr. Abbas's home looked markedly different from my previous visit. He had brought volumes and pages from years of his past work for us to analyze and cross-reference, and now the scholarly orderliness had succumbed to a hurricane of papers, as if the Library of Alexandria had exploded inside his modest living room. Every surface—chairs, tables, floor—had been colonized by documents arranged in concentric rings around a central point: me.

Abbas himself paced the perimeter of his paper kingdom, muttering calculations under his breath. His wife Fatima had finally embraced the typical Arabic hospitality, replacing her earlier thinly veiled contempt with practical efficiency. She'd supplied endless cups of tea, each stronger than the last, until I could feel the caffeine crystallizing in my bloodstream.

We worked in silence, until a sudden commotion caused us to jump.

The front door burst open with enough force to send several carefully arranged papers airborne. A rush of night air swept in, carrying the distinctive mixture of desert dust, faint perfumes, and the urban scents of Cairo.

I leapt to my feet, grabbing a letter opener from the desk, the cool weight of metal pressed against my palm.

Annie tumbled through the doorway, her round face tear-streaked but intact.

Behind her limped Benedict Quinn. His usually impeccable appearance was even more disheveled—collar askew and raw, scraped knuckles he tried to conceal within half-curled fingers.

"Annie!" I dropped the letter opener and rushed forward, heart fluttering. I enveloped her in an embrace. "Are you hurt? Did they—"

"I'm perfectly fine, Miss." Her voice wobbled unconvincingly. "Mr. Quinn was remarkably heroic. There were at least seven armed men—"

"Four," Quinn corrected, closing the door. "Though I appreciate the upgrade."

"—and he fought them all!" Annie continued, eyes wide with admiration.

"Four men against one, and you emerged victorious?" I raised an eyebrow. "That seems improbable."

Quinn's mouth quirked. "I didn't say I fought them. I bribed two, misdirected one, and only had to physically inconvenience the fourth. Violence is rarely the most efficient solution."

"Still," Annie smiled, "your technique was quite impressive. And not the training I'd expect from an antiquities dealer."

Quinn's expression flickered momentarily before resettling into casual charm.

Something in the way Annie said "training" brought a thought to the forefront. And I suddenly felt foolish for not having noticed it sooner—the way he moved, his situational awareness, how he always positioned himself with clear sight-lines to exits. Of course Quinn was more than he appeared.

Fatima bustled in with yet another tray of tea, the strong aroma of mint filling the room. She muttered something I strongly suspected was not a traditional Egyptian blessing upon her unexpected houseguests. She thrust the tray toward Quinn, who accepted the tea with grace.

Annie took a delicate cup and sank into a nearby chair.

"I'm developing an appreciation for your approach to problem-solving, Quinn," I admitted, arranging the scattered papers nearest me into a more organized system. "Though I maintain reservations about your methodology."

Quinn watched my hands with a knowing look. "Your reservations are duly noted and filed under 'Concerns to Address After Preventing International Conspiracy.'"

I grinned at his filing system. Perhaps I was improving him, after all.

Abbas cleared his throat. "Shall we return to the rather pressing matter of Operation Indigo?"

Quinn bowed. "Please."

"These entries," Abbas tapped Sutherland's journal with a reverent finger, "document a systematic pattern of forgery stretching back eighteen months. Your Dr. Sutherland was extraordinarily methodical."

I ran my fingers along the worn edges of the journal pages, feeling their slight oiliness from frequent handling—a tangible connection to Sutherland that made his absence palpable. "He would have appreciated that assessment."

I turned to a particularly interesting page and held it up. "And now we have proof that Sutherland was working undercover the whole time, trying to stop Hawke. It seems Hawke approached him initially to help identify valuable artifacts, and Sutherland played along to gather evidence against him."

Abbas nodded. "And now we also understand why he took your palette. When Clarissa discovered the blue pigment and those unusual New Kingdom markings, he suspected a connection to the other pieces Hawke was collecting."

I sighed. "He stole it to give to Hawke, to cement his undercover status," I said, my voice catching slightly as I read his remorseful words. "He felt terrible about it, especially because he knew it would damage my career."

I flipped the page. "But look—Hawke returned the palette to Sutherland a few days later, telling him to plant it in my tent to frame me because I was 'too nosy.' That's when Sutherland realized something was wrong."

"The forgery." Abbas adjusted his wire-rimmed spectacles. "He suspected Hawke from the beginning, but lacked concrete evidence until he started tracking pigment inconsistencies."

I nodded. "I think he must have been working in the monastery lab, figuring out that the chemical composition was wrong." I traced the neat columns of Sutherland's handwriting, my eyes burning from hours of focusing on his cramped script. "Modern compounds masquerading as ancient ones. And Hawke apparently didn't even know it was a forgery until Sutherland confronted him about it."

Abbas flipped to a page covered in chemical notations that he'd already been studying. "And it seems he was focused specifically on determining which pieces contained true lapis lazuli pigment versus Egyptian blue."

"Here's something interesting," I said, pointing to another passage. "Hawke was only collecting pieces with blue pigment that contained scientific notations. Sutherland never figured out why."

"Let me see your drawings of the original palette." Abbas patted a narrow empty space on the desk.

I pulled them from my satchel and laid them beside the photographs of the forged palette Sutherland had taken.

"Look there," I pointed. "The mathematical notations have been subtly altered in the forgery."

"Fascinating." Abbas shook his head. "Someone is not just forging these artifacts—they're changing the actual mathematical content."

I turned to the paper-ringed center of the room. "Sutherland's final entry shows he planned to meet Hawke the night before we found him murdered."

Quinn joined us, bending to examine the journal. "The meeting was to confront him," he traced the words with a finger that bore telltale scrapes from whatever "physical inconvenience" he'd delivered to Annie's guard. "He believed he had enough evidence to force Hawke to stop the operation."

"Instead, he got a personal demonstration of Hawke's approach to criticism." I flipped to the next page—blank, like Sutherland's future. For a brief moment, doubt clouded my mind—was I truly capable of bringing his undercover work to completion?—but I pushed the vulnerability aside.

"Why don't we go to the police with this?" Annie asked.

"Because Hawke controls them," I replied grimly. "Or at least, he has enough influence to ensure we'd never be believed. We've already seen how Captain Mahmoud treated us. No, our only chance is to make this public, just as all knowledge should be—not hidden away in private collections or buried by those with power."

Abbas pulled out a separate stack of papers covered in his own meticulous notes. "What's most remarkable is the pattern of artifacts being targeted—the advanced mathematical and scientific concepts. The Rhind Mathematical Papyrus alone demonstrates calculation methods Europeans wouldn't develop for millennia. Certainly an operation to suppress artifacts already documented could not have succeeded."

"Calculus in Ancient Egypt?" Annie looked skeptical. "Surely not."

Abbas's eyebrows formed a disapproving valley. "Your European education has limitations, young lady. The Ancient Egyptians were performing complex mathematical calculations while Europeans were still figuring out which end of a stick to sharpen."

A bit of exaggeration, but I chose not to correct him.

"Something's not adding up," I said, rearranging the documents. "Hawke is collecting pieces with blue pigment and scientific notations. Someone is analyzing them for Egyptian blue versus lapis lazuli content. Some are returned as forgeries with altered notations. Hawke didn't even seem to know they were forgeries initially."

"I've heard rumors of other forgeries turning up recently," Quinn continued. "All with lapis lazuli pigment, not the more common Egyptian blue. It's almost as if..."

"As if someone above Hawke is truly pulling the strings," I

finished his thought. "Someone's tracking a particular scribe's work—the one whose tomb we just found at Giza. When pieces with both scientific markings and lapis lazuli are found, they're forged, altered, and given back to Hawke."

"But why?" Abbas wondered.

"That's what we need to find out. But there's more." I showed Quinn a page I'd discovered, featuring a familiar name. "Rosamund Fairchild has been tracking the same artifacts."

"That's hardly surprising." He scowled. "She's as deeply embedded in this conspiracy as Hawke."

"Not necessarily." I tapped a notation Sutherland had made beside her name. "According to this, Fairchild was documenting the same forgeries but apparently working independently. Sutherland wasn't sure of her motives, but felt she was working to stop the thefts, just as she claimed."

Quinn squinted at the page. "Fairchild always has ulterior motives. Her career has been built on appropriating others' discoveries."

"Perhaps," I conceded, "but she seems to be on the side of good this time."

"So, what now?" Quinn sipped his tea. "If we feel we can't go to the authorities?"

Abbas tapped a newspaper on his desk. "Tomorrow's archaeological conference at the Continental-Savoy Hotel would be the perfect opportunity to expose Hawke's operation." He handed the paper to Quinn.

I had forgotten all about the conference. "The Annual Pan-Egyptian Archaeological Symposium. Every significant archaeologist and institutional representative in Egypt will be there."

What professional politics would be at play?

Professor Langley from Oxford—receptive to evidence but cautious of controversy.

Director Williams—firmly in the colonial camp.

Dr. Nasser—sympathetic to Egyptian claims but dependent on British funding.

"Including Hawke." Quinn was reading the article. "He's

scheduled to give the keynote address on 'Preserving Egypt's Cultural Heritage Through International Stewardship.'"

I snorted. "That's like Jack the Ripper giving a lecture on women's safety."

Quinn traced his finger along the newspaper photo of the hotel's exterior. "According to this, the conference will be held in the main ballroom, with Hawke's speech scheduled for noon. Security will no doubt be tight, both guards and British military."

"Walking directly into the lion's den," I mused. "Except in this case, the lion has a government position and armed security."

"You can't seriously be considering attending." Annie's eyes widened. "They're actively trying to kill you!"

"Which makes it the last thing they'll expect," I reasoned with a logic that seemed perfectly sound after eight cups of over-steeped tea. "Besides, we have this." I held up Sutherland's journal. "Concrete evidence of Operation Indigo, complete with names, dates, and forgery specifications."

"Evidence they murdered Sutherland to obtain," Quinn pointed out.

"But now it's evidence with an audience." I tapped the newspaper. "If we present this publicly, with journalists present, they can't simply make it disappear."

"Unless they make you disappear, before you even have a chance." Annie muttered.

"An excellent point," Abbas nodded, "which is why you need me."

I turned to the older man. "Dr. Abbas, we can't ask you to endanger—"

"I am already one of the speakers."

This announcement silenced us all for a moment.

He smiled, the look conspiratorial. "I am delivering a short lecture at twelve-thirty."

"Just after Hawke." Quinn's expression shifted to his plotting face—a realignment that somehow conveyed both mischief and calculation. "Perhaps you could alter the contents of your planned lecture?"

"Absolutely." Again the smile. "But Dr. Bell should also speak, so I believe I will simply provide the introduction and stand by her in support."

Quinn laughed. "I would pay to see this. Actually, I think I will. I have contacts among the Continental-Savoy's staff. I'll be sure to be there."

"More bribery?" I asked.

"Professional courtesy," he corrected smoothly.

I studied the article. "We'd need to ensure Sutherland's journal is considered trustworthy."

Abbas nodded. "I have colleagues at Al-Azhar University who would testify to the mathematical significance of these artifacts."

"And I have journalist contacts," Quinn added. "The *Egyptian Gazette*'s archaeological correspondent owes me a favor."

"Of course he does." I sighed. "Is there anyone in Cairo who doesn't owe you a favor, Mr. Quinn?"

"The newly-titled King Fuad." He winked. "And my hotel concierge, who remains stubbornly immune to my charm."

I fought a smile. The tension in my shoulders eased. I'd been kidnapped, chloroformed, and threatened, my career lay in ruins, and tomorrow we'd walk into imminent danger—yet somehow, Benedict Quinn's ridiculous confidence remained oddly comforting.

We continued to plan the showdown, both the timing and the truth we would use against Hawke.

Annie occasionally interjected with practical considerations like "But what if they shoot you?" which everyone politely ignored.

Fatima continued her silent tea offensive, each cup stronger than the last, until I felt I could potentially solve complex mathematical equations through caffeine-induced hallucinations.

"We will need copies of Sutherland's key evidence," Abbas

pointed to the journal, "distributed to trusted individuals before the confrontation."

"And an escape route." He glanced at Annie. "Just in case."

As the night wore on, exhaustion made itself known in our increasingly hoarse voices and slowed movements.

Quinn and I leaned over Sutherland's journal, our heads nearly touching as we mapped out timing and positions.

Through the small window of Abbas's study, I could hear Cairo beginning to stir.

"Clarissa." Quinn's voice was unexpectedly gentle. He moved closer, lowering his voice. "We don't have to do this. There are other ways to expose Hawke. If it doesn't work, your career—"

I met his gaze. "What other ways? Filing formal complaints with the same authorities who employed him? Writing sternly worded letters to academic journals controlled by the colonial establishment?"

"We could take this evidence directly to certain journalists," he suggested. "Or to the Egyptian independence movement. Things that don't involve you personally confronting Hawke."

"I need to be there," I said firmly. "Sutherland was my colleague. My friend. He deserved better than to be dismissed as an 'unfortunate incident' while his killers continue destroying evidence of Egyptian achievement."

Quinn studied me for a moment before nodding. "Then we'll make sure his evidence reaches the right audience."

"I still think this is madness." Annie twisted her handkerchief between trembling fingers. "These people are killers."

Abbas cleared his throat. "Dawn approaches. We should rest while we can."

I nodded, suddenly aware of the bone-deep exhaustion that had been waiting behind the tea-fueled adrenaline. My hands betrayed my exhaustion, and I wasn't sure if it was from caffeine, fatigue, or fear. "A few hours of sleep would be advantageous."

We separated reluctantly, each of us aware our next gathering would be under far more pressing circumstances.

Fatima appeared with impressive timing to show us to sleeping arrangements—Quinn and I were directed to opposite ends of the house with pointed emphasis that suggested she considered moral propriety a higher priority than collaborative convenience.

Quinn's hand brushed mine briefly as we parted—the contact so light it might have been accidental, yet it carried a weight of unspoken concern.

I settled onto a narrow cot in Abbas's study, surrounded by books in Arabic, French, and English, enveloped in the musty scent of old volumes—a scholarly cocoon both foreign and familiar. The small room created an almost womb-like sanctuary, allowing me to categorize the day's events with uncharacteristic uncertainty.

Benedict Quinn: Heroic rescuer or opportunistic rogue with military training? (Requires further investigation)

Rosamund Fairchild: Conspirator or independent investigator? (Evidence inconclusive)

Our Plan: Brilliant strategy or elaborate suicide? (Statistical analysis pending)

My Career: Utterly devastated or potentially salvageable? (Outlook pessimistic)

If we survived tomorrow, I would need to develop an entirely new classification system. One that could accommodate the blurring lines between academic pursuit and physical danger, between professional distance and personal involvement—and perhaps most disturbingly, between my long-standing distrust of Benedict Quinn and my growing, reluctant reliance on him.

The last thought I had before exhaustion claimed me was that archaeology had never prepared me for this particular type of fieldwork.

CHAPTER THIRTY-TWO

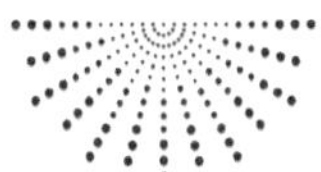

My fingers traced the restrictive high collar of my navy silk dress—chosen specifically for its sober academic respectability—as I fought the urge to loosen the pearl buttons that seemed determined to choke me. The Cairo heat made such propriety torturous.

The afternoon air hung heavy, the ballroom's attempts at ventilation failing miserably. My neck grew uncomfortably warm.

"Stop fidgeting." Quinn held my arm as we stood at the door. "You look perfectly normal."

"I look like I'm auditioning for the role of 'Repressed Victorian Governess'" I hissed back, scanning the room. "How is it you look like you've just returned from a refreshing holiday at a spa?"

Benedict Quinn did indeed look unfairly immaculate, not a hair out of place, his eye sponged back to normalcy by Annie's makeup genius, and not a visible bruise from his recent heroics. And the laws of perspiration must apply differently to charming rogues.

"Years of practice," he replied with a wink that did absolutely nothing to improve my currently homicidal mood. "One does learn to maintain appearances in my line of work."

"Yes, I imagine tomb robbing in a rumpled suit would simply be unprofessional."

"Antiquities redistribution specialist." He flashed his most charming smile at a passing waiter before snagging two flutes of champagne.

Our fingers brushed as he pressed one into my hand.

"And yes, it would."

The ballroom hummed with scholarly energy. Crystalline chandeliers cast prismatic light across the polished marble floor, their soft glow illuminating the tension beneath the veneer of academic civility. A stifling cloud of competing fragrances—bergamot, jasmine, and myrrh—made my nose twitch as I searched for fresher air. From a corner, a string quartet played classical pieces, their melody drowned by the hum of competitive conversations.

Academics in formal wear circled each other like territorial cats, occasionally hissing polite compliments that contained calibrated amounts of passive-aggressive subtext. Rivalries played out through innocent questions about methodology.

I backed toward the wall, seeking both tactical advantage and a momentary escape from the suffocating press of scholarly ambition.

At the head of the room, a small stage had been set up for the keynote presentations, with a backdrop of maps showing British excavation sites and glass cases displaying "rescued" artifacts. Egyptian staff moved quietly and efficiently around the edges while European academics dominated the center.

A waiter with a silver tray glided through the crowd, the path of his champagne flutes leading my eye across the room, where I spotted our target.

Quinn gaze had tracked with mine. "There's Hawke." He nodded toward the far side of the room.

Elias Hawke stood surrounded by admirers, resplendent in white tie and tails, looking for all the world like a benevolent patron of the arts rather than a man who'd recently tied me to a chair and threatened my friends. His silver hair caught the light, and his smile seemed genuine—if one didn't know it was the smile of a crocodile anticipating dinner.

"And one more of our players." I motioned subtly toward Rosamund Fairchild, who was engaged in what appeared to be an intense conversation with several museum security staff. Her elegant gown of burgundy silk rippled like liquid with her every movement.

I noticed something else—across the room, partially hidden behind a display of "rescued" artifacts, stood a woman whose distinctive profile sent a chill through me. Despite her formal wear and elaborate updo replacing her usual violet hat, I immediately recognized her: the woman from the train, from the Pompey's Pillar ambush, one of Hawke's trusted operatives. Her presence suggested whatever was happening tonight might be more orchestrated than we realized. I nudged Quinn and nodded subtly in her direction, his slight tensing confirming he'd seen her too.

"Remember the plan." Quinn tipped his champagne flute toward me as though toasting my existence. "We wait until Abbas's speech begins. Annie is positioned near the east exit with the documents. I've alerted my journalist contacts. Once his presentation starts, you—"

"Yes, yes, I recall the seventeen-step plan we spent all night constructing." I took a fortifying sip of champagne, its crisp dryness leaving a mineral aftertaste. "Though I still think my 'march up and denounce Hawke as a thieving imperial scoundrel' approach had a certain elegance in its simplicity."

"And a certain suicidal quality in its execution." Quinn half-smiled. "Position yourself near the refreshment table. I'll circulate."

I watched him glide away, seamlessly inserting himself into a conversation with the Egyptian Museum's assistant curator. His eyes strayed to me more than once. How did one learn to move through society with such fluid confidence? Was there a special Finishing School for Charming Rogues? If so, did it also feature courses such as "Advanced Smoldering Glances 301"?

As I watched Quinn work the room, I spotted Dr.

Montague from the Graeco-Roman Museum in Alexandria among the guests, chatting animatedly with several British officials. His elegant white beard was impeccably trimmed for the occasion. It was unsurprising to see him here—the colonial archaeological community in Egypt was ridiculously small, a tight circle of overlapping expeditions, museum appointments, and academic rivalries. Nearly all the major players were in attendance today, including the three I'd expected—Professor Langley from Oxford, Director Williams from the British School, and Dr. Nasser from Al-Azhar, who maintained his delicate balance between Egyptian scholarship and British patronage.

I made my way toward the refreshment table, carefully avoiding eye contact with several Cambridge colleagues. As I navigated between groups, I maintained a sightline to Quinn. A prickling awareness spread across my skin as I felt others' eyes following me.

The refreshment table offered little actual refreshment—imported European luxuries, like delicate morsels of smoked fish on crisp toast points.

Before I could find something worth eating, a voice boomed through the ballroom:

"Ladies and gentlemen, distinguished guests, may I have your attention please!"

The museum curator stood on the small stage, beaming at the assembled crowd. "It is my great honor to welcome you to the Archaeological Symposium sponsored by the Egyptian Museum. We are privileged to have with us today some of the finest minds in the field of Egyptology. Including our special keynote speaker."

The crowd applauded politely.

"May I please present our distinguished speaker, a man whose contributions to Egyptian archaeology and cultural preservation are unparalleled. Please welcome Mr. Elias Hawke!"

The applause swelled as Hawke mounted the steps to the stage, his smile as practiced as his posture. He gripped the podium with manicured hands that had, mere hours ago, been gesturing threats against my assistant's life.

"My friends and colleagues," Hawke began, his voice resonating with artificial sincerity, "I stand before you humbled by the majesty of Egypt's cultural heritage..."

Hawke's speech continued, a masterful performance of academic buzzwords and cultural platitudes. "...our sacred duty as stewards of history... preserving the past for future generations... respectful collaboration with our Egyptian colleagues..."

Each phrase made my blood boil hotter. This man who systematically erased evidence of ancient Egyptian achievement, who forged artifacts to maintain imperial superiority, who had Sutherland murdered—standing there preaching about preservation and respect?

For a moment, I hesitated, considering the imminent professional damage to my career. As a female archaeologist already fighting for credibility, such a public accusation carried enormous risk.

I twisted my head, seeking Quinn's gaze across the crowded room. He caught my eye and shook his head, clearly understanding my frustration.

In that moment, I spotted Rosamund Fairchild moving with determination from the opposite side of the room. Our eyes met across the heads of the assembled archaeologists. To my surprise, she gave me a slight nod—acknowledgment? Warning? Impossible to interpret, but I felt a conflicted mixture of professional respect and lingering suspicion.

"...and so, it is with great pride that I announce the British Museum's new initiative for cataloguing and preserving Egypt's most precious artifacts—" Hawke continued, oblivious to her approach.

"Mr. Hawke," Fairchild called out, her voice carrying across the suddenly hushed room. "Perhaps you'd care to explain how your preservation initiative handles forgeries?"

The crowd rippled with surprised murmurs. Hawke froze

mid-gesture, his expression flickering between confusion and anger before settling on patronizing amusement.

"I'm sorry, madam, but questions will be entertained after my presentation. If you'll just—"

"Or perhaps," Fairchild's cool voice cut through his response as she mounted the steps to the stage, "you'd prefer to explain Operation Indigo to our colleagues?"

Hawke's face drained of color so rapidly I had a moment of concern for his cardiovascular health, despite myself.

"This is highly irregular," the curator sputtered, looking between Fairchild and Hawke with panic.

In an impromptu decision, I took advantage of the confusion to climb onto the stage, the wooden boards creaking under my weight.

Hopefully the rest of my team would be ready to improvise as well.

I leaned into the public address system. "Eli Hawke has been systematically removing and replacing artifacts that contain evidence of advanced Egyptian scientific knowledge." I lifted my chin. "Dr. Gregory Sutherland discovered his operation and was murdered for it."

Gasps rippled through the crowd.

I spotted Quinn moving swiftly along the perimeter of the room, with a seeming instinct to position himself between me and potential danger.

Annie rose to the occasion as well, swiftly handing out documents to the critical journalists we'd identified for her.

"These are outrageous accusations!" Hawke spluttered, though his usual polish had developed noticeable cracks. "These women are clearly deranged—"

"Oh, I assure you, my mental faculties are in excellent working order," I reached into my satchel and withdrew Sutherland's leather-bound field notes with his characteristic cataloging system, artifact sketches with precise measurements in the margins, as well as his journal. "These contain Dr. Sutherland's documentation of your entire operation. The forgery workshop at Deir al-Matruh. The systematic replacement of artifacts. The suppression of evidence that ancient Egyptians possessed mathematical and scientific knowledge that predates Europe's by millennia."

The audience erupted into chaos, archaeologists shouting questions, museum officials looking horrified, journalists scribbling frantically in notebooks. I saw disbelief, outrage, calculation, opportunism.

I also saw Hawke's security men converging on the stage, their hands reaching ominously inside their jackets. This was the most dangerous moment of our plan—when Hawke would realize he was cornered.

What I didn't expect was Rosamund Fairchild stepping between me and the approaching security team.

"As representative of the British Museum's Antiquities Recovery Division," she announced, her voice cutting through the chaos, "I can confirm Dr. Bell's allegations. Mr. Hawke has been under investigation for months."

Personal feelings aside, I was grateful for the confirmation that Fairchild was working for Egypt and not against it.

"This is absurd," Hawke had recovered some of his composure, clutching the podium edge with whitened fingers. "I've dedicated my life to preserving Egyptian heritage—"

"By selectively erasing parts that didn't fit your preferred view of history," I countered. "By destroying evidence and having scholars who spoke the truth conveniently disappear or suffer 'accidents.'"

"I didn't kill Gregory Sutherland!" Hawke's control finally shattered, his voice rising to an undignified shout. "Why would I kill him? He was my man on the inside!"

The room fell suddenly, dramatically silent. Even the waiters had paused mid-service, champagne flutes suspended in air.

Hawke's eyes darted around the room, calculation replacing panic. "Sutherland worked for me. Has been for years. He identified pieces that needed... special handling." A cold smile spread across his face. "I had no reason to kill a valuable asset." He seemed to gain confidence in the silence. "He's been providing us with detailed information for months, including precise locations of items in deep storage at the Egyptian Museum. Why would I eliminate such a valuable source?"

Sutherland—a traitor after all? The man who'd treated me with respect, who'd championed my work?

"You're lying," I said, though uncertainty had crept into my voice.

"Am I?" Hawke's confidence was returning. "Ask yourself who had access to your camp. Who could easily examine artifacts without suspicion. Who could move freely between institutions."

My mind raced, re-cataloging evidence in light of this new information. Had I completely misread the situation?

Out of the corner of my eye, I saw Quinn attempting to push through the crowd toward the stage, his expression tight with alarm. Something was wrong.

Fairchild moved closer to Hawke, her voice low but audible to those of us on stage. "You've lost, Eli. The evidence is overwhelming. Your operation is exposed."

Hawke's laugh held no humor. "You think I'm the mastermind? I'm merely an errand boy." His eyes swept the room with disdain. "His plan existed long before I found a way to make the most of it."

"He?" I repeated. "Who is behind this?"

A strange calm settled over Hawke. "You're a clever girl, Dr. Bell. Haven't you figured it out yet?"

With that, Hawke made a desperate lunge toward the edge of the stage.

The crack of a gunshot froze everyone in place.

I flinched violently and dove for the floor.

"Quinn!" I shouted, but my warning was drowned in the sudden commotion.

But it was Hawke who staggered, a look of bewildered surprise on his face. He touched his chest where a rapidly spreading dark stain betrayed the bullet's path. His legs buckled, and he crumpled to the stage floor with an undignified finality.

Screams erupted. People scattered in panic. Security personnel belatedly drew their weapons, pointing them in all directions.

I dropped to my knees beside Hawke.

"Who?" I demanded, leaning close to his ashen face. "Who's behind all this?"

Hawke's eyes found mine, a surprising clarity in them as blood bubbled at the corner of his mouth. "He... he promised..."

His final breath rattled from his lungs, and the light faded from his eyes, leaving me kneeling in a growing pool of blood on the ballroom stage with a room full of panicking archaeologists.

I looked up, scanning the chaotic room for anyone who might make sense of what had just happened. My mind reeled, cataloging the fragment of knowledge Hawke had left me.

Only Quinn met my gaze, his face a mask of grim determination as he fought against the fleeing crowd to reach me.

CHAPTER THIRTY-THREE

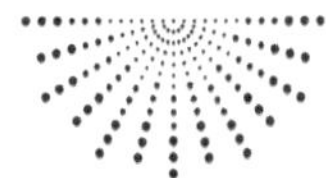

I remained kneeling beside Hawke's body on the stage, my dress now featuring an arrangement of blood spatters Annie would not appreciate.

Security guards swarmed the stage, weapons drawn. One grabbed my arm with unnecessary force, hauling me to my feet while barking questions I couldn't possibly answer.

My mind was stuck on Hawke's final words—the frustratingly vague "he promised."

"Stand back from the body!" The guard twisted my arm behind my back.

Quinn finally fought his way through the fleeing crowd, vaulting onto the stage with impressive athleticism for someone who spent most of his time seducing collectors over tea. "Release her!" He shoved between me and the guard. "She's with the Egyptian Museum's investigation team."

The security officer hesitated, clearly weighing the implications.

"Is that so?" Captain Mahmoud's voice cut through the chaos as he pushed through the stage door, flanked by Sergeant Aziz. "How fascinating, considering our standing orders to arrest Dr. Bell on sight."

I twisted to face Captain Mahmoud, my arm still trapped in the guard's iron grip.

"You may release her." Mahmoud did not take his eyes off me. "We will handle this... situation."

The guard complied with reluctance.

I massaged circulation back into my throbbing wrist.

Quinn stepped closer, his shoulder pressing against mine. "Captain," his tone was placating, "I believe we have a misunderstanding that could be resolved with—"

"With your arrest, Mr. Quinn." Mahmoud smiled. "Two fugitives at the scene of yet another murder."

A commotion at the back of the room drew our attention.

Dr. Abbas pushed his way through, waving papers like academic battle flags. "Captain Mahmoud! I have evidence of government conspiracy! These documents prove—"

"Dr. Abbas!" I interrupted, recognizing the imminent danger of a respected mathematician being arrested alongside us. "Perhaps this isn't the best moment for—"

"For justice?" Abbas's eyebrows rose in righteous indignation. "When better?"

The crowd had thinned to a core group of journalists, security personnel, and academics too invested in career-making scandal to flee. Among them stood Rosamund Fairchild, her expression a mix of horror and relief.

Annie materialized from the crowd, clutching a leather portfolio to her chest like a shield.

"Pardon me, Captain." Her voice was steadier than I'd ever heard it. "But I have the documents showing Dr. Bell and Mr. Quinn intended to bring the truth to this gathering." She thrust the papers forward, her chin raised.

Mahmoud examined the papers with narrowed eyes.

Annie stood her ground, shoulders squared. When she caught my surprised glance, a faint blush colored her cheeks.

I could have kissed her. Instead, I maintained my most dignified archaeological stance while mentally upgrading her classification from *Lady's Companion (Unexpectedly Useful)* to *Strategic Genius (Deceptively Unassuming)*.

Mahmoud's calculations were visible on his face—the political implications, the press coverage, the complexity of arresting foreign nationals with connections to British institutions. Finally, his shoulders dropped a fraction of an inch. "We will need statements. From all of you. Immediately."

~

The pink-orange late morning glow filtered through the canvas walls of my tent at the Giza dig site, transforming the humble space into something magical. The simple structure seemed to breathe with the morning light, the walls glowing amber where the sun struck them directly.

I sat cross-legged on my cot, surrounded by a sea of papers.

It had been exactly nineteen hours since Hawke's dramatic demise. Nineteen hours of police statements, journalist questions, and now, frantic sorting of evidence.

Yet here I was, alive, free, and back at the dig site with permission from Egyptian authorities to continue our work while the investigation proceeded. A miraculous outcome primarily attributed to three factors: Abbas's persuasive defense of us, Fairchild's professional prestige, and the political convenience of blaming everything on a dead man.

The tenuous peace between British archaeological authorities and Egyptian officials seeking control over their own antiquities had worked in our favor—for now. Captain Mahmoud clearly disliked releasing us, but the diplomatic complications of detaining British Museum affiliates outweighed his suspicions.

Quinn disappeared shortly after our release, muttering something about "loose ends" and promising to meet me this morning. I'd pretended not to care, which would have been more convincing had I not asked exactly what constituted "morning" and whether it meant Egyptian time or the more punctual British variety. My mental note of his absence now included entries under both *Irritating Behavior (Typical)* and *Concerning Disappearance (Potentially Dangerous)*—the latter category growing uncomfortably prominent in my thoughts.

As it turned out, it didn't matter whose clock, as he never showed up at all.

Now, I spread the papers recovered last night from Sutherland's room at the Mena House Hotel across my cot, studying his meticulous notes on Operation Indigo. Papers rustled beneath my fingers, the sound punctuated by distant calls of workers beginning their day and the occasional snap of canvas as morning breezes caught the tent walls.

The police seemed content to believe Sutherland double-crossed Hawke and got himself killed. But something didn't fit. If Hawke was telling the truth—if Sutherland had indeed been working for him from the inside—then why had he been murdered? Had Hawke figured out Sutherland's self-appointed undercover attempt? And most importantly, who was the mysterious "he" pulling strings behind Hawke's operation?

I didn't kill Sutherland. Why would I? It makes no sense...

Hawke was many things—antiquities smuggler, government conspirator, man with questionable taste in waistcoats—but his final assertion had the ring of truth.

I sat in the same tent where I'd once been relegated to sorting pottery by color, now faced with an even more daunting organizational challenge: the complete personal effects of Dr. Gregory Sutherland. Bradford had ordered everything from Sutherland's room at the Mena House Hotel brought to the dig site "for proper academic curation," which apparently meant "dumped in Clarissa's tent for sorting."

Bradford insisted nothing be discarded, however mundane.

The mountain of documents had the same chaotic energy as Benedict Quinn's hotel suite, minus the questionable antiquities and expensive cologne. Letters, notebooks, photographs, receipts, half-finished academic papers, and what appeared to be a collection of hotel stationery from every archaeological expedition since 1910 spilled across the floor like a paper tsunami.

"Right," I muttered to an audience of field notes and dust. "Let's solve a murder through the magic of filing."

I'd established four distinct piles:

1) Academic Research (subcategorized by excavation site)

2) Personal Correspondence (arranged chronologically)

3) Potential Evidence (items mentioning Hawke, stolen or forged artifacts, or anything to do with Operation Indigo)

4) Receipts for Unsuitable Meal Expenses (a category I created purely to document Sutherland's alarming fondness for pickled fish)

I applied stratigraphic principles to the layering of correspondence, treating each date stamp as a sedimentary layer revealing the evolution of relationships and events. Sutherland's meticulous record-keeping—standard practice for establishing provenance and academic priority since Petrie's innovations in the field—provided a surprisingly detailed timeline.

An hour into my exploration of Sutherland's paper trail, my back ached, the cramp in my fingers had progressed from annoying to painful, and a fine layer of desert dust coated everything, including my skin. The cool morning air was giving way to the warming interior of the tent, making the papers stick to my fingertips as I sorted them.

My fingers paused on the stack of correspondence, pulling out a bundle of letters secured with twine, the postmarks dating back nearly fifteen years. I ruffled through them, noting the names of the senders.

Then stopped midway through the stack, at the elegant handwriting bearing a familiar name.

Dr. Rosamund Fairchild.

I untied the bundle, spreading the correspondence across my makeshift workspace. There were seven from her, and I opened and read each in turn. The earliest letters were warm, collegial—two scholars exchanging ideas about methodologies, artifact dating, and the occasional academic gossip. The tone shifted gradually over the years, growing cooler, more formal, until they read like diplomatic dispatches between hostile nations.

The bombshell came in a letter dated only a month ago. As I unfolded it, my fingertips detected deeper indentations in the paper where Fairchild had pressed harder with her pen.

My dear Sutherland,

Your review of my monograph "Preservation-Centered Archaeology: A Framework for Future Excavations" has been brought to my attention. While scholarly critique forms the foundation of academic discourse, your assessment seems less concerned with advancing the field and more with burying my career. To suggest my minimal intervention methodology represents "archaeology for the timid and untalented" and that I am "hiding behind theoretical frameworks to mask a fundamental inability to distinguish a trowel from a teaspoon" goes beyond professional disagreement into the realm of personal attack. Your assertion that I "have likely never broken a fingernail on an actual dig site" is as inaccurate as it is insulting.

The timing of your review—mere weeks before the Museum Board considers my promotion to Senior Curator—bears all the hallmarks of academic sabotage rather than genuine scholarly concern. Perhaps most telling is your suggestion that I am "more interested in preserving my pristine reputation than in the messy work of actual discovery." Rest assured, I am perfectly capable of getting my hands dirty—though apparently not in the haphazard, site-destroying manner you seem to prefer.

Please direct any future correspondence through official Museum channels. I prefer to have several neutral intermediaries present.

Regards, Dr. C. Fairchild

I sorted and re-sorted the stack of correspondence, remembering another letter written to the British Museum.

Yes, here it was. I hadn't read it, since it looked to be only a rough draft, complete with crossed-out phrases and marginal notes.

Distinguished Board Members,

It is with profound professional concern that I bring to your attention serious inconsistencies in artifact authentication procedures currently employed by Dr. Rosamund Fairchild. Despite her vocal advocacy for "minimal intervention" and "preservation above all else" in field methodology, Dr. Fairchild appears to have no such scruples when it comes to authentication procedures.

During my recent examination of artifacts from the Deir el-Bahari collection, I observed that several items (accession numbers BM-4721, BM-4722, and BM-4735) certified as authentic by Dr. Fairchild show unmistakable signs of modern manufacture.

Most troubling is the stark contradiction between Dr. Fairchild's published methodological principles and her actual practices. She has consistently criticized traditional excavation techniques as "destructively invasive" while apparently approving items that any competent archaeologist would immediately question—assuming, of course, that competence rather than convenience was the guiding principle.

Given Dr. Fairchild's consideration for Museum appointment, these irregularities require thorough investigation before any advancement is confirmed. One cannot claim to be the guardian of archaeological integrity while systematically undermining it.

I've compiled comprehensive documentation supporting these concerns, which I will present during my scheduled visit next month. I trust the Board will approach this matter with the same rigorous standards Dr. Fairchild advocates in her writings, if not her practice.

Respectfully, Dr. Gregory Sutherland

"Oh, good heavens," I whispered, my heartbeat suddenly thudding in my ears, drowning out the ambient noises of the camp. My fingers tightened involuntarily on the paper, my pulse quickening as connections formed in my mind with the satisfying click of puzzle pieces locking into place.

This wasn't just professional disagreement; it was career

annihilation. And the letter was dated only three weeks before Sutherland's murder.

I spread more documents across the tent floor, my heart racing. Another letter—this one from the Museum Board acknowledging receipt of Sutherland's concerns and scheduling a formal review—had arrived at the dig site the very day before his murder.

Fairchild might have been uncovering Operation Indigo— but she'd also been protecting herself.

But was it enough proof?

I flipped through more papers, pulling Sutherland's small journal out again, the pages covered in his precise handwriting. The entry from three days before his murder sent a chill down my spine:

Meeting with R.F. on Saturday.

If Sutherland had confronted Fairchild...

A memory sparked, elusive and fading. I grabbed it... something Abbas's friend Nadia, the unofficial "tour guide" with the covert information, had said...

I heard she arrived on Wednesday to consult at the Giza site.

But at the hammam on Friday, Rosamund had told Quinn and me that she'd just come from Alexandria late the night before. If she actually arrived Wednesday, as Nadia said, it would have been *before* Sutherland's murder, not after.

The tent flap rustled, startling me from my thoughts.

I jumped, papers scattering, then snatched up the most damning documents and shoved them beneath a stack of innocuous field notes.

"Dr. Bell?"

Annie's round face appeared, bringing with her the welcome scent of morning coffee. Her expression vacillated between concern and relief. "Oh! You're already here. I was worried when I went to your lodgings and you weren't there." She stepped inside, eyeing the paper explosion with the traumatized expression of someone who organizes books by color and height. "What on earth are you doing?"

"Archaeological investigation of the paper variety." I held

up Sutherland's expedition journal. "And possibly solving a murder."

Annie's eyes widened. "But I thought it was settled? Everyone's saying Hawke was behind it all."

"Everyone is displaying a remarkable talent for jumping to convenient conclusions." I stood, stretching my cramped legs. "Hawke was many things, but in his final moments, he insisted he didn't kill Sutherland. I'm beginning to think he was telling the truth. I've found evidence that Fairchild and Sutherland had a bitter professional rivalry that recently escalated when—"

The tent flap opened again, bringing a change in temperature, as bright Egyptian sunlight silhouetted the crisp, immaculate figure of Rosamund Fairchild herself. Her face remained in shadow while the light illuminated the perfect cut of her suit, creating a momentary halo effect.

I couldn't have been more surprised, to see her materialize as if out of my suspicions.

"Dr. Bell," Fairchild said, her smile not quite reaching her eyes. "I've been looking for you."

My hand instinctively moved to cover Sutherland's journal, but the motion only drew her attention to it.

Her gaze lingered on the leather-bound volume, recognition flashing across her features before being quickly masked with professional detachment.

"I see you've taken over cataloging Dr. Sutherland's effects." She stepped closer. "How... thorough of you."

Annie glanced between us, sensing the sudden tension that seemed to compress the air in the tent.

"I should fetch more coffee," she murmured, backing toward the entrance.

"No need to leave on my account," Fairchild said, her tone pleasant but her eyes never leaving the papers surrounding me. "This won't take long."

I straightened my spine and met her gaze directly. "You're right," I said, reaching casually for my trowel amid the papers. "This won't take long at all."

CHAPTER THIRTY-FOUR

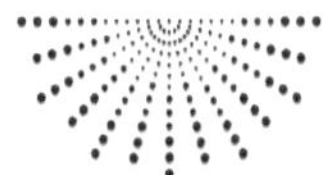

Fairchild eyed the trowel with upraised brows.

"Dr. Bell, the British Museum has appointed me to oversee the cataloging of Dr. Sutherland's professional papers."

I stiffened. "How convenient."

"Practical, rather." Fairchild surveyed the documents strewn across the floor, her expression unreadable. "His research belongs in proper institutional custody, not scattered across a dig site."

"Or scattered across a desk with his blood?" The words escaped before I could properly categorize them under *Thoughts Best Left Unexpressed*.

Fairchild's eyes narrowed fractionally. Sunlight streaming through the tent opening caught beads of perspiration forming at her hairline. "I understand you've been through a traumatic experience, Dr. Bell, but I suggest focusing on recovery rather than macabre details."

"Oh, I'm focusing on something very specific." I inched closer to the pile concealing Sutherland's most damning correspondence. "By the way, when did you say you arrived in Cairo? The day after his death? Or was it the day before?"

The atmosphere in the tent shifted palpably.

Annie edged toward the entrance, pressing herself against the far corner of the tent, her eyes darting between us like a cornered gazelle.

"I'm not sure what you're implying." Fairchild's voice maintained its cultured smoothness, but her fingers tightened on the handle of her leather document case. "But I assure you, my presence here is entirely professional."

"As was your relationship with Dr. Sutherland?" I raised an eyebrow. "Your correspondence suggests otherwise. Fifteen years of academic rivalry culminating in his threat to expose your questionable methods."

For a half-second, Fairchild's perfect composure faltered. Then her face hardened into something unyielding. "You've been reading private correspondence without authorization. Highly unprofessional, even for an archaeologist of your... unconventional standards."

The familiar dismissive tone sparked memories of my timid complaint when she hadn't acknowledged my work.

My heart raced, but I kept my voice steady.

"Less unprofessional than bludgeoning a colleague, I should think."

Fairchild's face paled. "You understand nothing." Her voice seemed suddenly less controlled.

The tent flap opened yet again, and we both turned.

Quinn.

His eyebrows rose at the palpable tension.

"Have I interrupted something?" The casual tone belied the alertness in his eyes as they darted between Fairchild and me. Though he appeared relaxed, his weight shifted to the balls of his feet, hands positioned at his sides, ready to act if needed.

"Perfect timing, actually." I stepped toward the document pile, extracting Sutherland's expedition journal and the damning letters. "I've been reviewing Dr. Sutherland's personal papers and found some fascinating correspondence between him and Dr. Fairchild. It seems they had a significant professional disagreement—one that prompted him to schedule a meeting with the museum board to discredit her."

Quinn's eyebrows elevated further. "How extraordinarily relevant to our recent adventures."

"Isn't it?" I turned back to Fairchild. "Even more relevant is this journal entry showing Sutherland arranged to meet with you the morning of his murder to discuss his concerns before reporting you to authorities." I hesitated, then added, "Concerns that included your pattern of claiming credit for others' work—something I experienced firsthand."

Fairchild's face remained a study in controlled aristocratic disdain, but a muscle twitched near her eye. "This is absurd." She reached for the journal. "Those are Museum property."

I stepped back, keeping the documents out of her reach. "They're evidence in a murder investigation."

"A murder investigation that's already concluded," she snapped, her cultured veneer cracking. "Hawke was responsible. The case is closed."

"Is it?" Quinn moved to position himself between Fairchild and the tent exit. "Hawke claimed with his dying breath that he didn't kill Sutherland."

"And you believe the word of a criminal?" Fairchild scoffed. "A man who orchestrated the systematic theft and replacement of historically significant artifacts?"

"I believe in evidence." I held up the expedition journal, with its margins filled with Sutherland's detailed sketches.

The tent fell silent except for the desert wind rustling the canvas and the sound of the dig team and workers beginning to arrive at the site. Through the tent opening, I could see the morning sun catching on limestone blocks where workers were beginning to uncover a new section.

Annie had pressed herself against the tent pole, her eyes wide as she watched the confrontation unfold from her position near the entrance.

"You've been remarkably clever, Dr. Bell." Fairchild's voice had developed a new edge—cold, precise, and dangerous. "I underestimated you from the beginning. A mistake I won't repeat."

"Is that a confession or a threat?" Quinn's casual stance had shifted subtly to something more alert, more predatory.

"It's an observation." Fairchild smoothed her immaculate jacket. "Some sacrifices are necessary for the greater good."

"The greater good?" I pressed, my mouth going dry as I faced her down. "Or was it personal revenge after he derailed your promotion and was about to expose how you've built your career claiming others' work as your own?"

"Both serve the Empire," she replied with chilling conviction. "My advancement ensures the continuation of policies that maintain order. Sutherland's so-called academic integrity was a luxury we couldn't afford—politically or personally."

"So you killed him." I said it not as a question but as the final classification of a complex artifact.

Fairchild's perfect posture somehow became even more rigid. "I protected British interests, as I've always done."

"By bashing in his skull?" Quinn's voice had lost all trace of charm.

"By eliminating a threat to stability." Fairchild's eyes fixed on his with disturbing intensity. "Just as I'll eliminate any threat that undermines my work." She smiled on me. "But don't imagine some grand conspiracy, my dear." Her voice tightened. "I went to confront him about his accusations—and about seeing him meet with Hawke. I thought he was involved in the thefts." She laughed bitterly. "The great irony is that I was wrong. He was investigating them. But when I confronted him that morning, we argued. He called me a fraud, said he had proof. He was going to ruin everything I'd built." Her voice dropped. "I didn't go there intending to kill him, but when he turned his back..."

The three of us stood there, mouths agape. Had she truly just confessed?

Fairchild smiled. "But of course you have no proof, no witnesses. My word against yours, and all that." She turned to go.

And faced yet another newcomer at the tent entrance. The distinctive figure of Captain Mahmoud of the Cairo Police.

"How fortunate." The captain's voice carried the satisfaction of a man who had just heard exactly what he needed. "I was coming with more questions for Dr. Bell about yesterday's symposium incident, but it seems I have arrived at an even more interesting conversation."

Fairchild's composure never wavered. She smiled on the police captain with the confidence of someone accustomed to institutional protection. "Captain Mahmoud. This is a misunderstanding of archaeological politics. Dr. Bell is overwrought after recent events and misinterpreting professional correspondence."

I waved the journal and letters. "Am I misinterpreting your admission to killing Dr. Sutherland? Or the fact that he was going to expose you to the British Museum Board?"

Captain Mahmoud stepped fully into the tent, his keen eyes taking in the scattered documents, Fairchild's rigid stance, and the strategic positions of everyone present. Behind him, several officers waited.

"Dr. Rosamund Fairchild, I am placing you under arrest for the murder of Dr. Gregory Sutherland." The captain's voice carried formal authority without a hint of the skepticism he'd previously directed toward me. "You will accompany us to headquarters for formal questioning."

As the officers moved to escort Fairchild from the tent, she turned back to me, her gaze locking with my own. "You're a wealthy amateur playing at scholarship, Miss Bell." She nodded toward Quinn. "And your choice of allies is questionable. Benedict has always played both sides rather skillfully. I wonder how much he's told you about his arrangement with Hawke—or about our previous... collaborations."

Quinn's expression hardened. "This isn't about me, Rosamund."

"Isn't it?" she replied with a knowing smile. "We all choose sides eventually, Benedict. I thought you understood that."

Mahmoud jostled her toward the tent flap.

"Ask your charming friend about his real allegiances sometime, Clarissa. You might be surprised by what you discover."

"That's the thing about archaeology." I met her gaze. "We're rather good at uncovering things people prefer to keep buried."

~

After Fairchild had been escorted away, the tent fell into a strange, hollow silence. Her expensive French perfume lingered momentarily before dissipating, leaving fresher air in its wake.

Annie sagged against the tent pole, looking as though she might faint from the dramatic revelation.

Quinn moved to squeeze my upper arm. "Well," he said, "that was remarkably less boring than pottery classification."

"I suppose murder investigations generally are." I sank onto an overturned crate, suddenly exhausted. Now that the danger had passed, I noticed my hands trembling. I quickly folded them in my lap.

After a moment, I began gathering the scattered documents, methodically restoring order to the physical space. Each paper represented a fragment of Sutherland's final investigation —a broken mosaic I was only beginning to piece together.

Quinn crouched before me, his eyes searching my face. The morning sunlight filtering through the tent canvas highlighted the stubble on his jaw. "Are you all right? You've just confronted a murderer with nothing but paper and razor-sharp deduction."

"I'm fine." I wasn't, not entirely, but I would be. "Just recalibrating my classification system."

"Your what?" Annie had recovered enough to join us, perching nervously on another crate.

"It seems I've spent my entire career—my entire life, really —categorizing people into neat taxonomies. Trustworthy academics versus questionable antiquities dealers. Respectable scholars versus opportunists." I glanced at Quinn, then immediately wished I hadn't. Something dangerous lurked in those eyes. "I had Fairchild filed under 'Admirable Female Archaeologist Who Succeeded in a Male System.'"

"Rather miscategorized that one," Quinn observed dryly.

"Precisely." I gestured to the papers scattered across the tent floor. "I never considered that someone could be simultaneously competent and corrupt. That success within the system might require sacrificing the very principles that system claims to uphold."

"People resist neat classification," Quinn said quietly. "Rather like history itself."

I looked up at him—really looked—seeing not just the charming, ambiguous antiquities dealer I'd first encountered, but something more complex: a man whose motivations remained as opaque as ancient papyrus. He'd been helpful, certainly. Protective, even. But there remained something inscrutable about Benedict Quinn that made my scholarly instincts twitch.

This murder had changed my understanding of academic politics and power. The rigid classifications I'd relied on—good scholars versus bad, ethical versus unethical—had proven woefully inadequate for the complex reality of human motivations.

"Some artifacts require more careful study than others," I conceded. "Speaking of which, there's still something I don't understand." I met his gaze directly. "What was *your* relationship with Fairchild, exactly?"

CHAPTER THIRTY-FIVE

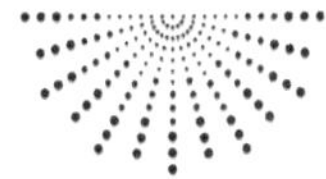

Quinn laughed at my question. "Am I still a suspect?"

I shrugged. "I watched you two together at the hammam. You seemed... very familiar with each other."

A shadow passed over Quinn's face, so quickly I might have imagined it.

"Professional acquaintances. As I told you. We worked together on certain... recovery operations for the British Museum."

"Just professional?" I pressed once more, hating the hint of vulnerability in my voice but unable to suppress it entirely.

Quinn's mouth twitched. "Fine. We occasionally posed as romantically involved when the situation required it. Makes moving through certain social circles easier. But no, despite what you may have seen, there was nothing genuine there."

"And your appearance at our dig site? The day I arrived? Another coincidence?"

He hesitated, the pause speaking volumes. "No. Not a coincidence."

"I thought as much." I gathered another stack of papers, focusing on them rather than his face. "You were investigating me, weren't you?"

"I was investigating everyone," Quinn admitted, with surprising candor. "Armand Bell's reputation for collecting Egyptian antiquities is well known in certain circles. When his daughter suddenly appears at a dig site, in an area where artifacts are disappearing..." He shrugged. "It raises questions."

"You thought I was stealing for my father?" I couldn't decide whether to be amused or offended. "The man I've spent my entire adult life trying to escape?"

"I didn't know that then." His voice softened. "I know it now."

Annie cleared her throat delicately and gathered her shawl around her shoulders. "I should, um... check on those workers arriving. And perhaps alert Dr. Bradford about... developments."

She scurried toward the tent flap, pausing only to shoot me an encouraging smile that contained multiple implied meanings, most of which made my cheeks warm.

As the tent flap fluttered closed behind her, the air between Quinn and me seemed to shift, rearranging into something new and undefined.

"Where did you learn to fight?" I asked abruptly. "Rescuing Annie at the warehouse. Surviving Hawke's men? That wasn't amateur hour."

"A gentleman never tells." His smile didn't reach his eyes.

"You're no gentleman."

"True. But I'm still not telling."

I narrowed my eyes. "You have training. Military? Did you fight in the war?"

"Everyone has a past, Dr. Bell." He deflected with practiced ease. "Some more complicated than others."

He took a step closer. "You know," he continued, clearly changing the subject, "Hawke mentioned 'a plan that existed long before me.' What if he wasn't being entirely melodramatic?"

"You suspect there's more to Operation Indigo than we've uncovered? Someone dealing above Hawke, pulling strings." I tried to focus on conspiracy theories, despite Quinn's signature smell of sandalwood and adventure, a combination no respectable archaeologist should find quite so appealing.

"There must be more." His expression shifted to something more serious. "The remaining artifacts are still out there —the genuine ones—including your scribe's palette. And someone very powerful wants them to stay buried."

"Someone with more institutional protection than even Fairchild or Hawke could claim." I nodded, my academic brain reluctantly engaging despite the competing signals from other, less scholarly parts of my anatomy. "And the woman in the violet hat? She was at the symposium last night. Do you think she's connected to whoever shot Hawke?"

"Almost certainly." Quinn's eyes darkened. "The question is whether she works for the same 'he' Hawke mentioned, or represents competing interests."

"Precisely."

Quinn's eyes held mine with an intensity that would have melted limestone. "So, I propose a partnership, Dr. Bell. A joint expedition to recover those artifacts and identify our mysterious mastermind. Your archaeological expertise, my... flexible approach to acquisition."

"A partnership?" I arched an eyebrow. "The last time I collaborated with you, I ended up kidnapped, chloroformed, and accused of murder. My academic standing now ranks somewhere between 'scandalous rumor' and 'cautionary tale at faculty meetings.'"

"Yet you solved a murder, exposed a conspiracy, and discovered evidence that could rewrite our understanding of ancient Egyptian achievements." His eyes dropped to my lips. "Admit it, Bell. You haven't been this intellectually stimulated since discovering that mistranslated hieroglyph in the British Museum catalogue."

"How did you know about—" I stopped, leaning closer. "You've been investigating me."

"Thoroughly."

The word contained enough implications to fill a museum wing.

Two weeks ago, I would have categorized his suggestion—the investigative partnership, not the other, more subtle implication—under *Absolutely Not* and filed it away in the dustiest, least-visited corner of my mental filing cabinet. But I was no longer the rigid academic who'd arrived in Egypt, expecting to find only pottery fragments and professional validation.

Perhaps I was learning that the most valuable discoveries often lay outside my carefully labeled taxonomies. That intuition could prove as valuable as analysis. That some risks were worth taking.

But there remained the question of trust. Quinn had his own agenda—he always had. The fact that our interests currently aligned didn't mean they always would.

"A *professional* partnership," I emphasized, testing the words. "With clearly defined parameters and boundaries. Focused solely on finding these artifacts and uncovering who's behind Operation Indigo."

"Of course." Quinn nodded with mock solemnity. "I shall maintain a minimum distance of one trowel length at all times. Unless, of course, you request otherwise."

His fingers brushed against mine as he gestured, causing a momentary loss of my train of thought. The simple contact sent an electric current up my arm entirely out of proportion to its significance.

"Your proposal has merit from a purely investigative perspective." I adjusted the collar of my dusty work shirt, which had suddenly become unreasonably constrictive. "The combined application of traditional archaeological methodology with your... alternative acquisition techniques... could prove effective."

"Dr. Bell," Quinn stepped closer, eliminating the proposed trowel-length distance with alarming efficiency, "are you accepting my proposal?"

"I'm considering the intellectual benefits of a temporary collaborative arrangement to pursue mutual research interests."

"Clarissa."

My name on his lips sounded like a precious artifact finally being recognized for its true value. I tried, and failed, to step backward.

He studied my face. "Stop cataloging and start feeling."

Before I could formulate a suitably academic response, Quinn closed the remaining distance between us. His hand slid behind my neck with decisive confidence, and then his mouth was on mine.

Specimen: Kiss (Unprecedented), Modern Era, displaying remarkable technical proficiency and unexpected thermal properties.

My initial instinct was resistance, hands flying up to push against his chest. But instead of pushing away, my traitorous fingers curled into the fabric of his shirt.

The kiss deepened. The taste of salt on Quinn's lips from the desert air felt only right. Categories dissolved, taxonomies collapsed, and meticulous organizational systems melted away like ice in the Egyptian sun. In their place came a flood of sensations too complex and immediate to classify—the slight roughness of his jaw against my skin, the pressure of his fingers at my waist, and the unmistakable taste of things I categorically should not want but desperately did.

When we finally separated, I discovered I'd somehow been backed against the tent's center pole. My breath came in short gasps that had absolutely nothing to do with the Egyptian heat.

"That was..." I blinked, struggling to reassemble my faculties, "...methodologically unsound."

Quinn laughed, a rich sound that seemed to resonate through places in me that had nothing whatsoever to do with my brain. "Is that your professional assessment, Dr. Bell?"

"My assessment," I said, finding my voice at last and placing my palm against his chest to create distance, "is that mixing professional and personal matters would be a catastrophic error."

His smile faltered. "Clarissa—"

"I have a career to rebuild." I stepped sideways, away from the magnetic pull of him. "And you still have secrets you're not sharing. Until I know exactly who Benedict Quinn is and what his true agenda might be, this..." I gestured between us, "cannot happen."

"You don't trust me." It wasn't a question.

"How can I?" I met his gaze directly. "You admit you've been investigating me from the beginning. You won't tell me about your training or your past. And there's still the matter of who you really work for."

"I work for myself."

"Nobody just 'works for themselves' in this business, Quinn. Not with your connections."

His expression shuttered closed. "Some secrets aren't mine to share, Clarissa."

"Then you can't expect me to share this." I gestured to my heart, hating the vulnerability of the moment but knowing it was necessary. "I need to focus on finding those artifacts and understanding why they're so important. I need to reclaim my academic standing. I can't afford... distractions."

"Distractions." His voice had cooled several degrees. "Is that what I am?"

"You're a complicated variable in an already complex equation." I straightened my shoulders, gathering my academic dignity around me like armor. "I accept your proposal for a strictly professional partnership to continue investigating Operation Indigo and recover the missing artifacts. Nothing more."

Quinn studied me for a long moment, then nodded, his expression unreadable. "As you wish, Dr. Bell."

That should have felt like victory. Instead, it felt like loss. I buried the sensation beneath layers of professional determination.

"Good. Then we have an agreement." I smoothed my hair, which had somehow become disheveled during our brief... interlude. "I'm particularly interested in finding the original scribe's palette. And determining what makes these lapis lazuli artifacts so important that someone was willing to kill to keep them hidden."

"And identifying our mysterious puppet master." Quinn

adjusted his cuffs, his composure restored with infuriating speed. "The 'he' behind Hawke's operation."

"And determining the identity of Violet Hat and her role in all this." I began gathering Sutherland's papers. "We'll need to start by analyzing these documents more thoroughly. Sutherland may have left clues about the original artifacts' location."

"A treasure hunt, then." Quinn's smile returned, though more guarded than before. "How very archaeological of us."

"This isn't about treasure," I corrected, though I suspected he knew that. "It's about truth. Historical truth that someone wants buried."

"Of course." He stepped toward the tent entrance. "I have some contacts to pursue. People who might know where the originals are being kept."

"Meet me tomorrow? Here?"

He nodded. "Tomorrow."

I followed him, to emerge from the tent into the bright Egyptian sunlight, the transition from filtered tent light to harsh brightness momentarily disorienting. The rising heat of the Egyptian morning had intensified, with the sun already beginning to shimmer off the distant pyramids, creating a mirage-like quality that made solid things appear insubstantial.

I'd come to Egypt to sort pottery and prove myself as an archaeologist. Instead, I'd been kidnapped, exposed a conspiracy, and solved a murder.

I'd also discovered that the most fascinating artifacts weren't the ones buried in the sand, but the living, breathing people who defied easy classification—particularly one Benedict Quinn, who remained as much an enigma now as when I'd first met him.

Some mysteries were solved, but others remained. Who shot Eli Hawke? What was the significance of the lapis lazuli artifacts? Who was the shadowy "he" pulling strings from behind the scenes?

And perhaps most dangerously: why did the memory of Quinn's kiss linger on my lips like the promise of adventures I absolutely should not pursue?

But those were discoveries for another day. For now, I was content to walk beside Quinn, maintaining a professional distance and ignoring the quiet voice inside that whispered I was making the biggest archaeological error of my career by not excavating whatever lay between us.

After all, didn't the best archaeological finds often come from the most unexpected excavations?

Specimen: Archaeologist (Female), Modern Era, displaying remarkable adaptability, surprising investigative talents, and a newly discovered preference for breaking rules over breaking pottery.

Classification status: Evolving.

SNEAK PEEK AT BOOK 2: PALM TREES AND POISON

Fresh from solving her first murder case in Egypt, archaeologist Dr. Clarissa Bell thought the most dangerous
thing about her new assignment would be authenticating
ancient pigments. She was wrong.

When a respected Egyptologist is poisoned at an elegant house party on the banks of the Nile, Clarissa finds herself trapped with a collection of suspicious guests—including the devastatingly competent Benedict Quinn, whose true profession remains tantalizingly unclear. With a second body discovered and a priceless artifact missing, the local police seem more interested in preserving diplomatic relations than catching killers.

As Clarissa applies her archaeological methodology to unraveling lies, she uncovers an international conspiracy that threatens Egypt's cultural heritage—and her father's reputation. But someone is always one step ahead, manipulating evidence and witnesses with the precision of a master archaeologist.

With suspects preparing to scatter across three continents and a deadline looming, Clarissa must prove her expertise extends beyond ancient pottery to very modern murder. The stakes have never been higher, and trust has never been more dangerous.

Some secrets, it seems, are worth killing for—repeatedly.

Order Palm Trees and Poison today!

Clarissa discovers that some adventures change everything—
and this one might just get her killed.

Get your free short story ebook right here:
https://BookHip.com/VFQXTLT

Dear Reader,

Thank you for taking an adventure to ancient Egypt with me! I hope you greatly enjoyed *Hieroglyphs and Homicide!*

You can find lots more about ancient Egypt on my website, along with travel journals of my trips there.

And in case you're curious, here's more than you want to know about me…

I've been writing stories since the time I first picked up a pencil. I still have my first "real" novel—the story I began at the age of eight during a family trip to New York City.

Through my childhood I wrote short stories, plays for my friends to perform (sometimes I had to bribe them), and even started a school newspaper (OK, I was the editor, journalist and photographer since no one took that bribe to join me). Then there were the drama years of junior high, when I filled a blank journal with pages of poetry. {{*sigh.*}}

In my adult years I finally got serious about publishing fiction, and have since authored nearly twenty novels.

When I'm not writing, life is full of other adventures— running a business, spending time with my kids and grandkids, and my favorite pastime: traveling the world. (I speak on cruise ships all over the world! How great is that?)

I started traveling to research my novels and fell in love with experiencing other cultures. It's my greatest hope that you'll feel like you've gotten to travel to the settings of my books, through the sights, sounds, smells, colors, and textures I try to bring back from my travels and weave into my stories.

I'd love to hear your thoughts about *Hieroglyphs and Homicide*, or ideas you have for future books I might write. Get in touch with me at tracy@tracyhigley.com.

Now, onward to another adventure!

(Be sure to join Clarissa's next adventure in Book 2, *Palm Trees and Poison*!)

HOW TO HELP THE AUTHOR

I hope you enjoyed *Hieroglyphs and Homicide!*

If you're willing to help, I would really appreciate a review! You can review the book right here: Leave a Review.

More than anything else, reviews help authors spread the word about their books.

It docsn't have to be long or eloquent – just a few lines letting people know how the book made you feel.

Thank so much!

BOOKS BY TRACY HIGLEY

The Seven Wonders Novels:

Isle of Shadows

Pyramid of Secrets

Guardian of the Flame

Garden of Madness

So Shines the Night

The Time Travel Journals of Sahara Aldridge:

A Time to Seek

A Time to Weep

A Time to Love

The Books of Babylon:

Chasing Babylon

Fallen from Babel

The Lost Cities Novels:

Petra: City in Stone

Pompeii: City on Fire

The Coming of the King Saga:

The Queen's Handmaid

The Incense Road

Standalone Books and Short Stories:

Nightfall in the Garden of Deep Time

Awakening

The Ark Builder's Wife

Dressed to the Nines

Broken Pieces

Rescued: An Allegory